Carrying her easily, Nicholas climbed the staircase and strode into her bedchamber.

"Put me down, Nicholas. I am perfectly capable of walking." Catherine struggled in his arms. He was difficult to resist, but resist she must, or risk everything she cherished.

"Easy, *ma petite,*" he murmured, his voice gentle. "Do not fight me."

He laid her down upon the counterpane and, tightening his arms around her, he kissed her, the tip of his tongue caressing her lips, then sliding inside, probing, tangling with her own, until an ache of pleasure scattered every sensible thought she possessed but one.

She had to stop him—before he discovered the secret her clan had preserved for centuries.

A moan slipped past her lips.

Something about the sound must have worried him, for he smoothed her hair. "Fear me not, Catherine. I will not hurt you."

With a surge of strength she clutched his shirt. "Leave, I say. I do not want you here. Go!"

Rather than answer, he kissed her again, his lips warm, persuasive, building the ache inside of her until she clung to him, her body quivering, eyes closed in unwilling surrender.

Too late.

Now he would see. . . .

TOUCH NOT THE CAT

TRACY FOBES

POCKET BOOKS
New York London Toronto Sydney Singapore

An *Original* Publication of POCKET BOOKS

POCKET BOOKS, a division of Simon & Schuster Inc.
1230 Avenue of the Americas, New York, NY 10020

ISBN: 0-671-02467-1

First Pocket Books printing October 1998

10 9 8 7 6 5 4 3 2

Cover art by Jamie De Jesus

Printed in the U.S.A.

TOUCH NOT THE CAT

Prologue

The Scottish Highlands, 1427

RIGHT HONOURABLE NEIGHBOR,—*I have received your honour's letter concerning these misfortunate accidents betwixt our houses, the like seen before in no man's day; but I am innocent of any wrongdoing. My friends went not within your honour's bounds, but only to MacKay-land,* where all men take their prey. *Sir, I have eight dead already, and twelve or thirteen under cure, and I know not who shall live or who shall die. I thought fit we meet at Bodhan's Pond, at the border between our lands, each attended by four horse only, to consider the trouble among us.—Sir, I rest yours,*

Aonghas Dhu, Earl of Bucharrie

Niall Roy nan Cath, third Earl of Kildonan, tucked the missive back into his leather purse and shifted on his saddle. Midsummer heat swirled around him but did little to banish the chill that had settled around both his tunic-clad body and his heart.

It did not sit well with him, what he'd planned today.

The McQuades had left him no choice.

As he rode through Kildonan's forest of oaks, morning

sunlight drifted through the leafy canopy above him and splashed against his face. Boulders, carpeted in green moss, crouched beside the trail like brooding sentinels. Wild things moved in the brush—grouse, pheasant, deer—but he did not, could not stop, despite the hunger that growled in his belly. He cast a glance at the men who rode behind him single file. There wasn't a MacClelland among them who hadn't lost a loved one to a McQuade reiving party.

Niall knew he could allow no more.

He shifted on his saddle again, the horse's plodding movements forcing a broadsword against his back with uncomfortable pressure. Connull and that damned sword! When would the lad learn to quarter his weapon properly? "Connull, will ye not move back?"

Niall's saddle mate jumped in surprise, his wild tangle of red-gold hair doing little to hide the bruises that darkened his face. "I canna! We havna the room."

"Then shift yer sword, before ye gut yer own laird."

Connull moved his broadsword to a less distressing position and slumped back into sleep. And a restless sleep it was, Niall thought, for the lad frequently cried out, his voice shrill with anguish.

Connull had suffered greatly, of that there was no doubt.

They'd found him that morning near the border of McQuade-land, his body stiff with abuse. Some time later Niall had received Aonghas Dhu's missive and left Rivendell—the stronghold he called home—with a four-horse war party. The scent of Highland heather pungent in his nose, he'd ridden into the moors with single-minded purpose.

Niall gripped the handle of his broadsword as his thoughts drifted toward his enemy.

Innocent of any wrongdoing, Aonghas Dhu, chief of the Clan McQuade, had claimed. Then how to explain the devastating loss of cattle, the torture of Connull by Aonghas's men? The pestiferous McQuade caterans had nearly brought the MacClelland clan to starvation with their burning and pillaging.

Went only to MacKay-land, Aonghas had said. And yet, Niall's own kin had espied those Highland demons on MacClelland-land at midnight, torches in one hand, hoggins of whiskey in the other.

Each attended by four horse only, Aonghas had requested. Niall glanced at the horses that followed him, a hollow smile twisting his lips. A man of his word, he'd brought only four . . . but seated two men on each horse.

Aonghas and his kin would die today.

As they drew closer to Bodhan's Pond, Niall kept a keen eye on the shadows between the oaks and pines. The handle of Connull's broadsword again began to press into his back. He decided to wake the lad, not so much from discomfort, but more because he needed every man alert. The McQuade devils could descend on them at any time.

"Wake up, lad." Niall nudged Connull in the ribs. "Soon ye'll have yer vengeance."

Connull opened red-rimmed eyes and moved his broadsword back on his belt. "I'll have the McQuade laird myself, Niall." His voice was fuzzy with sleep.

Niall slanted a glance at the red blotch that spotted the cloth near Connull's ribs. "Nay, yer tartan's soaked wi' blood. I shouldna ha' brought you wi' me. What other wounds do ye have that ye havna told me about?"

Jaw thrust forward, Connull sat straighter in the saddle. " 'Tis but a scratch."

"Scratch, my arse," Niall started to say, but a flash of saffron-colored linen in a gooseberry thicket caught his attention. He brought his horse to an abrupt halt.

"They've spotted us, lads," he said in a low voice to his men. "Let's have at them, before they turn tail and run!"

With a fierce whoop, he dug his heels into his horse. "Saint Catain preserve us!" His horse reared and jumped forward. The rest of the MacClelland clan followed with cries similar to Niall's own.

The scout ran in the direction of Bodhan's Pond, shouting, "Treachery, treachery!"

Niall and his men followed in a charge that shook the trees as they passed. They pounded into the clearing around the pond, their triumphant shouts startling the four McQuade clansmen and setting pheasants and grouse to flight.

Aonghas Dhu, Earl of Bucharrie, gray-haired, grizzled, as tall as the oaks that graced the forest, raised a bushy eyebrow. "Didna we agree tae four horse only?"

Niall studied the man. He appeared completely unruffled by the sight of eight MacClelland clansmen with swords drawn high and fury in their hearts. "I am a man o' my word, Aonghas. Do ye see more than four horse?"

"I see four horse and eight men."

"Ye see yer death." Niall dismounted from his horse and took two steps toward the McQuade laird. Niall's men circled the other three McQuades and relieved them of their broadswords.

"Several o' my clan attest tae ye burning my houses and stealing my cattle. Ye've killed my kinsmen," Niall said. "And Connull, here, has borne yer grievous sin. His blood still reeks upon yer dirk."

Aonghas nodded toward the younger MacClelland. "Connull blundered onto MacKay-land and intae our reiving party. My men took him for a MacKay and treated him as thus. 'Tis a shame we had tae let his blood, but we couldna let him tell he'd fared well at the hands o' the McQuades. We'd have every clan on this side o' the River Helmsdale after our cattle."

"In the same way, I canna let ye tell ye fared well at the hands o' the MacClellands." Niall pulled a dirk from his leathern belt. "Pick a man tae live, McQuade. The rest will die."

Aonghas stiffened. "Let our blood, MacClelland, and the feud between us will grow sae deadly it will know no match."

"Pick a man."

"My brother, Harailt." The McQuade laird nodded toward one of the men surrounded by Niall's clansmen.

Niall stepped forward, dirk ready. At the same time, Aonghas pulled his own knife. Rather than try to defend himself, the McQuade laird stabbed himself in the stomach. His mouth opened in a wide circle of pain but his eyes sparkled with unholy triumph. "Ye are damned, MacClelland," he breathed.

Niall, however, paid the words little heed. He heard only the sound of his clan's children weeping beside the burned husks of their parents. Even as Aonghas shuddered in death, he sliced the man across the throat, ducking to avoid the jet of crimson blood. Before Aonghas's heart had stopped beating, he'd gathered a small measure of blood in a gold filigreed goblet.

Snarling and kicking stones into Bodhan's Pond, the other McQuades twisted against the hands that held them. Ripples spread out across the pond's opaque surface.

The smell of McQuade blood acrid in his nose, Niall passed the goblet to Connull. Lips tight, the younger MacClelland ran two of the struggling McQuades through and added their blood to Aonghas's. He swirled the blood around in the goblet and returned it to Niall.

Niall lifted the goblet to his lips and drank, the liquid salty and thick on his tongue. He quashed the urge to gag and poured the rest of the blood into the stones before a cowering Harailt McQuade.

"Today, I take but a sip o' the Clan McQuade's blood. Hear me, Harailt McQuade. If ye and yer clansmen stray ontae MacClelland-land again, I shall take more than a sip. Be gone!" And with one mighty kick, he sent the McQuade on his way.

The MacClelland clan watched him scrabble through the thicket, in the direction of McQuade-land. When he'd disappeared, one of the Scotsmen spoke, his voice low. "Ye've dealt the McQuades a terrible affront. Do ye not think they'll harry us even more?"

"Aye, I've considered it." Niall mounted his horse and held tight to the reins while it sidestepped and pawed at the ground. "The McQuades are a superstitious clan, forsaking our Lord for their standing stones and chants. They'll not bother us for fear the blood I've drunk will give me knowledge o' the plans they hold in their hearts. May God have mercy on their souls."

Niall's kin grunted their agreement and, almost as one, they mounted and began the journey back to Rivendell. As they rode, an unusually cool wind hissed through the forest, cutting through the summer heat and stealing beneath Niall's tunic.

It reeked of McQuade blood.

One

London, 1817

Honey licked by flame.

Never had he seen hair precisely that color.

He could almost feel it drag across his bared chest, taste its warmth.

Nicholas, the twelfth Duke of Efington, felt his mien of polite boredom slip as he stared at the woman poised in the doorway.

Unfashionably tall, she topped the other ladies milling around Lady Wisborough's Egyptian-inspired ballroom by at least six inches. Her gown, a remarkable shade of green, sported a plaid sash across the shoulder. She stood out among the pastel gowns like a torch among candles.

Completely unorthodox. Utterly disarming.

He was not the only one to notice her. The heads of several elderly ladies immediately bent together in urgent gossip. Potted palms hid their malicious expressions but not their words.

". . . confirmed spinster at eight-and-twenty . . . hopeless recluse with a shrewish temper . . ."

Again, her hair drew his gaze. Streaks of red shot back from her temples and joined the riotous jumble of golden curls piled atop her head. He wondered how long it was, and for a brief instant thought about the pleasure he'd have unraveling it. Most of the women he'd known intimately had their hair cropped *à la Tite,* denying him that most sensuous of experiences.

"Quite a picture, ain't she?" The Honorable Harry Rappaport took up post next to Nicholas, a half-smile curving his pink lips. His stance was that of studied indolence, weight slung on one leg, the toe of his dainty-heeled shoe propped against the floor. A buck of the first head, his elaborately coiffed blond hair and heavy-lidded blue eyes stirred the pulses of dowagers and schoolgirls alike.

Nicholas gave Harry the briefest of nods. "Damned fine. Any idea who she is?"

"Deuced if I know. Scottish, if the tartan's any indication."

She paused near a marble column decorated with twining lotus flowers, her hand resting on the polished stone. Hieroglyphics covered the walls behind her and a lotus bowl chandelier swayed over her head. Scarabs and crocodiles crawled everywhere, and although Nicholas thought the decor droll, he was certain the Egyptians would consider it an affront.

Abruptly, the chattering knots of men and women around her parted, and a bear of a man dressed in tartan kilt, plaid, and dark coat joined her. Streaks of gray peppered his brown hair and neatly trimmed beard, and the hand he put on the small of her back appeared gnarled with age.

Harry leaned closer to Nicholas, his smile becoming derisive. "Scottish barbarians. Note the claymore dangling from his waist."

Nicholas raised an eyebrow. "Highlanders, you mean."

"Highlanders . . . barbarians . . . I see no difference."

They both fell silent as the old laird drew the woman onto the marble floor and began to dance the "Lord Dalhousie." Scottish dances were much in fashion that season, Nicholas reflected. It was too bad that most Englishmen's admiration didn't extend to the Scots themselves. Even intermarriage with the English aristocracy and the education of the lairds in England hadn't totally erased the opinion that Scots were boorish, dull men.

But no one could possibly accuse the woman who danced

so gracefully with the tartan-clad man of dullness. Rather, her refined yet lithe steps, coupled with that mane of burning gold, drew several appreciative male stares.

"She's no schoolroom miss, that one," Harry murmured.

Nicholas's gaze settled on the bosom that strained against the top of her gown. "No, indeed." In the past his taste had run toward females of a more theatrical nature. Tonight, however, he unexpectedly found himself intrigued by a woman whose very presence at Lady Wisborough's ball spoke of propriety.

The dance ended. The elderly man escorted her from the floor, leading her closer to Nicholas and Harry. Light from a chandelier revealed golden-red eyebrows that cut straight slashes across a forehead pale as moonlight.

"Damme, her dress may be a dozen years out of date, but she's a sweet morsel," Harry said.

Nicholas cast an amused glance at his cousin's tight-fitting Wellington coat, nipped in at the waist and sporting buttons as large as crown pieces. "God forbid should anyone fail to cut a dash."

"There's no need to look down your nose at me, just because you prefer to rig yourself like a priest." Harry transferred his attention to Nicholas's black evening coat—tailored by Weston himself—and poked it with an annoyed air.

Nicholas, whose restrained but tasteful mode of dress had excited such nobs of fashion as the Prince Regent, resolutely ignored him. Dandyism, he decided, was the only weakness in his cousin's otherwise engaging personality. Returning to his study of the Scotswoman, he rubbed his jaw with one lean finger.

A familiar voice broke into his reverie. "Nicholas, Harry, I'm so glad you've come." A woman with graying hair, her face wreathed in a smile, waded toward them through groups of chattering people. Ladies nodded and men bowed as she passed, her smart yellow gown and air of majesty giving her a presence only a true patrician could command.

When she reached their corner of the ballroom, Harry grabbed her gloved hand and kissed it. "Good evening, Aunt Annabella."

The Duchess of Efington narrowed her eyes and shook her finger at him. "Don't try to flummox me with your courtly airs, scamp. I'll not pay another of your debts until you've come up to scratch and wed Miss Schuler."

Nicholas rolled his eyes heavenward. His mother—forever the matchmaker. He leaned over and pecked her on the cheek. "I would have preferred White's to this crush."

Annabella gave her son a disapproving look. "Surely White's can withstand one night without you. Your presence here will mean so much to Clarissa."

Ah, yes, Nicholas thought, Clarissa. His blushing bride-to-be. Although he'd avoided actually offering for her, he knew he'd come to an age where it was natural for him to marry. He'd avoided the pitfalls of eager debutantes over the course of several Seasons, but the need for an heir, and for a wife to assume the duties the duchess now performed, made it imperative.

He supposed he could do worse than Clarissa Stonehaven. A more lovely English miss he had yet to meet. Small, delicate, she looked barely strong enough to support the wealth of sable-brown curls that teased her neck. Her eyes, a deep, chocolate brown, warmed him with their innocent promises, amid a complexion much like clotted cream. Light pink stained her cheeks, giving her the look of a delicious English confection.

Beauty notwithstanding, he knew no great love would develop between them. Simply put, Clarissa was incapable of it. Shallow and excitable, she worried more about the color of her gown than any of the recent crises that had so tested the English spirit. Even Waterloo had failed to gain much reaction, and that a moue of displeasure over the disruption to her social life. And she held not a jot of passion in her beauteous breast . . . a few stolen kisses had convinced him of that.

But it mattered not to him. Wealth, impeccable manners, and an extensive education in womanly pursuits would make Clarissa a perfect if somewhat frivolous duchess he could easily keep in hand. After the wild excesses of his youth—excesses that had damned near killed him—he only wanted to settle down to a predictable life with the woman of his choice: the docile yet beautiful Lady Stonehaven. And when the nights grew cold, he'd visit the mistress he planned to install on Torrington Square, a wench to warm his blood with a passion matched only by his own.

Unaccountably, his gaze strayed to a golden-red head.

Annabella tapped him on the arm, her eyes full of reproof. "I could see you ogling the MacClelland gel from across the room. Have a care, Nicholas. Clarissa will notice."

"Care to provide me with an introduction to the MacClelland gel, Mother?" He grinned as his mother's frown deepened.

"I will not. I barely know her, or her father."

Harry watched their interplay with an air of mild interest. "MacClelland, you say? What do you know of them?"

Annabella looked from Harry to Nicholas and sighed. "Her father, Iain MacClelland, is Earl of Kildonan. I met him at court in Edinburgh almost forty years ago. I remember it being something of a sensation he'd even appeared at court that year. The MacClellands are a reclusive bunch with a pack of rather odd legends around them."

Harry raised his eyebrows. "What type of legends?"

"Let's see." Annabella's forehead creased in thought. "Throughout the ages, all of their women have either devoted themselves to good deeds or entered convents."

"What a shame." Nicholas admired the contrast the Scotswoman's pale skin made against her deep green gown. Outmoded as she appeared, he secretly applauded her selection.

Annabella shot him a warning glance before continuing. "The MacClelland gel has followed her ancestors' example; the local Scots call her the 'Angel of Mercy.' "

Harry folded his arms across his chest and leaned against a column. "A bit too nunnish for you, don't you think, coz?"

"Perhaps." Most women Nicholas knew had experienced a man before they'd reached twenty. Those few who had waited longer were often less restrained in bed when they finally yielded their virtue. Instinct told him the Scotswoman would fall into the second category.

"Also," Annabella said, her tone quelling, "there's a story of a fierce Highlands wildcat, nearly the size of a leopard, called a grimalkin. Apparently this grimalkin ravages Kildonan's moors at periodic intervals, killing sheep and sometimes even people. According to legend, the grimalkin is the MacClelland clan's familiar."

"Barbarians, the lot of them," Harry pronounced.

"Sounds outlandish," Annabella agreed. "Nevertheless, the locals believe in the grimalkin wholeheartedly. I think it has something to do with an ancient clan they belonged to—Clan Chattan. Their motto is, in fact, 'Touch not the cat.' And that, gentlemen, is the limit of my knowledge."

His tone deliberately bored, Nicholas nodded toward the redhead. "What's her first name?"

"Catherine, I believe."

A black-clad butler approached Iain MacClelland and extended a note on a silver tray. After reading the missive, the Scotsman leaned down and spoke briefly to his daughter.

At the same time, two mamas, their oh-so-eligible daughters in tow, approached Nicholas from different angles. Leaving him no avenue of escape, they navigated the ballroom with more aplomb than Wellington at Vitoria. Silently Nicholas renewed his promise to offer for Clarissa soon, if only to discourage these damned title hunters.

Harry elbowed him. "Better fly, Nicholas, if you want to avoid dancing with a chit almost half your age."

"Surely a hunted fox has more options than I," he said as he scanned the room for a path to freedom.

The mamas drew near, their faces stretched in triumphant smiles.

His gaze fell on hair of honey and flame.

After a quick nod of greeting, he adroitly slipped past the women converging on him and strode toward Lady Catherine MacClelland.

She stood alone near the edge of the dance floor, her back stiff, the look in her eyes unapproachable. One glance at the pair of gray-haired biddies behind her, their mouths pursed with whispers, revealed the source of her outrage.

". . . choked on a piece of steak tartare tonight, quite unladylike . . ."

"Good evening, Lady Bickham, Mrs. Elphinstone," he said to the twosome, effectively ending their gossip. "I trust you're enjoying yourselves tonight?"

Without waiting for their replies, he tapped the Scotswoman on the shoulder. "This is our dance, is it not, my lady?"

She spun around and turned the full force of her green eyes on him, eyes that assessed him—at a most leisurely pace—from the tips of his polished black Hessians to the top of his head. "Why, I believe it is. Shall we?"

Something about the way she looked at him made him want to pull her into one of Lady Wisborough's unused rooms and kiss her senseless. She was too saucy by half, particularly for a confirmed spinster. He checked the impulse and, with a wry smile, placed a gloved hand against her back. Her velvet dress was soft, but he was willing to wager her skin was far softer. "You find me acceptable?"

"You'll do." With a neat twist she shrugged off his hand and led him onto the dance floor.

The little hellcat had an attitude about her, he thought, one that said she held her scullery maids in higher estimation than he. It was a novel experience, for women simply didn't treat him that way, and Nicholas felt a renewed urge to close her impudent mouth with a firm kiss.

He maneuvered her toward three couples who had joined for a country dance. She walked by his side, chin tilted upward, looking everywhere but at him. A delicate scent drifted toward him, that of heather and woodruff. She smelled clean, a rare thing in the malodorous, perfumed throng of society's finest.

An orchestra, hidden in an alcove, struck up a lively tune, and the lead couple began their figures. As they were the last couple in the set, Nicholas knew they'd have a good deal of time for conversation before they danced.

For once, he looked forward to it. He wanted to find out as much as he could about Lady Catherine MacClelland. "Pay Mrs. Elphinstone and Lady Bickham no attention. They gossip about everything and everyone . . . even the archbishop is fair game."

She threw her head back and looked him in the eye. "I don't know whether to thank you or scold you. You forget yourself, sir. We haven't been introduced." The faintest hint of a brogue colored her voice.

He could almost picture her in some secluded glen, surrounded by heather and fern, bathing, her hair floating on the water like liquid sunshine. . . . Nicholas stopped himself there, and hoped his casual smile hid the wicked thoughts running around in his head. "You looked as though you needed rescuing. I am Nicholas, Duke of Efington. You are Lady Catherine MacClelland. We are now introduced."

The duke gave her a slight bow, drawing Catherine's attention to his broad shoulders, tapering to a slender waist and long, muscular legs. He was very large, she thought, and twice as appealing. Six feet four if an inch, he had no need of the buckram wadding used so generously by the less-endowed bucks of the *ton*. Indeed, a body such as his would have sent da Vinci into raptures.

She nodded in return, surprised that this "noble," whose notorious exploits had reached her ears even in the Highlands, had chosen to dance with someone as unfashionable as herself. She'd hoped her gown would deter even the most persistent suitor, for she had no time for men or their games. Perhaps she could discourage the duke with her tongue.

"Your Grace. How wonderful to make your acquaintance. In fact, I feel as if I know you already. Tales of your escapades have reached even into the Highlands."

She searched his silvery-gray gaze for some sign of outrage. If he felt her barb, he gave no sign of it. Instead, he inclined his head toward her, giving her an excellent view of his profile—a strong jaw, straight Roman nose, and thick black hair brushed back in a vee from his forehead. He had the bold stance of an aristocrat, his tailored black evening coat and breeches emphasizing an unquestionable authority.

"Tell me, are you enjoying the Season?" he asked.

"Of course. What woman wouldn't enjoy a never-ending series of balls, visits, and dinners? Only in London would a hostess serve beef so rare it bellowed on the platter." She raised an eyebrow, daring him to contradict her.

Unlike the muslin-clad women who flitted about the room, she thought the Season a potentially deadly situation. If it weren't for her father's incessant prodding, she'd have remained in the Highlands—alone, safe, free. Every scrap of gossip she'd heard about herself came closer to the truth, chipping away at her secret, forcing her to remain on alert. Her head ached with the pressure of it.

"I also find it tiresome," he admitted, and bowed to a petite brunette who passed by with a snap of her fan.

"If that is so, what draws you to Lady Wisborough's tonight?"

His gaze flew to the brunette, who fanned herself near a refreshment table. Several dandies paid eager court to her, but she kept her attention on the duke. "A sense of duty. But let us talk of more diverting subjects. I understand you are known as the Angel of Mercy among your people, caring for your clan with a selfless generosity."

She choked back an unladylike snort. He made her sound like Joan of Arc! "Yes. When I'm not wearing this stunning gown, I don my white robes and halo."

His eyes widened for a moment, and he tried without success to smother a laugh. The sound, rumbling deep in his throat, was infectious, and she felt herself softening toward him.

In general, she cared not for the London dandies with their tiny waists and big heads. No, from a purely aesthetic viewpoint, she preferred men in kilts. But this man . . . well, were circumstances different, he might convince her of the appeal of Englishmen. She didn't find him handsome; his face was too thin and his nose too bold. Nevertheless, his hawkish looks, so different from Byron's perfection, were undeniably those of a sensual man.

A smile playing about his mouth, he tried another subject. "What part of the Highlands do you reside in?"

"The Strath of Kildonan."

"I've heard of it. A beautiful place, they say."

"If you enjoy rocks and moors."

"I have a passion for many things Scottish." The smile on his face changed somehow, became more intimate.

"How fortunate for Scotland." She wondered how it would feel to have those curving lips pressed against hers. He was no simpering dandy, this duke, with a kiss full of melodramatic feeling. No, he was a man, with a man's hard body and a man's uncompromising desires.

Quickly she chided herself for her fancy. She could see

why society called him the Dark Duke: He'd wrung a reaction from her despite her best intentions. But this time it would do him no good. She would never marry, never take a lover, for to do so would risk discovery of the secret that could send her to Bedlam . . . or even to the stake. Many times she'd wondered what it would feel like to have flames lick at her clothes, ignite her hair, and devour her flesh, leaving only a few bones as remnants. Nothing, she'd decided, could be more agonizing.

"Perhaps you'll invite me to your home once the Season has ended. I understand your grouse moors are quite the challenge to even an experienced hunter." His tone was dark, languid, full of promise.

She narrowed her eyes. She knew what he planned to hunt. The rogue hadn't an ounce of shame. "We do not entertain guests at Rivendell."

" 'Tis a pity, for I hoped to catch a glimpse of the grimalkin."

Grimalkin.

Catherine froze. Icy tendrils of alarm skittered down her spine. The word sounded so strange on his lips, spoken in a crowded ballroom. To her, it had all the power of an incantation.

As if sensing her change in mood, he leaned toward her, dared to put his hand on her arm. "My lady, are you all right?"

Flutes and a violin trilled a melody behind her, but she heard them with only half an ear. She attuned her every sense to the duke, hoping to smell the perspiration that suggested a lie, to hear a telltale quiver in his voice indicating a hidden motive. Smiling pleasantly, she removed his hand from her arm. "I'm fine. An errant draft momentarily chilled me. What do you know of the grimalkin?"

" 'Tis a fierce Highlands cat that ravages Kildonan's moors. Have you ever seen it?" His voice was guileless, as was his scent, that of Macedonian soap.

"I'm afraid I haven't. The grimalkin is nothing more than a tale used to frighten children into good behavior."

"I thought the local Scots believed in it wholeheartedly."

She worked hard to keep an uninterested tone in her

voice. "I cannot speak for others, but I am certain the grimalkin is utter nonsense."

His smile became playful. "Tell me the tale. I would like to hear it."

The duke, she thought, gave new meaning to the word *stubborn*. She began to feel like a trapped animal. "Why such persistence, Your Grace? Do you expect the tale to improve your behavior, as it does children's? Lord knows you are in dire need of improvement."

He leaned his head so close to hers that his warm breath—a heady combination of brandy and spices—fanned across her cheek. "As an angel of mercy, there is no better woman to provide guidance than you."

The man was simply outrageous. "I do not know why you've singled me out for your dubious company, Your Grace, nor do I care. You simply do not interest me. Now, I think it best I bid you good night." Satisfied she'd given him a ringing set-down *and* deflected his interest in the grimalkin, she began to march away.

"If I have in some way given offense, I apologize. I would have guessed you'd enjoyed our wordplay as much as I."

She caught the chiding note in his voice and spun back toward him. "Do not patronize me. You think me a wanton piece of goods, one you can flatter into your bed? Well, sir, you flatter only yourself. I assure you, I can think of nothing more distasteful. Good evening."

Heedless of the scene she was causing, she turned on her heel and crashed into the dandy she'd seen the duke talking to earlier.

The dandy grasped her arm, eyebrows drawn together in concern, but she pushed him away and hurried toward the entryway. The ballroom became hushed as society's leaders watched her hasty departure. She searched the staring crowd for a kilted form.

Where was Papa?

Silently she tried to recall whether or not Lady Wisborough was serving Scotch whisky in the gaming parlor. She'd identified many odors that night: brandy, ratafia, cigar smoke, the sweat of gambling, the unmistakable musk of coupling; but detected no trace of her father's beloved *uisge-*

beatha. If she couldn't find him quickly, she decided, she would return to the MacClelland residence alone.

Suddenly an arm went around her waist. Iain MacClelland drew her into the shelter of his presence, his gaze settling on the duke. "What happened, lass? Yer cheeks are as flushed as pippin apples."

"Nothing, Papa, that our return to Rivendell wouldn't cure. I am quite ready to leave." She shook her head, unwilling to say more.

Iain draped an ivory shawl over her shoulders. " 'Tis just as well, for my prize mare's in foal."

She risked a glance over her shoulder. Eyebrows lowered, the Duke of Efington was making his very determined way across the ballroom in her direction. "We must go *now,* Papa." She pulled the shawl over her head, shielding her face.

Her distress evidently communicated itself to Iain, for he shot her a discerning glance before hurrying her out into the moonlight. Her gaze fixed on the torchlit walk beneath her feet, she climbed into their barouche.

Her father settled onto the velvet squabs next to her. "Who was the fancy gent pursuing ye through the ballroom? He looked a wee bit perturbed."

"The 'gentleman' was none other than the Duke of Efington." Feeling much like a rabbit who'd barely escaped the jaws of a wolf, she closed the shades on the carriage window and pulled the shawl from her head. "He thinks himself irresistible. I purged him of that notion."

Iain began to chuckle. "Aye, I bet ye did, lass."

Nicholas reached Lady Wisborough's vestibule just as the MacClellands' barouche pulled away. Harry followed close on his heels.

"What the devil did you say to her, Nicholas? I've seen women run to you, but never from you." Out of breath from his mad dash across the ballroom, Harry rasped as he spoke.

Nicholas frowned, his annoyance with Lady Catherine fading as he considered his own disgraceful part in the affair. Ten years ago, he might have pursued a woman as vigorously as he'd just pursued Catherine MacClelland. Time, however, had mellowed him. At six-and-thirty, he'd given up his dissolute life in an attempt to heal both the physical and emotional wounds he'd suffered. Nevertheless, society continued to call him the Dark Duke, rehashing his past overindulgences with greedy enjoyment.

His behavior tonight, he thought with disgust, would no doubt reinforce his nasty reputation. He hadn't the faintest idea why he'd reacted so lustfully to the Scotswoman; something about her had loosened his tongue, made him want to wake her up, to see how hot her anger would blaze.

She stirred him in a way Clarissa never would.

Still, he owed her an apology, one he intended to make as soon as he was able.

Face red from exertion, Annabella joined them in the entryway. "Nicholas, good God! Whatever did you say to the MacClelland gel? Lady Wisborough is positively mortified."

His frown deepened. "I said nothing out of the ordinary."

"Nothing out of the ordinary, eh?" She put her hands on her hips. "You must have said *something* shocking. Everyone is agog with speculation. And Clarissa plans to quit the ball as soon as she can leave undetected."

He didn't like the tone his mother took with him—as if he were but a boy in a shortcoat. He gave her a severe look. "I simply suggested that a spot of hunting in Kildonan, after the Season had concluded, would interest me."

"Aha!" Annabella sounded victorious. "So, you angled for an invitation to the MacClellands' estate. No wonder the gel ran from the room. Nicholas, for pity's sake, you're spoken for."

"Mother, I'll ask you not to interfere in my affairs."

"Your *affaire de coeur*, you mean."

"What I do doesn't concern you."

The duchess gave a harrumph of disapproval.

Harry took up the reins of interrogation. "How did Lady Catherine reply?"

This evening had all the qualities of a nightmare, Nicholas thought, and decided he'd had enough. "She said she didn't entertain guests at Rivendell. Beyond that, I will answer no more questions." He gave Annabella a cold bow. "Good evening, madam. Tell Clarissa I will leave, so she may stay."

With a sharp turn, he strode away, only one purpose in

mind: Find out where the MacClellands were staying in London and visit them first thing in the morning.

As fate would have it, he found himself at the MacClellands' residence on Berkeley Street much sooner than expected. Directly after the debacle at Lady Wisborough's ball, he stopped at White's, where he learned Iain MacClelland had a prize mare in foal. A few club members had even placed bets against the mare surviving the foaling. Nicholas promptly placed a bet in favor of the mare and made his way to Berkeley Street, not only to soothe his conscience but to ensure his win.

A late-summer fog had descended upon London, dampening the moonlight and creating a halo around the oil lamps that lined the streets. Alert to the sounds around him—for London sported more than its share of ruffians, even in the best of neighborhoods—Nicholas passed the MacClelland residence and walked some distance before realizing he'd gone astray.

And no wonder, he thought, for despite its lofty address, the house was in a sad state of disrepair. The pink brick exterior had fallen prey to coal smoke, giving it a dirty, chipped appearance, and two of the windows in the porter's lodge had cracked. All of the shutters were closed, and a gate that hung on only one hinge creaked as he eased it open and stepped onto the gravel drive.

Drunken shouting drew him to the stable behind the house. Lanterns within the building revealed two men struggling with a mare, a leather hoggin of whiskey lying in the straw nearby. He identified one man as Iain MacClelland, stripped to the waist and his arm buried deep within the mare; the other man, a stablehand, held a lantern directly over the mare's belly.

"Argh, the wee beastie keeps slipping from my grasp." MacClelland grunted. Veins popped out on his forehead. "Get me a rope, and another swig o' yer fine whisky." He withdrew his arm, which appeared red and chapped, and grabbed the rope the stablehand proffered. With his other hand he lifted the hoggin to his lips and took several healthy swallows. "Ah, nothing like Macallan *uisge-beatha baoghal.*"

The stable housed at least twenty horses, all fine examples

of horseflesh, each standing on a soft bed of straw with a bucket of water nearby. Polished saddles and neatly stored tack leaned against a brick wall. If MacClelland was short of funds, as the state of his house and his daughter's wardrobe would suggest, the Scotsman certainly spared no expense in the stables.

The mare whickered softly, her eyes rolling. Nicholas knew her pain was great. He stepped into the light just as MacClelland began to fashion a slipknot. "May I be of service? I heard you're about to lose a prize mare."

The old laird wiped his hands on a rag and squinted through the darkness. "And who might ye be?"

"Nicholas, Duke of Efington." Nicholas braced himself for the laird's anger over the earlier scene in the ballroom, but none came.

Instead, the older man shrugged. "I appreciate yer offer. But what brings ye tae my house?"

"I came to apologize to your daughter for my conduct at Lady Wisborough's ball—"

"Catherine cannot be disturbed." Frowning, Ian turned away from him and gestured toward the mare. "This lass has her foal all bunched up inside her. Do ye have any experience with foaling?"

"I own and have bred several valuable horses," Nicholas said, diverted from his apology.

The stablehand, a Londoner if his accent was any indication, stepped forward with an eager smile. "Aye, His Grace is a crack whip with the horses . . . a bruising rider to the hounds, wins the Ascot every year." The words tumbled from his mouth in quick succession, and he repeatedly tugged on his forelock as if to accent each word with a show of deference.

A smile lifting the corners of his mouth, Nicholas nodded.

The stablehand's eyebrows suddenly drew together. "If I may be so bold as to ask, Your Grace, why do you always spare the fox?"

MacClelland leaned forward to better hear the answer.

" 'Tis simple. The cunning is not in the kill but in the pursuit. Why destroy an animal you cannot eat?"

Something flickered in the laird's blue eyes.

The mare snorted as if in agreement. Nicholas reached forward and rubbed her silky nose. "Easy, girl. We'll get you through this." He stripped the clothes off his upper body, the night air brushing against his skin with an invigorating chill.

MacClelland stepped back, his gaze fixed on the star-shaped birthmark just above Nicholas's rib cage. Nicholas had grown used to the attention his birthmark drew, but the laird's eyes seemed to reflect a particular curiosity.

"Have a tipple o' whisky, Yer Grace. The foal's in there tight—ye'll need it."

Nicholas took the hoggin and brought it to his lips, more to humor the laird than to satisfy a desire for drink. Smooth, single-malt, with a distinctive flavor, the whisky rolled down his throat and created a pleasant warmth in his stomach. With a sigh, he took another swig.

The laird grinned. "Compliments of the Macallan clan."

"Bought or stolen?"

MacClelland's grin widened. "Stolen."

Nicholas shook his head but couldn't keep a return grin from forming on his face. "I'll have to procure some myself . . . through traditional means, of course."

The Scotsman let out a guffaw that shook the walls of the stable. Then, without warning, he stumbled against a bale of straw, his face taking on a dangerously red hue. A low hiss escaped from between his teeth.

"Are you all right, man?" Nicholas stepped forward to offer support, should the laird need it.

MacClelland shook his head vigorously. "Nay, just a touch o' fire in the blood. It'll pass."

Within a few seconds, the Scotsman regained a normal color. After assessing him for a moment to make certain he had indeed recovered, Nicholas approached the mare. She lay on a soft mat of straw, her breath coming through her nostrils in fast snorts.

"Easy," he said again, and removed a ring from his finger. He held it out to MacClelland. "Will you hold this for me?"

MacClelland took the ring with a nod and put it atop a bale of hay.

Nicholas put one hand on the mare's haunch and, muttering soft words of encouragement, eased his other hand into the birth canal. He began to feel around. Two slick hooves and flanks jamming the opening . . .

A breech presentation. They were in for a long night.

For almost an hour, Nicholas maneuvered the foal, trying to pull the front two hooves forward. But the baby was slippery and resisted his efforts. Sweat dripped into his eyes and the muscles of his back and shoulders screamed with strain. During that hour he and the laird dropped all pretense of formality.

"The foal's a stubborn one." Nicholas grunted with effort. "Iain, the whisky. Another contraction is beginning."

MacClelland lifted the hoggin to Nicholas's lips. "Do ye want me tae have a go at her?"

"No, no, I'm almost there." He waited a full minute while the mare crushed his upper arm with the strength of an iron vise. Her contraction squeezed a low moan from him as the purest agony radiated into his back. Finally the contraction eased, and with a delicate pull he attempted to wiggle the foal into normal position. The mare raised her head to look at him, but her limpid brown eyes held nothing more than weariness.

"Ye have a fine touch wi' the lassies . . . ye can tell she's appreciative. But 'tis nigh ontae three in the morning. Ye've been at it for an hour, lad." MacClelland drank from the hoggin and dropped it with a frown. "Get us another hoggin," he ordered the stablehand. "We've drunk this one dry."

The whisky dulled Nicholas's pain, giving him the strength to endure in this task of unexpectedly Herculean proportions, but he feared the mare hadn't much time left. Just when he'd decided to let Iain have another try, the foal moved. Eagerly he grabbed the hooves that had eluded him for so long. With stunning ease, the foal's front legs and head appeared first, followed by the rump and hind legs as the mare pushed him out. He plopped, amid a gush of steaming fluid, into the hay, smelling much like newly made butter: soft, creamy, with a touch of salt.

Nicholas stared at it in blurry-eyed shock.

MacClelland gave a shout of joy. "Ye've done it, lad."

He slapped Nicholas on the shoulder and hefted the new hoggin to his lips. "And a fine colt it is! He's a beauty."

Nicholas collapsed into the hay, his muscles quivering like jelly. He really felt good, in a way he hadn't known for a long time. The sight of the mare nuzzling her baby had thoroughly restored him. MacClelland collapsed beside him, and together they watched as the mare gave her newborn one tentative lick.

MacClelland retrieved Nicholas's ring from the bale of hay. "Here's yer ring." He examined it in the light, some of the whisky-dullness leaving his eyes.

Nicholas held out his hand, but the laird refused to give it over.

"This is yer ring, ye say. Where did ye get it?" MacClelland's voice rang with strange intensity.

"It was my father's. Note the 'R.' . . . It stands for 'Ross.' "

"Did yer father give it tae ye?"

Nicholas eyed the laird as closely as he could, given the prodigious amount of whisky he'd consumed. "No, my mother gave it to me, after my father died. Said it was his."

"And yer mother, what's her name?"

"Annabella, Duchess of Efington. Why do you ask?"

MacClelland's eyes widened, as if Nicholas had just solved a particularly difficult problem. "Annabella," he breathed. "Ye didn't play fair, lass."

"Say again?"

Without warning, MacClelland leaned over and grasped Nicholas's arm. His eyes glittered with some nameless emotion. "Ye are going tae marry my daughter, lad."

The laird's fingers dug into his muscles with relentless pressure. Just as firmly, Nicholas removed them. "Your wits have left you, Iain. Perhaps another swig of whisky will straighten you out."

"Marry her ye will."

Nicholas narrowed his eyes. Had MacClelland gone mad? "I have no desire to be priest-linked to your daughter." As alluring as Catherine MacClelland was, he had no wish to marry a woman who had a penchant for causing scenes and whose temper burned even hotter than her hair. Besides, he had already committed himself—in his own mind—to Clarissa Stonehaven.

"Ye aren't betrothed, are ye?"

"Well, no . . ."

"Then ye'll marry my Catherine."

"Now, Iain . . ." Nicholas was about to protest further when the horses in the stalls behind him began to snort and paw the ground. The mare scented the air and struggled to her feet. Her frightened whinny echoed through the stable.

Nicholas jumped to his feet. "What in damnation . . ."

A large black shadow loomed near the door to the stable.

MacClelland struggled to his feet as well, sorrow warring with the alarm in his eyes. "Catriona," he whispered.

The shadow grew until it covered the door.

Nicholas's instincts screamed in alarm. He grabbed a pitchfork from the wall, his body getting colder and colder as the sound of sticks breaking and bushes rustling increased.

Something big was approaching the door.

The musk of a wild animal lay heavily in the stable.

The mare reared and plunged, her flanks heaving. Iain leaped back and pressed himself against the stall door.

Nicholas felt all the moisture in his mouth dry up as his mind chased around in circles, trying to guess what the shadow belonged to.

What he saw next nearly sent him reeling.

A pair of glittering green eyes observed him from about three feet outside the door. Shadows partially obscured its form, but the eyes alone made him question his own sanity.

They weren't human eyes.

They were the eyes of a wildcat.

As quick as it had appeared, it vanished.

The pitchfork dropped from his numbed hand. "Good Christ, what was that?"

MacClelland looked at the hay beneath his feet. "I saw nothing."

"It looked like a bloody leopard!"

"Ye've had too much whisky, lad. I'll have someone escort ye home."

"I think not." Nicholas raced outside and stared in all directions. Tendrils of fog, glowing beneath the moonlight, wove through a grove of birch and fir trees. All seemed peaceful.

He reentered the stables. "You saw it, MacClelland. Why do you refuse to admit it?"

"I canna discuss it further with ye. Thank ye for yer help wi' the mare. I must go now." MacClelland gave him one last intent look before retreating to his manse.

Pulling on his shirt, Nicholas found that fright had left him completely sober. On the walk back to Efington House, he turned the puzzle over and over in his mind. Maybe he'd seen a housecat, and his whisky-soaked wits had enlarged the cat until it gained the proportions of a leopard.

The problem was, he'd never felt more sober in his life.

But the idea of a leopard running loose in London was utterly ludicrous. Where could it have come from—a visiting circus? Perhaps all that superstitious talk about the grimalkin had brought on a hallucination.

A bitter chuckle escaped him as he turned the corner to Mount Street and Efington House. If he so much as dared to mention tonight's incident to any of his friends, they'd think he'd gone 'round the bend and recommend a stay at Bedlam.

It defied explanation.

And yet, he had a feeling MacClelland had seen the beast before. Why else would he remain so unconcerned, so downright saddened, as the thing had stalked toward the barn door?

Yes, MacClelland was hiding something.

But Nicholas didn't care to solve this puzzle. The hair prickling on the back of his neck at the memory of those weird eyes, he resolved to deliver his apology at the next public gathering he and the Scotswoman attended, and then stay as far away from the MacClellands as he could. The leopard he would put from his mind completely.

Lady Catherine, however, would not be so easy to forget.

Two

Catherine and Iain left London the following week to begin the journey back to Scotland. Their traveling chaise, pulled by four matched bays, couldn't move fast enough for her. A myriad of different odors—human waste, coal smoke, sickness, rotting food—had assaulted her delicate sense of smell and seeped into her pores. It left a disagreeable feeling no amount of scrubbing could remove. Indeed, the crowds of Londoners, even in spaces as open as Hyde Park, hemmed her in. She felt trapped, without an ounce of privacy.

How she longed for the Highlands. On those vast moorland hills she called home, she could roam as she wished, without fear of discovery. She was strong, free, untouched by man and untouchable. The red deer knew her, as did the grouse and pheasant, and the blood in her veins quickened at the thought of returning to them. She was as wild and unfettered as the Highlands themselves, and she reveled in it.

Catherine stretched against the chaise's leather squabs, the movement one of extraordinary flexibility and grace. So far, the trip home had been long and bruising, delayed by many a rainstorm. Throughout it all, she and her father had remained closeted together in the chaise's gloomy interior.

Despite the darkness, she saw her father's great weariness, his own longing for home. She felt it in the way he braced himself against one side of the coach, in the way he sighed. He'd spoken not once since they'd left London, and it worried her. Something troubled him greatly.

Suddenly he ended the silence between them and asked a most peculiar question, one that instantly set her on edge.

"What think ye of the Duke of Efington?" His voice seemed unnaturally loud within the confines of the chaise.

Without warning, an image of the duke popped into her mind—piercing gray eyes, devilish grin—and with it thoughts of his mouth pressed against hers, his tongue seeking hers, exploring her with a bold intimacy. His would not be a tender kiss; no, it would be hard, demanding, the kind that would crush all her good intentions to pieces. Damn the man, he'd put such tempting thoughts into her head.

She narrowed her eyes. "I think him a rogue."

"He saved my mare, lass, the night of Lady Wisborough's ball." Iain glanced at the moors that rolled past their window. "Brought her colt intae the world with all the tenderness o' a father."

Catherine stilled. "The duke visited our house while we were in London?"

"He came tae apologize tae ye, for his poor behavior."

She remembered the shouts, the calls for more whisky, the smell of blood. "Was that not the same night the grimalkin—"

"Aye."

Her heart gave a mighty thump. "Did he see—"

"He saw nothing."

She closed her eyes and breathed deeply. It did little to soothe the tumult in her chest. "Why did you not tell me about his visit sooner?"

"I didna wish ye tae fly from London before I'd accomplished unexpected business."

Privately Catherine agreed she would have flown at first opportunity. She'd thought the duke thoroughly routed at

Lady Wisborough's ball. A determined suitor would prove dangerous, indeed.

"I say good riddance to the duke and all men of his ilk. Did you know he dared to suggest I invite him to Rivendell for grouse hunting?"

He gave her a crooked smile, the first one she'd seen in quite some time. "Perhaps we'll take him up on it."

"You'll do no such thing!"

"He's got yer dander up, and that's a good thing. First man tae do it, in fact. But I can't fault yer taste. Those fancy-pants in Edinburgh were more concerned with money than morals."

"Don't remind me." Last year her father had turned a deaf ear to her protests and dragged her to Court in Edinburgh. Much to her disgust, the eligible young men had known about the MacClellands' financial troubles and looked at her more as a flirtation than a future wife.

In the end, however, it hadn't mattered. She would never marry. "Despite your suggestion, the duke hasn't angered me. Nor has he captured my interest."

"Ah, now, ye're lying, lass. We MacClellands are like smoldering fires. We only need a light touch and a bit o' breeze tae set us tae burning. Ye need someone tae bring ye tae life, and the duke may be the man tae do it."

"I cannot marry, knowing what I am. People are superstitious, Papa. They would not understand." She'd read the *Malleus Maleficarum,* penned by that old goat "Institoris," and knew the witch hunts it described had occurred less than a century before. If she were not burned at the stake, then surely the authorities would cage her at Bedlam for scholarly study. Either outcome horrified her. She had to protect her secret with every weapon available to her.

Her father, on the other hand, had the notion that without a husband or children, her life would remain empty, unfulfilled. Being a man, he had a higher opinion of men than she did, and insisted she could find a husband who would love her and refuse to betray her. It was an old argument, one they'd never resolved.

"Ye deserve some happiness, Catriona. I'll not have ye waste yer life wandering the moors barefoot."

She turned her attention to the heather-cloaked hills outside her muddied window. He referred, of course, to her habit of long walks through the heath surrounding Rivendell. It might be an odd thing for the daughter of an earl to do, but she liked to take off her boots and feel the warm grass beneath her feet. Many a solitary day she'd spent amid fragrant puddles of peat, listening to the bellow of Black Angus cattle as the crisp Highland breeze curled around her body. "I *am* happy, Papa. You have given me a life many would envy, one of utter independence."

He snorted, whether in disbelief or disgust she couldn't tell. "Och, lass, I'm afraid I've given ye too much independence. Ye've grown wild, with no one tae restrain ye. I indulged ye because I felt bad for ye, and guilty, too, for the burden ye must bear. I saw what it did tae yer Aunt Morag, and I wanted different for ye."

" 'Tis not a burden." She remembered little of Aunt Morag, only that she'd had white hair at the age of thirty. Her aunt had collapsed under the pressure of the curse and lived out the remainder of her life in a convent. Catherine, on the other hand, tolerated the change when it came.

It seemed the only logical way to survive.

She knew not what happened when she changed, and could remember little other than impressions—owls crying in the night, the smell of dew-dampened pine, rough stone beneath her feet. Nevertheless, the feeling of satisfaction when she awoke in her natural form, of muscles well-exercised and senses well-sated, left her relaxed and contented.

Iain looked as if he would spring off his seat at any moment. " 'Tis a burden for both of us. Do ye understand the worry I've known, wondering where ye are when the change is upon ye? Do ye understand how frail the web of lies we rest upon is? Ye'll be dead one day, shot by a frightened villager, and I'll have naught but tears tae remind me of ye."

"But I'm careful, Papa."

His voice rose several notches. "How can ye be careful when ye're but a beast? Good God, lass, 'tis a miracle ye're not dead already."

Catherine looked away, stung by his use of the word *beast*. Only he knew of the curse that had transformed her since the first day she'd become a woman. He'd helped her endure the agony of the change, protected her from the superstitious eyes of the villagers, made excuses for her. The only thing he hadn't done was discover how to free her from the curse.

She wasn't even certain if she could be freed.

He leaned closer, a strange determination burning in his gaze. "Things are going tae change, Catriona. Mark me."

"I am a Highlander, Papa. I will take no master." She set her chin stubbornly. Men and their double standards. "After all, 'tis you who's told me many times that a Highlander bows to no one. '*We are content with discord,*' you said, '*content with alarms, content with blood, but we will never be content with a master.*' Well, I might not be a man, but I certainly intended to follow your teaching."

Her father collapsed against the seat. "I see I've taught ye well. Too well."

Catherine silently cheered this small victory. Now, if only she could convince him to stop searching for someone to wed her.

Iain grew somber, his mood unbroken until they crossed the River Helmsdale. Soon afterward, the tangy smell of a peat fire and the cool scent of pine permeated the carriage, and the shingled roof of the Temperance Inn appeared over the treetops. Apparently unable to resist the beauty of his own lands, her father began to hum a lively tune, the same one he sang whenever in a spirited mood.

> *"My heart's in the Highlands, my heart is not here,*
> *My heart's in the Highlands a' chasing the deer;*
> *A' chasing the wild deer, and following the roe,*
> *My heart's in the Highlands wherever I go."*

Humming along with him, Catherine leaned forward to peer outside. The chaise lumbered beside a forest of oak and pine, one of the few in the Strath of Kildonan.

She knew this forest well, and knew what it held at its heart: Bodhan's Pond. The waters of the pond seemed silvery on the surface, but if she looked long enough, an errant ray of sunlight would illuminate its depths to a brilliant green. A turbulent burn flowed into the pond, depositing salmon and trout among the duck grass that danced deep beneath the surface.

Somehow, Bodhan's Pond was the very embodiment of a Highlander—taciturn and opaque upon a cursory inspection, but full of life and richness deep within. And her father, the chieftain of the MacClellands . . . he reminded her of the Grampian Mountains, purple in the lowering sun, surrounding the moors and forests with a protective embrace equal to that of a loving father for a child.

In centuries past, the MacClelland chiefs had ruled the Strath of Kildonan with an uncompromising fist. But times had changed. No longer did clansmen need to follow without question their laird's edicts. Nevertheless, Iain's men regarded him with the same blind devotion accorded past chiefs. His love of the land and his sense of responsibility toward his people were well-known in a time when lairds routinely ousted their clan from the land in favor of Cheviot sheep.

Iain—MacNiall to his clan—owned over one hundred thousand acres of what many in England called wasteland, but Catherine knew better. She need only walk to the little waterfall that emptied into Bodhan's Pond, and sit by the oak tree whose trunk glistened with spray, to know she'd come as close to heaven as anyone on this world could.

Of course, the McQuades claimed Bodhan's Pond as their own, for they, too, felt the pond's magical quality, and it sat upon their common border. The MacClellands and the McQuades had spent hundreds of years—and an equal number of lives—disputing that border, and each side was loath to give up the pond. It would be an admittance of defeat in a land where one clan simply did not submit to another.

Robert McQuade, the black-hearted bastard, had actually filed a claim in Helmsdale to settle the dispute once and for all. It was a foolish move, for a magistrate's order wouldn't end the feud between the clans. No, the sun would most likely cease to rise before the MacClellands and the McQuades called a truce. Catherine, after all, had the strongest reason to hate them, for it was a McQuade witch who'd cursed the MacClellands with the grimalkin.

And hate them she did.

In a short time they'd passed the forest and bumped their way onto Kildonan's main thoroughfare. Early evening sunshine slanted between two mountains, casting the village with a lurid glow. All of the buildings were constructed of gray stone, giving the impression that the village had thrust up from the earth itself, like some rough-hewn mountain.

What a difference from London's industrialized practicality, Catherine thought, where buildings—particularly in the poorer sections of the city—had all the charm of a boil on a sheep's arse. Here in Kildonan, the black peat smoke spouting from a dozen chimneys smelled of honest work, and the display tables laden with various goods—pewter mugs, pitchers, honeycomb candles—spoke of painstaking craftsmanship.

She craned her neck as they passed a cottage garden sporting a profusion of flowers. An old woman sat on a chair outside the cottage, a stool before her and a length of delicate material clutched in her hands. A few bee skeps and earthenware jugs tumbled beside her. Catherine waved to her. "Look, it's Old Queenie with her lace-maker and beehives."

Iain didn't answer. Wondering what had caught his tongue, she turned in his direction. His face had taken on a beet-red hue. "Papa, what's wrong?"

"Nothing, lass." He paused as the red leaked out of his face. "Just a touch o' fire in the blood."

"What do you mean, a 'touch of fire'? Shall I call for the surgeon?"

"Nay, I'll be fine."

She thrust her chin forward. "You're going to rest when we get home. I'll see to it."

He began to protest, but she cut him off before more than a few jumbled words escaped his mouth. "No arguments. Just bed."

A weak grin curved his lips. "Ye see why I'm always trying tae marry ye off."

She returned his grin despite herself. How could she be anything other than happy? They were almost *home*.

* * *

Iain slept on a massive four-poster bed fashioned from mahogany. His was a man's chamber, filled with the items he loved most in life: a collection of Shakespeare, several ancient dirks, a carefully folded length of the MacClelland tartan. Catherine, who sat beside him in a velvet-upholstered chair, placed his dinner on a side table. The slice of Hallowe'en cake, his dessert, lay forgotten. "You cannot die on me, Papa."

She held his hand in her own and watched leaves colored red, gold, and brown swirl past the windows opposite his bed. They settled on the ground far below, blanketing the earth for the winter to come.

Iain opened bloodshot eyes. " 'Tis not my wish, lass, but God's will."

" 'Tis my will that you live!" Hand trembling, she pushed the hair back from his brow. Her throat and chest felt tight, as if constrained by bands of iron. Thoughts of the future beat a dull monotone in her mind. *If I lose him, I will lose the only love I have in this world.*

"Half my body is dead. The rest will soon follow. 'Tis the way of things. Grieve not for me, for soon I'll join yer mother." His voice failing, Iain spoke with an odd lisp, a result of the apoplexy that had paralyzed him a week before.

A tear slipped down the side of her face. "Why did you not tell me you were sick?"

"I didna know myself. I thought it just a wee touch o' fire in the blood."

"Oh, Papa."

Fragprie, her father's factor, pushed the door open an inch. "How is he?" Short, graying, dressed simply in a linen shirt and plaid, the man had made repeated forays into the laird's bedchamber in the last week. Each time Iain had asked Catherine to leave.

"He is holding his own."

"May I come in?"

"No, you may not. Leave us be, Fragprie." She didn't know how long her father had left, but she planned to spend her every waking second with him, Fragprie be damned. Iain's factor was forever trying to put her in her place, but in a sneaky way, one that precluded open confrontation. She didn't like the man, and knew it showed on her face.

Fragprie nodded once and eased the door shut again. He had the attitude of a man who plotted, she thought. Iain and Fragprie had stirred up more than their share of trouble over the years, most of it directed at Robert McQuade. For once, she didn't care. Concern for her father consumed her night and day.

Iain lifted one shaky hand and touched her hair. "I shall not leave ye tae fend for yerself."

"Hush, Papa, you need your sleep."

The fire snapping in the hearth filled the room with warmth but also made it quite stuffy. She stood and cracked one of the windows open, certain fresh air would do a good deal to improve her father's mood.

"I've arranged a match for ye." The voice, weak yet stubborn, drifted from the bed.

She froze by the window, not certain she'd heard him right. "Arranged a match?"

"A husband, lass. Ye're tae be married." He closed his eyes for several moments, a rattling sound building deep within his chest.

She recognized how ill her father was, how close to death, but this was one subject she would not discuss with him. "I cannot make any promises about marriage, Papa. Rest now."

He struggled to open blue eyes filled with pain. "Listen tae me. Ye've got tae understand. Ye must marry him."

Fearing he'd lost his grip on reality, she indulged him a little. "Whom must I marry?"

"Nicholas, Duke of Efington."

"And what makes you think he will offer for me, should I agree to have him?"

"I've blackmailed him into it, lass."

Her mouth fell open. "You what?"

"He has no choice. Duchess of Efington you will be." He stopped speaking and closed his eyes again, the rattling sound becoming louder.

"Why have you done this? I have no wish to marry the Duke of Efington. And I'm quite certain he has no wish to marry me." Catherine shook her head, stunned at the depth of his deviousness, sick as he was. He'd put her very life in jeopardy! Why, *why* had he fixated on the Duke of Efington?

"Marry him ye must."

"Did you know they call him the Dark Duke belowstairs? Mary has supplied me with the gossip, and it isn't for the fainthearted."

"I care not for servants' prattle. Neither should ye, lass."

She felt her cheeks flush with heat. "Mary may be my maidservant, but she is also my distant cousin and a friend." Hands gripped together, she plowed on. "She says the duke gambled away half the Efington fortune before winning it back. That he kept two mistresses at once, *in the same house,* while carrying on with Lady Saunders. The man has bedded more women than the Prince Regent himself. You, Papa, wish me to marry a rakehell."

His voice grew huskier. "I canna leave ye here alone. Besides, he's a good man. Ye know that, deep inside. That's why ye respond tae him."

She shook her head. This was insanity. "Even if you hadn't set your sights on the Duke of Efington, I would not marry. I cannot."

"Ye will, lass, when you hear the rest. Lean close, now, for my strength is almost gone." His face filled with blood as he struggled to draw her closer.

"Papa, you must relax. Let me call the surgeon."

"Nay, I have no time for surgeons. Listen to me, Catriona," he implored, lapsing into Gaelic.

She tensed. Gaelic was the language of Iain's heart. For everyday affairs concerning Rivendell, for business transactions in Inverness and Glasgow, and in ordinary conversation, they spoke English. When something troubled him, or when he wished to speak of the things that mattered, he always used Gaelic.

"There's much I've been hiding from you. The duke is a McQuade. Other than Robert McQuade, only he can free you." He broke off as a rumbling gasp issued from his throat.

The sound reminded her of the mewling a deer made

when an arrow pierced its lungs rather than its heart. She drew the covers up over his chest, arranging and rearranging, as if a quilt could ward that arrow off. "The duke? A McQuade? How can this be?"

"He is a bastard. His mother Annabella had an affair with Robert McQuade and conceived his child. The duke's ring and birthmark prove it."

She felt her eyes widen. "A McQuade." Suddenly she realized why he'd chosen the duke as her mate and her mind whirled with the possibilities.

"Aye." He gurgled a sigh. "Do you remember the witch's rhyme?"

She nodded. How could she possibly forget? The rhyme was the key to life and death . . . the key to the torment MacClelland women had suffered throughout the centuries.

She'd heard it first just after her fifth birthday. She and her father had sat upon the branch of a large oak tree, its limbs covered with leaves as green as clover, the sun slanting down through the foliage to illuminate her father's face.

"Your mother is gone, Catriona," he'd said, "so I must tell you of the curse you will bear when you become a woman."

"What mean you, Da?" Giggling, she kicked her legs so hard she almost fell backward. Iain set her to rights but his face remained so serious she felt her own smile slip.

"We're a cursed clan, Catriona. Our men pass the seed down to the ones they love most—their daughters—and must watch them suffer."

She pulled a handful of heather from her apron pocket and sniffed it. "But seeds make flowers."

"Not this seed, lassie. Sileas McQuade, an ancient witch, sowed this seed in hatred for a terrible evil your ancestor committed."

"I don't understand, Da."

"The seed makes the grimalkin. I passed the seed to you. Right now the grimalkin sleeps, but when you become a woman, it will awaken."

She felt her eyes grow round at his revelation. "Will the grimalkin eat me?"

"No, lassie. You will become the grimalkin at night."

"I will become a cat?"

A peculiar sheen to his eyes, he smoothed her hair. "Aye."

A smile grew on her face. "Then I shall visit the mother cat in the barn and bring her kittens some scraps. Thank you, Da, for passing the seed to me." In her innocence, she'd found the idea of becoming the grimalkin wonderful.

But he'd looked off toward the distant moors, and a moment later, his frame had begun to tremble. When she'd heard the sobs erupt from his throat, she'd put her arms around him in a vain attempt to comfort him. After several moments had passed, he'd recited the rhyme to her in a choked voice.

Now she understood all too well why her father had cried for her that day. Hands clenched into fists, she began to recite:

"Killed my laird and killed my kin,
Only hatred beneath your skin,
Mixed and drank my family's blood,
Poured the remainder into mud,
A curse I place upon your daughters,
As the grimalkin they shall practice slaughter,
Until love grows between MacClelland and McQuade,
And the feud between us to rest is laid."

Silence, broken only by Iain's heavy breathing, lay heavily upon the bedchamber. She leaned forward, her heartbeat clamoring in her ears. Death hovered around him; like a shadow it smothered him, clouding his gaze, obstructing his airway, making his body tremble.

After several seconds, Iain said, "So chanted the witch Sileas before she threw herself on her husband's claymore to seal the devil's bargain." He paused, chest rattling. She strained to understand him, for his words were faint.

"You can expect no solace from Robert McQuade—he'd as soon slit his throat as fall in love with a MacClelland. But now you have a chance, lass. You must make the duke love you."

She stood and began to pace. For the first time in her life, she began to consider the idea of marriage. She knew it was a selfish thing to contemplate, forcing a man to wed a woman cursed as she was, but her intense longing for a normal life warred with the guilt that knotted in her stomach. "What reason did you give the duke for your blackmail?"

"I did not contact him directly. Rather, I sent his mother a missive. I know her well. She will be much more effective at coercion than anything I might do."

Clutching her hand in a viselike grip, he spoke with a peculiar force, as if he'd used the last of the air in his lungs. "I told her I will expose the duke as a bastard if he does not marry you before the Yuletide. She thinks we're after the duke's fortune."

" 'Tis easiest to tell the lie constructed of half-truths."

"Aye. But you cannot tell the duke more until he is ready. Fragprie will handle the details of the marriage." His gaze fastened on something she couldn't see. "Forgive me, Catriona, for leaving you." He sighed, his chest sinking in and becoming concave. It didn't rise again.

Motionless, she stared at him. He wasn't supposed to die. "Breathe, Papa." Her voice sounded so low she almost didn't recognize it. "Breathe, I say."

His hand slipped from her grasp. It still felt warm.

"Papa?" Fierce pressure began to build behind her eyes. She felt as if her head were going to explode. "Papa?"

A film settled over his eyes.

Drool leaked from the corner of his mouth.

"Please, don't leave me. I don't want to be alone."

Peck, peck. A sparrow, its small brown body quivering with life, clung to the windowsill and tapped on the glass.

Her father remained inanimate.

This isn't happening, she thought.

Oh, but it is, lassie, some corner of her brain taunted. *Your father is dead, and you are going to marry a man who will hate you like no other.*

She heard the voice and although she despised it, she knew it spoke the truth. Tears began to build, a turbulent river of them, promising bitter relief from the tension that coiled in her head. She pressed her face against her father's hand. "Good-bye, Papa. I love you."

The first agonizing jolt came without warning. It hit her with the force of a cannonball. She bent over double with the intensity of it, her mouth wide. A fire burned inside her, one so hot she was certain she'd disintegrate. It peaked and began to fade.

The grimalkin had awakened, without warning, as it was wont to do in times of strong emotion.

She left her father's body and raced into the hallway for her own bedchamber.

A second wave began to build. She managed to pull the door to her room open and stagger inside before collapsing onto the sheepskin rug. A window in her room stood ajar and she thanked the good Lord for it, for she hadn't the strength to open it herself.

Her bones were melting.

She kept her lips clenched tight to keep the scream bottled up inside. *Dear God,* she thought, *spare me this one time! I need to be with my father now.* But even as she formed the entreaty, she realized the change had progressed too far to stop.

After one tormenting minute, the ache dwindled. Knowing the next few moments were her final respite before the transformation, she crawled to the door on all fours and locked it. Beads of sweat trickled into her eyes, and she fought to draw air into lungs so hot they felt blistered.

The agony began to build, for the third and final time.

Unexpectedly, an amazingly clear image arrowed through the red haze filling her mind—a man's hawkish face, gray eyes darkened with passion, his careless grin making her quiver with need—and for an instant she felt nothing but yearning. Too quickly her yearning changed to regret, for in that instant, she also realized she couldn't use the duke as a pawn to gain her freedom. Her conscience simply wouldn't allow it. No, she'd travel to London at the first opportunity and release him from this farce of a betrothal.

The red haze obscured the duke's face and her ears began to ring with the beat of her own racing heart. Tendons popped and muscles stretched, reshaping themselves into something altogether different. Her spine lengthened and her skin tightened, itching with demonic intensity. She howled with the pain of it, but no human sound passed her lips, for she no longer had a voice.

Papa's dead, she thought. And yet, other thoughts, alien thoughts, began to intrude—the smell of black-footed sheep in Raonull's pasture, the disturbing clang of pots in the kitchen, the seductive glitter of moonlight on the wings of passing geese. These thoughts pushed her out, forced her to recede to a dark place that numbed her. And when she felt her muscles bunch to jump, she thought no more.

Three

Nicholas paused in front of the entrance to White's. Inside, men of all shapes and fortunes passed before the window, eagerly losing their blunt at gaming tables. He, too, knew what it meant to have gambling fever, for he'd nearly lost the Efington estate at a table of *jeu d'enfer*. But he'd conquered that weakness long ago, and now felt only saddened by the lengths to which some peers went to assuage their obsession.

The club's usher recognized him on the sidewalk and ran down the stairs to greet him. The oil lamp he held in his hand cast a dim glow on his sallow features. "Good evening, Your Grace. A fine night it is, too."

A cool October wind cut through the streets of the city, banishing the coal smoke and customary fog. Moonlight shone on leaves gilded with frost, lending a picturesque cast to an otherwise unremarkable section of London.

Nicholas nodded. "It is indeed."

"Thinking of joining us tonight? We expect both the Duke of Wellington and two ministers of the Crown."

"An impressive gathering. I believe I shall." He followed the usher up the stairs and into White's.

A large book lay open on a pedestal, the current date

printed on the top of the page. Various patrons had scribbled wagers beneath the date, some for guineas, some topping one thousand pounds. He paused to examine the most recent entry.

Ld. Lincoln bets Ld. Winchilsea One Hundred Guineas that the Dutchess Dowager of Marlborough does not survive the Dutchess Dowager of Cleveland.

Shaking his head at their callous disregard for something as sacred as death, he moved farther into the establishment, nodding to acquaintances as he passed. The gentlemen's club had spared no expense on the decor. The chairs and tables were handsome pieces done in the Sheraton style, and blue velvet draperies hung in luxurious folds over the windows.

A walnut table, surrounded by jolly, drunken peers, dominated the far corner of the room. Cards, sprung from a mechanical box, lay on the table in a distinctive pattern.

Faro.

Accepting a glass of Scotch whisky from the waiter, Nicholas sat at the table and began to play. Several hours later and many pounds richer, he broke his concentration from the cards and stretched. And noticed something odd.

A few of his acquaintances looked at him with speculative glances. Some of the younger bucks of the ton even stopped in midspeech as his gaze settled on them, as though they'd been discussing him.

He glanced down at his coat of blue superfine, at the snowy folds of his linen neckcloth, at the waistcoat from which a single gold fob descended. Had he dropped a dollop of whisky on his shirt, or disgraced himself in some other manner?

No, as far as he could tell, his clothes were spotless. His valet had done an impeccable job that night, as usual. What in damnation was going on?

Suddenly a familiar face pushed through the crowd. "Nicky. I thought I'd find you here." Harry Rappaport gave Nicholas an easy smile and brushed an imaginary speck of lint from the sleeve of his puce-colored coat. His heavy-lidded eyes, evidence of distant Italian ancestry, reflected a hint of curiosity rather than their customary ennui.

" 'Tis not hard to find me. You need only follow the stares."

Harry raised one languid eyebrow. "What have you done, coz, to incur such interest?"

"I'm not certain. Shall we investigate?"

"By all means."

The two men began to circulate around the room, Nicholas hoping to find someone willing to fill him in on the latest *on-dit*. As the gossip apparently concerned him, however, the other gentlemen met his inquisitive gaze with blank stares.

Harry, however, had better luck, for within minutes he returned to Nicholas's side. "Lord Webster mentioned a certain wager he'd placed in the betting book within the hour. I suggest we examine the book immediately."

Nicholas led the way to the ledger that lay open upon the pedestal. Directly beneath the wager regarding the longevity of the dowager duchesses of Marlborough and Cleveland, he found a new entry:

> *Mr. Gilmartin bets Ld. Webster Two Thousand Pounds that Lady Catherine MacClelland, "Angel of Mercy," shall reform the "Dark" Duke of Efington within one year of their marriage.*

"What nonsense is this?" Nicholas raised a disbelieving eyebrow. How could Lord Webster make such a tremendous error? Never, not even for a moment, would he consider marriage to Catherine MacClelland. In a spouse, he wanted docility, for God's sake, not a tart-tongued shrew. He pitied the man who would dare marry her.

Harry shrugged. "We'd best find Lord Webster."

The two men began to search White's for the unfortunate peer. Nicholas couldn't help but wonder how he'd again become linked to the Scotswoman.

In the three months since the debacle at Lady Wisborough's ball, he'd considered his behavior that night carefully. It had been a complete departure from his usual attitude of polite boredom, so different that he would have blamed it on sorcery if he weren't an enlightened man. First his uncontrollable desire for the wench with hair of honey and flame, his ballocks tightening like those of a stag in rut; then his absurd sighting of a leopard at the MacClelland residence.

He found his lack of control disgusting. It reminded him of earlier days, days spent drinking, nights spent with members of the Hell Fire Club. . . . He felt nauseated just thinking about it. All that wine and debauchery; thank God he'd gotten hold of himself before he'd put himself into an early grave.

But not before he'd collected a few ghosts. The young prostitute splayed on the altar, her cries for mercy twinged with a Cockney accent—she still haunted him at night, drove him to the bottle on particularly lonely evenings. He hadn't wanted it to happen, hadn't actually participated in the ceremony, but damn it, he hadn't stopped it, either.

The girl had shown a remarkable resemblance to Clarissa Stonehaven.

The morning after the ceremony, he'd returned to the labyrinth to find her, to help her in some way, but discovered only blood and the remnants of a buckram petticoat. Either she'd disappeared into the teeming throngs of the London unwashed, or someone had buried her.

The smell of her terror and the salty tang of sex lingering in his nose, he'd gone home and examined himself in the looking glass—eyes ringed with circles, hollow cheeks, a three-day-old beard on his face—and sworn to turn his life around.

That had happened over four years ago. From that day forward, his life had remained moderate, even boring. Nevertheless, he preferred boredom to the specter of a young girl's eyes wide with shock. He didn't know what had happened to him the night of Lady Wisborough's ball, but for his own peace of mind, he'd stayed away from Catherine MacClelland ever since. He hadn't even sent her an apology for his behavior, as he'd planned to do. Around her, he threw caution to the winds and let his body rule him.

That made her dangerous indeed.

Nicholas and Harry found their prey seated at a game of

loo, a glass of wine at his elbow. Nicholas approached him with a heavy frown. "Good evening, Lord Webster. I would like to discuss a certain wager with you."

He gestured to a more private corner of the room, and Lord Webster—a portly gentleman in his early twenties—hurried from the table, deserting his cards. "Of course, Your Grace."

Nicholas kept his voice to a low murmur, but he couldn't quite remove the outrage from his tone. "Explain the wager you placed with Mr. Gilmartin."

Lord Webster's brown eyes widened. "Your Grace, I apologize for using the term 'Dark Duke,' but I didn't mean it in a negative sense. We all think you're superlative, a Nonesuch, and we admire you greatly, especially your touch with the horses. We bet on Ladyfair at the Ascot—"

"Yes, yes, I took no offense at the term. Will you explain the wager?"

Appearing even more agitated, Lord Webster clasped his hands. "If the betrothal isn't common knowledge, I apologize, but Mr. Gilmartin assured me banns will be posted in tomorrow's *Gazette,* and we found the match so intriguing, particularly after your long courtship of Lady Clarissa Stonehaven, and Lady Catherine MacClelland a spinster at eight and twenty—"

Nicholas felt his heart rate increase ever so slightly. A noose was tightening around him, one he couldn't see but felt at his throat. He cut in again. "You are correct, Lord Webster. My betrothal isn't common knowledge, primarily because I haven't asked the lady yet. And the lady is, indeed, Clarissa Stonehaven, not Catherine MacClelland."

Even as he paled, Lord Webster's eyebrows drew together in confusion. "But how can this be? I assure you your mother has posted banns in tomorrow's *Gazette*. Mr. Gilmartin has connections in the *Gazette*'s publishing department, and it is he who suggested the wager. He knows the MacClelland family from court in Edinburgh, says he struck up a flirtation with Lady Catherine only to have her chide him for bad manners . . ."

The invisible noose began to choke Nicholas, robbing him of breath, but at least now he knew who pulled it tight—his own dear mother. Why would she want to promote a marriage between him and Catherine MacClelland? Had she even met the Scotswoman? Cursing Annabella silently but fervently, Nicholas dismissed Lord Webster with a curt nod. "I see I shall have to take this matter up elsewhere."

"Good evening to you, Your Grace," Lord Webster replied. Rather than return to his cards, he made for the exit.

"What will you do now?" Harry grabbed a glass of wine from a passing waiter and took a sip.

"Speak to my mother, of course."

"I'll drive by tomorrow morning to make sure Efington House still stands."

After giving Harry a humorless smile, Nicholas left White's and headed straightaway to Efington House and his deceitful mother. Moonlight had given way to storm clouds, and by the time his barouche stopped outside his residence, a wet, freezing rain had begun to pelt the city.

Efington House was one of London's great Palladian houses and sported numerous steps leading up to the door. It looked quite splendid but was hardly convenient, Nicholas thought, as he raced up the stairs. The storm wet him to the skin and blew him to bits before he reached the door, improving neither his appearance nor temper.

A footman stationed in an alcove jumped to open the door. Nicholas strode into the great marble foyer and began to strip off his sodden outer garments. Another footman caught each piece of clothing before it hit the floor.

"Merriam," Nicholas shouted, and accepted dry clothes proffered by yet a third footman.

Merriam, his bald pate gleaming beside the candle he held aloft, walked in with a serene expression. He held himself regally, as befitted the butler of a duke. "Your Grace. How good to see you this evening."

" 'Tis five in the morning, man! Don't stand on ceremony. Where is the duchess?"

"Upstairs in her suite, Your Grace. Shall I announce you?"

Nicholas ignored his butler's offer and took the steps two at a time. How convenient, he thought, that Annabella had returned early from the ball she'd attended. Not bothering to knock, he barged into her rooms and strode over to her canopied bed. "Wake up, madam," he said in as rude a tone as he could muster. "You and I must talk."

"Wha? Wha?" Gaping like a beached fish, Annabella sat up, a frilly cap askew on her graying curls. "Who is that? Nicholas? How dare you barge into my bedroom, boy, and wake me from a sound sleep! What devil has gotten hold of you?"

After lighting an oil lamp, he scrutinized her with cold impatience. "I might ask the same of you, madam. I find myself sick to death of your meddling in my life."

Bluster replaced some of the outrage in her gray eyes. "You come in here at . . ." she paused to squint at the ormolu clock on the mantelshelf, "five in the morning, to issue threats to an old woman? You'll put me in my grave, and that ain't a thing for a son to be proud of."

He leaned close to better look her in the eye. "You have posted banns of my marriage without my knowledge or consent. If that isn't beyond the pale, you have me priest-linked to that MacClelland wench, not Lady Clarissa Stonehaven. Have you lost your mind?"

Nicholas's stony gaze locked with Annabella's defiant one. Neither he nor his mother looked away for several seconds, until, much to his surprise, moisture filled her eyes. Then, as if someone had punched the air out of her, she simply caved in. Shoulders bent, fingers folding and unfolding the ivory counterpane, she began to cry. She looked frail, as delicate as the yellow tea roses papered on the bedchamber's walls.

He tried to hold on to his anger, without success. Annabella had cried in front of him only three times in his life: when his father had died, when her friend had lost her first baby, and when an Arabian had broken its leg racing the Ascot. Each time, he'd felt horrible. Tonight was no different. He softened his tone and sat next to her on the bed. "Tell me, Mother, what has happened."

Her tears began to flow in earnest, dropping from her chin and wetting the top of her nightgown. "Oh, Nicholas, there is so much you don't know, so much you won't understand. Or forgive. . . ."

He put an arm around her shoulders and gave her a little squeeze. How bad could it be? "Nothing you tell me will make a whit of difference to my affection for you."

A tremulous smile formed on her lips and, much to his relief, the flow of tears decreased somewhat. "You're a good son. If only your father had given you a chance—"

"Please, let us discuss the issue at hand." His father was a sore spot in Nicholas's heart, a wound that continued to pain him if prodded. He still heard the tinkling sound of the pianoforte his father had insisted he learn to play, felt the sting of leather across his backside when he'd refused. Ross, eleventh Duke of Efington, aroused nothing but revulsion in his son.

Nicholas closed the door on the memories before they could surface and distract him from his mother's confession. "Why have you posted banns of a marriage between myself and Catherine MacClelland?"

The duchess took out a square of linen and blew her nose into it. "I don't know if I can tell you."

"You must. And spare not a single detail, for if I am to extricate us from this mess, I need to know *everything.*"

A knock interrupted them.

Nicholas mouthed a few oaths. "What is it?"

"I brought some refreshment, Your Grace." Merriam's voice drifted through the door that separated them.

"Come in."

Merriam glided in, a tray laden with a delicate Wedgwood tea service and a decanter of brandy in his hands. He poured tea for the duchess, but refrained from filling Nicholas's snifter when Nicholas waved him aside.

"Will that be all, Your Grace?"

"May I remind you, Merriam, that I did not ask for refreshment?" The butler's face held concern, and as it was unusual for him to display any emotion, Nicholas curbed the desire to shout at him. "Nevertheless, your instincts are superb, as usual. That will be all. The duchess and I do not wish to see anyone until I inform you otherwise."

Merriam inclined his head and made a gracious retreat.

Annabella took a swallow of tea and straightened her

back. Light from the oil lamp created hollows beneath her eyes, making her look far older than her fifty-eight years.

"Almost forty years ago, Ross and I traveled to Edinburgh, ostensibly to court," she began. "Your father was actually in the service of the king, investigating rumors of corruption. A few Scots peers had complained of a dishonest patronage system thriving under Henry Dundas, who was then the Scottish lieutenant."

After filling his snifter with brandy, Nicholas nodded, encouraging her to continue. She'd mentioned this trip several times, most recently at Lady Wisborough's ball. But how did the MacClellands fit in?

She took another swallow of tea. "Specifically, Robert McQuade, the Earl of Bucharrie, had made several outrageous statements to the House of Lords, all concerning Dundas. According to the earl, 'Dundas was the pharos of Scotland. Who steered upon him was safe, who disregarded his light was wrecked.' The king asked your father to cultivate the earl, find out what he knew about Dundas's patronage system, and report back."

The duchess's voice had begun to tremble, most notably when she mentioned the Earl of Bucharrie, and Nicholas wondered what the Scottish earl could have done to arouse such fear.

"Your father did just that," she continued. "He became fast friends with Robert McQuade. Throughout our time in Edinburgh, we stayed at Kinclaven Castle, the seat of the McQuades." She broke off and began to pleat the counterpane, folding and unfolding until he could stand it no more and covered her hands with his own.

"It's all right, Mother. Tell me." He used as gentle a voice as he was capable of.

When she looked up at him, her eyes pleaded with him to understand. "You know how uncaring, how cold your father was. Robert McQuade had the fire of the Scots in him, and he was a compassionate man, concerned for my well-being. One night, when Ross fell asleep . . ." Her face twisted, and she stopped, the tears flowing again.

Nicholas sighed deeply. He could see where this was

going. Fear hadn't caused her lips to tremble over the name Bucharrie.

Annabella remained silent for several moments, evidently trying to work up the courage to tell him what he'd already guessed. Finally, she choked out, "Robert and I became lovers. Even as your father used me each night, I thought of the moment when I could sneak away to Robert's rooms."

Although he had braced himself for exactly that piece of news, her revelation still hit him with the force of a sledgehammer. Not because she'd found solace from a loveless marriage in the arms of another man, not because she'd bedded two men beneath the same roof, at the same time. He, of course, had kept Valerie and Lydia within his Torrington Square residence for over a month.

No, what frightened him most was the suspicion that had suddenly popped into his mind when she'd uttered the word *lovers.* He released her hands and sat back, a terrible burning in his gut. Even though the liquor would only add to the burning, he picked up his snifter and drank the remaining brandy in two tremendous gulps. Then he looked away, lost in the grimness of his thoughts.

Annabella did not notice his reaction. Now that she'd made her confession, the floodgates opened, and words poured forth so quickly he had to strain to understand them.

"Ross was cruel, you must understand that. Not cruel in a physical sense, but in the way he made me feel. As if I were dirty, worthless, uglier than the flotsam that drifts along the Thames. Robert treated me so differently, so reverently. He respected me and understood me at a time when I'd given up hope. How I loved him." She broke off for a moment and her face glowed with the memory. "You are a child of love, Nicholas, never forget that."

There, she'd admitted it.

He was the by-blow of a Scottish earl.

Good Christ, a bastard!

He closed his eyes for a moment, trying to assimilate the true proportions of the disaster, his mind working slower than it ought. Each revelation, as it came to him, was like a physical blow.

This house didn't belong to him.

He was not the duke.

The Efington lands didn't belong to him.

He had no right to take a seat in the House of Lords.

In short, his entire life was a sham, built upon deception. Even worse, shame filled him: he was naught but the product of a tawdry affair.

There must be some mistake, he thought, at the same time realizing he was grasping at straws.

Annabella touched his face with her palm, much as she had when he'd been little and his father had hurt him. "I'm sorry, Nicholas, for what I've done to you this night. I would have kept the secret forever, if possible."

He pulled away from her touch, and the pain of his rejection showed in the way she flinched. He couldn't help it—he had his own wounds to tend right now. "Are you absolutely certain I'm the spawn of some Scottish Highlander?"

"Yes. The star-shaped birthmark on your stomach makes me so. Robert McQuade has the same mark on his own skin. 'Tis an inherited mark, one carried by the McQuade chiefs for centuries. But Nicholas, 'tis no shame being the son of a McQuade. Robert is honorable, kind, from a long line of men like him." Her voice was a whisper, filled with regret. Nevertheless, he caught a hint of defiance in the way she set her chin.

Clenching his hands, he stalked to the marble fireplace and stared at the glowing embers within. Only the *tick-tick-tick* of the clock on the mantelshelf broke the silence in the room.

"Your ring, too, is a McQuade heirloom," she tentatively offered. "The 'R' stands not for 'Ross' but for 'Robert.' Robert gave it to me in parting, as a token of his love."

He swung around to face her, blood pounding through his veins. It seemed his life was a lie down to the smallest detail. Narrowing his eyes, he said in an even voice, "You told me that ring was from my father."

"It was, Nicholas." She dropped her gaze and examined the counterpane again.

The tenuous control he'd had on his temper snapped like a thread in a gale-force wind. He wanted to take her by the arms and shake her, but instead he removed the ring and slammed it onto the mantelshelf. He poured his anger, his sense of betrayal into the words that erupted from his mouth. "Goddamn it, Mother! How could you do this? We stand to lose everything."

Annabella looked at him, her eyes such raw pools of pain that he felt his rage weakening even as he cursed her. She was as much a victim as he, caught for years in an evil maelstrom named Ross Efington.

Lips quivering, she smoothed the counterpane. "Oh, Nicholas, I'm sorry. I dreaded this moment because I knew I'd lose you forever, and now I have. I love you so dearly—you're the only thing I have left to remind me of Robert. Please, try to forgive me, try to understand. Robert gave me a few months of joy in an otherwise hellish existence."

She stood and moved to the window, her back to him, and sighed bitterly. "If only Iain MacClelland had kept silent."

"You have not lost me," he said, jaw clenched. He did not yet understand how Iain MacClelland fit in, but he'd be damned if he'd let the laird ruin their lives.

Relief swept across Annabella's face. Shivering, she grasped the decanter of brandy and refilled her cup. The embers in the fireplace didn't throw much heat into the room, and Nicholas knew her prim cotton nightgown wouldn't keep her warm. He retrieved a blue velvet wrap from her wardrobe, which she gratefully accepted.

Once they'd sat down, Nicholas on a straight-backed chair and Annabella on a yellow damask sofa, he stared at the cup in his hand and said, "Does McQuade know about me?"

She shook her head vigorously. "No. I dared not tell him, for his hatred of the Sassunach is second only to his familial loyalty. If he had discovered he'd sired a son, he would have insisted upon claiming you, if only to raise you as a proper Highlander."

The invisible noose around his throat loosened a bit. McQuade's ignorance made the situation more tolerable. "I must say I'm relieved. Now tell me how MacClelland became involved."

Sighing, she looked to the ceiling, as if searching for words. "Robert and Iain are old enemies. The blood feud between their clans goes back centuries. Iain took particular delight in causing as much trouble for Robert as he could. One night . . ." she paused, her cheeks reddening, "Robert and I decided to make love by a pond near the border of McQuade lands. 'Tis said that the pond has a special property, that of fertility. Of course, I discounted it at the time, thinking it an old wives' tale, but nine months later I paid the price for my carelessness."

Nicholas winced at the reminder of his undesirable beginning: He was a by-blow, a mistake, born of two people who'd enjoyed an illicit union.

Grimacing, she continued, "One of Iain's men, a Scot by the name of Fragprie, had been spying on Robert and followed us to Bodhan's Pond. The bastard stayed to watch us make love, revealing himself only when he startled a pack of grouse to flight. Robert identified him but couldn't catch him. Obviously Fragprie informed Iain of our tryst, but Iain has kept the knowledge of the affair to himself . . . until now."

Nicholas frowned, his dislike for Iain MacClelland growing to new levels. Now the laird's peculiar interest in his birthmark and ring the night they'd birthed the foal made appalling sense. "And the price for his continued silence is marriage?"

The clock chimed six, its notes echoing eerily throughout the bedchamber. Annabella wrung her hands, tears beginning to flow again. "Yes. He wants you to marry his daughter, Catherine."

"Why did you not come to me with his threats in the first place? Why embarrass me before my peers by posting banns in the *Gazette* without my knowledge?"

"I know you well, Nicholas. You would sooner hang yourself than submit to blackmail. But I'm not as strong as you are. In fact, I'm a coward. I cannot face the ridicule of the women whose friendships I prize. I do not want to give up my position in society, and I refuse to live on Fleet Street. If word of your true parentage leaks out, the *ton* will cast us out and your title and lands will pass to your cousin Harry. I thought if I forced the marriage by posting banns, you'd have to marry the MacClelland gel."

He shook his head. How could his mother have such a

low opinion of him that she thought he'd throw her to the dogs? If his interests alone were at stake, he'd never surrender to MacClelland's blackmail. He would rather the laird expose him as a bastard and live with the consequences. After all, his reputation was already as black as Satan's.

But his mother—he loved her, wanted to preserve both her reputation and the life she'd grown accustomed to. If for no one else, he'd fight MacClelland for his mother's sake. "From now on, come to me before you attempt anything like this. I'm sure I can find a way to come to terms with him. Did he give you a reason for insisting on this travesty of a marriage?"

"The MacClellands are in terrible financial straits. Iain expects you to restore his various properties and support his clan."

His spirits suddenly lifted and a harsh chuckle escaped him. Annabella jumped at the sound.

"So, the old codger wants blunt. Well, blunt he shall have. I'll have my solicitor contact him first thing in the morning." He'd thought it was going to be the very devil to extricate himself from this engagement, but now realized it would be far easier than he'd dreamed. He would bargain with the laird, delivering blunt yet refusing the marriage, and ultimately buying time. MacClelland would have the capital to restore his estates and at the same time keep his daughter free from the unwanted, lecherous attentions of the Dark Duke. For once, Nicholas was thankful for his rakehell reputation.

Annabella shook her head. "I thought of that, too, Nicholas, but MacClelland adamantly rejected my offer. He wants you to marry his daughter."

"He'll change his mind after I tell him what I'm going to do to her."

"I don't like that gleam in your eye, Nicholas. It makes you look positively wicked."

"The MacClellands deserve all the wickedness I can send their way." He stood up and began to pace, already embroidering the tale of lewd desires he'd regale the laird with. The damnable part of it was, he really would like to perform each and every indecent act with the man's daughter, so hot had she stirred his blood.

He even toyed with the idea of sending Catherine a message directly, one that promised he'd bed her wherever and whenever he wanted if she forced him to wed her. After all, she should expect as much from a Dark Duke. But such a message was improper in the extreme, the act of a desperate man, and he'd write it only as a last resort.

"Your father never knew about my affair with Robert McQuade," Annabella said, ending his reverie. "He was mean through to the bone, and made your life miserable for the sheer joy of it. You have not a drop of his blood in your veins, thank God."

A knock saved Nicholas from having to make a response. "What is it now, Merriam?" He wondered why in hell the butler had ignored an explicit order.

"Lady Clarissa Stonehaven is downstairs, Your Grace. She is most distraught, and refuses to budge until she sees you." The butler rasped, as if he were in pain.

A low growl rumbled in Nicholas's throat. She was, quite possibly, the last person he wanted to see. "Show her to the drawing room and tell her I'll be down in a moment." He turned to his mother. "I shall return later to finish this discussion."

Nicholas stalked from the room and brushed past Merriam. The butler struggled to match Nicholas's stride, hobbling in a way suited to a man far more advanced in age.

Noting Merriam's difficulties, Nicholas slowed. "Are you ill?"

"I had to restrain Lady Clarissa Stonehaven. She tried to rush up to Her Grace's rooms. She was most enthusiastic in her resistance, Your Grace." A militant sparkle had entered the butler's eyes.

Nicholas looked to the ceiling, his patience ebbing away. He did not think he could withstand any more female theatrics this night. As he approached the drawing room, he heard muted sobs. Tensing, he took only two steps into the room before a slender female form bowled him over. Her face reddened and puffy from crying, she buried her nose into his neckcloth. A mint-green ribbon wound through her brown curls, giving her an absurdly youthful look that grated on his nerves, particularly since he now felt so old and worn.

He frowned at her, her tears provoking him further. "Clarissa! What are you doing here?"

Clarissa raised limpid brown eyes to his, her lashes spiked with tears. "I am affronted, Your Grace," she said in a coarse whisper. "You have cast me aside for a Scottish dowd."

He felt his eyes widen at her rather melodramatic choice of words. Catherine MacClelland was indeed Scottish, but a dowd? Never. Secretly, he thought Catherine had a spark of life that Clarissa lacked—hell, she was a conflagration, not a spark.

He supposed he'd have to calm Clarissa down before he hurried her out the door. With that in mind, he enfolded her in a paternal embrace and wondered how he was ever going to take her to bed once they'd married. "What have you heard?"

"The Honorable Mr. Gilmartin of Sussex has just informed me that you have posted banns of your marriage . . ." she paused for dramatic effect, her face screwing up for a rush of tears, "to someone other than me. To a heathen, redheaded Scotswoman, in fact."

Exasperation kindled in him at the girl's jealousy. If her diaphanous mint gown—belted beneath her slight breasts and sprigged with embroidered ivy—was any indication, she must have rushed straight to Efington House from whatever party she'd attended. Her timing was as awful as Merriam's was impeccable. " 'Tis simply a misunderstanding between myself and my mother."

"Misunderstanding or not, the banns will be posted in tomorrow's *Gazette.* It is difficult, indeed, for a gentleman to break an engagement once it has been formally announced." Something close to panic appeared in her eyes.

"I will have them print a retraction the following day," he assured her.

"But the Scotswoman, her reputation will be ruined."

"I do not care." A thread of steel ran through the words, and Clarissa gave him a tremulous smile.

He released her from the impromptu embrace and escorted her to the door. She clutched his wrinkled evening coat with a possessive hand, the gaze she bestowed upon him having much in common with that of a cocker spaniel's. "Thank you, Your Grace. You have put my mind at ease."

"My pleasure." He plucked her hand from his coat and sketched her a slight bow. Then, feeling like he'd barely averted calamity, he led her into the front hall, where Merriam had cornered her aunt. "I shall call upon you in two days to inform you of my progress."

Forcing a smile to his lips, he turned her over to her aunt, who was muttering all sorts of dire imprecations. After they'd left, he closeted himself in his study, where he set to cleaning up the mess his mother had made.

The real disaster, however, had yet to come.

Four

"Och, Cat, ye've lost yer senses. The duke will thrae ye out on yer arse, and I canna say ye doan deserve it. Tae go tae a man's house and tell him ye'd rather marry a toad! He'll think ye a nasty piece o' baggage." Mary placed her hands on her bombazine-covered hips and nodded once for emphasis. Her white cap sat crookedly on her head, revealing a demure chignon of soft brown hair.

"Don't call me Cat. You know how I hate that name," Catherine said, her back stiff. "And as far as the duke is concerned, I was speaking figuratively. I have no intention of comparing him unfavorably to a toad. But I do plan to visit him today at Efington House and tell him the marriage is off."

Once again installed in her bedchamber in London, she stalked to the window and, awash in early afternoon light, read the missive clutched in her hands:

Dear Lady,

That you have attempted to blackmail me is disgraceful enough. If you force me to wed you, our marriage will not be one in name only. I shall bed you whenever, and wherever, I please, and you shall beget me an heir. And think not the Efington coffers will be open for your imprudent use. You'll have my hand and title, but you'll not get a sou more.

Most Respectfully Yours,
Nicholas, Duke of Efington

That hateful man! Her fist clenched around the paper and she fought the urge to shred it into a dozen pieces. So, the duke planned to use her as his whore. Let him try it. He'd receive a taste of the dirk she'd tucked into her wool garter.

Some two weeks after her father's death, the duke had called at Rivendell. She hadn't spoken to him herself, preferring not to risk her secret, and instead ordered Fragprie to release the duke from their engagement. For an entire day the duke and Fragprie had remained closeted in the study. Fragprie, despite her wishes, had secretly continued to blackmail the duke into marriage. Evidently her father had settled a monthly allowance on Fragprie, one he could collect only after she and Nicholas Efington had married.

The following morning the duke had left for London.

His letter had arrived in Scotland about a week later.

She jammed the parchment into her reticule. "In fact, I've changed my mind. I *shall* call him a toad."

A dreamy expression entered Mary's eyes. "A toad, say ye? Have ye seen him? If I were ye, I'd marry him right quick, I would. He's a fine eyeful . . . strong, tall, with a fair wicked smile . . . aye, I'd like tae see him in a kilt."

"Hush, Mary, you're spouting nonsense."

"Nonsense? Have ye got no eyeballs in yer head?"

"Not for a man who promises to bed me at every chime of the clock, without regard for my own wishes."

Mary's eyebrows almost disappeared into her hairline. Her surprise dissolved into a barely contained giggle. "And ye find the thought o' an attentive lover troublesome?"

Catherine gave the girl a severe frown. Mary was almost ten years younger than she, her mind and tongue fixed incessantly on men. "You should be angered on my behalf. It is a most improper thing for any man to say to an unmarried woman. And I would not describe the duke as an attentive lover."

"If ye don't want him, I'll have him in my bed, then." Giggling louder, Mary fled from the room.

Catherine shooed her on her way and shut the door behind her. Truth to tell, she could understand Mary's fascination with the duke. He had a powerful charm; she'd felt its bite all too keenly the night of Lady Wisborough's ball.

And that arrogant letter he'd sent her—it fairly made her cheeks burn. Despite her most determined efforts to put him from her mind, she wondered what it would be like to have him love her in a dozen different places—on a secluded stretch of heath, in the waterfall near Bodhan's Pond, drenched in moonlight, in sunlight, on the sheepskin rug in her room . . . on her very own bed . . .

Swallowing, she realized Mary was not the only woman he'd cast a spell on. Thoughts like these could only lead to disaster.

Pulling determination around her like a tartan cloak, she examined her reflection one last time in the looking glass. Mary had piled her hair atop her head in a cascade of appealing curls, and despite her mourning gown of black and white tartan, she thought she looked passably well.

She could delay it no longer.

Time to beard the lion in his den.

Things were looking deuced bad. Over the past several weeks, Nicholas had done his utmost to clean up the mess his mother had wrought, to no avail. He'd even gone so far as to travel to Rivendell. MacClelland and his daughter had refused to talk to him, as if he were a lowly messenger unworthy of their attention, and had sent Fragprie instead. Fragprie, for his part, had refused to bargain, and discreet attempts to place pressure on MacClelland through his duns had failed utterly. The laird may have been bankrupt, but he commanded a certain loyalty and respect Nicholas found ludicrous in the face of his efforts at extortion.

The entire village, in fact, had been unusually silent about MacClelland. Nicholas thought it rather odd.

With a violent expletive, he tossed the contents of his snifter into the fire. Fed by brandy, flames leaped at him through the fireplace grate, casting deeper shadows on the leather-bound volumes lining the study's walls. He slouched down into his overstuffed chair and grabbed from a side table the letter MacClelland had sent his mother.

He skimmed its contents for the tenth time.

If he didn't bring Catherine MacClelland to the altar by December first—exactly two weeks away—MacClelland would label him a bastard. The old laird would produce witnesses and point out the origins of Nicholas's star-shaped birthmark and ring, both described and documented in the McQuade family Bible.

His fingers curled around the letter, crushing it into a ball. He threw it into the flames.

His thoughts darted to his mother. Just a few weeks ago she'd changed her mind, told him she could withstand the disgrace, the reversal of fortune, if he chose not to marry Catherine. Particularly since the trouble was of her own making. Although he thought it a noble gesture, he hadn't considered it for even a second. Desperate to save her reputation and her standard of living, he had begun to understand he had no choice but to marry the wench and be done with it.

Goddamn it, how he hated having his hand forced like this.

Eyebrows lowered, he stood and began to pace. Never had he known such frustration. Fragprie, who possessed the killer instincts of a terrier running a brock to ground, had listened to each of Nicholas's alternate offers and, with an amused twinkle in his eye, had refused him. Nothing swayed the man, not compromises, not even threats to his mistress. When Nicholas had stated his intention to enjoy Catherine in every lustful way he could think of, Fragprie had sighed and said, "Aye, she's a bonny lass, Scotland's finest."

Nicholas had come away from Rivendell with the distinct impression that nothing, and nobody—not even Catherine herself—would confound MacClelland's plans to wed his daughter to the Duke of Efington.

In fact, he'd all but resigned himself to the idea of marrying her. He would make the best of it, knowing he'd preserved his mother's reputation. Clarissa, of course, would be crushed . . . she'd had her heart set on being a duchess.

Although he'd never proposed to her, he'd raised her hopes with his attentions and had set certain tongues to wagging about engagements. Nevertheless, he was certain she'd land on her feet, snaring a man with a title equal to his—or better.

He glanced at the Hepplewhite desk before him, at the chairs upholstered in burgundy velvet, at Hogarth's *Calais Gate* hanging on the wall. If he were penniless, the old laird wouldn't have had the slightest interest in him. But as it stood, the MacClellands had cornered him, trapped him like a wild animal, left him no way out. Adrenaline surged through him anew at the knowledge, and he felt a need to strike out at something, anything, if only to relieve some of the pressure building in his gut.

Merriam knocked on the door, his muffled voice shattering the charged silence in the room. "Lady Catherine MacClelland is here to see you, Your Grace. Shall I send her in?"

Nicholas froze. "Lady" Catherine MacClelland was here, in this house, right now?

He could hardly credit his ears.

Could he trust himself in her presence?

No.

"Send her in, Merriam. And see that we're not disturbed."

"Right away, Your Grace." Merriam returned a scant minute later with a stiff-backed, green-eyed beauty. "Will that be all?"

Nicholas nodded. "Yes."

Merriam bowed and closed the study door with a soft click.

"Good evening, Your Grace." Chin tilted upward, she challenged him with a defiant glare.

Nicholas allowed his gaze to rove from the hem of her skirt to the top of her head, much the same way she'd examined him at Lady Wisborough's ball. With her usual disregard for fashion, she'd gowned herself in an ugly black and white dress, the colors emphasizing her translucent skin, the soft pink of her lips. But it was her hair that drew his gaze, made him ache to touch her all over again. Honey and flame, tumbling down her back, promising warmth, sweetness, silky delight. . . .

A slow throbbing built in his loins, and he cursed his wayward erection. This swindling Highlander was bilking him of his future. How could he think about sex at a time like this? "Come to gloat, dear lady?"

Green eyes blazed into his, and she clutched her reticule tightly, as if she intended to swing it at him. "Are you such a prize, then, that I should gloat over you? I think not." Pert nose in the air, she dug into her reticule, withdrew a piece of paper, and slapped it against his chest. "You, sir, are reprehensible. What explanation have you for this?"

The paper fluttered to the ground and lay between them like a gauntlet. Recognizing the ducal crest at the top of the sheet, he didn't bother to pick it up. Instead, he clenched his jaw and battled the urge to smother her insults with one devastating kiss. *"I* am reprehensible? *I?* Do you mean to suggest my sin of penning a letter is greater than yours of extortion?"

"Only a coward would send a letter of this nature."

"Shall we talk of cowardice, then? Why did you refuse to see me when I visited Rivendell?"

She tossed her head. "I thought Fragprie more than capable of handling you. I had far better things to do with my time."

Nicholas felt a flush creep up into his face. The wench went too far. Attempting to rein himself in before he did damage, he looked upward and focused on the cherubs and angels that frolicked on the ceiling. Painted in gold and sky-blue tones, they gazed at him with gentle smiles.

Lips tight, Catherine retrieved the letter and watched him with wary eyes.

He took a few deep breaths and forced a semblance of civility into his tone. "Why don't you sit down, Lady Catherine, and I'll ring for tea."

"I am not here for tea, Your Grace. Nay, I have come to tell you that the marriage is off."

The hand he'd raised to ring for Merriam dropped abruptly. "Pardon?"

"I do not wish to marry you. Indeed, on the day you

called at Rivendell, I had ordered Fragprie to release you from our engagement. Unfortunately, Fragprie chose to promote my father's wishes rather than my own."

"What sort of game are you playing now?"

She waved the parchment at him. "In this letter you demanded your freedom. Well, now I offer it to you. I promise you, Your Grace, I will say nothing of your . . . heritage. We do not need to marry."

"You promise to keep quiet. Tell me, how trustworthy is a promise from an extortionist?"

"What would you prefer, my signature in blood?"

He chuckled, the sound a dangerous one, with not a jot of humor in it. So, the two blackmailers no longer agreed on their plan. Had she suddenly decided money wouldn't compensate for a husband who despised her? In any case, he couldn't risk his mother's reputation. He had to assume MacClelland would follow through with his threat to expose him if he didn't marry Catherine. "Delude yourself no longer. We will stand before a priest within the next two weeks. Afterward, you won't dare say anything of my heritage. 'Tis a simple matter of self-preservation. If you damn me, you damn yourself."

"So you think to silence me by marrying me?"

"You and your father have left me no choice."

"I would rather marry a toad." Two bright spots of color burned in her cheeks.

He stepped closer to her, the movement slow, remorseless.

Eyes wide, hand on her throat, she took a step backward, maintaining the distance between them. Something leaped in her eyes . . . not fear, no, something else. He'd seen the look before, the hunger, the denial, the excitement, but never with quite that intensity. . . .

She wanted him, perhaps as badly as he wanted her.

The knowledge was a revelation, transforming his fury into desire that burned equally as hot. "Ah, Lady Catherine, are you sure about that?" He reached forward, tangled his hand in one long, silky curl, and rubbed it against his lips. Its soft vibrancy was too hard to resist.

He tasted it.

She stared at him, openmouthed.

Her reticule dropped to the floor.

Woodruff, heather . . . she was sweet, clean, oh so delicious. "Come here." With one lean hand, he grasped her elbow and drew her closer. She pulled away, but not nearly as hard as he'd expected, and for one tiny moment she was pliant against him, the fullness of her breasts pressed against his chest. He thought of licking them, devouring them, dipping his face into that silky white cleavage and surrounding himself with luscious female flesh.

Unable to help himself, he leaned down and flicked his tongue across her left breast.

She gasped at the contact, her eyes wide, her lips a pink O of surprise. "How dare you!" Without warning, she drew her arm back and slapped him.

He did not flinch, but took the blow, her hand warming his cheek. Then, deliberately, he dropped his gaze to her breasts and ran one finger along the edge of her bodice, enjoying the feel of warm skin against cool black silk. "You tasted delicious, dear lady."

"Oh!" She narrowed her eyes and drew her hand back again, but this time he stopped her arm in midmotion and pulled her hard against him. She twisted in his grasp, the sleek curves of her hips brushing against his rock-hard erection, setting him further aflame. A laugh rumbled in his chest, and, openly delighted, he trapped her face between his hands and kissed her deeply, thoroughly, touching her with his tongue, enjoying the way she fought him at first but then clung to him, her body quivering, eyes closed in unwilling surrender.

Never had a kiss given him such pleasure.

She was molten, a wildfire, scorching his loins, so drenched in honey sweetness his lust knew no bounds. He wanted to explore every square inch of her delectable flesh—licking, touching, smelling—and would not rest until she opened to him and gladly allowed him access to her body's innermost secrets.

He had to have her. It was that simple.

"Ouch!" Blinding pain seared through his foot.

A satisfied expression on her face, Catherine ground her

heel into his boot, kept grinding until he pulled his mangled toes away.

Eyes narrowed, he rubbed his injured foot. Her slender frame hid the strength of a balky mule. "You little vixen. I ought to—"

She moved back several paces and put a chair between them. "If you thought to kiss me into submission, you have underestimated me, Your Grace."

Their tussle had released her hair, and now it tumbled down her back in a golden-red waterfall. Breathing heavily, a pink flush on the tops of her breasts, she looked so beautiful in that moment his throat ached.

"We have a lifetime of kisses ahead of us," he grated, "and I fear I shall be closing your mouth quite often with my own, if only to stifle your shrewish impertinence."

Catherine felt her chest tighten with wrath. Not only had he dared kiss her between his insults, but he'd left her wanting more. Her own body had betrayed her, turned traitor and allied itself with the duke.

That, in itself, left her particularly vexed.

The man was a demon, straight from hell.

At the same time, she realized she'd made a grave tactical error coming here today. She was no match for the duke's logic, his bold confidence, his pure magnetism. She had to escape and regroup.

"Mark me, Your Grace, we will not marry. Beyond that, I have nothing more to say." Her reticule lay on the floor, a tangible reminder of her loss of control. After snatching it up, she stalked toward the door, his gaze boring a hole through her back.

She felt at a disadvantage, almost as if she'd turned her back on a dangerous predator, and she strained to hear his footsteps following her.

Instead, his voice—low, forbidding—froze her limbs.

"I will not allow you to leave this room, Lady Catherine," he said, "until you promise me you will remain at your London residence, where I can easily find you."

Slowly she turned to face him. He seemed barely civilized, poised behind his desk, muscles bunching beneath his white linen shirt and fawn-colored breeches, gray eyes reflecting an implacable will, lips thinned to a harsh line.

He looked ravenous, and she felt like dinner.

"I can't make such a promise."

"Can't, or won't?"

The urge to taunt him was too strong to resist. "Won't."

"Ah, then, I see I shall have to lock you up."

She watched him, eyes wide, wondering at the meaning of his words, while he rang for a servant.

A bald-headed man, his face impassive, answered the duke's summons.

"Prepare a room, Merriam," the duke said, an unholy gleam in his eyes, "for Lady Catherine. She plans to stay with us for a few days."

"I do not!" Catherine stamped her foot, outraged by the mere suggestion. "Merriam, your master has taken leave of his senses. Call the constable at once."

"Will the Gold Room do, Your Grace?"

The duke bestowed an appreciative smile on the servant. "A perfect choice. We shall be along in a moment."

Merriam turned on his heel and walked off, presumably to prepare her jail cell.

"You cannot do this. You are kidnapping me."

"And *you* are blackmailing *me.*"

She stared at him, her mouth working. How neatly the duke had corralled her. She could say nothing, do nothing, without incriminating herself.

A familiar ache began to build in her bones.

Oh, no, not now! Not in this hateful man's study, before his very eyes!

Nausea blossomed in her stomach at the thought of the duke actually observing the change, watching her shed her clothes and become an ugly, primitive animal. He would be shocked at first, disbelieving, but that would soon change to disgust, the kind people felt when viewing freaks in a circus. How long would it take him to turn her over to authorities? How soon would she find herself locked in a cage in Bedlam, prodded with surgeon's knives?

How soon would flames begin to devour her flesh?

Clenching her jaw so hard her teeth ached, she pushed

the bitter thoughts to the back of her mind, drained the indignant retorts that had sprung to her lips, and closed her eyes.

I am home, on the moors, she thought, *the wind is curling around my body, the smell of heather is heavy in the air.*

I am calm.

By small degrees, the ache receded.

She'd ensured her own safety, at least for now.

When she opened her eyes, the room shimmered for a second before settling down into normalcy.

He looked at her with a curious expression. "Is something wrong?"

She read concern in his gaze, tangled with a good deal of puzzlement. "Oh, and are you worried about me now? Shall I add hypocrisy to your list of faults? I will run out of paper before long."

"You are precariously close to another kiss, Catherine." He leaned forward, as if to make good on his threat.

She put one slender hand on his chest. "Lock me up if you must, *Your Grace,* but I warn you, I will consider it a declaration of war."

"Then so be it." A rude smile on his face, he took her by the arm, led her up a grand staircase, and deposited her in a handsomely furnished room.

An oak bed, surrounded by gold hangings, took up a full half of the room, while a wardrobe, pitcher, and washbasin stood near another door—presumably opening to a sitting room. She sauntered into the room, made sure the windows opened, and checked the distance to the ground. About two stories—a paltry jump, for the grimalkin. She would escape before the sun rose the following morning. Yes, the plan was dangerous, for a passerby might observe the grimalkin, but she thought it far more dangerous to remain here, helpless.

"Is this my jail cell, then?"

"Only until we wed." Unaccountably, he shifted from one foot to another, and his smile faltered.

He appeared uncomfortable, Catherine thought, and he ought to, imprisoning her like some feudal lord. She strolled to the bed, ran a hand over the lace counterpane, opened a wardrobe door, and peered inside. Her inspection complete, she gave him an unconcerned shrug. "I shall remain your prisoner until that glorious day arrives."

Staring at her hard, he grasped the doorknob with one hand. "I'll collect your things from your London residence and send a maidservant up to attend to your needs. Good evening, Lady Catherine."

Preferring not to answer him, she presented him with a stiff back.

The door closed softly behind her. She heard a key turn in the lock.

Several hours later, Nicholas reentered his study and slapped a special marriage license on the desk. Now that he'd resigned to wed the wench, he wanted the ceremony over as quickly as possible.

He'd arranged a discreet affair at St. Giles's for eight in the morning, rousing a snoring deacon and depositing several pounds in his pocket to ensure his cooperation, and had invited both Harry Rappaport and his mother to witness the ceremony.

Afterward, he'd stopped at the MacClellands' London residence, marched up to Catherine's bedchamber, and, to an accompaniment of missish gasps from a maidservant, selected a silk gown for Catherine to wear. A most delicate shade of ivory, the gown would emphasize Catherine's own vibrant loveliness. It was a perfect wedding gown, and he viewed it with a cynical twist to his lips. For all her protests, Catherine had obviously planned to marry him. Why else would she have such a dress in her wardrobe?

While at Catherine's town house, he'd also run into Fragprie, who'd evidently arrived in London separately from Catherine. He'd given the man an abbreviated explanation of the day's events and told him of the impending marriage. Fragprie had appeared unperturbed at the idea of Nicholas holding his mistress hostage, and had promised to pass the message along to MacClelland. Catherine, Fragprie had explained, had flown to London without informing her father, and Fragprie insisted MacClelland would wish him to continue with the marriage ceremony even though the laird wouldn't arrive in time to attend.

Nicholas stabbed into the steak Cook had thoughtfully prepared for him, his gaze settling on the embers in the fireplace. The night had been incredibly long and trying, but he'd accomplished all he'd set out to. Now he had nothing to do but lean back in his chair and wait for the sun to rise.

At seven o'clock in the morning, he sent a maidservant into the Gold Room, bearing both the ivory dress and a tray of hot chocolate and croissants.

The maidservant returned to him three minutes later, her lips curving in a frown. "The room is empty, Your Grace."

"Empty?" He jumped up from his chair. "Lady Catherine is gone?"

She looked at the floor. "Yes, Your Grace."

"Was the door locked when you brought the tray up?"

"Yes. I used the key you gave me to open it."

"How the devil . . ." He left the sentence unfinished and ran for the Gold Room, taking the stairs two at a time. He remembered Catherine's nonchalance when he'd shown her the room, her arch smile as she'd gladly become his prisoner. The hoyden had even then planned her escape. Could she have picked the lock and slipped out with no one the wiser? It didn't seem possible, for without a key, one could lock the door only from the inside.

When he reached the Gold Room, an open window caught his attention. Rapidly he reviewed the house's layout in his mind. No trellises affixed to the walls, no roof to walk on, no drainage pipes to shimmy down, and a two-story drop into the gardens. She hadn't made a rope from sheets and descended that way, for the bedcovers weren't disturbed, and he saw no sign of a rope. The only evidence of Catherine's imprisonment, in fact, was the tangled pile of her clothes heaped atop a chair.

And yet, the window, other than the door, seemed her only option.

How in *hell* had she escaped?

Deciding that it didn't matter how she'd escaped—at least for the moment—he raced back down the stairs, yelling for his phaeton on the way. His first stop was her London town house; the second, Rivendell.

He would drag her to the altar if he had to.

Pushing his set of matched bays to the limit, he arrived at the MacClelland town house less than half an hour later, daylight only serving to emphasize the estate's ramshackle appearance. Darkened windows, leaning shutters, and a lack of visible servants—grooms, gardeners, footmen—made the house seem deserted. He maneuvered his phaeton to the curb and tried to open the gate blocking the drive, but someone had clamped it shut. Shaking his head, he tied his team to a lamppost.

If the stakes weren't so high, he thought, he'd hoot with laughter at the utterly ludicrous situation he now found himself in. Catherine had a maidservant—he'd seen that youngster the previous day, when he'd fetched her dress—but where, for God's sake, were the rest of her servants?

His footsteps determined, he climbed the stairs, rapped sharply on the door, and, without waiting for an answer, pushed his way into the foyer. Motes of dust swarmed in a shaft of sunlight, adding to the gloomy atmosphere and settling in his nose.

He sneezed, the sound explosive in the silent house.

At last Catherine's maidservant hurried to greet him. She stopped several paces away and tangled her hands in the white apron belted around her waist. "She's not here, Yer Grace, she's traveled tae her aunt's, said she'll contact ye at her earliest convenience. . . ."

"Do you think me an idiot?" He stepped around the girl and charged up the stairs, heading for the bedchamber he'd visited mere hours before.

"He's coming, lass, away wi' ye," the maidservant shouted and followed hot on his heels, tugging at his coat.

Nicholas banged the bedchamber door open and stopped two feet into the room, the maidservant crashing into his back with a thump.

Hair in riotous disarray, half-dressed in a traveling costume, Catherine froze, one hand suspended above a trunk.

"Preparing for our bridal tour, *lass?*"

She stared at him, her eyes red, as if she'd had little sleep or had spent a good deal of time crying. This situation wasn't easy for either of them, he thought. Never able to remain hard-hearted before a woman's tears, he relaxed his guard. "Come with me, Catherine. It will not be so hard to bear."

She bent over, apparently to smooth her skirts, her hands busily adjusting the hem. "I am but half-dressed, *Your Grace*. Please allow me a moment to array myself properly."

"A very ladylike sentiment. I understand fully. Take as much time as you need." Unfastened in the back, the bodice of her gown gaped open, revealing to his greedy eyes an expanse of white flesh. Silently he admitted their marriage would not be so hard to bear at all. Even if things didn't work out between them, they could go their separate ways, married but living independently of one another. Although the thought of Catherine taking a lover stuck in his craw, they wouldn't be the first couple of the nobility to reside in different houses, with different paramours.

In a moment, she straightened, one hand hidden in the folds of her skirt.

Relieved that she'd decided to act reasonably, he proffered a hand.

Snarling like a wildcat, she withdrew a wicked-looking dirk and swiped it across his palm. He winced at the stab of pain that careened up his arm.

"Ha! You have underestimated me again, Your Grace. Now remove yourself from my house at once." Keeping the dirk pointed at his chest, she nodded at her servant. "Mary, call the constable."

Eyes wide, lips trembling, Mary hesitated.

Catherine's voice rose a notch. "Call the constable at once, I say."

"I canna, Cat. I fear for ye."

"Have you gone daft, Mary?"

Nicholas intervened, his tone silky. "I'd say she's the only female in the room with any sense. Put the knife down, Catherine."

Taking deep breaths, she backed away. "I shall not."

"Put it down."

"No."

Aware they'd degenerated into a childish shouting match, he took a step nearer.

Inexplicably, the air around her shimmered. Nicholas halted his advance. A warm draft blew across his face, and he smelled a fresh, penetrating odor, as if lightning had discharged just outside the window.

"Go, Mary," Catherine ordered, her voice low-pitched and trembling.

The maidservant scuttled from the room.

He watched his wife-to-be closely. Lips pressed tight, her throat working, she seemed to suppress some wild emotion. "Catherine?"

For one insane moment, he thought he saw her green eyes blaze with unholy fire, pupils elongating into something . . . impossible.

His breath caught in his chest.

She closed her eyes, her face stiffening into a granite mask.

"Catherine?"

He sensed he was on the verge of a momentous revelation, one he would rather not know. The urge to turn tail and run was almost too strong to deny.

She began to shake like a leaf caught in a gale-force wind.

They both teetered on the edge of a precipice too shadowy and deep to climb out of, and he, for one, didn't want to fall in. He had to stop whatever had dug its claws into Catherine. With a strength born of fear, he wrapped his arms around her trembling form, grabbing the dirk at the same time.

Catherine became utterly still, her body stiff as a wooden plank. A few seconds later she relaxed against him.

"You win, Your Grace. For now." Her voice sounded rusty, unused.

"What in hell just happened?" He escorted her to a chair and forced her to sit.

Catherine grasped for a plausible explanation. " 'Twas a touch of fire in the blood—an affliction peculiar to the MacClellands. It makes me terribly uncomfortable and leaves me quite cold when it passes."

Dear God, she thought, how close she'd come to revealing

her secret to the duke. Twice now, she'd wobbled on the edge of the change before him, the ache tearing through her bones, demanding surrender. That she'd remained human was a miracle. It was almost as if some part of her wanted him to see, to know, to understand.

Had she fallen for him, on some deeper level? She found him difficult to resist, of that she had no doubt. He'd dressed completely in black, with a white linen shirt and neckcloth, the simplicity serving only to emphasize his hard, muscled body. The carriage ride had tousled his black hair most attractively, and wind had put a ruddy glow in his cheeks.

He looked healthy, vital, undeniably male.

His brow creased for a moment, and after a lengthy pause he nodded. "Your father complained of the same affliction. Have you seen a surgeon?"

"Aye. There's naught I can do about it. 'Tis but an annoyance, nothing more."

Blood flowed from his wounded hand, spotting her gown. Nostrils quivering, she again suppressed a whisper of the change. Blood. An utterly nauseating and frightening smell, but a heady fragrance to the grimalkin.

"Nevertheless, you look quite drained," he said, as he bound his hand with a linen handkerchief. "Allow me to assist you in dressing. The deacon awaits, dear lady."

She began to deny his offer, but he put one warm finger against her lips, effectively silencing her.

Resolve darkening his gray eyes to the color of steel, he stripped the traveling costume off her shoulders, pulling it down over her hips, his fingers lingering a second too long near the tops of her silk stockings. She hadn't bothered with pantalettes this morning, and now she regretted it. Her senses, heightened by the near-change, magnified his every caress until she was in an agony of pleasure and expectation. The hard grip of his fingers against tender flesh, the softness of his breath against her half-naked breasts, made her throb with need.

She shivered, felt weak, hated herself for wanting his touch so badly that she'd couple with him at a moment's notice, hated him for arousing such a passion . . .

Needed him to love her.

Ever so gently, she touched his hair.

If he felt her caress, he gave no sign of it. Instead, with jerking movements, he slipped pantalettes on her legs, snorted as he relieved her of the dirk's sheath, forced her into a velvet dress the color of sapphires, and buttoned her with all the skill of a lady's maid.

Throughout it all, she wondered if they would ever come to *like* each other. Love seemed an unimaginable goal.

Leaving her hair unbound, he bundled her into a velvet cloak and hustled her out of the house. He practically threw her into his phaeton, and a few moments later they were flying through the streets of London, panhandlers and drunks cursing as the phaeton kicked up great sheets of mud. Throughout it all, Catherine remained silent, her body throbbing, her conscience clamoring, her eyes on the duke's uncompromising profile.

St. Giles's Church, a moderately sized brick affair, hunched on the edge of respectable London. Its doors stood wide open, despite the early hour, and two empty carriages—a barouche and phaeton—rested in front of the attached cemetery. Catherine recognized the Efington crest on the barouche, but the phaeton remained unidentified. She had no time to think on it, however, for as soon as the duke pulled his team to a halt, he hopped from their phaeton and hustled her into the church.

His fingers gripped her arm far too tightly. She risked a glance in his direction and noted his narrowed eyes, compressed lips, and stiff jaw.

His mood, it seemed, had become positively frosty.

A black-robed deacon waited for them near the front of the church. His frowning, liver-spotted countenance, along with a few sputtering candles and a cloud of musty-smelling incense, created a dour atmosphere indeed. As the duke hurried her to the altar, Catherine caught a glimpse of both the duchess and the dandy she'd seen at Lady Wisborough's.

At least the church didn't crumble when the duke entered, she thought.

Arm clenched around her shoulders, he stopped before the silk-draped altar. The deacon gave her bodice a prolonged glance, the tip of his tongue moistening his lips.

The duke stiffened. "Are you deacon or whoremaster?"

Eyes widening for a moment, the deacon uttered a loud "Ahem" and began to intone in Latin, the words blending together in a low, numbing buzz.

This must be a dream, she mused. She couldn't really be marrying the Duke of Efington. If he discovered her secret, he'd turn her over to the authorities, and she'd die. It would be a rather effortless way for him to rid himself of an unwanted wife.

The deacon paused and gazed at her expectantly. With a start, she uttered the words he wanted to hear.

The duke repeated the marriage vows as well, his voice emotionless.

He grabbed her cold hand and slipped a ring over her finger.

He tilted her chin up with one lean finger and pressed his lips against hers, a chaste kiss before God.

The deacon announced their married status to rows of empty pews.

Hand shaking, writing nearly illegible, she affixed her signature beneath the duke's in the parish register.

He took her arm and led her down the center aisle, the dandy and duchess following behind them. "We are now bound together, Catherine," he snarled as he led her out into the sunlight. "Legally, irrevocably, *forever.*"

The gold wedding band burned on her finger.

Five

The duke assisted Catherine into the phaeton, his touch none too gentle. He refused to look at her, instead concentrating on his team of four. They pranced and pawed the cobblestone street, as if their master's severe mood distressed them.

"We are returning to Efington House for the remainder of the day," he said, his voice cold. "Tomorrow, at first light, we travel to Rivendell. After I have toured my new holding, I shall return to London. You will remain in Scotland."

Catherine sat as far away from him as she could, perching precariously on the edge of the high-sprung seat. She felt numb.

She was now Duchess of Efington.

She had a husband.

How long would it be before he discovered the curse that ruled her life? Could she hide the grimalkin from him? Possibly, if he left her in Rivendell and returned to London, as he'd indicated.

But it would be a difficult time indeed. She could keep the grimalkin at bay for a month or so, but beyond that, all wagers were off. On only one other occasion had she prevented the change for more than a month—at fifteen, when she'd caught pneumonia and had nearly died.

If she could not get rid of the duke quickly, he would surely learn her secret.

There was one other option, of course—make the duke love her. If he loved her, he might take pity on her and protect her from those who would seek to end her life, should the truth be known. But she had no illusions on that score. She could see how much he hated her, that hatred tempered only by a lust equally as great, one he obviously planned to indulge at every opportunity.

No, love was a gamble she wasn't willing to take.

Her best bet, she decided, was to act as disagreeably as possible toward the duke, to fan his hatred until he left Rivendell, never to return.

A frigid wind rushed down the cobblestones, promising the first snow. Casting a glance at the leaden sky, she pulled her sapphire cloak tighter around her body and huddled within its folds. "I prefer not to wait until tomorrow. I'll leave now, with Mary. You may join me in Rivendell."

Eyes narrowed and as dark as the storm clouds overhead, he took up the reins and set off at a bruising pace. "There are many things you must understand, dearest Catherine." His voice was softly menacing, and the gaze he suddenly turned on her was filled with contempt.

Catherine glared at him, her chin tilted upward. Let him shoot his mouth off, she thought, and then return the favor in equal measure. *To hell with love.* "Please, enlighten me."

"It is true, I have married you, and you are now Duchess of Efington. But you are also my wife. As such, you will do what I tell you, when I tell you."

So he planned to make her his prisoner. Well, she thought, he'll find that a bit difficult. "Go to the devil."

Stiffening, he spurred his team on to greater speed with a flick of the reins. " 'Tis obvious you haven't known an ounce of discipline in your entire life. I intend to change that." The phaeton seemed to take wing, moving faster than it ought, barely avoiding a hackney.

"Bloody cobb." A hackney's driver shook a fist at them

seconds before the hackney barreled into a cart loaded with apples and potatoes.

The duke paid the fracas no attention. Frowning, eyebrows lowered, he swung the phaeton around a sharp corner.

Catherine expected their carriage to tilt onto two wheels. She gripped the seat, her knuckles white. "Trying to kill us? Or just me?"

"Neither. I'm simply in a hurry to return to Efington House, where I shall fully taste the goods I have bought today." He threw her a look of such wrath that she wisely shut her mouth and remained silent for the remainder of the trip. She wanted to arrive in one piece; there would be time later to flay him with her tongue.

They came to a screeching halt outside of Efington House, and Catherine alighted before the duke on shaky legs. She had her doubts he would have offered assistance even if given the opportunity.

"Come, Catherine, meet the family." He seized her by the arm and pulled her up an endless flight of stone stairs, into a great marble foyer.

She'd visited Efington House once before, but its opulence still left her speechless. Burgundy damask walls niched to hold statues of former monarchs—Henry the Eighth, George the Third—stretched up to a painted, arched ceiling that would have made Michelangelo proud. Sumptuously carved settees upholstered in navy blue, mirrors, and stools were arrayed discreetly, conveying a feeling of rich privacy.

The duke lived like a king.

She realized her mouth was hanging open and closed it with a snap. "Well, it isn't Buckingham Palace, but it's better than a finger in your eye."

"Don't get used to it," he informed her, eyes glittering. "This will likely be your first, and last, night here."

Merriam glided into the room, a woman cowering behind his black-clad form.

Catherine caught sight of a serviceable lilac gown and demure chignon of brown hair. "Well, Mary," she said, "or should I call you Judas? I see you've joined forces with my husband."

"Oh, no, Cat, I wouldna do that." Her maidservant stepped forward, her hazel eyes pleading. "I packed yer trunks, ye see, for we're tae travel back tae Rivendell. His Grace's footman brought me here. A fine place it is, too."

"His riches have turned your head."

" 'Tis likely the riches I placed in her pocket have turned her head."

Catherine gave him a sweet smile, determined not to let on how much Mary's betrayal bothered her. "The infamous Efington charm didn't work, then? You resorted to bribery to gain her favor? You must be losing your touch, *Your Grace.*"

He seemed to sense her discomfiture and, based on the grin that flickered across his lips, took great delight in it. "Bribery is a subject you had best not broach, my lady."

She looked down her nose at him, at a rare loss for words.

The duke raised an eyebrow. "What, nothing to say?" At her continued silence, he chuckled.

Narrowing her eyes, she put her hands on her hips. "I can see your mood has improved, *Your Grace,* at my own expense. If you're finished taunting me, I'd like to retire to my room."

"Spoken like a true general. When outmaneuvered, retreat."

She whirled to the butler. "Merriam, please show me to my bedchamber."

The duke gave Merriam an imperceptible nod and then smiled most wickedly at her, his eyes dark and smoldering beneath half-closed lids. With his great height, he easily dominated the room and made the handsome Kent furniture seem drab in comparison.

Fists planted against his thighs, he was standing close to her, so close she could feel the warmth of his body, smell the horseflesh, dust, and brandy that clung to him. She remembered the hard pressure of his lips, forcing hers apart, his tongue probing, thrusting against her own. She remembered how he'd tasted her hair, licked the soft curve of her breast, his tongue like hot silk, leaving a tingling dampness on her skin.

She tried to forget.

"I will join you directly," the duke said.

Refusing to shrink under his hungry gaze, she tossed her head. "I await your pleasure." Then, reddening at the unintended double entendre, she whirled and followed Merriam up the staircase, Mary trailing in her wake.

She'd climbed no more than ten steps before a frenzied pounding on the door echoed through the foyer. Merriam did an about-face and glided back down the stairs, his face composed, reaching the door seconds later.

A wild sobbing replaced the pounding.

" 'Tis a banshee, come for our souls," Mary whispered, and crossed herself.

Apparently Merriam had a bit of drama in him after all, for he took his time unlatching the door. But he'd opened it no more than halfway when a slight female form dressed in pink exploded through and rushed the duke.

A graying, well-dressed woman—the dowager duchess—raced through next and valiantly tried to restrain the girl, her face red with effort. The duke's dandified friend brought up the rear, his customary air of indolence replaced by a most remarkable urgency.

"Quite a parade," Catherine muttered.

The yelling, disruptive throng surrounded the duke, who looked at them as if they'd all gone mad.

"Silence!"

His short, barked command had the effect of a whip cracked over their heads. Sniffling, a wounded look in her eyes, the young girl grabbed his arm but ceased her caterwauling. The dowager duchess wore a formidable frown, as if she'd like to call the constable, and the dandy looked shocked at his own display of emotion.

The duke gave them a severe look. "Have you all lost your wits?"

Everyone started to talk at once. The duke cut them off with a furious hand gesture.

"The study, Your Grace?" Unaffected by the chaos, the butler gestured to an arched door off to the right.

"Yes. Bring some tea, Merriam."

"Right away, Your Grace."

The duke led the boisterous trio into the study and closed the door.

Dismissed, Catherine thought, and thank goodness for it. She turned and began to climb the stairs again, Mary behind her, but suddenly a deep voice stopped them.

"Please join us, Catherine." The duke stood in the doorway, a frown etched across his face.

"Must I?"

"Yes." His voice brooked no denial.

"Prepare my bed, Mary. I shall be up in a moment," she said loud enough for the duke to hear, and then made her way to the study. All of its occupants assessed her as she entered, the girl's eyes filled with spite, the dowager duchess's with interest, and the dandy's with cold speculation.

The duke stood with one foot propped against the fireplace, his expression weary, as if he held the weight of the world on his shoulders.

She gave each one a cool nod and sat in a thickly cushioned leather chair.

"Look, she sits in the duke's favorite chair." The girl stalked toward her, her fingers hooked like claws, her soft brown eyes mere slits. "You will tell me how you forced him to marry you."

Catherine felt her own eyes widen slightly as she realized the depth of the brunette's animosity. Was this one of the duke's mistresses? Perhaps an actress? No, if the girl were a lightskirt, she'd realize the duke's marriage would have little impact, if any, on their illicit relationship.

Obviously the brunette was quality and had expected the duke's own hand in marriage. How unfortunate. Her father had destroyed a budding romance with his blackmail. Well, Catherine thought, judging by her melodramatics in the hall, she'd guess the brunette would have caused the duke untold amounts of trouble. And the duke's temper made him a dubious prize as well. Both were probably better off as things stood.

Besides, the dandified gentleman seemed more than willing to replace the duke in the brunette's affections. The glances he bestowed upon her spoke of a deep regard.

"That's enough, Clarissa. She is my wife, and you will accord her the respect due a duchess. Sit down."

Grudgingly, Clarissa took the chair the duke indicated, her eyes promising that the war had just begun.

"Catherine, this is the Honorable Harry Rappaport, a friend of many years, and incidentally my cousin."

"Delighted." Harry bowed, his cravat so stiff and tall he moved like a wooden soldier. He took a seat next to Clarissa.

Catherine guessed he felt anything but delight; regardless, she stood and sketched him a curtsy.

"My mother, Annabella, Dowager Duchess of Efington," the duke continued.

Face inscrutable, Annabella gave an imperial nod, nothing more.

Catherine curtsyed more formally for the dowager, and resumed her seat.

"And this," the duke concluded, "is Lady Clarissa Stonehaven, daughter of the Earl of Stonehaven."

Clarissa shot her a look of pure hatred.

Catherine didn't bother to curtsy.

With introductions completed, the duke pulled a chair next to Catherine and sat. "Now, Clarissa, please tell us why you charged into Efington House with all the manners of a spoiled child. I grow weary of these scenes."

Evidently taken aback by his frosty tone, the girl looked as if she might begin crying again. "I heard the most shocking rumor, that you'd wed this Scottish dow . . . lady," she amended. "I couldn't believe it was true, but on the way here I met Harry and Her Grace, and they confirmed it, and oh, Nicholas, how could you do this to me?"

She hunched her shoulders, put her face in her hands, and began to sob pathetically. Catherine thought her abject misery patently false.

Harry, on the other hand, seemed decidedly upset by her dramatics and insisted on waving a handkerchief in her face, which she swatted away.

The duke's stern countenance began to waver. "The circumstances of my marriage to Lady Catherine were unusual; nonetheless, she is now my wife and Duchess of Efington, and both she shall remain." He put an arm around Catherine, pretending affection that neither of them felt but for which she was grateful. "I am prepared, Lady Clarissa, to offer you a substantial settlement."

Clarissa ran to the duke and threw herself into his lap. She clutched the lapels of his jacket, her thick lashes spiked with tears. "Have I displeased you in some way? Is that why you've abandoned me?"

Refusing to give the girl any satisfaction, Catherine turned and looked out the window.

Jaw clenched, gaze stony, the duke stared at Clarissa for a moment before trying to set her on her feet. The jade clung so tightly to him, however, that he tangled himself in her arms and dumped her unceremoniously on the floor. The dowager gasped, and Harry jumped to his feet.

Catherine silently cheered.

Gasping, the girl sprawled on the floor like a broken doll, her shoulders hunched, her face buried in her arms, playing up the moment for all she was worth.

"You go too far, coz," Harry hissed, and picked the limp Clarissa up. She clutched his shoulders, sobbing again, but this time it sounded quite real.

After all, Catherine mused, a rather big fish—the duke—had just escaped her net.

"You're deuced lucky I consider you a friend, Nicholas, or I'd call you out." With a glare in the duke's direction, Harry tightened his arms around her and left the study.

A thick silence reigned as the remaining occupants digested Harry's parting comment. After what seemed like minutes, the duke slumped and poured himself a full snifter of brandy.

"I apologize for subjecting you to such a display," he said to Catherine, his voice tired. "Had I known she would go to such lengths, I would not have asked you to attend."

"A piece of baggage we are best rid of," the dowager duchess announced. "Good day, Nicholas, Catherine. I shall see you tomorrow, before you depart."

Catherine curtsyed as the dowager duchess left the room,

and then assessed the duke. He seemed preoccupied, his gaze far away, his fingers wrapped around the snifter.

Rather than feel miffed by his lack of attention, she felt sorry for him. After all, in a space of ten minutes, he had not only lost a good friend but had formally broken with a woman he'd intended to marry. Deciding to give him a bit of privacy, she tiptoed toward the door.

"Just a minute, Catherine. We still have a matter left to discuss."

"Of course, Your Grace." She turned and resumed her seat, noting the way the firelight flickered on his black hair, casting shadows on his face, reminding her of the statues that graced the foyer. He leaned against the mantelshelf and rubbed his forehead, as if trying to banish a headache. The uncompromising gleam in his eye warned her the subject he planned to introduce was anything but casual.

"I have followed your father's instructions and married you. I have a contract I demand he sign—one in which he states he knows nothing of the relationship between my mother and Robert McQuade, and furthermore vows never to speak of that relationship to anyone."

She raised an eyebrow. "Who do you wish to sign it? Fragprie?"

Gently, every movement controlled, he placed his snifter on the mantelshelf. "Don't play games with me, Catherine. I want your father's signature, not Fragprie's. I tire of dealing with Iain MacClelland's servants."

Surprise left her bereft of words for a long moment. "I'm afraid you'll have to talk to Fragprie, Your Grace. My father died a few days before Samhain."

Face arrested, posture suddenly stiff, he stared at her. "What did you say?"

"My father is dead." Her voice trembled despite her best efforts to control it. "Did you not know?"

He clenched his hands into fists as if he thought to strike something, and his entire body vibrated. His eyes, a turbulent gray, promised retaliation. "Fragprie told me your father will arrive in London any day."

"He is dead, Your Grace. Fragprie told *me* he had informed you of Iain's death the day you visited Rivendell."

"If I knew your father was dead, I wouldn't have married you. Did you not wonder why I would insist on this farce of a marriage, if your father could no longer speak out against me?"

She pressed her fingers against her temple. She felt faint. "When I came to this very house and told you the marriage was off, you insisted on marrying me to ensure my silence."

He took a menacing step toward her. "You did not know my mother, nor were you alive when her affair with McQuade took place. Furthermore, you are a recluse, a spinster from Scotland known for her strange ways. I would not bother to marry you to ensure your silence, for your word means nothing."

Her heart pounding in her ears, she crossed her arms over her chest. He looked ready to strangle her. She searched her mind for something to convince him he hadn't sacrificed himself in vain. "Perhaps it is best we both complied with Papa's wishes. Not only is Fragprie loyal to Papa, he is also receiving a monthly allowance from my father's estate, one which commenced when we married and will stop if we divorce. He knows the details of your, ah, heritage, and wouldn't hesitate to come forward if he thought we'd thwart Papa's will—"

"Get out of my study." Fury radiated from him, surrounding him in an almost palpable aura.

Back stiff, she walked toward the door.

"You shall travel to Rivendell alone," he growled. "Pack your things and be gone by midday tomorrow."

Determined not to cower before him, she faced him squarely. "I shall intrude on your hospitality no longer."

Evidently unable to bear the sight of her, he turned to the fireplace.

Head tilted proudly, Catherine left the study. If she'd wanted to fan his hate, she thought, she'd succeeded admirably.

Why, then, did her heart ache as if squeezed by a giant fist?

Had any man ever been a bigger fool than he? Nicholas shook his head, disgusted by his own gullibility. Lady Catherine, with her fiery hair and clear green eyes, had blinded him to her lies with her tempting smile and lively impertinence. She claimed she hadn't known he was unaware of her father's death. She claimed Fragprie had kept the information from him without telling her. She was, as she would have it, innocent as a newborn lamb.

He took another swallow of brandy, some corner of his mind noting he'd done nothing but drink brandy and whisky since he'd met the wench. She'd even affected his health—for the worse. With an oath, he threw his snifter into the fireplace, smashing the Waterford crystal into a hundred glittering shards.

Speculation created an ache behind his temples. He wondered if she had been as ignorant as she'd claimed, or if she had cooked up these lies to sweeten his attitude toward her. It was one thing to marry a conniving adventuress, and quite another to marry a poor lass duped by her father and a servant. Did she hope to snare him with her guileless act and dig even deeper into his purse?

"Little bitch," he muttered, wondering if even now she snuggled into her bed, content in the knowledge she'd gained the title of Duchess of Efington and had a wealth of money at her disposal and society at her feet.

The fire leaped and crackled with uncommon energy, emitting a strange blue glow, and the crystal began to melt, becoming red and smoky. Casting a jaundiced eye at the burning logs, which threw off enough heat to warm three rooms, Nicholas yanked off his waistcoat and neckcloth. He felt his own temper heating up, too. Here he stood, on his wedding day, his delectable wife curled up in one of his bedchambers—but he couldn't touch her.

Pride wouldn't allow him. Making love to Catherine was tantamount to surrender. If he touched her, he'd implicitly be accepting this farce of a marriage, forgiving her of her lies and schemes. Besides, his chances for annulment would fly right out the window if he consummated the marriage.

Nevertheless, he could not banish the image of Catherine in the Gold Room, sprawled upon the giant oaken bed, surrounded by golden drapery, her long, pale legs tangled in the lace counterpane, her honey-flame hair spilling over the pillow and hanging halfway to the floor.

He squeezed his eyes shut as the lust he'd denied for so long made him harden, torturing him with need. *Ah, Catherine,* he thought. The soft blush of sleep would color her cheeks . . . her lips would be pink and slightly parted, beckoning, tempting, inviting exploration. . . .

With a low growl, he plucked his gold wedding ring from his pocket and flung it into the fire, too, where it joined the pooling rivulets of melted crystal. "Goddamned tease," he snarled, and, realizing he had several hours to wait before Catherine left for Rivendell, he opened one of the windows—for the study had become hot as an oven—and hoisted the decanter of brandy to his lips.

Night fell and then gave way to early morning sunshine before Nicholas fell into an exhausted slumber, slouched in a chair, boots resting on his desk. At noontime, he heard a brief flurry of activity in the foyer, but as the drums of a hundred orchestras boomed in his head, he remained in the study and waited for the affliction to pass. Merriam glided in after teatime and placed an attractive plate of cold fillet of beef, dressed beet root, and pastry rolls before him.

Nicholas, however, felt only nausea. "Has my wife left for Scotland?"

"Yes, Your Grace." Merriam busied himself by lighting the various candelabra in the study, banishing twilight's shadows. "Will that be all?"

"Tell Rupert to prepare my evening clothes. I shall return to my apartment to dress within the hour."

Merriam nodded and left the study.

Nicholas had every intention of resuming his old life—attending White's, visiting the theater—and perhaps he would even select a new mistress. He was married now, and the fact ought to give him a great deal of new freedom. He need no longer worry about some conniving female trapping him into marriage.

He, after all, had already been trapped.

Smiling grimly at his own wit, he picked up his fork and prepared to do battle with the queasiness in his stomach. But before he'd even touched the beef, a soft, golden twinkle from the embers in the fireplace caught his attention. He put the fork down and, groaning at the pressure in his head, stood and prodded the charred logs with a poker. Feeling slightly foolish, yet even more curious, he pushed the logs back, searching, digging.

Sparkly, gilded, half-hidden beneath the ashes . . .

What in hell was that?

He moved the ashes aside as best he could with the poker, but when the job became too tedious, he reached in and scattered the soot with his fingers, burning himself on an ember, but he didn't care, for the twinkling object had a diamondlike beauty. It was just within his reach and suddenly—

He touched it. It was small, warm, as smooth as his wife's skin, as clear as a teardrop and shaped like one, too, with a gold filament trapped inside.

Holding it in the palm of his hand, he straightened and polished it with his shirttail. Where had it come from? Perhaps his mother or one of her guests had lost a necklace, although the idea of her entertaining in his study was unusual at best.

He examined it more closely. The gold filament within the teardrop had the same shape as the symbol for infinity, a circle set on its side and twisted into a figure eight.

Not a filament. A ring. A gold ring.

"Preposterous," he whispered, staring at the teardrop with a bemused frown.

Logic told him there could be only one explanation for the teardrop. It was made of crystal, crystal from the snifter he'd tossed into the fireplace last night. He remembered the unusual heat, the frenzied glow of the fire.

The crystal had melted and then congealed around the wedding ring he'd later thrown into the flames. Somehow, the fire had twisted the gold into the symbol for forever.

A shiver raced across his flesh, raising bumps in its wake. He clenched the teardrop in his hand so hard his knuckles grew white, and closed his eyes.

Had he misjudged Catherine? Had he wronged her by sending her away?

Were they fated to marry?

No! It was coincidence, nothing more.

Although he'd experienced many strange things lately, all in connection with the MacClellands, he refused to yield to foolish superstition. Since he'd broken with the Hell Fire Club, he'd renounced all things supernatural and become a man of science. The enormous intellectual advances of the previous one hundred years, fostered by Bacon, Voltaire, and Descartes among others, had convinced him of natural law and universal order. He now used a scientific approach to political and social issues, and extensive study had convinced him of the rightness of his decision. Everything could be explained.

There were no "mysterious forces" at work, be they God's or Satan's.

Lips firm, he slipped the crystal pendant into his pocket and stalked out of the study.

He had no time for this kind of nonsense.

White's awaited him.

Six

Nicholas fought the urge to think about his new wife, to hope she had reached the safety of Rivendell's walls, for since she'd left London he had received not a single letter from her, nor a voucher. He threw himself into all the pleasures the city had to offer, including the charms of a certain Sarah Spencer, an actress playing the princess of France in a Drury Lane production of *Love's Labour's Lost.*

His mother reminded him repeatedly that he'd promised to join Catherine in Scotland. Unaccountably, she seemed to have taken a liking to his new wife and constantly spoke in her favor. He shrugged off such reminders and arguments and went on his not-so-merry way, to his gaming clubs or to the arms of Sarah, with whom he had yet to make love. Catherine, even when absent, had the ability to spoil his attempts at lovemaking by popping into his mind at the most inopportune moments.

Christmas came and went, as did Hilary Term, Candlemas, and Easter; still, he did not leave for Scotland. All through that woefully long winter he debated whether or not to annul his marriage to the Scotswoman, as Clarissa had suggested when his mother had first posted the banns. His pride demanded he nullify the union, for she'd used him as surely as any pimp used a whore. But something he couldn't quite define made him hesitate.

Lust, he eventually decided. Lust, pure and simple, kept him from erasing Catherine from his life forever. He pushed the dismay to the back of his mind and blamed it all on his burgeoning manhood.

Finally, at the opening night of *The Taming of the Shrew*, a Drury Lane production in which Sarah Spencer played Katharine, Nicholas decided upon his future. Miss Spencer wore a wig of honey-red curls, and staring at the creation that couldn't even come close to the beauty of his wife's own hair, and hearing the name "Katharine" on Petruchio's lips as he kissed the actress, Nicholas knew he could deny himself no longer. Why settle for a substitute when he could have the real thing?

Annulment wasn't an option, he told himself. Fragprie had proven a Scotsman to the marrow, loyal to his laird and country. Nicholas didn't think he could bribe the man, and knew the servant would inform society of Nicholas's illicit beginnings, should he think the allowance MacClelland had settled on him at risk. Although the factor's testimony would have less credibility than an earl's, it would damage the Efington name nonetheless. No, he'd have far better results if he asserted his authority at Rivendell and found another way to bring Fragprie under heel.

His plan to bring Catherine around was more pleasurable. Even though he'd insisted her word meant nothing, in truth she was the daughter of an earl and, if she set her mind to it, could wreak a great deal of mischief. He had to put a child—preferably a boy—in her belly. Not only would he finally have an heir, but with her own son's inheritance in jeopardy, she'd be less tempted to reveal his bastard heritage.

He checked the impulse to rub his hands together and settled for a smile instead. A trip to Rivendell was definitely in order. Only there could he ensure the true circumstances of his birth remain a secret.

Seated in his private box, Lord Ramsey at his elbow and a pair of curvaceous twins at his back, Nicholas felt his smile widen into a wicked grin. All around him, women dabbed the tears from their eyes as Katharine and Petruchio avowed love for one another, and he guessed his own expression looked very strange. He didn't care. Excitement snaked through his limbs, energizing him for the first time in months. Yes, there were many reasons to journey to Rivendell, and the resolution to his problem was so simple he couldn't believe he hadn't realized it before now.

And so, he spent the following week wrapping up his affairs. Remembering the state of Catherine's wardrobe, he visited a modiste who supplied him with gowns suited to a duchess. The frilly things strapped behind his carriage in trunks, he set out for Scotland, amid the red tulips and pink lilies of May Day. He wondered if Catherine would be surprised to see him. As five months had passed since they'd parted, she probably thought he'd abandoned her.

The notion stayed with him all the way across the Great Glen and into the Highlands. He saw little of the emerald lochs, the flower-strewn moors, the hills cloaked in purple heather. Rather, atop the traveling chaise with his driver, he thought of a pair of green eyes that often glittered fury, but at times seemed strangely vulnerable. When the chaise finally lumbered up the gravel drive to Rivendell, followed by two more carriages containing his valet and luggage, his gut tightened in anticipation.

His traveling chaise approached Rivendell from the side, its medieval beauty fascinating him all over again. Gray stone turrets, topped by iron finials, stretched toward the sky, doubtlessly providing an unparalleled view of the countryside. He imagined the notched battlements, which crowned the outside walls of the castle, hid catapults and other ancient weapons of war. A pair of barn owls swooped around the giant hawthorn growing just outside the castle, giving Rivendell a mythical aspect; he expected King Arthur to emerge from the great wooden door and greet him at any moment.

Instead, a female figure, dressed in sprigged cotton and wrapped in an ivory shawl, stood outside the portal watching them approach. Overgrown clusters of sweet William, lady's thumb, and astilbe crouched at her feet. She hugged her breasts as if marauding invaders charged up the drive.

Did she have a cannon trained on him, too?

The carriage stopped, and he alighted. Despite weeks of travel, he felt strong, in command, ready to do battle.

"Ah, the prodigal husband returneth," she mocked, sarcasm heavy in her voice. Her green eyes held the wrath he'd expected, and strands of honey-flame hair whipped about her face in the early summer breeze. Her breasts were fuller than he remembered, pressing against her thin cotton dress like bonbons awaiting his appetite. Rarely had he seen beauty such as hers, a wild beauty matched only by the Highlands themselves.

She was breathing heavily, apparently ready to do battle, too. But the thought dismayed him not. In a strange way, he had hoped for exactly this. He realized he thrived on their sparring. She may be a scheming wench, but she had backbone, and he admired her for it.

He swooped down and planted a hard kiss on her unsuspecting mouth. Feeling more than a bit randy, he slipped his tongue between her pink lips and tasted her spicy sweetness seconds before her teeth clamped down. Thankfully he'd had the foresight to withdraw in time.

As always, the kiss left him unbelievably hard, throbbing, a heaviness in his groin he intended to satisfy very soon. Tonight, perhaps.

Grinning, he bowed deeply. "I could stay away no longer, dear lady."

She snorted and put her hands on her hips, color flying high in her cheeks. "And have you brought Miss Spencer along?" Audaciously, she eyed his crotch, and he felt himself swell even larger. "No, I can see you haven't. You found no barmaids to relieve yourself on? No willing innkeeper's wife? Then you shall most regrettably suffer until you return to London. And I assure you, you *will* return to London."

Silently he cursed the gossips who had evidently informed his wife of his supposed indiscretion with Sarah Spencer. He didn't dare try to defend himself, for surely Catherine wouldn't believe a word he said.

Instead, he eyed her imperiously, pulling the cloak of dukedom about his shoulders, even as amusement twitched at his mouth. "You forget, Catherine. We are married. I am now lord of this particular manor."

"On the contrary, Your Grace, I have not forgotten that unfortunate fact. Would you prefer I call you laird? Or perhaps Macniall-mor would suit you better?"

Unaware of the intricacies of the clan system's form of address, Nicholas nevertheless guessed she'd just dealt him a keen insult. "I prefer you to call me Nicholas." Wanting to end the hostilities before they flared too high, he looked pointedly at his traveling chaise. "I trust you have servants here at Rivendell? I shall need some assistance in unloading my trunks. Rupert, my valet, will need a room."

He nodded toward the diminutive Englishman who had traveled with him. Dark circles bagged beneath Rupert's eyes, evidence of a bout of sickness induced by the swaying carriage. "Where are the laird's apartments, by the way?"

She looked startled. "You wish to sleep in the laird's apartments?"

"Of course. As shall you."

A mysterious smile on her face, she took him by the arm. "The long journey from London is fatiguing, I know. Come inside, Nicholas. I'll show you to the laird's apartments, where you can rest. I can't think of a more fitting place for a nobleman of your stature to reside."

She nodded toward two footmen, who began to unload his trunks, and drew him into the central hall. Everywhere he looked he noted evidence of financial difficulties. A threadbare plaid rug, displaying the MacClelland colors—yellow, orange, green—covered an equally worn wooden floor. Cotton stuffing leaked from chair cushions sporting the same plaid pattern as the rug, and he could actually detect sunshine through the once-sumptuous velvet draperies that shrouded the windows.

Mentally he catalogued the improvements he'd need to make as they passed through the reception hall and into a long corridor, mullioned windows on one side and two wooden doors on the other.

She stopped before the first door. "This one leads to the laird's apartments," she said almost gleefully, "and the other leads to the wine cellar. The MacClelland lairds liked to keep an eye on their drink. Will that be all, Your Grace?"

"You're not a servant, Catherine, to ask for dismissal. And please call me Nicholas."

"I'll have the footmen bring your trunks up, and once you've settled in, I'll assemble the servants. When you're ready, you will find me in the gardens." She didn't wait for his response but turned on her heel and, nose in the air, stalked off down the hall.

"Have your own belongings brought down, for as my wife, you, too, belong in the laird's apartments."

"We'll talk of it later," she replied, not bothering to stop, treating *him* like a servant.

That woman had a real knack for getting under his skin, he thought. Sourly he pushed the door to the laird's apartments open and took two steps into the room.

Utter disbelief froze him in place.

Iain MacClelland had definitely not slept here.

Vines snaked in through broken windows, twining along the wall and disappearing beneath wrinkled, cracked tapestries of dull brown and red. Doves roosted within broken sections of the wall, their soft cries of alarm filling the room with a mournful song. Currents of wind whistled along a ceiling at least sixteen feet high, and a rotting wardrobe topped by busts of dead Scotsmen looked ready to topple over.

This place wasn't fit for a vagrant.

Each step cautious, he walked into the room and stopped by an ancient bureau. Bottles containing a dried scum of perfume lay like fallen soldiers on the mottled wood, and cobwebs wrapped around a silver jewelry box. He opened the box and it played a cold, tinkling melody; moths had eaten the ruby velvet lining. A miniature in a carved wooden frame stood next to the jewelry box. He brushed the dust from the painting and stared at the two people who smiled at him.

A man, Iain MacClelland in his younger days, posed with a young woman, her hair a mass of honey-gold curls. Nicholas couldn't mistake the woman's resemblance to Catherine. Her mother? Perhaps. He didn't know much about Catherine's past, he realized, but planned to remedy that deficiency as soon as he could.

He replaced the picture on the bureau and, scowling, wandered through his new quarters. He'd be damned if he'd ask Catherine for a different set of rooms. She thought it a great joke, no doubt, to show him to an apartment unfit even for pigs, but he planned to turn it around on her. He would restore these noble apartments to their former opulence, becoming the Laird of Rivendell in action as well as name.

He did not bother to find Catherine when he'd finished his survey. Rather, he cornered Fragprie in the study and ordered him to gather the servants. Dressed in a kilt and loose shirt, Fragprie measured him with a cool blue gaze, raised one eyebrow at his peremptory tone, but didn't quibble. He simply put his quill down and did the duke's bidding.

A short time later Nicholas stood before a small staff of about thirty servants, from Fragprie, who served as house steward as well as factor, to footmen and scullery maids. Other than Fragprie, all wore shabby clothes, the women in frayed dresses, the men in patched breeches, herdsman's boots, and ancient livery coats. Rupert, too, had come at Fragprie's beckoning, but stood several paces away from the Scots. They in turn shot suspicious glances his way.

He introduced himself to the motley assemblage and explained what he expected from each and every one of them. Their faces, sullen and inattentive, told him they'd not yet forgotten Culloden, but his promise to raise their wages perked more than a few up. With care, and time, he would win the whole household over.

Afterward, he met with Fragprie, who in rather sonorous tones described the failings of the estate. Shockingly, he discovered the entire MacClelland estate brought in only nine thousand pounds yearly, as compared to Robert McQuade's thirty-seven thousand. Catherine did not, it seemed, run a very tight ship.

But a more thorough look convinced him she had not much to work with, having spent less than a year at its helm. The monies collected from rent, produce, and the docks at the mouth of the Helmsdale River, plus the interest from stocks, shares, and royalties, wouldn't even cover the housekeeper's list of necessary improvements.

Sighing heavily, Nicholas tore into the problem, and when Fragprie informed him dinner would be served within the hour, he felt he had a good grasp of the situation, if not the entire estate in hand.

"Good evening, Lady Catherine. I see you're at the books again." Fragprie strode into the dining hall and took his customary place near the mahogany server. Paying her little attention, he began to heap poached prawns onto a plate.

Catherine spared him a quick glance before returning to her study of Rivendell's finances. She could not abide formal dinners. Rather, she preferred buffet-style affairs where she served herself, and at the same time pursued those matters that needed her attention. As Fragprie had always dined with the family in the past, she continued to permit the tradition. Privately, she vowed to dismiss the man as soon as she discovered a way around the provisions her father had left Fragprie in his will.

Luckily for Fragprie, the blue ledgers held not a jot of chicanery, instead reinforcing her desperate predicament. The MacClelland properties had brought in a paltry sum last year, not nearly enough to support the household, immediate grounds, and tenanted lands.

Without the necessary agricultural improvements, her clansmen would starve within a few years. Even so, she refused to oust her kin in favor of Cheviot sheep, as so many of the other Highland chiefs had done. There had to be other alternatives.

She pushed the books away and rubbed her eyes. Although the duke now owned Rivendell, she knew she could expect no help from him. He'd already told her he wouldn't give her a sou, the tight-fisted bastard. Perhaps she ought to start cataloguing Rivendell's valuables. The dining room contained several likely prospects: a Hepplewhite tea table, two ancient claymores, chairs displaying carvings of Pictish battle scenes. Surely the great table, a bulky creation of marble and mahogany, would fetch a good price at an auctioneer's block. Even the mounted stags' heads might sell.

Queasy at the idea of selling family heirlooms, she contemplated the server. Trout Drambuie, poached prawns, Beef à la Royale, Lowland lamb, Dunlop cheese, rowan jelly, unleavened bread, and the inevitable plate of haggis created a fragrant, steaming cloud that normally would tempt her appetite. Today, however, she decided she could stand no more than a cup of tea and poured herself one from her mother's Wedgwood tea service.

The sun hovered low on the horizon, its orange rays lighting the room with a muted glow. She wondered what had happened to the duke. She'd waited in the courtyard for quite some time, braced for his anger over the state of his rooms. Eagerly she'd anticipated his request for new quarters, which she'd grant only after asserting herself as the master of the castle. But she'd waited in vain.

Fragprie burped, the discreet sound bringing her back to the situation at hand. "I see the finances have worsened," she started.

Busy shoving prawns into his mouth, Fragprie shushed her with a distracted gesture. "Once the duke completes the improvements he's planned, our income will increase markedly."

She brushed a wrinkle from the skirt of her black mourning dress. The gowns delivered to her bedchamber earlier—gifts from her new husband—remained snug in their trunks. "The duke has no intention of spending even a sou on Rivendell."

He raised an eyebrow, fork suspended in midair. "Do tell."

"Even if he did offer to provide funds for my use, I would not accept them. I do not wish to owe him anything."

Fragprie made no reply; he simply resumed his rather gluttonous chewing. As he obviously didn't agree with her, she tried to appeal to the Scotsman in him. "He is an Englishman, Fragprie, an Englishman who now owns one of the most ancient, respected Scottish estates. How could you side with him?"

"Now, lassie, you're being pigheaded about this. He is your husband."

Evidently the duke had already sweet-talked Fragprie into

crossing battle lines. Outmaneuvered again, she thought. Impotent fury pooled like acid in her stomach. "And you are fortunate my father protected you in his will. If not, I would have dismissed you long ago."

A gleam entered Fragprie's blue eyes. "Oh-ho, you've your father's temper, there's no doubt about that. If I were but a few years younger—"

"Enough, Fragprie," a deep voice said. "My wife is not only your employer, she is Duchess of Efington. And you are a servant. As such, I find your behavior disreputable. I would tread carefully if I were you."

She shivered as a cool gray gaze swept over both her and Fragprie. Fragprie chewed more slowly, his appetite noticeably dwindling.

The duke strode into the room, his presence filling the air with energy. Sweat clung to his black hair, making it curl at the ends like a boy's. He had removed his jacket and waistcoat, revealing a casually tied neckcloth and full linen shirt that bagged where he'd tucked it into his waistband. Dirt smudged his black boots and mud spotted the gray breeches that clung to his muscles like a second skin.

His proud carriage as he stalked into the room, the commanding manner in which he surveyed both Fragprie and herself, and his magnificent size—that of a warrior who'd spent years honing his strength and agility—reminded her of the ancient kings of Pictish Scotland. He needed only a kilt and claymore to complete the illusion. For one delicious moment she pretended the duke was, indeed, a laird, and she his lady love, together guiding an ancient, respected clan.

Good Lord, she thought, to have a man like this return your love. To have that leashed power, that hard, sinewy body all to yourself.

She felt his gaze on her, probing, questioning, and tore herself from the fantasy. *Get rid of him,* she silently told herself, *before he discovers your secret.*

"Why, Nicholas," she said, an innocent smile curving her lips, "you look as if you've been cleaning. I hope you found the laird's apartments to your satisfaction."

He sat next to her, settling his big frame into the delicate chair with a degree of difficulty. "They're splendid."

Her smile widened. "I'm sure you're quite hungry. Mrs. Finlay has prepared Beef à la Royale in your honor. It is quite tasty."

"Delicious, in fact," he murmured, showing not the least interest in Beef à la Royale. He didn't even glance at the mahogany server. Rather, his silvery gaze never left her face. He appraised her, his eyes heavy-lidded, indolent yet attentive, reminding her of a jungle cat that had brought down a particularly juicy meal.

He looked ready to take the first bite. Only the duke didn't bite; no, he kissed, and those kisses wrought far more devastation than any bite could.

She fought the urge to fan herself, for the room felt far warmer than it should. "How long do you plan to remain in Scotland?"

Leaning close, he brushed her ear with his lips. "Until you are with child."

She reared away, her shocked gasp startling Fragprie. The Scotsman's fork clattered to the table.

The duke wore a satisfied grin.

"Until I am *what?* Have you lost your senses?" She stared at him as if he'd sprouted horns and wings, the rules of the curse blaring in her mind. She could never have a child. Never. Every woman who'd possessed the seed of the grimalkin and had dared to give birth had died in the attempt.

"Leave us, Fragprie," the duke ordered, and the Scotsman jumped from the table, abandoning his half-eaten dinner.

Catherine didn't wait for Fragprie to close the door behind him. "You will have a difficult time, indeed, putting a child in my belly, because you and I will not share a bed."

He didn't answer. Rather, he stood and piled a selection of meats, fish, and vegetables on his plate, forsaking the Beef à la Royale. His large body, as he leaned over her to reach the wine, dwarfed her, making her feel so small, so . . . feminine. She felt his chin brush her hair as he sat back down.

A contemplative gleam in his eye, he took a sip of wine and murmured, "You can make it enjoyable, or you can make it uncomfortable. Either way, you will beget me an heir." He speared a slice of lamb on his fork and lifted it to his mouth.

"We shall see, sir. We shall see." She glared at him as she took a sip of tea.

"I've had enough of surprises, Catherine. Don't try to spring any more on me, for you'll not like the consequences."

"I wish only to return to the life I knew before I met you."

" 'Twas your scheming that brought this marriage about," he reminded her.

"I did not want to marry you, Nicholas. My father insisted upon it."

He snorted. "If you want my respect, you'll have to start telling the truth."

An errant ray of dying sunlight fell across his face, as if the sun itself wanted to touch him. She glanced out the window and noted the sun had all but disappeared below the horizon. If memory served her correctly, the moon would be full this night, mysterious, radiating an attraction the grimalkin could not ignore. A flutter of unease in her stomach, she stood, walked to the windows, and pulled the draperies shut.

Primarily to show the duke his arrival hadn't affected her in the slightest, she then gathered a plate of prawns, Dunlop cheese, trout, and bread.

He poured her a glass of white wine as she sat down. "Afraid of the dark, Catherine?" His tone was one of amusement.

She hesitated for a moment, searching for an explanation he wouldn't question. Finally she decided to go along with the one he'd already provided. "Aye. 'Tis a fear I've had since early childhood, one my father and the servants learned to indulge." She lowered her eyes and curled her lips in an embarrassed frown, hoping a bit of playacting would strengthen the lie.

"I'll wager your father indulged far more than your fears. You're naught but a pampered Scottish princess, used to getting your own way."

"How little you truly know me."

A spark of interest flared in his eyes. "Quite right. 'Tis a shortcoming I'd like to remedy immediately. Tell me about your mother. How old were you when she died?"

She eyed him narrowly. This subject was fraught with danger. "She died when I was born."

"Your father raised you, then?"

"Yes."

"Here, in Scotland? Your brogue is very slight, almost unnoticeable."

"Fragprie graduated from Cambridge. He taught me how to speak the King's English. My father thought it important."

Rubbing his jaw, he digested this comment for a moment. "Any aunts? Uncles?"

"No."

"Ah, now, Catherine, you're lying again." Shaking his head, he rebuked her as a tutor might scold a recalcitrant pupil. "In London, when I came to collect you for our wedding, your maidservant tried to fob me off with some Banbury tale of you visiting your aunt."

She thought fast. "My aunt is dead. I thought you meant living relatives."

"Oh. And your aunt's name?"

"Morag."

Eyebrows drawn together, he shifted on his chair. "Can you tell me a little about her?"

"She died at the age of forty, in a convent."

He remained silent for a long time, staring at her so fixedly she felt heat rush to her face. Fidgeting in her chair, she desperately searched for a way to change the subject without being too obvious, but her brain felt numb. She could only sit there like a fly beneath a glass.

"What are you hiding from me, Catherine?"

She jumped, his soft, silky tone cutting straight through her skin and piercing her hard-won poise. "Hiding?" Her voice squeaked, and she winced. "I'm hiding nothing, Your Grace. I simply dislike talking about myself."

"Secrecy is the badge of deceit," he said.

"A profound thought. Have you considered the cloth? Surely others beside myself could benefit from your sermonizing."

A muscle ticked in his jaw. "I am far too hedonistic to consider priesthood, as you will tonight discover."

Shaking her head, she slowly rose from the table. "Oh, no, I think not."

He stretched, his plate empty, other appetites evidently awakening. "You need not wait up for me. I'll rouse you when I've finished going over the books with Fragprie."

Her attention diverted from his threat of lovemaking to his equally hazardous threat of taking over Rivendell, she took a step closer to him, to better look him in the eye. "I myself reviewed the books a mere hour ago. Everything is in order, I assure you. I do not wish you to interfere."

"But, Catherine, I own Rivendell now." A lazy smile played about his mouth. "The MacClelland estates need a firm hand and a great deal of work before they will turn a profit. I intend to make these lands financially sound."

Hands on her hips, she thrust her chin forward. "In your letter, Your Grace, you said you would not give me a sou. Well, I do not want your money. I have extensive plans to improve Rivendell, not only to turn a profit but to enhance the lives of my clansmen. I shall sell off a few family trinkets to raise the necessary funds."

His eyes narrowed, became more gray than silver, and she thought she saw a flicker of anger within their depths. "I will not have the Duchess of Efington running an auction. Perhaps we can discuss it tomorrow, after I've toured the estate. Would you like to join me? I leave at dawn."

"I have no wish to join you, not for any reason."

He pushed back from the table and regarded her closely. "I cannot understand why you are balking at my every suggestion, Catherine. I've married you, I've even stated an intention to restore the MacClelland lands. Still, you act as if I'm a marauding invader. I've simply given you what you've asked for, and the only thing I want in return is a child."

His argument sounded so logical that she couldn't think of a single way to refute it, without revealing the grimalkin. How could she make love to him, night after night, without him witnessing the change? Sometimes it came without warning, hitting her with such strength she barely had time to get to her bedchamber.

Dear God, what if she changed while making love to the duke? And what if he got her with child? She would die in childbirth.

As if thinking about the grimalkin had invoked it, she felt a whisper of the change twist around her spine, exerting a slight pressure she knew would blossom into a tortuous ache. Mentally she calculated the last time the change had come upon her and realized the grimalkin would prove difficult to control.

Back stiff, she turned to face him. "I am tired of arguing with you, tired of having to defend myself from you. I am going to bed. As far as providing an heir for the Efington title and fortune, I need another night to think on it. I shall give you my answer tomorrow morning, when I join you to tour Rivendell." She would spend the entire night devising a scheme to send him packing at once.

He stood as well and placed his hands on his thighs. A determined gleam had entered his eyes, and his aristocratic face was stern. "For several months I have done nothing but think about you. I married you, then stayed away and considered annulment. I tried to make love to other women but could not, for when I held them in my arms, I saw only your face. Finally I could stand it no more. I journeyed to Scotland to claim what is mine. I am not talking about Rivendell, Catherine. I am talking about you."

Lips parted, she stared at him, stunned at the depth of passion in his husky voice. He exuded a sensual magnetism that pulled her against her every instinct, seeking to make her his abject slave. "I thought you hated me."

He touched her lips with one lean finger. "I can think of nothing but kissing you."

"You're tired, exhausted. Let me show you to a comfortable chamber—"

"I do not need sleep. I need only you."

"Please—"

"I want to make love to you."

"Nicholas—"

"I want you to have our child."

She felt hot, overwhelmingly so. "Do not talk to me like this. It is wrong."

He balled his hands into fists and leaned closer, so close she could almost smell the sweat that dampened his black hair, almost taste the wine on his lips. "How can talk such as this be wrong? We are man and wife, our marriage not yet consummated, and I will wait no longer. I can barely eat dinner with you nearby, and when we accidentally touch, I want to howl like a savage."

"But my father forced you into this match. Our marriage is one of convenience only." She longed to flee, but the duke had trapped her with his sensual mouth, a mouth that murmured persuasive words and shattered her resistance with a single kiss.

"I am too polite, I think. I should have claimed you the day I first saw you."

"Just one night, please; tomorrow I shall give you my answer." She remained perfectly still, her heart beating a rapid tattoo in her chest, the grimalkin's ache spreading to the rest of her limbs. Her mouth felt dry at the prospect of the duke watching her melt into an ugly, primitive animal. And yet, her need to touch that powerful body, to tangle her fingers in the black curls on his chest, to entwine her legs around his trim waist, was equally as strong.

He scowled. "No, Catherine. Patience has deserted me. I must have you tonight. Together we will force you to acknowledge your own passion. I can see it in your beautiful green eyes, taste it on your soft lips. Deny me no longer."

"I cannot, I will not—"

"We shall. Now." Abruptly, he placed an arm around her back, put his other arm behind her knees, and in one lithe movement, swung her up into his arms. "Which way to your bedchamber?"

Helplessly, she nodded toward the stairs. He was quite impossible to resist, but resist she must, for the grimalkin wanted to take her as badly as the duke.

Carrying her easily, he climbed the stone staircase and, following her direction, stopped before her door.

"Put me down, Nicholas. I am perfectly capable of walking." She felt him bury his face in the soft curls at the back of her neck.

"Easy, *ma petite,*" he murmured, his voice flowing over her like warmed honey. "Do not fight me." Freeing one hand, he twisted the knob, strode into the room, and kicked the door shut with a booted foot.

He tightened his arms around her and kissed her, the tip of his tongue caressing her lips, then slipping inside, probing, tangling with her own, until an ache of pleasure started between her thighs and joined the pain of the grimalkin's coming. She groaned, unable to pull away, her senses intensifying, nostrils full of his virile, salty scent, the smell of her own need heavy in the air. Her fingers found the crisp hair beneath his linen shirt and, pressing her cheek against his shoulder, she stared up into eyes nearly black with passion, hair painted silver with moonlight.

The windows stood open, revealing a moon that rode high and full in the sky, lighting the giant hawthorn outside her window with pale shadows.

Mary had neglected to close the draperies.

The duke nuzzled her neck for a moment and inhaled deeply. "You smell like flowers," he murmured, and carried her to the bed, pushing aside the lace bed-curtains.

He laid her down gently upon the lilac counterpane and took off her dainty shoes. He slipped his hand up to her thighs, pulled her garters down, and then found the tops of her silk stockings. When she felt his fingers brush against the sensitive flesh of her inner thighs, she jumped, pleasure nearly drowning out the change. But the grimalkin was upon her, hard and heavy, and the stress of revealing it to his horrified eyes proved too much for her. Pleasure gave way to an agonizing ache.

She moaned. Something about the sound must have worried him, for he sat back and smoothed her hair. "Fear me not, Catherine. I will not hurt you."

"Please, leave."

"I cannot. Things have gone too far."

With a surge of strength she sat up and clutched his shirt. "Leave, I say. I do not want you here. Go!"

Rather than answer, he kissed her again, his lips warm,

persuasive, building the ache inside of her until pleasure and pain and the grimalkin mixed as one.

She could no longer stop it. The duke had made his choice, insisting on remaining with her. Now he would see the demon she struggled to keep at bay. Throwing him a wild look, she began to tear off her clothes, popping buttons, ripping fabric, running a race with the change, knowing she would lose.

He sat back from her, eyebrows drawn together, frowning. She could smell his confusion, feel the heat that radiated from him. Outside, a barn owl swooped past her window, landing in the hawthorn, its yellow eyes piercing the darkness like a beacon, meeting hers like an old friend's. She heard Mary's voice in the servants' quarters, heard the duke's heavy breathing, listened to a hare squealing in its death throes, the weird, ululating cry calling to her.

She spiraled downward, into the dark place, the grimalkin finally gaining control.

Far away, she heard a man call her name.

Seven

"Catherine?" Nicholas paused, hand in the air, ready to touch her, instinct holding him back.

Something about the way she'd pulled her clothes off felt damned odd.

A fresh, penetrating odor blew through the room, and the air around her shimmered like heat waves above a hard-baked road. For one precious second, she lay before him, her skin pale against the lilac silk counterpane, her clothes thrown about the bed in wild disarray. Moonlight sliced through the lace bed-curtains and dappled her body with patterns of silver, and her hair seemed to quiver, each honey-flame strand sleek and vibrant.

He ached to smooth his hand along her long, well-formed legs, over the gentle curve of her hips, around the small waist and up to her breasts that rested as full and luscious as he'd imagined. But he dared not touch her. He felt danger around him, swelling, ready to burst like some noxious mushroom, Catherine at the center of it. What was it about this woman that clouded his reasoning? Around her, nature's precepts seemed to fall apart, leaving intuition as his only guide.

The penetrating odor grew stronger as the draft curled

around his body and a golden glow began to suffuse the room. At first he thought one of the servants had hidden in her bedchamber with a candle, for the glow seemed to emanate from a point unseen. With a little jolt he realized the glow came from Catherine herself, surrounding her body in a pulsating nimbus of light. She began to writhe, pulling up the lilac counterpane, tangling herself in the sheets, a soft moan escaping her lips.

His passion died a quick death. The energy crackling through her had nothing to do with sexuality—or any other normal human experience. And yet, to some remote area in his soul, the spell enrapturing her felt vaguely familiar.

It reminded him of his years in the Hell Fire Club.

He froze, and for one second an image of a young girl on an altar replaced the reality of Catherine on the bed. Stomach churning, he shook the image and reminded himself that he'd quit the Hell Fire Club years before. He no longer practiced the occult, and whatever had dug its claws into Catherine had a wholly reasonable origin.

The glow around her intensified, and she stretched mightily, her body longer than it should be, her legs and arms shortening, joints grinding as they changed position. Clicks and pops filled the room, the sound of bones reshaping themselves, of cartilage breaking and mending itself. Her spine stretched up through her skin, elongating, curving, becoming . . . something other than human.

He took two steps back from the bed and stared, transfixed, the scene before him denying all logic.

I am a man of science, he told himself. *Everything can be explained. There are no "mysterious" forces at work, be they God's or Satan's.*

He clamped his jaw shut to prevent his teeth from chattering.

Even as her body contorted to nightmarish proportions, she raised one hand and stared at it. Golden hairs sprouted from her skin like seedlings beneath a summer sun, each strand wavering and dancing with a life of its own. Fingers shortening, palm widening and toughening to a sandpaper texture, nails hooking into claws, her hand became that of an animal's.

Cruel spurs of fear rode up and down his back, jabbing him until he bent nearly double with the force of it. A low groan built in his chest, growing and swelling until it became a shout, a denial of the horror before him, an affirmation of everything he'd believed in until this moment.

"No!"

She looked at him then, a vestige of humanity in her gaze, and slow tears trickled from the corners of her glittering green eyes.

Good Christ, on some level, she knew! She knew what was happening to her.

She blinked, and suddenly he stared into eyes that seemed oddly luminous in the darkened room, eyes with elongated, black pupils . . .

Cat's eyes.

Recognition hit him like a bolt of lightning.

The MacClellands' estate, London, the night of the ball.

Mouth dry, beyond speech, chill after chill racing across his body, he remained an unwilling audience to a spectacle he was certain would drive him insane.

Bands of tawny fur erupted from her skin, racing across her legs, enfolding her arms, masking a torso that had all but flattened, each hair glowing, golden, alive. Her nose compressed even as her jaw stretched forward, producing a wet grinding noise that scraped in his ears like metal against an exposed nerve.

He tried to reach out to her, but his arm muscles refused to work. He could not even move his head. And yet, the violent thuds in his chest, the cold sweat dripping down his brow, the burning pain in his lungs as he gasped for air reminded him he was made of flesh and blood, not granite.

Fairy magic, he thought wildly, the term dredged up from childhood, from his nurse's tales of wood elves and beanstalks and princesses.

And wolves.

Suddenly the glow increased, becoming so bright he had to protect his eyes or go blind. With a strength born of self-preservation, he broke the enchantment that held him immobile and lifted an arm to shade his eyes. Eclipsing anything he'd known previously, the brilliant glow radiated through his body before fading away, leaving him unharmed but drained.

A mysterious silence replaced the cacophony of clicks and pops, of bones grinding and vertebrae squeezing. He could no longer smell clean, pungent air. Instead, he detected a musky odor, one that conjured images of steaming tropical jungles. Drawing on a reservoir of courage deep within, he lowered his arm and looked at the bed.

At first he saw nothing. The blinding light had burned into his retinas, leaving a white, hazy afterimage. Slowly, his pupils expanded, adjusting to the darkness in the room, and the bed came into focus: lace bed-curtains, lilac silk counterpane . . .

An explosive puff of air left his lungs.

He fought a sense of unreality.

His wife had disappeared. A leopard, one that watched him with an interested green gaze, had taken her place.

Somewhere between five and six feet long, she lounged on the bed, her deadly looking claws only partially sheathed. A thick layer of red underfur, topped by tawny hair, covered her body, now sleek and powerful. Her legs appeared short and thick, made for jumping, and a soft white fur covered her underparts. A faint radiance surrounded her, as if fairies had sprinkled her with gold dust.

He remained perfectly still, staring into the beast's eyes for some sign of recognition. She returned his gaze with equal fervor, taking his measure. Shock gave way to a realization of his own danger. What in God's name would he do if she decided to rip his throat out?

In one supple move she jumped off the bed. A mere three feet away from him, she easily stood taller than his waist. Whiskers pointed forward and up, she chuffed the air softly, her green gaze never leaving his. He didn't dare look away, for he knew she'd interpret such a move as a sign of submission and would probably attack.

Seconds ticked by, and still their gazes remained locked. Pressure built in his head until he thought he'd explode. He couldn't bear the anticipation, the waiting, the wondering. Evidently she'd had more practice at this particular game than he.

She stopped chuffing, but her mouth remained slightly open. Almost mesmerized, he didn't realize at first that she'd lowered her body to the ground and had assumed a crouch. He balled his hands into fists and waited for her assault, knowing he'd be lucky to remain alive but determined to hurt her only as necessary. Somewhere inside that tawny fur his wife lay hidden.

Her back legs quivered, muscles visibly bunching.

In another second, she'd have him pinned to the ground.

"Catherine?" His voice trembled, and he braced himself.

An eternity passed.

Suddenly a barn owl swooped past the window, its white, heart-shaped face and yellow eyes ghostly in the moonlight. She caught the movement out of the corner of her eye and turned her head to follow its progress. With a great flapping of wings, the owl stopped to roost on the hawthorn.

He waited.

Whoo-whoo-who-who-who-whoooooo.

Almost as if calling to her, the barn owl opened its beak and hooted insistently, the sound rising and falling on the night air. It flapped its wings again and stared through the window, as if interested in the proceedings. Abruptly, she sat back on her haunches and looked at him with markedly less enthusiasm.

Whoo-whoo-who-who-who-whoooooo.

She padded over to the window.

Hope flared in his chest. Alert to every nuance of movement in her feline body, he allowed his own muscles to slacken. Indeed, his legs quivered so much they seemed ready to collapse.

With one last glance back at him, she crouched and sprang through the opening in a smooth leap. He heard a puff of grass and leaves as she hit the ground below.

Gasping, he lurched to the window and searched the moors for a catlike form. Irregular shadows danced through the gardens and patches of heather. In the valley below, lights from the village of Kildonan winked and flashed through the trees. Somewhere in the distance, a sheep bleated.

Nicholas felt his heart begin to slow.

He put a hand to his forehead.

It seemed the grimalkin was more than just a legend.

The first rays of daylight poked through oak trees and gooseberry thickets, glistening on the sandy shore of Bodhan's Pond, cutting through the mist that hovered above the water. Butterflies, their wings a patchwork of blue and black, sunned themselves atop a boulder and flitted among the patches of astilbe and lady's mantle. A gurgling brook tumbled over rocks and emptied into the pond, coating the trunk of an oak with spray.

The spray drifted, settling on Catherine's face, waking her to the chill of early morning. Surrounded by stone, she stretched, her bare feet pushing against cold granite, her fingertips scraping the wall behind her.

As usual, the grimalkin had left her in a cave, lying atop a mat of dried leaves, on the shores of Bodhan's Pond. Why the cat always chose Bodhan's Pond as the place for transformation, she did not know. Experience, however, had taught her to keep a spare dress and cloak in the cave, for regardless of season or circumstance, she awoke here.

A quick glance at her naked body told her the grimalkin had restrained itself, for she hadn't a smudge of dirt anywhere, nor could she detect any blood. Her fingernails remained clean, unbroken. She wouldn't need a swim in the pond today, thank God. Even in summer, those waters could be terribly cold.

Every muscle aching, but in a pleasant way, she reached for the leather bag that held her clothes and opened it. A few brown spiders scurried out with her dress and, grimacing, she swatted them away.

Something nagged at her, something she should remember.

Eyebrows furrowing, she pulled on the cotton muslin and buttoned it, her touch deft. As she dressed, a vague worry grew in the pit of her stomach, squeezing her insides, forcing her to take a few deep breaths.

Something *bad* had happened.

Pulling brambles out of her hair, she tried to reconstruct the moments directly before the previous night's transformation, but a haze clouded her mind. She went back further. In the morning, she and Mary had visited Old Queenie, trading lace for liniment. At lunchtime, she'd picnicked alone on the moors, enjoying the smell of things growing, the heavy sweetness of flowers heating in the sun. Later, she'd . . .

The thought trailed off as an aristocratic face formed in her mind, the eyes turbulent with passion, lips curved in a provoking smile . . .

The duke. He'd finally arrived at Rivendell.

Hands trembling, she pulled the wool cloak about her and stepped past the brambles that concealed the entrance to the cave, her toes curling into the moss.

What then? Her mind raced on, faster and faster, her chest tightening with dread.

She'd quartered the duke in the laird's apartments, they'd had dinner . . .

He'd nearly made love to her . . .

She put one slender hand to her throat.

She'd changed before his very eyes.

Her heart seized up. She staggered against a boulder and clutched an indentation, her gray cloak swirling around her ankles.

Trouble had found her, trouble of the direst kind.

Although she'd dreaded this moment for years, she tried to think calmly about it. The duke had watched her change and would no doubt try to brand her as a witch. Still, it was his word against hers. She would do her best to convince the clan that the English interloper lied about her being a witch; that he had, in fact, made up the entire tale to discredit her. Loyalty ran deep in Scotland, and hatred of the English flared hot.

Yes, she would lie like the most reprehensible wretch, without an ounce of shame, her tongue spinning falsehoods as her father's used to do, and pray it would be enough to save her own life.

Legs shaking, she pushed away from the boulder and began to run, across the sandy shore, into Kildonan's forest of oaks. She had two miles to travel before she reached the stronghold, three if she avoided the main thoroughfare. The sun's rays had brightened, reminding her that each second she remained away from Rivendell gave the duke more time to assemble the villagers, drawing her closer to her own death.

She knew the way home all too well, and years of walking had strengthened her legs, giving her an endurance few of the landed gentry could match. Avoiding brambles and thickets of berries, she slipped past exposed roots that sought to trip her, and twisted between oak trees whose height and girth spoke of great age. Grouse clucked in the bushes, as if scolding her for her precipitous flight, but she paid them little heed. Instead, she drew in deep breaths of air laced with the smell of forest loam, and ran to the edge of the trees.

There she stopped, and scanned Rivendell. It loomed high on a knoll, about a mile away, the gray stone awash with early morning sunshine. She could not detect even a flash of activity. Rather than reassure her, it made her even more uneasy.

What had the duke planned for her?

She crept up through the outlying trees, into the gardens, and through the servants' entrance.

Mrs. Finlay had already arisen, her thin cheeks red from steam that poured from a kettle. Bits of oatmeal spotted her serviceable dress and apron. "Up already, are ye, lassie? An' I see ye've been out walkin' barefoot again. Macniall-more wouldna be pleased wi' ye."

Catherine froze at the sound of her voice and waited for the muttered oaths she knew would come: "Witch!" "Devil's spawn!" She could see the flames in the oven, and imagined how they would feel licking her flesh, burning her hair away, turning her into a charred skeleton. But not a trace of alarm or guile appeared on the elderly woman's face, and her hands remained steady as she stirred the kettle of steaming porridge. Apparently the duke had yet to raise an outcry. Why was he waiting?

After forcing a smile to her lips, she grabbed a bannock from the pile of breakfast pastries on the table and took a bite. It tasted like paper: dry and utterly tasteless. Even so, her stomach grumbled.

Mrs. Finlay looked horrified. "Och, ye'll be needing heather honey on it."

" 'Tis fine as it is." She slipped the rest of the bannock into a pocket in her cloak and made for the servants' staircase.

"All this sneaking 'round, 'tis not seemly," the elderly lady mumbled, her pinched features becoming even more grim. Since Catherine's mother had died, she'd fussed around Catherine like a hen with a chick. "Aye, if Macniallmore could see ye now, roaming the moors with yer husband up, waitin' on ye tae tour Rivendell, he'd likely spank ye proper."

Catherine paused, hand on the railing. "Did you say the duke is waiting for me?"

"Since dawn, the man's been sittin' by himself in the laird's apartments, cleanin' like a chambermaid and bletherin' about fairies like a bairn just out o' the cradle."

"Fairies? The old tales?"

"Aye, and talk about the grimalkin. I told him tae hae done with such-like nonsense and got him a tray. He asked for ye tae come tae the laird's apartments as soon as ye returned."

Catherine turned in the direction of the laird's apartments, but her feet refused to move.

Mrs. Finlay stamped her foot. "Away wi' ye. Yer husband's waitin', lassie. Bring him this, 'twill warm his gullet." She placed a hoggin of Highland bitters—whisky infused with spices—in Catherine's hand.

Aware of the soft note in the woman's voice, Catherine approached the laird's apartments. She knocked on the oaken door, her lip caught between her teeth, the stomachic of bitters trembling in her hand. Would he spit vile epithets at her? Perhaps even try to ward her off with a cross? No, sonorous accusations were more appropriate when confronting a witch. An image of the duke, bewigged in long white curls, wrapped in a justice's black robe, formed in her mind, and she almost laughed at the absurdity of it.

Almost.

At the very least, he'd regard her with absolute revulsion. She was an animal, a thing whose body melted and then reformed in the most grotesque manner. She'd watched her own hands and feet as they changed, and it wasn't an appealing sight.

A masculine voice interrupted her reverie. "Get in here, Catherine."

Face tight, blood pumping heavily through her veins, she straightened her back and pushed the door open.

He stood near a thickly cushioned damask sofa, in leather riding boots, fawn-colored breeches, and brown riding coat, his linen shirt open at the neck. Eyebrows lowered over a stormy gray gaze, he looked like a surly bear who'd awakened prematurely from hibernation. Brown smudges beneath his eyes testified to a long night without sleep, and his unshaven cheeks and chin gave him a decidedly piratical look. Nevertheless, his magnetism energized the room, and she couldn't have taken her gaze off him even if she wanted to.

Suspense drawing her nerves as tight as a bowstring, she sauntered into the room and paused by the fireplace, her bare feet luxuriating in the thick carpet that now covered the floor. She could smell beeswax, and beneath it a sour undertone of whisky.

Peering at her with a belligerent glare, he stalked over to the door and shut it behind her. "Well, Catherine, we have much to talk about, no?"

She shrugged. "Any subject in particular, Your Grace?"

A muscle began to tick in his jaw. "Why don't we start with last night."

"Last night." She pressed a finger against her lips and pretended to think deeply. "We ate dinner. You stated a desire to get me with child, with or without my consent, and then proceeded to carry me upstairs. You'd drank so much whisky I thought for certain you'd drop me on my arse. Indeed, this morning you have the look of a man who has had nightmares, the kind that come with an unsettled stomach."

"How odd. I don't remember drinking whiskey until much later in the night. And my stomach feels quite normal." He joined her by the fireplace and leaned against the mantelshelf, his posture stiff. "What happened after I brought you to your bedchamber last night?"

"Why don't you tell me?"

His throat worked. Seconds passed. When he finally spoke, his voice sounded hoarse. "You became the grimalkin."

She forced a laugh. "Pardon?"

"You transformed into the grimalkin. Don't pretend innocence, Catherine. You know damned well what happened."

Her eyes wide, she examined him with an expression she might reserve for a madman. " 'Tis clear to me the whisky has addled your brains."

"Your father said much the same thing in London," he snarled. "Made me think I hallucinated the entire incident."

She knew the duke and her father had met while in London, but beyond that she didn't know what in heaven he was talking about. "Not hallucinations," she said slowly, as she would address a child, "nightmares. Nothing more."

"Nightmares." He began to laugh, a low, tortured sound. " 'Twas no more a nightmare than you, standing before me now, are a dream."

"Think about what you're saying, Your Grace. You are accusing me of becoming a four-footed animal. A wildcat."

He dragged a hand from his forehead to his chin. "Yes, I am, and I stand by it."

"I daresay you will have difficulty convincing others of your charge." Her heart pounding in her chest, she knew she walked along the edge of a precipice, one he could easily nudge her into if she didn't persuade him otherwise. "Many of us here in Kildonan have dreamed of the grimalkin. I have myself—'tis the Scottish air that does it."

"I don't understand how or why, but I observed your transformation with my own eyes. You can't fool me, Catherine."

She forced another laugh. Beads of sweat gathered along her brow. "What utter nonsense." As casually as possible, she set the stomachic of bitters next to him on the couch. "From Mrs. Finlay. She seems to have taken a liking to you. Why, I can't imagine."

Her sally failed to provoke a retort, a grimace, or even a

snort from him. He remained completely silent, studying her as a scholar might study an insect beneath a magnifying glass. He thought her a repulsive monster; she could see it in the way he looked at her, in the stiffness of his body.

Throat tightening, she strolled around the sitting room, touching the furniture he'd dusted, noting he'd removed the cracked tapestries and ivy that had twined through broken windows. Indeed, the room held several pieces of the fine mahogany furniture her father had packed into the parapet years before. In the space of less than twenty-four hours, he'd nearly made the sitting room livable.

Act as normal as possible, she reminded herself, and injected a bantering note into her voice. "A laird that cleans his own apartments. Most unusual."

"Admit it, Catherine. Admit you transform into the grimalkin, or I will gather evidence to prove it myself."

She pretended she didn't hear him. "I see you've raided the parapet for furniture. I must say, I applaud your selection. I've been keeping these pieces for auction."

His unwavering gaze drilled into her. "Fragprie is sending a freemason up to repair the windows and stone walls. Within a week I expect to have these apartments completely restored."

"So you're staying, then?"

An inordinate amount of time passed before he answered. "How can I leave with such a mystery plaguing me?"

She shrugged. "I see I shall have to devote a considerable amount of energy toward ensuring your departure."

"You might secure my departure by telling me the truth."

"But Your Grace, I have told the truth," she said with wide eyes.

He snorted. "Then I shall remain in Scotland for a very long time indeed. I've found Rivendell fascinating. An unexpected challenge, in fact." His tone lightened somewhat, and a gleam entered his gray gaze, one she found wholly disconcerting. He turned to stare out one of the broken windows. "Have you breakfasted yet?"

Unconsciously she'd been holding her breath, and at his question she sighed gustily. Apparently he'd realized no one would believe him if he insisted she transformed into a beast. She wondered if he even believed it himself. For once, the extraordinary nature of the curse had worked in her favor.

The tightness in her throat eased. Today, at least, she would remain free. She would have to be extra careful to ensure he never gathered evidence against her, as he'd threatened. With luck, in a month or so he'd grow bored and frustrated, and leave Rivendell on his own accord.

She smiled at him. "I walked the moors this morning without eating, as I usually do. I admit I'm quite hungry."

"Mrs. Finlay prepared me a tray, one with enough food to satisfy a hundred clansmen. Go ahead, eat."

A silver tray sat on a satinwood table. She lifted the cover and sighed, her mouth watering. Cold mutton ham, Orkney cheese, eggs, smoked salmon, baps, oatcakes, and a selection of currant jams greeted her delighted gaze. After a night as the grimalkin, her appetite often rivaled Fragprie's. She turned to make sure the duke's attention remained on the gardens, and began to stuff oatcakes into her mouth.

Minutes later, she'd neatly devoured the remaining food on the tray. Covering her mouth with one hand to smother a ladylike burp, she glanced at the duke. Eyes wide, rubbing his jaw with one finger, he stared at her.

"You have quite an appetite. Do all Scots eat with such enthusiasm, or might you have another reason?"

She looked at the empty tray and felt warmth suffuse her cheeks. "An early morning walk in the moors does wonders for one's constitution."

Eyebrow raised, he glanced again at the tray. "Is that so? Well, we had better begin our tour of the MacClelland lands, then. I find my own appetite has evaporated. While you change into your riding habit, I'll have the groom saddle horses for us." Without waiting for her approval, he strode toward the door.

"Your Grace, wait."

He paused and looked back at her.

"I have no riding habit."

Sighing heavily, he shook his head. "Of course, I should have guessed. Why would a woman who flouts conventionality at every turn own something as prosaic as a riding habit?"

"I do not ride," she said, her voice soft. Animals appeared to know the grimalkin lurked within her, based on her scent, and often reacted unpredictably in her presence. Horses, in fact, detested her. Often she'd wondered how it felt to ride atop a horse, to feel surging muscles beneath her legs, to let her hair fly behind her like a banner as she raced across the moors.

Unfortunately, she'd never know that particular delight.

His eyebrows drew together. "What? Surely you jest. Your father stabled some of the finest horseflesh in all of Scotland. He never taught you to ride?"

" 'Tis more than that. Horses and I . . . we do not get along. They frighten me. My father and our servants learned to indulge me at a young age. They keep the horses away from me, and I remain clear of the stables."

He looked to the ceiling, as if trying to find a measure of patience. "Does the entire household cater to your every whim?"

"I don't appreciate your attitude, sir."

"Come outside with me," he ordered, his eyes mere slits.

She hesitated, but he had, after all, granted her a reprieve of sorts and for that she was grateful. Footsteps slow, she trailed behind him as he stalked down the corridor, through the central hall, and out the front entrance. She lagged even farther behind him on the flagstone path leading to the stable.

Attached to the side of the castle, the stables appeared well-kept, the building's gray walls neatly patched in some places, its roof missing not a single tile. Horses whinnied from inside the building, their contented snorts filling the air as they munched oats from wooden buckets. An ancient groom in patched blue livery—a Scotsman by the name of MacDuff—sat atop a bale of straw outside the stable, polishing leather tack. When he espied the duke, he jumped to his feet and doffed his frayed tam-o'-shanter.

The duke spoke to the old man, who eyed Catherine and shook his head vigorously. Eyebrows drawn together, the duke placed his hands on his hips and spoke more sharply.

Catherine couldn't hear his words, but she recognized their air of authority.

Shaking his head, MacDuff disappeared into the stables.

Finally she reached the duke's side.

Nostrils flared slightly, he stared down at her with an implacable gaze. "Your servants show a deplorable lack of training."

"MacDuff, Mrs. Finlay, Mary . . . they are all related to me. We are the clan MacClelland. I encourage their familiar attitudes because I have no immediate family of my own."

He frowned. "We shall discuss your servants in more detail later. For now, I will teach you to ride. I've instructed MacDuff to saddle two horses: an even-tempered mare for you and a mount suitable for me. Several horses from my own stables shall arrive within the month."

"But, Your Grace, 'tis not so easy as that—"

"Nicholas, damn it. Call me Nicholas."

"Aye, Nicholas, I'm sorry, but we'll have to walk—"

"Walk? We have hundreds of acres to cover, a task accomplished much easier on horseback."

"I walk these lands every day. 'Tis not so hard as you'd imagine. Please, don't force me to ride."

Just then, MacDuff drew two horses from the stable, one a gentle gray mare, the other a hoof-stomping, fire-breathing black monster. Catherine felt her heart begin to thump in her chest at their approach.

"Here's Annie for the lassie," MacDuff said, "and Beelzebub for ye, Yer Grace."

The duke snorted. "A fitting choice. I'm surrounded by devils. God has decided to punish me at last."

She eyed him cautiously. "I did not take you for a religious man."

A humorless laugh erupted from him. "I'm not, dear lady. I'm not."

A breeze blew into Catherine's face, carrying her scent away from the horses. The smell of manure, horseflesh, and leather mingling in a pungent cloud around her, she remained stiffly alert, waiting for the wind to change. She didn't bother to swat the wasp that buzzed over her head.

MacDuff, witness to previous debacles between her and

the occasional horse that strayed in her path, tightened his grip on the bridles. The horses, plagued by gnats, swished their tails against their flanks. "I've saddled Annie wi' a flat saddle, as ye requested."

"Good man." The duke extended a hand to Catherine. "You and I will ride together on the mare until you feel comfortable enough to ride on your own. We'll take Beelzebub with us, although I'm sure he won't appreciate following us on a lead."

She took his hand, but pulled back, resisting his effort to draw her to his side. "What male willingly follows a lady's example?"

A gleam entered the duke's gray eyes. "Quite so."

Exerting relentless pressure, he forced her to stand next to him. Soft wind blew against her back, fluttering her skirt, ripping tendrils of hair from the casual chignon at the back of her neck. Her scent traveled across the flagstone path and directly to the horses.

Beelzebub's great round eyes became rounder. He issued a warning snort. Nostrils quivering, the mare lifted her head.

The duke stepped closer to the pair and reached for the mare's reins, but MacDuff refused to give them over. "Ah doan think ye understand, Yer Grace. The lassie, here, she canna ride, for the horses frighten her. Aye, since she was a wee bairn, she's stayed away from the stables—"

A heavy frown crossed the duke's face. "I understand that you've given in to her every shameless demand. Today she will learn to ride."

"As ye say." Eyes wide, MacDuff handed him the reins.

Beelzebub stomped the ground in cadence, his hooves pushing aside huge clods of dirt. Whinnying softly, the mare responded to Beelzebub's warning and tried to back away, but the duke held her firmly. With Catherine pulling on one of his hands and the mare pulling the other, he seemed in imminent danger of splitting in two. Still, he shushed the mare and stroked her mane, which seemed to quiet her a bit.

"Now, Catherine, I am going to seat you atop the mare, and then I'll mount behind you. To keep your balance, you may hold her mane or the saddle, here, and . . ."

He spewed out a series of instructions that she payed not

the least attention to. The horses had captured her gaze, their insistent snorts boding ill for both her and the duke. Now the mare had begun to stomp in rhythm, too, and her flanks heaved.

"Are you ready?"

"No, I shall not ride. You cannot force me—"

Ignoring her, he put his hands around her waist. Abruptly, she was in midair, her backside directly above the leather saddle.

Beelzebub chose that moment to let out a shrill whinny. The mare jolted to the side, and both Catherine and the duke pitched forward, her backside landing on a pile of dirt between the horses rather than a saddle. Spine tingling from the collision, she tried to gasp, but the fall had knocked the air from her lungs. The gasp came out as a tortured moan. She couldn't breathe.

Eight large, muscled legs bucked and plunged around her, their hooves showering her with clumps of dirt. The horses seemed to come within inches of crushing her head, her legs, her feet. Curled into a ball, she closed her eyes, certain the beasts would render her a bloody pulp. Earsplitting whinnies pierced the stableyard, mingling with her own moans and the shouts of MacDuff and the stablehands.

An ache blossomed along her spine, snaking around her bones, pulling, rearranging, coming fast and powerful, like a beast threatened. She arched in protest, the movement forcing air back into her lungs. Her lips formed a single, unspoken word: *No!* She thought no longer about the horses that flailed around her; rather, she fought the change with every ounce of strength she possessed.

A body suddenly pressed down on her, covering her from head to toe, molding her to its own shape. Muscular arms wrapped around her waist, pulling her back against broad shoulders. She smelled a salty-virile scent, heard a muttered command in her ear.

"Hold on to me."

Nicholas. He would save her.

She looked up at him through shimmering air. He recoiled for one tiny moment, the movement undetectable to a human but more than obvious to her heightened senses.

Nevertheless, his arms remained around her, and she clung to him as he drew her out of the fracas, Beelzebub kicking him on the buttocks in the process.

When they reached the safety of a small fir tree, he set her upon the grass and sat down next to her. MacDuff and two other men still fought to grab the horses' bridles, their colorful oaths reddening the face of Mrs. Finlay, who'd come to the front door to view the spectacle. Finally the groom managed to calm Beelzebub and Annie, and, with one fierce glance at Nicholas, led the horses back into the stables.

She fought off a rush of tears, but a few managed to leak out. Hand shaking, she grabbed the hem of her dress and wiped them away, showing muddy pantalettes in the process.

"Good Christ, Catherine," he said, his voice husky, his gray eyes dark. "Those horses acted as though a snake had wound its way through their hooves."

"The stallions my father breeds are often high-strung—"

"I know a frightened horse when I see one."

"While you were explaining how to mount, a wasp buzzed around my head." Her stomach a cold, hard knot of fear, she pointed at a small paper wasp's nest that hung from the barn roof. "Perhaps it stung the mare and her alarm affected the stallion."

"Stop making excuses. We both know why the horses reared."

Lips quivering, she mustered a defiant look. "And why is that, Your Grace? Because I have a beast within my soul, as you suggested in your apartments? These tales of the grimalkin have affected your judgment."

He eyed her speculatively.

"You are imagining things," she insisted.

Silence reined.

Abruptly, his touch businesslike, he ran his hands over her legs and arms, presumably checking for broken bones. "Everything feels as it should."

Relief washed over her in a wave. For the moment, she wouldn't have to spin any more lies about the grimalkin. "Almost everything. I don't think I'll sit for a week."

Frowning, he tucked a stray curl behind her ear. "Liniment works wonders for bruises such as yours. Not only do

I have a jar of my jockey's prized recipe, I would be more than happy to apply it for you."

Heat curled in her stomach at the thought of those fingers stroking fragrant oil into her bare bottom, the part that ached the most.

Damn him for doing this to me, she thought.

"You had best apply it to your own arse, Nicholas. Beelzebub dealt you a hard blow. If you do not feel it yet, you will within the hour, I assure you." She smiled at him, the knowledge he'd be hurting more than she sweetening her temper.

"I'll take you up to your room," he grumbled, and helped her to her feet. In one lithe movement he lifted her into his arms and carried her back into the castle. He swept her through the central hall and, amid her groans over her tender bottom, climbed the stairs and stopped in front of her bedchamber.

Not once did she ask him to put her down. She had denied herself the pleasure of his lovemaking, and would continue to do so, but she couldn't help indulging herself a little before he returned to London. Her flesh was weak, and his relentless, erotic assault on her senses didn't help matters any. Besides, she felt wonderfully safe and secure in his arms, surrounded by the heat of his body and the sound of his heart beating steadily beneath her ear.

Gently he set her on her feet.

"Thank you," she said, her gaze fixed on his broad chest. Unaccountably shy, she could not look him in the eye.

He placed one lean finger beneath her chin and tilted her head up. "For better or worse, you are my wife."

Slowly, he leaned forward, lips hovering above her own.

Surely she could indulge herself a little more, she mused, and closed her eyes. She waited for the feel of his persuasive lips against her own, and, the smell of him thick in her nose, she moistened her lower lip with the tip of her tongue.

Kiss me, Nicholas, she silently pleaded.

Seconds ticked by. Finally she opened her eyes and stared down an empty corridor.

The scoundrel had disappeared.

Eight

Crouched with his back against cold granite, Nicholas huddled beneath the leaves of the giant hawthorn. A cool night breeze slipped beneath his kilt, and he cursed the garment, wondering how Scotsmen endured the snows of winter. Even the ancient skean tucked into his belt seemed determined to make him uncomfortable, its sharp, double-edged point poking him whenever he moved. The damned thing needed a scabbard, he thought, and vowed to procure one first thing in the morning. In fact, he would have brought his pistols from London, but who'd have thought he'd need to protect himself from a wildcat?

The moon hovered high and full above him, playing hide-and-seek with ponderous rain clouds that raced across the sky. Must be about midnight, he decided, and pulled the homespun plaid closer about his shoulders. Anytime now, the grimalkin would make its appearance, and he was determined to follow it, on this mid-September eve.

Over four months had passed since he'd witnessed the grimalkin, four long months in which he and Catherine had exchanged barely a word. At first she'd avoided every question he'd asked her about the grimalkin, stubbornly denying its very existence, but now she simply avoided him. Indeed, they met only at dinner, Catherine burying her nose in Fragprie's ledgers, and he concentrating on dated copies of the *Scotsman,* a weekly Edinburgh newspaper.

The wildness had changed everything between them.

He'd decided to call the strange magic that transformed his wife the "wildness." It seemed a fitting term for something neither a priest nor the most brilliant scientific minds could have explained. He closed his eyes at the memory of her body stretching, her bones popping, tawny fur erupting from silky white skin. He tried to bring the vision into sharper focus, for since that fateful night it had faded, as if his mind shied away from it.

Oh, that night had shocked him to the very core of his being. The sight of the wildness emerging from Catherine had nearly destroyed his entire belief system, one based on science and discipline. For years he'd studied empiricism and had eventually tamed the ghosts he'd collected while in the Hell Fire Club. He told himself he hadn't sold his soul to Satan. After all, there was no Satan.

Science can explain everything.

That had been his mantra.

John Locke would have been proud of him.

But Catherine, with her fairy magic and her power of transformation, had—in mere minutes—done more damage to his carefully constructed world than an earthquake. Outrageously, the morning after her romp as the grimalkin, she'd come to the laird's apartments looking as innocent as a newborn babe. He—the rational one—felt like the dung scraped out of a horse's hoof, while she—the wildcat—appeared as fresh as a rose.

A drop of water splashed on his head. The rain clouds had gathered, blotting out the moon, dashing across the heavens with ominous speed. He looked up at the window to Catherine's bedchamber, noting a soft glow, perhaps that of an oil lamp. He felt certain if there was a grimalkin, it would appear tonight. As on the night he'd last seen the wildcat, Catherine had displayed an unprecedented edginess at dinner. He'd noticed a fresh, penetrating odor in the dining room and a warm draft without a discernible source.

Tonight he was determined to learn once and for all if

the grimalkin existed, or if he'd dreamed the beast, as Catherine had suggested. And afterward, if the grimalkin proved real, he could annul his marriage should he desire to. Catherine and Fragprie could no longer blackmail him without serious consequences. He might be a bastard, but she was something much stranger.

Accordingly, he'd procured a disguise—a scrubby plaid and kilt—from MacDuff, and prepared to follow the wildcat, if and when it appeared. The kilt and plaid felt quite reckless after a lifetime of breeches, but at least he'd prevent talk about the strange Englishman who skulked around the moors beneath a full moon.

A sudden flash of brilliant white light spewed from her window, and instinctively he raised his arm to shield his eyes. The light illuminated the hawthorn and surrounding grounds with all the power of a miniature sun, and for an instant Nicholas felt drained, as if the grimalkin had drawn strength from his own body.

He hadn't dreamed it.

The grimalkin did, indeed, exist.

He dropped his arm and, with a sound like a razor stroking leather, pulled the skean from his belt. He wondered if she would attack him. Would injuring the cat also injure the woman beneath? His hand began to shake at the thought. He remembered her tears the night he'd seen her transform, the agony that had etched lines into her face, and something in him twisted with sympathy. Clearly she suffered. Her life, he thought, must be one of loneliness, filled with the constant fear of discovery.

Despite the trouble between them, he abruptly wished he could ease her burden a bit.

Moments later, a black shape hurtled down toward him and landed on the grass not ten feet away. Tawny fur glowing and alive beneath the moonlight, muscles rippling from the impact, she regained her balance and sniffed the air. The breath froze in his throat, and, his heart racing in his chest like a thoroughbred just out of the starting box, he stared at her.

Evidently catching his scent, she turned to face him, her

green eyes wide, whiskers forward, ears up, and tail resembling a scorpion's: curved, high in the air, ready to strike.

He tightened his grip on the skean and hid it behind his back.

She took a step in his direction. And another, and another, until she stood a mere three feet away. Even up close, she projected extraordinary grace and beauty, her body a contrast of hard sinews and soft fur.

He could smell that same musky odor he'd detected in her bedchamber four months previous, and it reminded him of the very real danger he now faced. Suppressed power vibrated through his body, and even as she readied to pounce, his own muscles bunched. The skean seemed to burn in his hand with a fire all its own.

A low growl rumbled from her throat.

He tried to imagine sinking the skean into her fur.

Instead, he remembered the vulnerability he occasionally glimpsed in her green eyes, eyes that usually regarded him with pride and defiance.

He thought again of her tears.

A low sigh, almost a groan, escaped him.

He could not hurt her. Not even to save himself.

Slowly, he dropped the skean and held his hand out to her, palm up. Her growl modulated to an even hum, and to his utter shock, she rubbed her face against his outstretched hand. Soft, silky, smelling like newly mown hay, her fur tickled his skin. Her brilliant cat's eyes never left his as she leaned into him, her throaty hum as soothing as a lullaby.

Every movement controlled, his face betraying none of the raw excitement building within, he stroked her, his fingers buried in tawny fur, her soft glow making his hand appear golden. He could have maimed her, and she him, but instead, this strange tenderness grew between them. How ironic, he thought, that the grimalkin cleaved to him more eagerly than the woman inside.

Without warning, a high, piercing whinny sliced through the air. Both Nicholas and the grimalkin froze.

"Away with ye, Beelzebub, ye black bastard. The mare's not for yer pleasure." MacDuff's voice, heavy with annoyance, drifted from the stables, and on its heels, Beelzebub's distinctive challenge rose above the sound of snorting and cursing.

Smash!

Somewhere a board broke, and the stallion gained his freedom.

The grimalkin dropped low to the ground and, with her ears back, padded off into the grass. Each paw placed very carefully on the ground before shifting any weight on it, she crept silently into the moors, leaving not a mark.

Cursing MacDuff and Beelzebub for ruining what could have proven a definitive moment in his life, Nicholas scrambled to pursue her. He stumbled over boulders and tangled himself in unseen patches of heather, and felt utterly graceless in comparison to her sleek beauty. Peat bogs sucked at his buckskin brogues and slimed his kilt until he smelled like a swamp dweller. Still, the grimalkin padded on, heedless of her clumsy companion, surveying her territory with all the aplomb of a laird inspecting his holdings.

He wished he had paid more attention to the terrain during his recent expeditions—upon that devil Beelzebub—through MacClelland lands. He and Fragprie had toured the land these past weeks, the long rides upon the moors a balm to his wounded spirit. He'd also worked alongside Kildonan's ironsmith and freemasons, renovating the castle and its outbuildings. The physical activity had not only improved his disposition but initiated a friendship with the MacClelland clansmen, who evidently admired men unafraid of hard labor.

Catherine, of course, had glowered at every one of his improvements, apparently viewing them as an effort on his part to undermine her authority in the castle and with her clan. She still didn't realize he had no desire to replace her at Rivendell, but was simply trying to cope with the grimalkin's existence and all it implied.

Distant thunder rolled over the Grampian Mountains, shaking the ground beneath his feet and drawing him from his thoughts. They'd walked to the border of a forest thick with trees and brush. Eyes so luminous they appeared lit from within, the grimalkin tracked into the trees.

Navigating exposed roots and thorny brambles, Nicholas

identified landmarks where he could and waited while the grimalkin scratched marks on oak trees, displaying daggerlike claws that slit the bark like a razor through silk. As they passed around a pond, crossed a waist-high stone border, and emerged onto the moors again, he realized they'd left MacClelland lands and had probably trespassed onto those of his erstwhile father.

Sheep's throaty cries replaced the clucks of grouse and pheasant that had permeated the forest. A few more raindrops pattered against his head, and the wind picked up, becoming even colder, as if sweeping down from the North Pole. His gut tightened as they approached a ramshackle wooden barn, bleats echoing from within, and he speculated that the wildcat planned to make her first kill of the night. How fitting, he thought, that she would choose to slay McQuade sheep rather than her own clan's, for the old groom had enlightened him about the blood feud between the MacClellands and the McQuades.

The grimalkin lowered her body even closer to the ground and picked up speed, reinforcing his assumption that she approached her prey. A moment later the storm broke, pelting the moors with a torrential downpour, obscuring his vision for all but a few feet. He raced in the direction she'd disappeared, buffeted by winds and rain, the night as dark as a subterranean cavern. The moors seemed endless, their deep purple shadows relieved by flashes of lightning.

"Catherine," he shouted, his voice barely audible, his hair dripping in his eyes.

Only the wind answered, wailing across the hills like a banshee.

Guided by touch alone, he stumbled into two standing stones, one of them leaning against the other and providing a niche of sorts. He huddled in the niche and hoped the grimalkin would have similar luck in finding shelter, for even a wildcat must kneel before the tempestuous forces of nature.

"Catherine!"

A cosmic peal of thunder rolled over the land. For a few seconds after it died away, the moors seemed preternaturally quiet. Then, faint and far, he heard a defiant growl, the throat of a wildcat convulsed in song. . . .

Nicholas gripped the wet stone next to him.

She did not kneel.

For one startling moment, a wild longing thrummed through him. Chills that had nothing to do with the rain shivered across his body, and suddenly he understood.

She roared back at the thunder, bold to her very core, primal, at one with nature, filled with an innocent joy for the majesty of life.

Oh, to know such delight.

As the grimalkin, she simply expressed the very essence of her being. And although he considered himself a rational and knowledgeable man, on the most basic level he, too, remained an animal, with a drive to hunt, mate, and survive. Nature had given them both the right to express themselves as they must, and anything that stood in the way of that freedom, be it science or superstition, must be set aside.

The wonder that comes with a simple truth raced through his veins. Exhilarated, battered by the stinging downpour, he lifted his face to the sky. A tremor built deep within his diaphragm and rumbled up through his chest, finally breaking free as a primitive howl, the sound as savage and vital as a Highland war cry.

I am here, he said in a language without words. *I am with you.*

Eagerly he awaited her answer. The storm calmed to a steady pattering of rain, and as the minutes passed, he realized she had chosen not to recognize him. But it bothered him not, for there would be many more nights such as these.

Good Christ, she made him feel so alive.

The cobwebs of doubt and reserve in his mind disintegrated, leaving only a burning desire to understand her intimately, to possess her in her human form and taste the moors on her lips. The carnal attraction he held for her—one he'd tried to dampen over the last few months—burst forth like a Roman candle. Like those who taught sparrows to eat seed from their palms, some fundamental part of him wanted to tame the wildness within her while compromising none of her glorious pride or defiant will.

Silently, braced between stones raised by ancient Druids, he vowed to woo her, to understand her magic and make her his own. Of course, the practical side of him insisted, his desire to join as man and woman wasn't without its problems. He would have to be very careful not to get her with child, for he couldn't withstand the worry of knowing she shapeshifted with his son or daughter in her belly.

At some point he'd have to consider the problem more thoroughly, for he needed an heir to the Efington fortune. But he didn't want to think about that now. He only wanted to anticipate that moment when he held Catherine in his arms and claimed her body and soul.

A subtle glow on the horizon announcing the coming of day, he began to walk back toward Rivendell.

Catherine wrinkled her nose at the mud that covered her from head to toe. Partially dried, it had tightened her skin like an old crone's. She brushed off the leaves that stuck to her body and sighed. Apparently the grimalkin hadn't enough time to clean its fur before transforming.

Either she'd have to brave the pond's cold water or take a bath at the castle. Since she didn't relish having to explain bathwater as dirty as that of a pig's trough, she opted for the pond and counted the weeks until winter. When snow and ice froze the earth, the grimalkin had no opportunity to pad through mud, reducing her difficulties tenfold.

Grumbling, she peeked through the brambles that concealed the entrance to the cave and noted the first rays of sunlight slanting down through the trees. A shallow trench filled with twigs and chaff ran directly past the front of the cave, mute testimony to the strength of the downpour last night. She had a vague recollection of thunder, and an even stranger memory of a barbaric roar—one that reminded her of a savage entering battle—but beyond that, nothing.

An imprint near the shore of the pond caught her eye. From a distance she couldn't identify it, but the mark looked out of place. Warily she scanned the outlying trees and, finding nothing out of the ordinary, struggled into a yellow dress and hurried over to the imprint.

She touched it with a trembling hand.

A footprint. Probably a man's, based on its size.
Again she scanned the trees. Everything appeared normal.
Had someone looked behind the brambles and found the grimalkin's lair?
She dearly hoped not.
Regardless, whoever had trespassed here left long ago, she decided. A few red deer lapped water on the far side of the pond, and sparrows pecked for seeds among the brambles hiding the cave. If someone hid nearby, surely the animals would fly for cover.
Wincing at the cold pebbles beneath her feet, she stuck one toe into the waves lapping against the shore.
"Cold as a kelpie's heart," she muttered.
Growing daylight prodded her on. She pulled the dress off and waded into the pond, her feet sinking into muck, fronds of duck grass tickling her legs. So cold it made breathing difficult, the pond swirled about her thighs with an embrace that again brought the kelpie to mind. Lips set, she splashed water against her neck, washing the last of the mud from her skin. Without wasting a second she emerged from the pond and began to dry herself with the sack.
A pheasant clucked an alarm from the bushes.
A length of tartan flashed from behind an outcrop of boulders.
Frost chased through her veins.
Someone was watching her.
She dove for her gown and dragged it over her head. Then, decently if not fashionably covered, she examined the outcrop and the brush in its immediate vicinity. "Reveal yourself at once."
The sound of water tumbling over rocks filled the clearing.
Mind racing, she washed off the mud that spotted her gown and yanked a cloak around her shoulders. The trespasser saw nothing more, she firmly told herself, than the earl's daughter swimming in Bodhan's Pond. He'd likely tell a bawdy tale at the Temperance Inn, and eventually—through Mary—it would reach the castle. Mrs. Finlay would give her a good scolding, Fragprie would raise a derisive eyebrow in her direction. . . .
What would the duke say?

A sour frown crossed her face. Fiddling with the hooks and eyes on her dress, she decided the duke would say nothing. They barely spoke anymore, and on the rare occasions when they exchanged a few words, he invariably prodded her about the grimalkin. Her father had been mad to trap her into a marriage with the Duke of Efington, mad to think the duke could ever fall in love with her and break the grimalkin's hold on her.

Irritated at the mere thought of the duke, she marched over to the outcrop and peered behind it. Nary a footprint marked the earth, and the tufts of grasses that grew between the boulders appeared untouched.

Somewhere in the brush, the pheasant clucked another warning.

"Silly bird," she muttered, and began the walk home.

When she reached Rivendell, the sun had climbed higher in the sky than usual, and her stomach grumbled in protest. She boldly strode through the front entrance and made straight for the dining room, noting the new velvet drapes at the windows and the ivory Aubusson carpet beneath her feet. Not content with the worn MacClelland plaids, the duke had replaced both carpets and curtains with those more to his liking.

Damn the man, but she liked the new decor better, too. Was there nothing he could not do? And the servants—Mrs. Finlay, Mary, even MacDuff—had all become his devoted vassals. Thank goodness he'd chosen to breakfast elsewhere, she thought, for if she saw him right now, she might not be able to restrain an urge to kick his shins.

She swept into the dining room, her daffodil-colored dress rustling against the mahogany server, and stopped short at the sight of two very long shins clad in ivory breeches. The duke had seated himself at the breakfast table, a fine plate of grilled herring, porridge, eggs, and girdle scones at his elbow. Looking damnably large in the fragile Hepplewhite chair, his hair damp with a recent bath, he smiled at her. He actually smiled at her.

"Did you enjoy your walk on the moors this morning?"

She raised one eyebrow at him and, with hands that shook

ever so slightly, made a quick adjustment to the lace tucker that concealed her bosom. "Aye, 'tis a fine day for walking."

He traced the curves of her body with a heavy-lidded gaze, and for one dangerous moment she wished he would lay her back against the table, right there amid the sunshine and silk and porridge, and touch her as he wished. She wanted to see his dark head nuzzled against her white skin, to feel his lips against her, warm, compelling . . .

With a supreme effort, she banished the fantasy from her mind, grabbed a plate of bannocks and jam, and sat in her accustomed chair.

After a few more seconds, he ceased his examination and stretched, the movement displaying every athletic inch of his long legs. He'd neglected a jacket this morning, and wore an ivory linen shirt that revealed a vee of black hair at his neck. He turned to refill his plate, the muscles of his back and shoulders visibly bunching beneath his shirt.

Catherine stuck her tongue out at him. Oh, he exuded masculinity, this duke, his red-blooded passion attracting her like a bee to a flower. And yet, she couldn't act on that attraction, for to do so would risk her secret yet again. She might convince him he'd dreamed the grimalkin once, but twice? The duke was no fool.

Frustration had been her nightly companion ever since his arrival.

She wondered at his friendly attitude, after months of sulking. Perhaps he had some new plan to improve Rivendell and wanted to sweeten her up a bit before broaching the subject. But then again, the duke hadn't consulted her on any of his improvements so far. Indeed, he'd become so involved in restoring Rivendell and the surrounding lands she despaired of ever getting rid of him. She'd spent the last three months keeping away from him, fearing the sensual chains he so easily bound her with.

Loneliness, too, had been her nightly companion since his arrival.

"Are you and Mary planning a visit to Kildonan this morning? If so, I'll accompany you." His voice held none of the ill humor she'd come to expect. Rather, he acted as if a heavy burden had fallen from his shoulders.

More mystified than ever, she took a dainty bite from a bannock. Her stomach raged with audible gurgles, and she fought the urge to gulp her breakfast. These mornings after the grimalkin were always so difficult. "My rounds in the village with Mary are terribly boring. We talk of jams, and heather honey, and the effectiveness of slippery elm bark in curing chilblain. Surely you have more lordly things to do. Why don't you ask Fragprie to show you the docks at Helmsdale?" She smiled bitterly at him, his alliance with Fragprie annoying her to no end.

"I would prefer to accompany you and Mary," he reiterated, his gray eyes revealing an iron-willed determination.

"But—"

"Is there a reason why you'd rather I not go?"

She caught her lower lip between her teeth for a moment and realized she had no choice. "We'd be honored, Your Grace." Damn, now what was she going to do? She and Mary had loaded the cart up two days ago with MacClelland antiquities. This morning, they'd planned to drop the valuables off at Mary's brother's, and later arrange for their shipment to Helmsdale for quick sale. The smuggling scheme had brought thousands of pounds into the Rivendell coffers, all without the duke's knowledge.

How she'd gloated these past months. And how good it had felt. The duke thought he was spending his own precious money to restore Rivendell, when actually he hadn't spent a sou. She'd financed every one of his ventures with money she'd received from the sale of antiquities. At some appropriate point in the future, she planned to throw his money back in his face and tell him what an idiot he'd been.

She didn't need the duke's money. Or his love.

Just then, Mary entered the dining hall, dressed in a pleated skirt made of the MacClelland tartan and a simple cotton blouse. She held a cloak over one arm, as the nip in the air promised a cool day. Her eyes widened when she saw the duke, and she looked to Catherine for reassurance.

Catherine stood and took her arm. She hoped the smile she'd pasted across her face looked more real than it felt. "The duke plans to accompany us today, Mary. Is that not grand news?"

Mary blanched.

Eyebrows drawn together, the duke examined them both.

Hurrying her cousin toward the door, Catherine put a plate of girdle scones in her hands. "I don't believe Mrs. Finlay has yet packed our basket. Why don't you help her. We'll bring these scones, and make sure you include a tincture of elm bark for Old Queenie."

"Aye, I've packed yer basket, lassie." Beaming, Mrs. Finlay chose that moment to enter the room, a large hamper grasped under one arm. "His Grace told me of yer plans tae sup on the moors, so I've prepared a feast tae dae ye proud—potted hough, stovies, cloutie pudding—wi' a stomachic of bitters tae wash it all down. 'Tis good tae see ye both talking again."

Hardly sparing a breath, the cook turned to the duke and said, "Why did ye not tell me ye wanted a bath? The laird of Rivendell shouldna be swimming in a pond before daybreak."

He cast a glance at Catherine and a playful smile curved his lips. "My wife chooses to bathe in the pond at daybreak. Why shouldn't I join her?"

Catherine sputtered, but Mrs. Finlay smiled widely, the duke and she clearly in harmony. "Aye, I understand now, Yer Grace."

"I'm afraid I don't understand at all," Catherine said, a thousand outraged questions crowding her mind. That damned rogue had indeed been spying on her. But where had he hid? And why had she seen a flash of tartan rather than a glimpse of a somber-colored coat? Well, she didn't plan to quiz him in front of Mrs. Finlay and Mary. Belowstairs had enough gossip to fuel it through the winter, without her heaping more coals on. Instead, she focused on the other gem Mrs. Finlay had dropped, and shot the duke a questioning glance. "Lunch on the moors?"

"Mrs. Finlay is evidently a matchmaker at heart. It was she who suggested we sup *al fresco.*"

The old dame had the grace to blush.

Sizing up Mrs. Finlay with a single glance, Catherine spoke in a manner reminiscent of her father delivering a stern lecture. "I'll have no more interference on your part,

Mrs. Finlay. Your expertise, may I remind you, is in the kitchen. Now, I need you and Mary to pack a basket for my trip into Kildonan. Fill it with jams, honey, the usual items."

Mrs. Finlay appeared perplexed. "A basket? I thought ye used a cart on yer trips."

Mary bleated and looked ready to faint.

Good God, Catherine thought, *the secret's near to spilling.* A wary eye on the duke, she pushed both women out the door. "Mary, help Mrs. Finlay prepare a basket for our trip to Kildonan. We shall leave within the hour." Then she leaned closer to Mary and in an undertone said, "Have MacDuff drive the cart down to your brother's. I'll sneak away from the duke and meet Harailt later."

Her lips quivering, Mary nodded, but both she and Mrs. Finlay hesitated near the door.

Catherine mustered a quelling tone. "Go."

Finally they hurried off toward the kitchen, and she shut the dining room door on them.

"I smell a rat," the duke said, his words contradicting his casual tone. "What are you up to now, dearest Catherine?"

After resuming her seat, she munched on another bannock and reminded herself an offensive strike was often the best defense. "I might ask the same of you, Your Grace. After months of reticence, I find your jolly mood somewhat . . . disconcerting. First I discover you've been spying upon me during one of my most intimate moments, and then you announce a desire to accompany me on my rounds. Why have you appointed yourself my guardian?"

"To keep a closer eye on you, of course. You appear to need it, based on the scene I've just witnessed."

"Oh. Tell me, Sir Guardian, who will protect me from you?"

His voice dropped to a more intimate level. "No one would dare. You'll have to trust me."

She snorted. "Trust you? Have you lost your wits? I would rather trust a hungry wolf."

"Or a leopard," he added, his eyes heavy-lidded.

Silenced for a moment, she stood and refilled her plate, even though her appetite had deserted her. Once she'd marshaled her thoughts, she set the plate on the table with more force than necessary and gave him a measuring look. "How much did you see at the pond?"

He pushed back from the table and propped his boots up on its green marble surface. "I saw every glorious inch of your naked body."

"And why did you not reveal yourself?"

His grin was unrepentant. "Because I wanted to savor each moment."

Lips tightening, she clenched her hands into fists. "You, sir, are an unprincipled bastard."

After a moment of thought, he nodded. "An epithet I've become used to." Then, as if he'd grown tired of the discussion, he uncurled his large form and stood, looking much like a dark Apollo descended to earth. "Mary awaits. Shall we?"

He held out a hand to her, an unreadable expression sparkling in his gray eyes, tension suddenly apparent in his stance.

Nose in the air, she stood as well and brushed past his outstretched hand. "Come if you must. I daresay Mary and I will tolerate your presence."

His low, amused chuckle ringing in her ears, she sailed out the door and through the central hall, calling for Mary on her way.

Nine

The village of Kildonan was small, primitive, and isolated, a drover's society nestled in a glen between three mountains: Morven, Beinn Dhorain, and Ben Griam More. Cottages, their worn stone sides girded with timbers, hugged the main thoroughfare, and behind many a home, pantaloons hung next to breeches on makeshift clotheslines. The bleats of sheep and desultory conversation filled the air, as groups of people clustered at the marketplace, examining wool, purchasing crates of turnips and wild spinach, or simply gossiping about the latest news from the town of Helmsdale. Together, the people and their buildings gave their small corner of the Highlands a domesticated appearance.

And yet, a certain fierceness permeated the village. Mist shrouded the mountains and wafted down into the valley, concealing both clansmen and the ghosts of cattle thieves in its damp, cool embrace. Gullies cut through the mountains themselves, each furrow so deep and straight it seemed as if giant talons had scratched across the rock. It was a village of contrasts, of sunshine and raging storms, of boisterous brawls and kindhearted deeds, a place where each man tried to reconcile the ancient thirst for bloodshed and revenge with the more genteel rules of the nineteenth century.

As she and Mary trod down the path toward the village, Catherine felt the spirit of the place enter her heart. The sheer perfection of everything she saw—the purples and greens of the moors, the stalwart gray of the village, the quiet honking of geese flying overhead in a vee—struck her anew each time she experienced it.

Still, the village was not without its own ill wind, for the patches of ground beneath each clansman's tillage had become infertile. Only the land closest to the cottages was manured, and if a clansman reaped one seed where he'd sown four, he counted himself lucky. Without the new agricultural techniques employed in England, the people of Kildonan would suffer a very long winter, indeed. She shifted her basket from one arm to another and wished it held more than just coins and medicines. She needed a king's ransom.

The duke walked before them, his pace easy. Carrying the picnic hamper Mrs. Finlay had prepared, he navigated twisted hawthorns and firs, stepped over peat bogs and ditches filled with stone, and waded through patches of thrift, the petals of the blush-colored flowers so thin they appeared made of paper. Catherine picked a few stems of thrift on the way and put them in her basket, all the while keeping a vigilant eye on the duke.

He dodged hidden stones and depressions in the turf that should have tripped a man who only months before had considered Vauxhall Gardens his hunting grounds. Odd, that he fit in here so easily, she thought, as if he'd known this land all his life. And yet, he looked like he belonged. A breeze ruffled his black hair, which had grown well past the collar of his cotton shirt, and he'd discarded his necktie and jacket, the casual attire only enhancing an indisputable toughness. Gray eyes alert, black boots spotted with mud and dust, he commanded attention with every lithe stride.

He was, in short, a superb male animal.

They crossed a stone bridge and entered the village square. The duke stopped by a fountain, which provided water for both man and beast, and drank from a ladle. All around them, people busied themselves at the marketplace, studying the smithy's cast-iron pots, picking through the apples and pumpkins, examining the fine wool tartan the village women had woven. Ostensibly brushing dust from her skirt, Catherine peeked up at the duke only to find his attention diverted to the cottages beyond.

Matrons and virgins alike had suddenly decided to sweep their front porches or gather vegetables from their gardens. She didn't like the interested gazes they bestowed on him or the half-smile that curved his mouth. She didn't trust him. Hadn't he chased Sarah Spencer within weeks of their marriage? As long as they remained married, she refused to let him cuckold her again, particularly in her own home.

Chin tilted up, hands on her hips, she glared at him. Much to her annoyance, her pugilistic stance threatened him not, for with a more pronounced smile, he continued his review of the village maidens.

Ye'll catch more flies with honey than vinegar.

Mary's unwanted advice suddenly surfaced in her mind. The girl had repeated the phrase again and again as she'd tried to coax Catherine into marriage with the duke. At the time, Catherine had violently refuted the idea of seducing the duke to gain his favor, but now it didn't seem like too poor a notion.

Certain she could handle the temptation just this once, she loosened a few tendrils of hair and adjusted her lace tucker, showing more of her bosom than she'd ever before dared. "Have you visited the village yet, Nicholas?"

He grinned at her, his white teeth flashing in the sunlight. "A few times."

She longed to stroke his jaw, shaded as it was by a day's growth of beard, and feel the sandpaper texture of his skin beneath her fingertips. Instead, she placed her basket on the ground and drew Mary aside. For now, she wanted the duke all to herself. "Continue on to Old Queenie's, Mary. I shall join you there within an hour or so."

"But Cat," Mary whispered, "what of my brother? He plans a trip to Helmsdale, to purchase ale for tonight's celebration."

Catherine leaned closer. "Celebration?"

"Aye. MacDuff has a new grandson."

"Tell Harailt I will visit him tomorrow, then."

Mary let out the breath she'd been holding, nodded once, and hustled off in the direction of her brother's cottage.

When Catherine looked back to the duke, she found him watching her, eyebrow raised. Unwilling to explain her dismissal of Mary, she sought to divert his attention to more acceptable channels. She leaned down and plucked a cluster of lady's bedstraw, fully aware she revealed half of her bosom in the process.

Some distant corner of her mind shouted a warning; she was enjoying this little seduction far too much. Nevertheless, she wanted to claim him before the women who dared smile at him, some of their invitations innocent, some of them openly covetous. With a smile of her own, one that spoke of softness and femininity and surrender, she teased the tops of her breasts with the flowers, leaving a golden dust on her skin.

"Would you like to meet some of my clansmen?"

Much to her satisfaction, his gaze fell unerringly to her bosom. He crossed his arms, the gleam in his eyes telling her he knew her game and liked it, too. "Would you like me to kiss you, here, in front of all these good women? Shall we sneak off into the bushes?"

"Well, no, I . . . you're teasing me."

"And you're teasing me. A smile such as that doesn't belong on your lips."

She couldn't decide if he'd complimented or criticized her. A moment's thought, however, convinced her he'd both insulted and rejected her in some subtle way. She threw him a look that would have shriveled a lesser man. "I withdraw my offer. Introduce yourself to the MacClelland clan. I hope they throw you out on your Sassunach arse."

"Ah, much better." A wicked grin curving his lips, he grabbed her by the arm and crushed her to his chest. "I would much rather turn your snarl into a purr of delight."

Imprisoning her with one arm, he forced her lips apart with his own and thrust his tongue forward, filling her mouth, claiming her before the entire village. He smelled of warm straw, of sunshine and sweat and dust, the male scent of him intense. She pulled back and stared up into stormy eyes, and read an unmistakable challenge, one she could not ignore.

Resisting the flutter in her belly that demanded she yield to the pleasure he so boldly offered, she summoned every last ounce of willpower she possessed and bit down on his tongue—not hard, but enough to force him to withdraw.

He released her, an appreciative gleam in his eyes.

Several villagers, their attention caught by the lusty scene, had paused in their dealings to see the outcome. Their stares hot on her back, she scowled at the duke and took a menacing step in his direction. "You, sir, are most wicked."

A chuckle shook his broad chest, damn him. "Finish your rounds, wife, and attend me at Rivendell when you're done."

The urge to spit on the ground by his feet almost overwhelmed her. "Aye, Great One. I shall count the moments until we are together again." Back stiff with outrage, she turned on her heel.

His hand landed against her bottom with a light slap, the sound muted by the fabric of her dress but sounding like a thunderclap to Catherine. She saw the approving nods of the men—her own clansmen—and stalked away without retaliation, her stomach tight with resentment.

She loved these Highlands, and remained proud of the Highlanders' independence and fierce pride, but couldn't abide the belief that every woman needed a man to keep her in hand. They all had the same notions her father had entertained. Without a husband, a woman's life was empty and unfulfilled. Would men never emerge from the Dark Ages?

She left the village square and walked down a road made of gray stone sunken into mud. Painfully conscious of the duke's stare, and the villagers' equally interested gazes, she felt a flush of heat stain her cheeks. The need to have revenge on him, even in the smallest way, gained strength when she saw two matrons huddled by a cottage garden, giggling, their sly glances flying from her to the duke.

She gave the older of the two women an annoyed frown. "Sileas Macleish, do you not have more important tasks than to ogle my husband? Where is your bairn?"

The matrons abruptly stopped giggling and busied themselves in their respective yards. Sileas, however, persisted in her distant flirtation, swishing her plaid skirt in a most provocative manner. Catherine sighed and continued down the street, determined to put some distance between herself and the duke. She had a lot to accomplish this morning—many people to visit, coins to dole out to the poorest of Kildonan, ointments and tinctures for the sickest.

She paused by a stall displaying lamb's-wool blankets, purchased one in the palest shade of blue, and had it sent to MacDuff's newest grandson. A small boy ran past, his quick "Morning, Miss" drawing a smile to her lips. He clutched two loaves of dough in his arms, evidently bound for the public oven. She exchanged greetings with others who passed, spoke to a carpenter about fixing the water wheel that splashed in its sluiceway, and chatted with the baker, who operated Kildonan's small gristmill. The village may be small, she thought, but it had everything a hardworking family could need.

She took pride in this village and pride in the people who lived here. Many of the nobility in London had mocked the Scots' dull-witted, barbaric lives. And yet, even the poorest Scotsman lived better than some of the culls in the East End of London. Much to his credit, the duke had remarked upon these very facts one evening during dinner, to his boot-licking minion, Fragprie.

Yes, he'd shamelessly courted her clansmen these last months, flattering them and charming them with his promises and his improvements, making her appear incompetent in the process. Someday she'd tell them she'd sold MacClelland valuables, with Mary's and Harailt's help, to finance the duke's improvements and raise their wages.

She had not deserted them or allowed her responsibilities to slip into another's hands. Indeed, she planned to purchase new agricultural equipment and institute revolutionary techniques as soon as she sold the latest cartfuls of antiques.

Antiques! Perhaps, if she hurried, she could find Harailt before he left for Helmsdale. She wanted that furniture on the next ship to London. Delighted by the continuing opportunity to thwart the duke's will, she finished the last of her rounds and maneuvered through a tight alleyway behind the Temperance Inn.

As she squeezed by, she could hear the lilting drone of the bagpipes and bodhran and Uillean pipes. The local musicians were preparing themselves for tonight's celebration, and silently she vowed to slip away from Rivendell and join them, as she'd done so many times in the past.

Without the duke, of course.

Soon she stood before Harailt's door. She raised her hand to knock, but before she touched wood, the door opened and a feminine hand pulled her in.

"Ye took a great risk coming here wi' the duke about."

Catherine squinted through the darkness. Mary had pulled the shutters closed and stuffed sod into the few remaining cracks. Other than the narrow shaft of sunlight that sliced through the doorway, the cottage remained gloomy. "Why all this subterfuge, Mary? Your strange behavior, rather than any initiative on the duke's part, will give my secret away."

Gesturing to the shadowy pile behind her, Mary shut the door and lit an oil lamp. "I canna stand the suspense. What would the duke say if he peered through nigh window? Is there nae ither way?" She lifted the oil lamp high to illuminate heavily carved walnut and mahogany bureaus, settees whose rich damask upholstery had scarce begun to fade, and chairs in the Sheraton style that had once graced the laird's apartments.

Catherine heard the tremble in the girl's voice and felt a spasm of guilt. She had undoubtedly put a great deal of stress on Mary, and implicated her brother as well. After this shipment, she decided, she would cease her smuggling efforts and find another way to raise the funds necessary to drag the MacClelland clan into the nineteenth century.

She gripped Mary's hands to still their fluttering. "This will be the last shipment, Mary. I cannot tell you how much your and Harailt's help has meant to me. In fact, I wish to leave this for Harailt's wife." She retrieved an enameled jewel box from inside one of the smuggled bureaus and opened it. Within, a pair of ruby earrings—her mother's—lay nestled against black velvet. She willingly gave the earrings away, for she had no memories of her mother and knew her only by the miniature in the laird's apartments.

Mary touched the earrings with one reverent finger. "Oh, Cat, 'tis so kind of ye, but he wouldna accept it. He serves ye because ye are the laird's daughter and are good to yer clan. Many call ye the Angel of Mercy."

Catherine placed them in Mary's hand and forced the girl to close her fist around them. "Nonsense. I insist he take the earrings. 'Tis but small payment for the help he's provided."

Mary shook her head. "I will not argue with ye—"

A piercing scream cut off the rest of her sentence.

Catherine froze at the sheer terror in the voice. "Good Lord in heaven, what was that?" She grabbed Mary by the arm and pulled her out into the sunshine, her pulse quickening at the sound of distant shouts and enraged whinnies.

Eyes wide, Mary stared in the direction of the village stables. Several people ran toward the fenced-in enclosure that quartered nags and geldings alike. Catherine rushed off with them, a sense of disaster building inside. Several of her clansmen—Alasdair, the smithy; Raonull, a drover; Gearald, the innkeeper—stood near a gate, gesticulating wildly, their Gaelic sharp and full of urgency. Sileas, whom she'd berated mere minutes before, clutched the fence, her gaze frantic.

When she reached the gate, Catherine pushed the men aside and peered into the enclosure. Two stallions, Beelzebub and a roan she'd never seen before, charged each other in the middle of the clearing, rearing and clashing with their front hooves, neighing, drawing blood, doing their best to maim each other. Dust swirled around them and blanketed the three mares that stood off to the side, nervously prancing and sidestepping, their eyes rolling.

The smell of sweat, horseflesh, and blood hung in the air like a miasma. Catherine felt her pulse quicken at the stallion's primal battle, and deep within her the grimalkin stirred.

Shuddering at the sight of the roan's left ear hanging by a thread, she put an arm around Sileas. Already she had forgiven the woman for trying to flirt with her husband, and wondered at the tears that now streaked down her plump cheeks. Did she own the roan stallion? Beelzebub had given him a good beating. "What idiot put two stallions in the same pen with three mares?"

Her throat working, Sileas could only mutter, "My bairn."

Bairn? Eyes squinting, Catherine tried to see through the dust, and suddenly, between the stallions, she glimpsed a small girl, about four years old, with soft black hair that hung to her waist. Dirt and grass stained the white cotton dress she wore, and she had only one boot on. The toes of her naked foot curled into the dirt, and tears ran from her blue eyes, tracking through the dust on her cheeks.

Catherine's heart did a flip-flop and landed in her throat. Lileas! How had she managed to wander into the enclosure?

The child stumbled across the dirt, limping, hemmed in by the enraged stallions, trying to the best of her ability to avoid their hooves. Catherine could see a large hoofprint on her apron, evidence that one of the horses had kicked her, and marveled that the girl could even manage to stumble. But what affected Catherine most was the feeble cries that came from Lileas's mouth. She bleated, much like a lamb who'd become lost on the moors, the sound hopeless, abandoned.

Those stallions would stomp her to little more than blood and gristle.

She could not fault the horses for fighting over the mares, for they were animals, living as nature had intended them to. And yet a great anger hammered through her, that this small girl could suffer and die so young, before satisfying whatever purpose had placed her here on earth.

Gearald, the girl's father, worked the rope that held the gate shut, trying to free the knots. His ham-handed attempt had only managed to tighten them further. She slapped his hands away and picked at it herself, her nimble fingers having much more success. "Fetch a musket," she ordered to no one in particular. "If we can't get Lileas out, we'll shoot the horses."

His whole frame quivering, Gearald watched with anguished eyes as his daughter courted death. "I wanted tae jump in there myself, but Sileas, she wouldna let me, said the beasties would pound me intae the dirt, too. What else am I tae dae?"

"Sileas is right," Catherine said as she freed one of the knots. *One more to go.* "We'll open the gate and force them to bolt."

"Raonull wanted tae breed his mares wi' Beelzebub," Gearald continued, his voice no more than a tortured whisper. "The duke gave his permission and MacDuff brought him doon this morning. I doan know who owns the roan. You ken yoursel' they're going to kill my bairn."

"Stop it, Gearald, your daughter will be fine." The tips of her fingers felt raw from pulling on the knot. Fortunately, Raonull dashed to her side and, his face red with effort, cut through the remaining knot with a knife. The gate swung open, and the mares ran through as if pursued by demons from hell.

Another hoof struck the child, this time on the back, and she fell down softly, slowly, like an angel descending to earth, her blue eyes suddenly sweet and fearless.

Lileas would die soon. Catherine saw that clearly now. She stared at the stallions' surging hooves, the bloodlust in their brown eyes, and gathered her courage. She would go into the enclosure herself and distract the stallions, giving Gearald the time to rescue his daughter. Not for a second did she doubt the effectiveness of her plan, for horses regarded her as a predator, even in human form. She would force them away from the girl as a wolf separated his prey from the pack, and hope they did not stampede her in the process.

And yet, even as she made the decision to move, her limbs refused her, as if someone had nailed her feet to the hard-packed dirt. She did not fear the physical injury the stallions might inflict, for she knew pain—each time the change came upon her she suffered the purest agony. Nor did she fear death. Surely there was no cause more worth dying for.

More precisely, she feared the horses' ability to detect her strangeness. They knew her secret, and without too much effort, an onlooker—one who knew horses well—might discern the strangeness in her as well.

Even so, these were her clansmen, her family. As the daughter of the MacClelland chieftain, she had a responsibility to save Lileas, no matter what the consequences. And she felt that responsibility even more keenly, for devoting herself to her clan's welfare was the only way she could atone for the impulses that drove her in the grimalkin's form.

Swallowing, she gauged the distance between herself and the stallions and determined the best way to herd them toward the gate. Then, her limbs trembling ever so slightly, she leaned over and spoke slowly to Gearald.

He argued with her at first, but she played upon his loyalties and at last he nodded in acceptance. Some of the panic left his eyes, replaced by a grim determination.

She put one foot inside the enclosure and, the gazes of her clansmen urging her on, turned back to Gearald. "Remember, if you interfere between me and the horses you will cause me more trouble. Do not worry about me. Save your daughter."

He began to protest, but she cut him off and edged past the gate.

Without warning, a large hand clamped down on her shoulder and yanked her out of the enclosure. "What in hell do you think you're doing?"

The duke's eyes held the gray chill of winter within their depths, and he held a flintlock musket in his hand. Sweat ran down from his temple and over the muscle that ticked in his jaw.

Did he care about her that much?

She wanted to throw herself into his arms and let him face the danger. But she refused to back down from the challenge she'd set herself, particularly in front of her clansmen. No, he'd made that impossible with his earlier taunts. "Release me. I'll distract the stallions and allow Gearald to rescue his daughter."

Surprisingly, he removed his hand, only to prime the musket for firing. "Don't be an idiot. I'll shoot the horses from here."

"My plan has less chance of harming the girl," she insisted.

"And more chance of killing you. I won't allow it, Catherine." He grabbed her by the arm and pulled her behind his large body. With a soft click, he drew back the trigger and aimed at the roan stallion.

Around her, several clansmen fell still, momentarily diverted by this struggle for dominance between Catherine and the English interloper who'd shown a generous yet firm heart. Catherine saw a look in her clansmen's eyes she'd never seen before, one that made her shrivel inside. Without further thought, without plan, she broke free of his grasp and raced into the enclosure, knowing only the pounding dread of dishonor, feeling only the cold sweat that trickled between her breasts.

Bang! The duke's shot went wild, cutting off a few leaves before lodging in the trunk of an oak tree. She risked a glance backward; he had dropped the musket and was charging after her.

He reached her side and grabbed her arm. "Damned fool! Do I have to drag you out of here?"

"Let me do this," she said, and tried to yank free from his grip. "I owe it to my kin."

"You don't owe them your life."

Anger surged through her, vibrating from the tips of her toes to the hair on top of her head. He would do as she commanded, or she'd call the grimalkin, God help her.

"Release me at once."

Something in her voice must have given him pause, for he looked at her with a peculiar intensity.

"Let me go," she said again, her voice low and furious.

Unaccountably, he pulled her against his body and held her for several seconds before releasing her. "All right, we'll try it your way. But if either of those horses moves so much as an inch toward you, I'll shoot them. Understand?"

"Aye." She nodded, shaken by his closeness despite the circumstances.

The duke backed away, giving her the freedom and trust she so desperately needed. She moved forward until she stood about ten feet from the horses. The girl lay in a tangled heap between them, her apparently lifeless body forcing Catherine to admit she may have waited too long.

"Get away from her," she growled, and waved her arms to get the stallions' attention. Carefully, her back to the villagers, she reached for the dark place in her mind and tried to rouse the grimalkin. Only once before had she deliberately called the wildcat—the night she'd escaped from Efington House—and the feat had exhausted her. Swallowing, she focused her every thought, every ounce of inner strength she possessed into forcing it to surface.

Her face grew hot and she began to tremble with effort. Now that she needed the beast, the damned thing stayed quiescent.

Lileas twitched. Her lips opened and a tiny mewl drifted out. The stallions jumped around her, their attention divided between her and Catherine.

"Quiet, baby," Catherine whispered, frustration and panic burning in her stomach like a raging fire. She wanted to scream. To shout. The fire in her stomach twisted, crept along her spine, and suddenly—

The change began.

It invaded her bones with a muted ache, and the air around her shimmered. A warm draft blew her skirts around her ankles and stirred up even more dust.

Abruptly, the stallions separated and fixed their gazes on her. Beelzebub snorted, perhaps recognizing her as an old adversary, and began to back away, his nostrils flaring, the roan temporarily forgotten.

She took another two steps forward. The grimalkin pulled at her bones, trying to reform them with a sleepy insistence. As before, she had forced the beast to life. Now she had to gain control of it, or transform before the entire village. Her chest tight with dread, she forced herself to breathe deep, to concentrate, to adjust her mental hold on the grimalkin.

The beast settled down, seeking the dark place like a bear roused prematurely from hibernation.

Confidence blasted through her, along with a perverse need to torture the grimalkin. Oh, the joy she knew in wrecking its sleep! Eyes narrowed, she called upon it yet again, allowing the change to progress a bit more. Suddenly she could no longer see colors: everything appeared a different shade of gray, and yet more defined, more vital. She could see less, but she could see more.

She looked through the grimalkin's eyes.

The roan gave a frightened whinny and began stamping the ground, drawing her back to the present.

With renewed determination, she assessed the horses and realized she had their undivided attention. Now she had to force them away from the child. Circling around, she locked eyes with the stallions and moved even closer. They backed away, clearly threatened, and Catherine briefly wondered what the villagers were thinking. Had her ability to intimidate two mighty stallions startled them? Had more than a few of her clansmen finally discerned her secret?

The child was almost clear of the stallions, and Gearald circled around, too, his gaze fixed on the horses, waiting for a moment to scoop his daughter up in his arms. Confused by the joint attack, the roan and Beelzebub sidestepped, their agitated snorts indicating their confusion had just about come to an end. In another second they would flee, perhaps trampling Gearald, Lileas, and herself in the process.

Violently she surged forward and swept the child up in her arms, crushing the grimalkin back into the dark place at the same time. Beelzebub reared up at her unexpected attack and narrowly missed her head on the way down. Scrambling, the girl's limp form clutched to her chest, she backed out of the enclosure and stumbled into Sileas's plump form. Immediately she placed the child in her mother's arms.

Sileas rocked back and forth and began to moan, "My bairn's dead," over and over, her tears falling on the girl's face and washing the dust from her cheeks. Only Catherine had felt the soft, hesitant beat of Lileas's heart and knew that she lived. "Take her to Old Queenie," she said, and collapsed against the fence.

The villagers clustered by Sileas. As the Scotswoman gathered her child up and began to walk toward Old Queenie's, an old man looked back at her and tugged at his cap. Another sent her a grateful smile. A few women curtseyed in her direction. She sensed admiration in their eyes and manner, rather than fear.

Her secret evidently remained safe.

An arm went around her. She looked up and felt the pressure of the duke's gaze, his eyes dark with some unnamed emotion. His face pale, he touched her cheek with one finger, and she gave in to an earlier impulse. She threw her arms around him and hugged him close.

"That was a damned foolish thing to do, Catherine," he said, and she felt the trembling in his body and wondered at it. His arms tightened around her and he buried his nose in her hair. She imagined the warmth that emanated from him had nothing to do with lust.

"Thank you for trusting me," she said, her cheek against his dirt- and sweat-stained shirt. She felt his heart beating beneath her ear and for one startling moment glimpsed a possible future: days in which she and Nicholas picnicked on the moors, bathed in sunshine and heather, long nights spent talking before a crackling fire, Nicholas protecting them with his strength and tenderness, loving them.

"I ought to bring you home and give you the lesson you so richly deserve," he muttered, and the moment was gone.

Sighing, she pulled away and squinted at him through the noonday sunshine. "I did what I had to do, Nicholas. Berate me no longer." He did not appear angry with her. No, his face held a strange expression, as if some sort of hunger consumed him, one that involved neither lust nor food.

"Do you think you can walk home, or shall I carry you?"

"I am stronger than you think. I prefer to walk."

A soft voice spoke behind her. "Ye did a brave thing today, Cat. The whole clan is proud of ye." She turned to find Mary standing with the lunch hamper in her hands.

"Thank you, Mary. We are returning to Rivendell. Care to join us?"

"Nay, I shall remain at Harailt's until he returns from Helmsdale."

"We'll take the hamper, then," the duke said, and, with a nod for Mary, took Catherine's hand and led her away from the village.

Nicholas watched her closely as they walked down the flower-strewn path, searching for signs of injury. He felt quite certain he'd never done anything more difficult than let her stay in that enclosure at the mercy of those two beasts. Good Christ, how he'd feared for her. His finger had trembled on the trigger of the musket, and many times he'd come near to firing, but somehow he'd held back and believed in her.

And now he knew he'd made the right decision, for not only had she routed the stallions and saved the child, but given him a hug that had nearly turned his legs to water. No one had ever held him like that before—without passion, without lust, but with a simple trust. Damn if he didn't want to drop to one knee and pledge his eternal troth to her, like some besotted medieval knight.

Evidently she'd avoided injury, for she trod with a sure step, her honey-flame hair flowing down her back in soft curls, the tip of her nose smudged with dust. Prettier than the pink and gold flowers in the meadows surrounding them, she looked far too feminine to have just challenged two stallions and won.

He knew how she'd done it. He'd felt the grimalkin's presence, not as strong as he'd grown accustomed to, but there nevertheless, and her control over the beast had impressed him. Even as he applauded her, though, he chided himself, for he felt more than a bit culpable. He'd practically goaded her into rescuing the girl. She thought he was undermining her authority, and he'd confirmed the impression with his heavy-handed orders.

Up ahead, the path diverged, going back to Rivendell in one direction and to Bodhan's Pond in the other. As he was loath to return to the castle and give her up, he touched her arm with his free hand and said, "Would you care to join me for a brief repast? It seems a shame to leave Mrs. Finlay's carefully prepared feast to waste."

"I would join you, but I fear you will continue to scold me."

He took her hand, her fingers long and white and delicate within his. "I scolded you only because I feared for your life, and despite your convictions, I do not want to attend your funeral. In fact, I'm not certain I shall ever let you go."

She seemed shocked by his admission, almost as shocked as he. She searched his face, her green eyes seeing far deeper than his skin. "You cannot 'keep' me, Your Grace. I am not a possession you can place on your shelf, nor am I an animal you can lock in a cage."

"Call me Nicholas."

Even now, he mused, when nothing more than a little frown crossed her lips, she teased him. A cool breeze blew through the trees, plastering her skirt against her body, revealing legs so long he wondered how they'd feel wrapped around his waist. He and his wife would fit well together, he was quite certain, and he so longed to experience that heady pleasure that the mere thought of it damn near drove him mad.

He glanced at the ripped seam along the side of her bodice and discovered an expanse of white skin hidden by neither camisole nor stays. Her feet, tucked into worn buckskin brogues, were otherwise bare, suggesting she'd neglected stockings and pantaloons as well. He felt himself tighten at the thought that beneath this ripped yellow dress she was completely naked.

How she tempted him.

They had reached the point where the path diverged. She pulled from his grasp and headed toward Rivendell. He let her go. "I realize I shouldn't have challenged your authority in front of your clansmen," he said to her retreating back, "but I did not think you so insecure in their loyalty. They love you, you know."

She stopped and turned to face him, one golden eyebrow raised above suspicious eyes.

" 'She is as pretty as she is good,' they say. Based on what I've learned so far, 'tis high praise coming from a Highlander." He shifted on his feet. "Lunch with me, and teach me more about this land you love so."

When she hesitated, he knew he'd won. He smiled his most beguiling smile. "Please, Catherine. Do I ask all that much? I will remain on my best behavior."

Her step slow, she rejoined him. "All right, Nicholas, I'll trust you this once. Do not disappoint me."

Ten

"I'm going to show you Dun Strathnaver," Catherine said as they left Bodhan's Pond behind and approached mountainside grazing lands.

His breeches wet from walking through soggy patches of heather, Nicholas heard the distant bleat of sheep and had a strange feeling he'd visited this place before.

" 'Tis nothing more than a few standing stones and a broch from pre-Roman times," she continued, "but it has an atmosphere I think you'll find appealing. Not many know about it." A lilt had entered her voice, and her stride easily matched his. Evidently she considered Dun Strathnaver a special place indeed.

"I'm pleased you're willing to share it with me."

A smile lit her face, and in an unprecedented gesture of friendship, she clasped his hand. He returned her grip gently, aware that if he held her too tightly, she would surely fly from him. Yet gone were the distrust and contention that had been so much a part of their marriage, at least for the moment.

He walked with her for almost another hour, the hamper clasped in his free hand, Catherine pointing out the various landmarks she used to find her way through the moors. At length they topped a grassy knoll, and he suddenly realized why this landscape seemed so familiar. She'd brought him to the same place he'd huddled last night, battered by stinging rain, listening to the sound of the grimalkin's roar.

She stopped and looked at him with an eager gaze, waiting for his reaction.

Taking it all in, he spun around. In daylight, the area looked quite different. The standing stones still leaned upon each other as he remembered, but now he discovered they stood about ten feet away from an ancient circular dwelling that had long ago fallen to ruin.

"Well, what do you think?" she prodded.

Not a word would come to his lips. All those feelings he'd had mere hours before now blazed through him with stunning force—exhilaration, longing, an innocent savagery—and the breath froze in his lungs. He turned from the broch and stared into her green eyes, eyes that saw far beyond normal human perception, and for one desperate moment he wanted to tell her what he'd experienced, reveal his knowledge of the grimalkin, ask her how it felt to roam the moors in a beast's form.

Sweat broke out on his brow. *Not yet. She's not ready, and neither are you.*

"Nicholas? Is something wrong?" She frowned at him, her eyes gaining a hint of distrust.

Sunlight beat down upon her uncovered head, turning the streaks of red in her hair to molten copper, and her skin appeared even whiter than usual and utterly flawless beneath that heartless glare. He could see the delicate tracery of veins on her eyelids, and imagined himself planting kisses along the fragile-looking angle of her shoulder blades. She was both beauty and beast, clotted cream and bitter whisky, strength and fragility.

Desire swelled in him, closing his throat, forcing his heart to thump in his chest. Could a man die of need? If so, then he stood with one foot in a coffin. Mustering every ounce of resolve he had, he quashed the urge to kiss her senseless and gave her a warm smile instead.

"Quite an impressive sight."

The suspicion fled from her gaze and she answered his

smile with another of her own. She seemed determined to put their differences behind them, and he agreed wholeheartedly with the gesture. The earlier scare he'd had in the village had made him appreciate her that much more, and besides, who could remain angry on such a glorious day?

"I thought you'd like it." She tugged on his hand, drawing him into the dwelling. Large blocks of drystone formed the broch's walls, which stood almost two feet thick in places and sported a showy mantle of chamomile, mountain silk, and sage. It had once housed many families, Nicholas thought, for stone outlines of individual chambers still existed, but now sheltered only doves and deer, their nests and droppings mute testimony to their presence.

Fascinated, much as Catherine had predicted he would be, he entered the dwelling and touched the lichen that clung to the stone wall. It crumbled against his fingers, coating his skin with mint-green dust. Everywhere he noted signs of deterioration. Fungus clung to the remnants of a ledge that had once supported a wooden floor, dark puddles of peat-slimed water lurked between tumbled stones, and ferns grew between the cracks in the ruined walls, tenaciously clinging to the soil that had begun to seep into the interior.

The broch was decrepit with age, a somber gray between the greens and purples and pinks and yellows. And even though he found the sight quite pleasing, beneath all those flowers and lichen and ivy he saw the skeleton of a dead behemoth.

"I agree," he said. "This place abounds with atmosphere."

Catherine wandered through the broch and selected a spot free of puddles and thorns. She took the hamper from him, removed a tartan blanket, and spread it out between patches of purple thyme.

He sat and helped her arrange the food on the blanket. Mrs. Finlay had outdone herself, for the aroma coming from the earthenware bowls and glass jars had his mouth watering.

A secretive smile curved her lips. "Potted hough, stovies, cloutie pudding, brown bread . . . Mrs. Finlay must think highly of you, Nicholas. I cannot remember the last time she made cloutie pudding." Tracing the pattern of the blanket with one finger, she added, " 'Tis clear my servants know you better than I do myself. Perhaps, one day, you will put aside the lordly attitude and let me see what you hold in your heart."

Good Christ, why did she suddenly insist on flirting with him? He didn't dare respond in kind, for he feared he'd lose control of himself and make love to her with all the abandon of an untried youth, her protests be damned.

She stirred the dish and lifted a spoonful to his lips, her eyes containing a shy invitation that set his teeth on edge. Nevertheless, he obediently opened his mouth and savored lamb spiced with dried fruits and cinnamon.

"Do you like it?"

"More than you can imagine," he said, his tone intense.

Her eyes narrowed, she gazed at him for a moment. "You are most strange at times, Nicholas."

When he didn't respond, she helped herself to a piece of brown bread and asked, "What would you like to know about the Highlands?"

Grateful she'd turned the conversation to less dangerous subjects, he settled back against his elbows. Many things about Rivendell had perplexed him, and here stood the perfect opportunity to discover why Iain and Catherine had made such uneconomical decisions.

"Well, first I'd like to know why you persist in farming the MacClelland lands, when Cheviot sheep are so much more profitable. The richest lairds—Glengarry, Sutherland, Chisolm—have relocated their clansmen and turned their tillage into grazing lands. They now boast overflowing coffers."

She looked out across the moors, and the smile slipped from her face. "Ah, Nicholas, you bring up a difficult problem."

She paused, evidently at a loss for words, and folded her hands in her lap.

Silence grew between them. At length, she continued.

"After Culloden, each clan chief became the sole owner of his lands. They joined English society and acquired expensive tastes. When their clansmen could no longer afford to pay rent, the lairds evicted them from their homes and brought in sheep." Her tone hinted at distaste and subdued anger.

He heaped some more cloutie pudding onto his plate. "You sound as if these lairds committed a crime." The practical side of him understood that life was seldom fair, and to survive, a man had to change with the times. " 'Tis not a crime to relocate families in order to save an estate."

"Aye, it is a crime." She put her own plate down and gave him a direct look. " 'Tis murder most foul."

"Murder? That is a serious accusation, indeed."

"I stand by it," she said, her eyes dark, her voice low and uneven. "The lairds you speak of have not merely 'relocated' their clansmen. Nay, they burn the homes of their own flesh and blood, giving them but a few minutes' warning. Indeed, the old and infirm often die within the flames, for they can't move fast enough to avoid the fire, and those who light it do not care.

"They give no compensation for homes burned or the possessions destroyed within, and those dispossessed souls must do their best to survive without food or shelter. *Clan* means family, and yet Glengarry treats his sheep better than his own kin. Aye, these Cheviot are naught but four-footed clansmen who browse contentedly on ground soaked with clan blood. 'Tis a shameful crime, and my father and I refuse to put money before our kin."

He sat up, affected by her passion, sensing the fury she barely kept leashed. He did not doubt for a second the truth of her words, and he finally understood why she'd fought him so hard to retain control of Rivendell. "You thought once we'd married I would follow Glengarry's path and evict your clansmen."

"Aye. You'd have the right to do so." Her back stiff, she looked out to the moors again.

He admired her decision to trod the higher, yet more difficult, path in life. Despite the grimalkin, or perhaps because of it, she'd put family and responsibility before a greed that went by the name of improvement. "Catherine, I would never clear these Highlands against your will."

Hesitantly, she turned back to face him, her eyes softening

with a strange glow. "But the improvements you've already made . . . not once have you sought my opinion on them."

"No, I did not consult you on whether or not to fix the south wall, or to replace the draperies, or to restore the laird's apartments. These changes I made were positive yet inconsequential."

She thought this over, her bottom lip caught between her teeth, and at length she nodded, as if some inner dilemma had finally resolved itself. "Nicholas, I . . . think perhaps I've misjudged you to some degree."

He pushed an errant curl of honey-flame hair away from her face. "And I, you. I thought you a spoiled wench who cared only for herself, but now I can see why your clansmen love you."

The smile that she gave him sparkled in the sunlight, filling him with warmth, making him ache to reach out and gather her close to his chest.

She leaned forward and grasped his hand between her own. "I have so many ideas." She positively bubbled, the grim mood of moments before forgotten as she plotted how to improve Rivendell without resorting to sheep. Her ideas came fast and he had to strain to keep up with her. "The infield and outfield must be manured yearly, and crops must be rotated. I've marked several iron plows, scythes, and a threshing machine for purchase in Helmsdale, and once in use, they should increase our output dramatically. Once I've abolished runrig farming, each clansman—"

He cut her off, laughing. "Please, Catherine, you're making my head spin. Why don't we return to Rivendell, and discuss it in the study. We can make notes, perhaps even plan a trip to Helmsdale together—"

A dark shadow fell over them, momentarily blotting out the sunlight, and he looked up to find a very large, red-faced Scotsman staring down at him. The man had appeared from nowhere, perhaps sprung up from the earth itself like some moldering shade. Dressed fashionably in a dark green riding coat and leather breeches, his gray eyes held such wrath that Nicholas wished for a musket.

"Get up, trespassers, and hie thee off my land!"

Nicholas jumped to his feet and tried to pull Catherine

behind him. She avoided his grasp and stepped toward the Scotsman, her chin thrust forward, animosity sparkling in her eyes. "And who are you to speak to me that way, Robert McQuade?"

About to take a step in the Scotsman's direction, Nicholas stilled. His gut began to burn. Eyes narrowed, he stared at the man who had enjoyed an illicit affair with his mother and filled her belly with a child.

Catherine moved in front of him, as though protecting him with her slender form. The secret of his patrimony loomed over them like a thundercloud. He hoped McQuade would never learn he'd sired a bastard. He would not claim this man as his father, nor accept any overtures from him.

"I heard about the petition you filed in Helmsdale," she said, "and I shall fight it with every breath in my body. Dun Strathnaver does not sit upon your lands. It is mine."

Hands clenched into fists, Nicholas realized he and Robert McQuade did not look all that much alike. McQuade had gray hair streaked with red and a cleft in his chin; if not for his gray eyes and large physique, Nicholas himself might have doubted the veracity of his mother's claim. According to Annabella, McQuade didn't know he'd sired a bastard.

McQuade chuckled. "Aye, little wench, fight it with your last breath. I shall enjoy watching you bluster."

"Perhaps you'd like to meet me privately to settle this matter," Nicholas said, his voice cold, as he maneuvered in front of Catherine. He didn't care if his mother loved the man. He still yearned to knock the Scotsman on his arrogant arse.

"Pistols at dawn, eh? And who are you?" His gaze insolent, McQuade examined Nicholas from head to foot. "The English whelp she married?"

Nicholas felt his temper rise even higher at the crude insult. "As my wife said, we are not trespassing. I suggest you remove yourself from this broch at once."

Catherine laid a restraining hand on him. "He is my husband, and your social better. Meet the Duke of Efington, McQuade." Then she turned to Nicholas, took him by the arm, and whispered, "Do not let him goad you any further. He is not worth the time."

Nicholas, however, paid her little heed. He kept his gaze on McQuade, noting the man's curious reaction to his title. When she'd mentioned Efington, McQuade's eyes had widened and his face had paled.

McQuade took a step closer. "Annabella?" he breathed.

Nicholas nodded, and felt his stomach begin to churn. Did McQuade know he'd sired a bastard, after all? "That is my mother's name."

"Is she here, in Scotland?"

"What business is it of yours?"

The Scotsman clenched a fist. "Answer me, damn you!"

"No, she has remained in England." Nicholas had endured about all he could without swinging at the louse. "Return to Kinclaven. We will discuss this border issue at a more propitious time."

"Aye, we will," the Scotsman said, regaining some of his aplomb. He nodded toward Catherine, who'd finished packing the hamper, and chuckled. "But before I do, I want to thank the wee lassie for refurnishing Kinclaven."

McQuade had the audacity to flick a finger against her chin. "The MacClelland furniture and antiquities you've been selling in Helmsdale look quite splendid in my study." At Catherine's horrified stare, he nodded. "Aye, I've bought every single shipment. But I must admit, I've wondered what you sit on each night."

He slanted a glance at Nicholas, who had stiffened in disbelief, and with another chuckle walked back into the moors.

Catherine closed her mouth with a snap and waited for the storm to break. It hit with more fury than even she had expected.

"Why, you lying Scottish jade." Nicholas's gray eyes had widened at first and then become as dark as the clouds that brought killing snows to the moors. "You've been auctioning off furniture behind my back. You and Mary. Do you deny it?"

She felt terribly guilty, as if he'd caught her in some heinous sin. Even so, she lifted her chin and stared down her nose at him. "Nay, I do not deny it. But you cannot blame Mary. She had no choice in the matter."

He raised one cold eyebrow. "And what have you done with the money you've earned?"

She winced at the outrage in his voice, and realized her chance to throw the truth in his face had finally come. Why, then, did she feel so damned miserable, like someone had punched a hole in her heart? Perhaps because she'd seen another side of Nicholas today—a caring side, a trusting side, an honorable side—and she liked this new Nicholas very much. With him, she had glimpsed a future that was warm, and safe, and very beautiful.

"Well, I bought drapes, and paid the freemason for fixing the south wall, and I restored the laird's apartments—"

"Don't toy with me, Catherine." He grabbed her arms as if he wanted to shake her.

"I have visited each man who holds one of your notes of credit and paid him off," she said, her tone bitter, her breath stuck in her throat. "That is what I have done with the money. Are you satisfied?"

He let her go and took two steps away from her. She saw the betrayal and regret in his eyes and withered inside.

"Yes, I am more than satisfied," he said, his voice shaking. His face had taken on the hue of a bleached skull. "For a few minutes I had thought you honorable, but now I see you're naught more than a self-centered brat. Obviously I need to watch the finances much more closely."

He leaned down and yanked the hamper off the ground. "Good day to you, Madam."

Jaw clenched, Catherine watched him walk away. Soon he disappeared over the knoll, and she had only the doves for companions, their mournful coos of sympathy making her feel even worse. Part of her wanted to cry . . . no, to sob, to flood the broch with her tears.

Never.

Pride kept her mouth shut and her eyes dry except for a suspicious sparkle. She asked herself why she wanted to weep over a man who had married her against her will, stated a desire to use her as his whore, come to Scotland and taken over her home, and called her a self-centered brat whenever the mood came upon him.

She wiped her face with the hem of her dress and noticed

the gown's dirty, torn appearance for the first time. *Look at her,* she thought. She wore a dress unfit for even an urchin. A gentleman would have mentioned a rip in a lady's bodice, but the duke had kept silent, no doubt ogling her at every opportunity.

That man was a blackguard.

Nay, a traitorous voice inside said. *Look at the situation through his eyes.*

Unwillingly she remembered the other Nicholas she'd discovered this day, the one who had treated her gently and sought to protect her. Indeed, other than the kiss he'd given her in the village square, his conduct had remained beyond reproach. And truth to tell, she couldn't complain about the lusty kiss, for it had satisfied her own desire to lay claim on him before the village matrons.

From his standpoint, she thought, he'd had to endure several nasty tricks since they'd first met. He'd been forced to marry her and had played the part of fool—before all her clansmen—as she paid off his vowels. Worst of all, he'd been tricked into marrying a woman who had a beast within her soul.

Of course, her desire to keep that very beast secret had been at the root of her mischief, but Nicholas didn't know that. That he'd restricted himself to mild epithets such as "lying Scottish jade" was a miracle. Incredibly, he'd refrained from forcing her into the marriage bed, restored her lands, and even stated a desire for her to bear his child. Rather than lock her in a parapet for her misdeeds, he'd asked her to teach him about the Highlands. He'd borne up well through it all, and she abruptly understood why her father had called him a "good man."

With growing conviction, she decided she'd made a complete cake of their marriage. But how to repair the damage without encouraging him and putting her secret in jeopardy? She sighed and pressed her fingers to her temples. Theirs was a tangled knot, one that didn't offer any immediate solutions.

Even so, a great shadow lifted from her mind, and, her steps brisk, she, too, began the journey back to Rivendell. A little song burst from her lips, startling the doves to flight.

When I see him, she thought, *I must talk to him, tell him how much I appreciate what he's done for Rivendell, and perhaps even apologize.*

In a short amount of time she reached the castle, called for Mary, and glided up to her room. The girl arrived out of breath, her eyes sparkling with the anticipation of gossip.

"Did ye enjoy yer picnic with the duke?"

Catherine closed her eyes, remembering the appreciative curve of his lips, the interested sparkle in his gaze. "We had a terrible row," she said.

"Och, don't tell me ye two were fighting again." Mary put her hands on her hips and shook her head. "Can't ye make peace wi' him? He's a fine man, one worth keeping."

"I intend to do both. Make peace with him and keep him." The words surprised her as she uttered them, but they felt so good she didn't bother to dissemble.

Mary gave her an odd look. "Ye've been fighting, and yet ye look like he bedded ye." She thought it over, and without warning, her mouth opened in an O of surprise. "Did he?"

Laughing, Catherine drew back the lilac counterpane on her bed and stretched on the white sheets. "If you must know, the duke found out about our little smuggling scheme," she admitted. "Robert McQuade has bought every single shipment of MacClelland antiquities, and he visited our picnic to tell me so. The duke was, I think, more than a bit perturbed."

Mary's eyes widened at first, but as the news sunk in, she clutched the bedpost for support. "Oh, no, he'll force me tae leave for sure."

"Hush, Mary, I absolved you of wrongdoing." Catherine dearly hoped the maidservant would forgo hysterics, for she wanted nothing to spoil the happiness growing within her. "I bear all of the guilt in his eyes. Now, wake me in two hours, and warn Mrs. Finlay to set the kettle to boil, for I should like a bath before dinner. Later, I shall join you when you leave for the Temperance Inn. And please shake out the blue silk gown the duke bought for me, for I plan to wear it tonight."

A mischievous smile curved her lips. Shot with gold thread, the blue-violet gown looked like the heavens on a clear night when stars blanketed the sky. She thought she looked quite becoming in it; it brought out the highlights in her hair, and its heart-shaped bodice, the point center front, revealed a daring amount of shoulder and cleavage.

Mary collapsed on the bed and sat, evidently trying to digest all of this at once. "If ye're fighting wi' the duke, why do ye want tae start wearing his dresses? The blue silk is the kind o' dress tae wear if ye want a tumble—"

"Nevertheless, wear it I shall."

"And ye know the duke wouldna be pleased with yer plans tae visit the Temperance Inn. Why, the men will be rowdy, and the ale flowing fast, and the music loud—"

"I will invite Nicholas to join me. He would enjoy celebrating the birth of MacDuff's grandson along with the rest of my clan."

Mary pursed her lips, her eyes full of doubt. "I don't understand ye, miss. Ye've been fighting wi' the duke, and yet ye're as happy as a clam. Ye embarrass him before all the clansmen, but ye plan tae invite him tae a clan celebration. . . ." She clasped her hands together. "His Grace, he doesn't take kindly tae mischief—"

"Enough chatter, Mary. Please, let me sleep." Catherine closed her eyes to emphasize her request, and she felt the bed bounce when Mary stood up.

"And Mary?"

Her cousin let out a tolerant sigh. "Aye, Cat?"

"Thank you."

Catherine felt a hand pat the bedcovers. "Have a good rest, then."

Three hours later Catherine sat and ate dinner in an empty dining room. According to Mrs. Finlay, the duke had decided to sup in the laird's apartments and had invited Fragprie to join him. Slumped in her chair, she sawed through the venison on her plate, lifted the meat to her lips, and found it utterly without flavor. The evening had lost its sparkle, and she realized how much she'd been looking forward to winning Nicholas back during dinner.

Perhaps it was too soon to attempt an apology, she mused. No doubt he still smarted from the blow she'd dealt him earlier today. Rather than tell him about the clan celebration at the inn, she decided to go on without him and give him a chance to let off steam. If she invited him, he might think she did so only to gloat over his predicament further.

She pushed the meat around on her plate and, in an effort to banish him from her thoughts, watched the tall case clock tick, the candles flicker in the draft that clung to the ceiling, the steam rise off a plate of haggis. When a maidservant brought a large platter of apple tarts and cream into the dining room, Catherine bade her to take it back. She'd had enough of loneliness and frustration, and now just wanted to relax among the company of people who understood and accepted her.

And so, a short while later, she and Mary made their way to the Temperance Inn, Catherine disguised in an old brown cloak and hood that also blocked her sight of the moon. She felt certain she could control the grimalkin, for it had roamed the moors just last night and sated its every need. Even so, she didn't want to tempt fate by strolling through the moors beneath a hunter's moon, the last full moon before Samhain.

Sounds of revelry greeted her ears as she and Mary approached the twinkling lights of the village—pewter mugs clinking, villagers talking, an occasional drunken shout, the low drone of the bagpipes. Firelight wavered through the inn's glazed windows and created a latticework shadow on the bushes outside. Avoiding the wooden lintel that seemed better suited for children, Catherine and Mary ducked their heads as they entered the establishment.

Inside, the rough stone walls dripped with moisture, perspiring from the heat and excessive talk. Catherine shed her brown cloak and hung it up on a peg near the door, satisfied she fit in perfectly with her clan. She'd stripped off the blue gown in favor of a simple plaid skirt, peasant blouse, and arisard draped in graceful folds over her shoulders and fastened at the neck with a golden circlet. Fine leathern brogues covered her feet, and her dirk, tucked into a wool garter, nestled against her thigh.

Candles set in crude pewter sconces flickered wildly upon

the gathering, their flames caught in the updraft of merry-making. Men and women, some dressed in silk plaid, others in grimy wool, clustered around rough-hewn wooden tables and lounged near the bar. A merchant bent over several sheets of food-splattered parchment, a quill and inkwell near his elbow, his hand fondling the breasts of a well-made brunette Catherine had never seen before.

Somewhere near the back of the inn, a fight broke out, and Gearald—the innkeeper—hustled the cursing, bleeding miscreants out the door. On his return, he espied Catherine and grasped her in a bear hug.

"Thank ye for saving my Lileas," he said. Smiling, he plunked a tankard in her hand and called a toast:

"Here's to a bottle and a bold lassie!
What wad ye wish for mair?
The friend we trust, the fair we love,
Na h'uile la gu math diut!"

Amid cheers, she drained her tankard and remembered Scots ale had a potency bested by whisky alone. A cough shook her slender frame, and with tears in her eyes, she pushed away the additional tankards proffered in her direction.

MacDuff sat on a stool near the musicians, a foolish smile on his face, a tankard of ale clasped in his hand. Several of his kilted cronies, who stood in a loose circle around him, refilled his cup after his every sip, interspersing their jokes with hearty thumps on the poor man's back. MacDuff looked in danger of toppling over.

She joined him, and the ale, a pool of warmth in her stomach, loosened her tongue. She lapsed into a brogue. "Och, MacDuff, ye'll be kissing the floor before the night has truly begun."

MacDuff squinted at her through a haze of smoke billowing from the fireplace. "And where might yer husband be, lassie? Yer a sight for sore eyes, and ye ken it weel. The laddies will be after ye like bears after honey." His gaze roved over the outlines of her body, barely hidden by the tartan skirt and soft cotton blouse.

"I'll forgive ye for yer own roving eye, for ye be fair dommered, but in return, I'll ask ye not tae bring up my husband." Her brain hurt from thinking about the man, and she didn't want to compound the problem by talking about him, too.

His gaze owlish, MacDuff nodded. "Ye ask so nice, lassie, how can I tell ye nay?"

She smiled at him and pulled his tam-o'-shanter lower on his brow. Then, the acrid stench of sweat, warm ale, and charred mutton thick in the air, she wandered among the sturdy tables, calling greetings to those she recognized and nodding to those she didn't. Occasionally she took a sip of whisky or of ale, to ease the dryness in her throat, and paid little attention to the lassitude that stole along her limbs.

After a good deal of mingling, she sat next to Mary on a deacon's bench and brushed away the cobwebs that hung near her head. The musicians' loud, discordant rehearsal thrumming in her ears, she waited for the entertainment to begin.

As if on cue, the bagpipes, bodhran, and Uillean pipes began to play in harmony, their trilling melody setting her foot to tapping. A large, red-faced woman set two claymores on the floor, their blades crossed, and the first man—a drover in a tattered frieze coat and breeches—began the ancient Gillie Callum dance. His feet hopping nimbly about the swords, he spun about, one hand on his hip, the other raised in the air. It was a dance of warriors, of victory, and for one magical moment the drover seemed more a prince than pauper.

Ale and whisky flowed copiously from the bar. One by one, both men and women took the stage and danced the sword dance, or the Highland fling, and within a short time the mood within the inn had progressed from merriment to absolute recklessness. When several sets of hands urged Catherine onto the floor, she took position between the swords with only a minimum of doubt.

She knew the Gillie Callum well, had danced it several times on this very floor. Nevertheless, as she waited for the music to start, a faint ache bloomed deep within her bones, for the ale she'd drunk and her high spirits had roused the grimalkin from its lazy slumber. Surprised at the beast's strength, she spent a full ten seconds breathing deeply, forcing it back to the dark place, trying to keep relatively calm.

The music started, a song with a heavy, rolling beat. Tension filled the air at the sound of the drum. It penetrated the room, like the beating of a titanic heart, and arrested conversation in midstream. She closed her eyes and reveled in its pure beauty.

Shouts urged her on. She raised one arm in the air, placed the other on her hip.

Looked out across the sea of faces.

Saw Nicholas sitting at a table in the far corner of the inn.

The dance fled from her mind.

Firelight cast deep shadows on his face and made his hair appear even blacker, giving him a distinctly Satanic aspect. He had propped his boots up against the table, and when he caught her gaze, he lifted his tankard high in the air, as if to toast her. His mouth curved in a smile of contemptuous amusement.

A brunette—the same one who'd dallied with the merchant earlier—sat near his side, her low-cut dress revealing most of her ample breasts. He didn't touch her, didn't even seem aware of her presence. Even so, the woman wore a triumphant grin, as if she'd already bedded him.

The drum prodded Catherine on, commanding her to move. But she remained frozen. She couldn't tear her gaze away from Nicholas's. The chill she'd seen in his gray eyes earlier that day had thawed to something much warmer but even more dangerous. She had a sudden, ominous premonition that she'd finally pushed him too far.

He crossed his legs at the ankles and took a swig of ale from his tankard. His piercing stare, however, gave the lie to his casual position.

The mournful wail of the bagpipes and dry thrum of the bodhran shook her from the spell she'd fallen into. She began to leap and spin about the crossed swords, her movements as stately and graceful as those before her. The song flowed through her, like a warm, silky fluid, and she felt the stares of the men lingering on her legs and breasts and face.

A fever blossomed within her, fanned by the admiration she saw in so many male eyes and by her new perception of Nicholas. She remembered all the times he'd claimed her with one single, shattering kiss, the sweet, persuasive words he'd uttered as he begged her to have his child. In that instant, she realized just how much she wanted to smash the wall between them and feel his naked strength pressed against her.

She held one hand out to him as she danced, inviting him to join her.

The curious turned their heads to see whom she'd tempted. He took another swig of ale, his gaze never leaving her face. The brunette issued a challenge of her own by snuggling up next to him and pressing her bosom against his arm.

Not easily bested, Catherine twisted to the drumbeat, her dance becoming more sinuous, her breasts thrust up against the peasant blouse, her eyes daring him to come and take what she so blatantly offered. Inspiration struck, and she reached up and pulled the ribbon from her hair. Curls fell to her waist in a gleaming, silken waterfall, tickling her bare shoulders and swirling about her hips. She threaded her fingers through the soft tresses and pulled her hair up, revealing that most vulnerable of spots—the nape of her neck.

The audience goaded her on, clapping and stomping their feet in time with the drum. Appreciative whistles cut through the music and added to the furor. Vaguely she realized she was behaving outrageously, but she didn't care. The duke's disdainful reserve challenged her very femininity.

He put the tankard down and pulled his boots from the table. The contemptuous smile had slipped from his face, replaced by an intent frown that made her feel hot and cold at the same time. She had finally gotten through to him, but what had she roused? Anger or desire?

The drum rolled through the inn like a fierce storm, and her dance became equally untamed. Reveling in her power over him, she slid her hands down the sides of her breasts and over her hips, not caring that she was making a spectacle of herself. She'd forgotten the sword dance in her passion for him, and knew only a desire to soothe the ache that vibrated along every nerve in her body. Her face half-masked by silken tresses, she held her arms out to him.

Dear Lord, how she wanted him. She loved his face, his body, the way his mind worked . . . she loved how he tried to dominate her, failing utterly in the process. She loved his gentleness and his need to protect her, loved the way his eyes became silvery with laughter, loved how he'd shown her respect, in spite of all the mischief she and her father had engineered.

Without warning, her pirouette became disjointed and she stopped, in counterpoint to the ever-increasing frenzy of the drum. She felt hopelessly vulnerable, poised on the floor, the music crashing around her head.

Good God, she'd fallen in love with him.

Frantic, she sought his gaze across the room.

He tossed back a long swallow of ale and stood.

Her hands fell to her sides, the drumbeat forgotten, her clan forgotten, everything forgotten but the dark Englishman who strode forward to claim her. His big body easily dwarfed those who stood around him. Most of the villagers got out of his path. Those few who didn't see his glowering approach suddenly found themselves pushed aside.

In a short time he reached her side. The look in his gray eyes sobered her instantly. She'd never seen him so angry.

Lips compressed to a thin line, he wrapped his arms around her waist and tossed her over his shoulder. "You dance only for me," he said amid a chorus of cheers.

Her backside nearly scraped the timbers that supported the roof. "Put me down, Nicholas. You're making a fool out of me."

"You've made a fool out of yourself, wife."

The blood rushed to her head, and the grimalkin awoke for the second time that day. She squeezed her eyes shut, trying desperately to control it. "Put me down," she ordered, louder this time, and wiggled in his grasp.

Rather than answer her, he gave her a mild tap on her backside. A wicked chuckle that had nothing to do with happiness rumbled through his chest, and the drunken cheers became lewd shouts of encouragement.

"Aye, laddie, ye can tame her!" a male voice shouted.

"I've ne'er seen a dance like that."

"Bring her tae heel!"

"A woman needs a strong hand tae keep her in line."

She gasped, outraged at this unexpected maneuver. Yes, she'd fallen in love with the brute, but she'd be damned if she'd tell him so. Nevertheless, she held on to him as he grabbed her brown cloak and carried her out into the frosty air.

Eleven

He did not let her down in the yard outside the inn. Rather, he hustled her up the path that led to Rivendell. After a painful minute, he dropped the brown cloak in a patch of heather and laid her on top of it. Tufts of grass and small sticks prodded her through the cloak, and the smell of crushed heather, moist and fragrant with dew, swirled around her. She looked beyond him to the sky. Never had she seen so many stars, or dared a moon as bright as this one.

Tension churned through her insides as the grimalkin struggled to claw its way up from the dark place. Her anger and outrage paled next to the danger Nicholas had put himself in, simply by holding her now, under the moonlight. She focused on him, on every beloved plane of his body, and clung to her self-identity. She wouldn't let the grimalkin take her, not this time. She'd controlled the beast once and could do it again—

"You will tease me no longer," he said. His voice held not fury, but an implacable determination.

"Nicholas, I—"

"You will show your body to no one but me." His gaze burned across her breasts and down to her thighs.

Budding desire joined the hard knot of anxiety in her stomach. "I have no wish to show anyone but—"

"Quiet. I have more to say."

She closed her mouth firmly, cutting off the explanations that had threatened to pour out. Although she wasn't ready to risk her pride and trust him with the knowledge of her love, she had at least wanted to justify her appearance at the celebration without him.

He knelt down next to her and sat back on his heels. The moon, hovering behind his shoulders, created a silvery aura around him and threw his face into darkness. "I have known you for more than a year, and since that day we met, I have thought of nothing but thrusting deep within you."

Her gasp cut through the air, shattering the stillness around them, finally fading and leaving the night even quieter than before. A long moment passed.

"I plotted ways to tumble you between my sheets, thought of stroking the perfect, honey-flame cleft between your thighs," he continued, his voice growing soft. "All this time I waited, because I wanted you to come to me willingly. You are like a wild bird, and I thought if I went slowly, you'd gentle to my touch."

A peculiar giddiness curled in her stomach. The ale, she told herself. She'd had far too much ale.

"At the inn, I watched you. You looked so beautiful my muscles ached, my throat tightened, and my desire to have you grew so strong I nearly put my fist through the table. Does this shock you?"

"No," she whispered, her thoughts scattering like leaves on a hurricane wind. He crouched next to her, his body a silhouette against the oaks and hawthorns that rustled behind him. Even in that compact position, he was so very large, every pore of his body exuding a raw masculinity. Her nipples tightened and rubbed against her cotton blouse at the thought of those hard lips against hers, the sensation like a delicate caress.

"Tonight, I will have you." His gaze dropped to her breasts, and she realized that although he stood in shadow, the moon illuminated her fully. He could clearly see his effect on her, but he refused to move back and give her a chance to collect her wits. "Are you a virgin?"

A slow flush crept up into her cheeks. "The moon, Nicholas, oh, look at it. It is so very beautiful. Do you have such a splendid view in London?"

He leaned forward and grasped her arms. She thought she might faint. "Are you a virgin?"

"Aye." She looked away.

Gently, he held her chin with one hand and turned her to face him. His mouth hovered a hairsbreadth above hers. "It pleases me that no man has had you before this night. I will be the first, and the last."

She felt a touch of panic and struggled halfheartedly against him. "Do not think I am submitting to you."

His fingers gentle, he stroked her brow. "This is not a war, *ma chérie*. There are no winners and losers. We are simply doing what nature intends us to do, as husband and wife."

"Will it hurt?"

A soft chuckle escaped him, the sound of a man who knows the game is won. "Tonight, I'll teach you about the pleasure a husband can give his wife. I'll taste and stroke every inch of your flesh until you take me in your hand and force me to thrust within you. At first it will hurt, but then all else will pale as you feel the ecstasy that love can bring."

"Nicholas, I'm . . . frightened." He would never know how much it had cost her to make that admission.

"Trust me."

She took a deep breath. "Promise me we will not create a child this eve."

He stilled, the hand stroking her brow arrested midmotion. "There will be time for children later."

She stared deep into his eyes, and beneath the lust she saw easy acceptance. She wondered why he hadn't showered her with questions or angry denials. But then he dragged his fingers across her neck and downward, leaving a trail so hot she forgot everything but how good he made her feel.

The faint presence of the grimalkin pushing against her spine, she snuggled against him and brushed her lips against his, her touch lighter than a butterfly's wing. She kneaded his broad shoulders with trembling hands, traveled down to his trim waist and across his buttocks, savoring the hard muscles, the firm flesh. In his own way, he'd teased her just as relentlessly, and now she wanted to explore that large body, to worship his magnificent strength. She would give him everything, while compromising nothing.

He vibrated beneath her hands, full of suppressed power, his lips twisting as if in pain from her hesitant exploration. When she fondled the heated fabric at his groin, he growled low in his throat, and lowering his mouth to hers, he kissed her, his lips firm against her own, his tongue like hot, wet silk, reaching inside and plundering her hidden recesses with shocking familiarity. Her mind whirling with the whiskyed taste of him, she followed his lead, touching his tongue with her own, listening for his groans, learning what tantalized him most.

"You are a natural, made for love," he murmured as he trailed kisses from her ear down to her neck.

He untied the laces on her blouse, pulling at the cotton, softly tormenting her taut nipples. Within seconds the blouse lay in a milky heap upon the heather, and cool night air drifted across her bare skin. Greedy for the pleasure she knew would be hers, she pulled his dark head to her breasts. There was something so scandalous about the sight of him pressed against her skin that the almost painful tingle between her thighs grew to unbearable levels.

Tendrils of mist crept around them and mingled with the earthy scent of their passion. She yielded to his gentle words of encouragement as he stroked and licked, his mouth moving from her breasts and across her stomach. Her nipples throbbed in the aftermath of his attention, and with shaking hands, she touched them. Swollen and tender, they ached for more.

He reached the barrier of her wool skirt, unhooked it, and pulled it down her thighs, gazing reverently at each new inch of flesh that appeared. "So beautiful," he whispered, "so perfect. I'm afraid to touch you, for fear you might vanish on me."

His words helped her forget the faintest brush of embarrassment that had touched her when her skirt, garter, and dirk joined the blouse in a heap of wool and metal. No man had ever seen her naked before, and she felt utterly vulnerable, her most sensitive parts exposed before him, in this public place, while he remained fully clothed. And yet, something about it felt titillating, too, and perhaps even naughty.

Breathing raggedly, his face sharpened with desire, he stared at her, his gaze wandering from the tips of her toes, up past her calves, lingering on the thatch of curls between her thighs, stopping at the top of her head. She rejoiced in the effect she had on him—in her mastery over him—and stretched upon the scratchy cloak like a rose opening beneath the summer sun.

"Good God, you provoke me." He dropped a kiss on her stomach, and then pulled her silken tresses across her body, arranging it artfully, revealing more than he'd hidden. "I want to touch you with my mouth, there," he said, and rubbed his thumb against the soft flesh between her thighs, "but we'll savor that pleasure another night."

She cried out at the sudden burst of sensation that shot through her, and thought she would die if he did not assuage the ache soon. "Do what you will."

Sighing raggedly, he planted a swift kiss on her lips. "If I taste you there tonight, I will lose all control and take you too quickly." Then, resting between her thighs, he continued to torment her with his thumb.

She moaned at the soft, circular motion that made her tingle and throb, building a honeyed lassitude along every nerve in her body. Probing her, his every movement gentle, he stretched her, seeking to make his ultimate entry less unpleasant. Still, he remained clothed, and the need to see him naked grew until she could stand it no more. She sat up and tugged on his shirt, even as the tip of his thumb entered her and pressed against her barrier. "Please, let me see . . ."

He glanced up at her, his lips compressed, his face stark with unspoken passion. Evidently he read the mounting excitement in her eyes, for with a speed that popped the studs on his shirt and buttons on his breeches, he rid himself of his clothes. For one moment he stood still beneath the moonlight, and his glorious perfection struck her anew. She saw every individual muscle girding his arms and shoulders, and the thick mat of hair covering his chest did little to hide the ripples that spoke of a rugged virility.

Too soon, he reclaimed her mouth with his own, kissing her hard, rolling her on top of him and crushing her against his chest. Her arms and legs felt heavy and loose, yet filled with energy. She wanted to feel him in every cell of her being, wanted to lose herself in the gray need of his gaze. She tangled her fingers in the black curls on his chest and smelled him, licked him, worshiped every square inch of his magnificent form as she'd so longed to do.

Finally she raised her head and gazed at him. Nostrils flaring with each breath, he'd squeezed his eyes shut. The furrows in his forehead spoke of a man experiencing utter pain and pleasure without comparison. The sight of his tightly leashed passion inflamed her more than words ever could. She pressed against him, her breasts heaving, her legs wrapping around his waist of their own accord.

"I can wait no longer."

"Guide me, my love," he said against her ear, and eagerly she grasped him in one hand. She brought him to her, and snuggled him against her moistness. Still, he refused to thrust forward. Sweat beaded his brow and ran down his temples, and his face had darkened even further with strain.

"Please," she begged, arching against him, seeking the completion only he could bring.

He groaned, the sound low, tortured.

She could take no more. With one shaking hand she grasped him and pushed him inside. Instantly she felt as if she'd taken a knife to her flesh, and cried out even as her muscles tightened, resenting his intrusion. A warm stickiness spread across her thighs, and she recognized it as blood.

A sudden, powerful ache unfurled in her bones, and she stiffened, the scent of her own blood magnified in her nose, her eyes wide. Pain, pleasure, blood, sex . . . they mixed as one and she cried out again.

The grimalkin had awakened—and roared within her—like a beast threatened.

"Shhh, it is done," he whispered, and began to thrust forward with delicious slowness, soothing the pain yet building the ache, bringing delight beyond compare. She groaned with hunger, a strange hunger she'd never felt before, one that made her want to spread her thighs wider, to melt into his large form. She had no pride, could offer no resistance in the face of this kind of pleasure; she could only thrust her own hips up to meet his, urging him on, rising with the bubble of ecstasy swelling inside.

She would do anything he wished, anything to ensure he'd continue this sweet torture. As if he sensed her complete and utter surrender, he gripped her shoulders and thrust deeper, harder, faster, claiming her, marking her . . . and she wanted more.

"Ah, God," he cried, and withdrew from her just as the bubble within her began to burst, pleasure swamping her every pore. He began to shudder, and his seed spilled into the heather beside them and she realized amid the shattering delight that he'd deliberately avoided getting her with child.

A breeze blew around her, rustling through the moors and catching pieces of chaff in its wake. The tingling in her limbs gave way to an increasingly devilish itch, and her fingers began to hook into claws. The trees, they looked so different in the moonlight, she thought, each leaf outlined with silver. She caught the profile of a grouse perched in a thicket, its soft, melodious clucking telling her it had fallen asleep. Nicholas's breath grated heavily in her ears; in the distance, a mouse squeaked, caught between the paws of a pine marten. She smelled the overwhelming musk of human coupling and, more subtly, the scent of a roe deer.

Nay, don't make me leave him now.

She smothered a wail as a terrible pain shot through her back, as if someone had yanked her spine from her body. All around her, the landscape lightened, becoming shades of gray, and yet more defined.

He lifted himself onto his elbows and looked at her through heavy-lidded eyes, a tender smile curving his lips. "Never have I felt—"

Suddenly he gasped, the sound slicing through the preternatural stillness like an alarm bell. "No, Catherine, not yet, please. Control it! I will not lose you, not now."

"Forgive me," she groaned, and then the wail broke free, howling through the moors, the cry deafening in her own ears.

Concealed behind a gooseberry thicket, Nicholas peered through the thorns and watched the tawny cat drink from Bodhan's Pond. Fog hung in a layer above the water, congealing in spots and hiding the teals that ducked down for a morning snack. Although the sun had yet to appear, the skies had a gray-purple cast that banished the stars. Dawn was not far away.

Over the last few hours, he'd followed the grimalkin on her nightly rounds, some of his fascination with the beast tempered by the trouble it brought. He'd damned near swallowed his heart when he realized she was transforming right beneath his very naked, very vulnerable body. And though he found the sight of her transformation compelling, the pain that had radiated from her as she twisted to a new shape had left him feeling nauseous and utterly powerless to help her. Worst of all, he'd lost to that blasted beast the precious chance to hold her after taking her virginity.

He wondered how he and Catherine could ever share anything meaningful together if she transformed during every crisis. Or how he could know the joys of fatherhood married to a woman whom he didn't trust to carry his child. Or how he could ever have a night's peace knowing she put her very life at stake each time she transformed. What if a zealous villager shot her? What if they captured her and watched her transform at dawn? She'd be dead before the sun cleared the horizon. For the first time, he understood how enormous a problem the grimalkin posed.

Her thirst satiated, the grimalkin padded over to several bushes and disappeared behind them. He circled around the gooseberry thicket and inched closer to the bushes, but froze when a brilliant light erupted through the leaves, momentarily blinding him and startling the teal to flight.

The light faded and all became quiet once again. Hesitantly he pushed the bushes aside and peered into a cave.

Catherine lay within on a mat of dried leaves. She looked like a wood nymph, her hair fanning about her in a tangled honey-flame mass, mud covering her hands and feet. Her limbs—long, white, and slender against the gray backdrop of the cave—sprawled carelessly, revealing her femininity to the casual eye. His gut twisted at the thought of some Scotsman stumbling upon her in this pose.

She looked so defenseless, her one hand half-curled into a fist, her forehead smooth, her pink lips smiling, that a great protectiveness welled within him. He didn't know when she'd awaken, but he was damned if he'd sit here and watch her until then. A cool breeze cut through the cave, and even though she slept, goose bumps erupted across her skin. He wondered how she'd survived all these years without falling prey to pneumonia.

Well, she need not worry any longer, he thought.

After ducking his head to avoid the stone ceiling, he entered the cave and espied the brown sack she'd hidden in a crevice. Spiders clung to the fabric as he yanked it from the niche and opened it. Within, he found a sapphire cloak, which he immediately wrapped around her. Then, fatigue and lack of sleep throbbing in his head, he carried her limp form back to Rivendell.

Mrs. Finlay held the door open as he approached the castle, concern evident in her gaze. "Ye two've been gone all nicht. What happened tae the wee lassie?"

He mustered a smile. "Too much ale and celebration, I'm afraid. We passed the night under the stars." Catherine's servants, he reflected, took some getting used to. Even so, he found himself warming to their familiar attitudes and the concern they expressed for his well-being. He felt like he'd moved in with a gaggle of benevolent aunts and uncles. And according to Catherine, many of them were exactly that—relatives.

"Well, then, away wi' ye tae the laird's apartments," the old dame said, her hands on her hips. "I'll have water brought, and a nice breakfast, too."

After giving the cook a weary nod, he made his way to the laird's apartments and found Rupert asleep in a chair by the fire. The valet, Nicholas knew, felt left out amid all the bonhomie in the castle and hadn't yet accepted the MacClelland servants' attitudes, either. Nicholas felt sure he never would.

"Rupert," Nicholas said, "wake up, man."

Rupert flew out of the chair, adjusted his braces, smoothed his hair, and buttoned his waistcoat. "Your Grace. I apologize for falling asleep. Can I assist you in any way?"

"No, that will be all. You may go."

Betraying not the slightest bit of surprise at the sight of Catherine's naked feet peeping from under her cloak, the valet beat a hasty retreat.

Nicholas laid Catherine on the ancient mahogany bed and threw a red velvet counterpane over her. Fatigue closed in on him and he collapsed next to her. He pulled her sleeping form close and buried his nose in her hair.

He must have dozed off, for a soft knock awoke him. His vision blurry, he sat up. "What is it?"

"I've brought ye water for a bath, Yer Grace."

He invited the maidservant in. Eyes averted from the bed, she poured a bucket of hot water into a ceramic basin. Steam billowed upward, creating a hazy spot on the washstand looking glass. "Yer breakfast will be up in a minute, Yer Grace," she muttered, and hurried away.

The first rays of dawn slanted through the arched windows, flooding Catherine's face with a reddish light. She stretched restlessly beneath the counterpane, the sun rousing her from her enchanted slumber. Soon she would awaken and they'd have to discuss the grimalkin. He dreaded what he might discover this day, feared the beast might prove too much an obstacle in their marriage.

After throwing a thick towel over his shoulder, he grasped the basin and brought it to the bed. Slowly, he drew the counterpane back, savoring each inch of her silken white flesh. Spots of dirt marred her perfection, and after dipping the towel in the hot water, he sponged the dirt away. His hand trembled as he washed the spots of blood dotting the inside of her thighs—proof of her virginity.

Her eyelids fluttered, arresting his hand in midmotion. Without further warning, she sat straight up, her green eyes wide, her hair a mane that tumbled to her waist. She looked around the room, looked at him, looked at the dirty towel in his hand, and clutched the counterpane to her breasts.

"Where . . . what . . . how . . ."

He dropped the towel and grasped her hand between his own. "You are in the laird's apartments—"

"I can see that," she snapped, her stomach rumbling audibly. "What am I doing here?" She pulled her hand from his grasp and pressed her fingers to her forehead. "I can't remember."

Eyes narrowed, he sat back in his chair, amazed that she would pretend ignorance of last night's events. Did she think him that much of a fool? Good Christ, she'd damned near transformed beneath him. "You remember all too well, Catherine. And don't try to persuade me I'd drank too much ale. This thing between us, we must discuss it."

She gave him a frightened look and clutched the blanket to her body, convincing him her memory loss was not just a convenient ploy, but related in some way to the grimalkin. After taking a few deep breaths, she leaned against the mahogany headboard and closed her eyes, her eyelashes golden against cheeks tinged with pink. "I went to the Temperance Inn with Mary," she whispered, "and I talked with MacDuff." A moment passed, and she swallowed. "I danced the Gillie Callum."

"Yes, you did," he agreed, one eyebrow raised.

Her eyes flew open. "You were there."

"Of course. When Mary told me you planned to attend the celebration alone, I immediately left for the inn. I arrived before you, in fact."

"Why didn't I see you?"

"I didn't want you to see me, at first."

"Oh." She chewed this over, her face reddening as more memories evidently rose to the surface. A bittersweet smile came to her lips, and she slanted him a thoughtful glance that had him wishing he could read her mind.

The clock atop the bureau ticked away the seconds.

"You smacked my arse before my entire clan. Brute!" she suddenly exclaimed, her eyes narrowed, her hands curling into fists.

"Aye," he said, lapsing into a feigned brogue. "It takes a

strong man tae bring a woman like ye tae heel." He loved teasing her, loved the way her green eyes sparkled when he provoked her. "But you need to remember the rest," he hurriedly added. "Do you remember the way you teased me?"

Lips compressed, she glared at him. "Do not mock my clan, or the Scots tongue."

"I have the utmost respect for Scotland. But let me prod your memory. Yes, I smacked your luscious backside. You deserved much more. Do you not recall the way you unfastened your hair, and thrust your breasts up against that flimsy peasant blouse you wore, before all your clan—"

She cut him off. "Aye. I remember."

"And I carried you out of the inn and laid you in the heather, and we—"

"Made love." Fixing him with an accusing stare, she frowned at him.

He remembered the moment that her slender hand had grasped him and pushed him into her velvety softness, and gave her a decidedly appreciative smile.

Eyes closed halfway, she looked down at the counterpane. "I have never lost control so completely before, forsaking my pride, losing all inhibitions."

Inside, he chuckled. "You are a beautiful, seductive woman who enjoys the pleasures of the flesh. 'Tis not a crime, Catherine. Indeed, the fact that you acknowledge your sensual nature pleases me greatly."

Silence grew between them, a lazy tension in which he recalled her dance at the inn, her breasts pressed against tissue-thin cotton, her shapely calves flashing beneath her plaid skirt, her arms held out to him, beckoning, tempting.

It was a silence he was loath to break, but break it he did, for he had more pressing matters to discuss. "Do you remember what happened next?"

"Aye. I saw the moonlight against the trees, heard a grouse clucking in the bushes, could smell a roe deer . . ." Her face paled.

"And then?"

Her gaze darted from the basin filled with muddy water to his face. "You know," she breathed.

"Yes." Watching her carefully, he felt his chest tighten with suspense. The sunlight streaming through the window suddenly seemed too bright, a cold, merciless glare that banished the secrets in the room and laid each corner naked for the world to see.

Abruptly, she pushed back from him on her hands and feet in crablike fashion and stared at him with wild eyes. "You know. You saw!" Her glance flew to the door. "Are they coming for me, even now?"

He, too, stared at the door, expecting a demon to burst through. He'd seen so many strange things lately he didn't dare discount her alarm. Seconds passed, however, and nothing untoward happened. "Who in hell are you talking about?"

She refocused on him, her breath whistling through her lips. "Let me go, Nicholas. I'll leave through the servants' entrance. You'll never see me again. Allow me five minutes."

As on the night he'd first witnessed her transformation, he felt danger all around them. He couldn't tell if he was reacting to her dread or if a buried instinct of his had detected looming disaster. He grabbed her, trapping her within the velvet counterpane, and crushed her shaking form against his chest. "Shhh. No one is coming for you. No one would dare take you from me. You are safe. Safe."

She struggled against him. "You don't understand. I will not die in the flames."

"Flames? What flames?" *Was the bloody castle on fire?*

She didn't bother to elaborate. Rather, her efforts to break loose became more panicked, and she succeeded in freeing one arm. Wildly she struck out at him, delivering a glancing blow to his ear that set his head to ringing.

He held his aching ear with one hand and tried to restrain her with the other. "Damn it, Catherine, you're safe."

Lips curled in a snarl, she pounded his chest, all the while trying to drive her knee into his groin.

"Good Christ, you are a wildcat." He began to think she'd succumbed to hysteria, and had drawn him in as well. Indeed, she'd turned him into a gibbering nitwit. He grabbed her about the waist, threw her on the bed, and pinned her down with his own body.

She continued to struggle ineffectually for several seconds until she evidently realized he had no intention of letting her go. "You hate me so much, you would see me burn at the stake?"

"Burn at the stake?" He felt like an idiot, constantly echoing her statements, but other than reflecting some vague threat to her person, they made no sense. "Who are you frightened of?"

"Has no one told you of Isobel Gowdie? She burned because she recited this spell:

'I sall goe intill ane catt
With sorrow, and sych, and a blak shott;
And I sall goe in the Divellis nam,
Ay will I com hom againe.' "

Everything suddenly became clear. His face lowered inches above hers, he stared into green eyes filled with resignation and sighed. "If you will remain still for one minute and listen to me, I would much appreciate it."

She turned her head away.

"Will you listen to me?"

Seconds passed.

"Aye," she finally said. Her tone held defeat.

Moving slowly, he released her and sat up. "I am aware the grimalkin is more than a legend. I also know you possess a strange magic that transforms you into the grimalkin." His voice wavered as he spoke, for the words sounded outlandish, the very idea impossible. Part of him wished she would deny it. "I have known this since that first night I watched you transform."

A small noise escaped her, perhaps a hastily smothered outburst. Still, she refused to look at him.

"I do not understand the origin of this bizarre magic, or what you have done to possess it, or why you would wish to. But I do know this. Since we met in London, you have consumed my thoughts, my dreams." He ran one finger along the side of her perfectly formed jaw. "I cannot let you go. And I do not think you a witch."

On sudden impulse, he leaned down and kissed the pert tip of her nose. "Look at me, Catherine."

"Nay."

"Have you not more courage than that? Where is my bold wench?"

As he'd expected, she turned to face him, her green eyes luminous.

He cleared his throat, some of his cool authority slipping. "Your secret is safe with me. I . . . have come to care about you."

A teardrop leaked from the corner of her eye and ran down her cheek. Her lips trembled. "Do you not think me evil?"

He felt her pain, saw her eyes fill with more tears, and quietly cursed the grimalkin. "I think you a brazen, pigheaded Scotswoman who cares for her clan with a selfless generosity and has more courage than most men." Lips twisting, he remembered how he'd called her an angel of mercy. Abruptly he understood how cruel a name it was, how she must have cringed every time someone in London had mentioned it.

She began to cry in earnest and, wrapping her hand around his neck, pulled him to her. He held her tightly, feeling ineffectual, wishing he could do something to ease her distress. Hopelessness filled him as he realized the grimalkin would likely stand between them forever, preventing them from sharing a normal life. Much to his amazement, he found himself embracing the thought of a life with Catherine. He imagined long nights with her, snuggled beneath a velvet counterpane, the shouts of their children awakening them on a sunny morning.

By God, it wasn't fair.

Her sobs lessened to hiccups, and her teardrops spotted the velvet counterpane, reminding him of another teardrop, one born in fire and anger. He wiped her face with his thumb and whispered, "I have something to show you."

Evidently intrigued by the mystery in his voice, she

rubbed her nose and rearranged the counterpane against her breasts.

He stood and rifled through the bureau near the bed. When he found the velvet bag, he returned to her side.

"I found this in the fireplace in Efington House the day you left," he said, dropping the bag into her lap. She drew open the silk cord and peered inside the velvet.

"I threw a crystal goblet into the fire, along with my wedding ring," he continued. "The fire melted the crystal and wedding ring, forming a teardrop pendant."

He'd brought the teardrop to a jeweler and had it mounted with a gold chain. She pulled the crystal out by the chain and dangled it in a ray of sunlight. The crystal projected a rainbow of colors against the wall, and the ring within seemed to glow in its crystal prison.

" 'Tis a thing of great beauty," she said, her voice haunted. She rubbed the crystal with her thumb. "It seems so familiar. As if I've seen it before."

"Why don't you try it on."

Hesitantly she settled the chain over her head. As soon as the teardrop touched her skin, a brilliant golden light exploded from it and she cried out.

Good Christ, he thought, the pendant had scorched her! Blood pounding through his veins, he reached forward to rip it from her neck.

"Nay." She blocked the motion, a smile growing on her lips. "It tickles."

The golden light began to ebb away. "It *what?*"

"My insides are tingling with a strange radiance. Fingers of warmth are reaching down into my stomach. 'Tis a most peculiar feeling."

"Take it off." Nothing—outside of her transformation to the grimalkin—had frightened him like this before.

Her lips curved in a thoughtful frown. "I feel as if I must wear it. It seems right."

"Catherine—"

"You have asked for my trust this day," she said, her tone firm. "Now I ask you to trust me. Allow me to wear it."

A deep unease shivered through him. "Magic, enchantment . . . they cling to you like a wet cloak. I don't understand."

"I'm afraid I know little more than you. I will tell you what I do know, if you wish, but first I would like to dress." The crystal seemed to have revived her, he thought. She had regained some of the stubbornness she normally displayed.

He didn't want to let her out of his sight. "I'll have Mary retrieve a dress for you."

"I would rather sneak back to my bedchamber, with no one the wiser."

"In what, a sheet?"

"You have a point. But I do not want the servants to find me naked in the laird's apartments. They will draw the most embarrassing conclusions."

Unsure he'd heard her right, he eyed her askance. "Embarrassing? It is embarrassing that a husband should make love to his wife? I intend to make love to you again and again, and I don't care if all of Scotland knows about it. Indeed, if it weren't for the grimalkin, I would have erased the pain of our first coupling with several well-placed kisses."

She pinkened prettily. "I would have liked that."

Heat rushed to his loins at her admission. To think of the additional pleasures he could have shown her last night, of the excitement he'd have known watching her experience them for the first time. Never had he dreamed of a more potent fantasy, a fantasy he could have fulfilled, if it weren't for that beast. "That grimalkin is a damned nuisance," he muttered.

Her eyes widened and she stared at him. Suddenly she began to giggle. He thought about what he'd said, and he wondered at how absurdly commonplace the remark had sounded. But then the humor of it hit him, and he began to chuckle, too.

"You have no idea," she choked out between giggles. She began to shake with laughter, and he joined in, until she grabbed him around the neck and pulled him close and laughter cleansed his soul.

"Thank you, Nicholas," she whispered.

Twelve

Mary arrived at the laird's apartments some minutes later with a breakfast tray. Catherine broke away from Nicholas, her giggles finally trailing away. She felt as if she were floating upon a cloud.

This was a splendid day, indeed.

She examined Nicholas from beneath her lashes. Despite his mussed black hair, the shadow that covered his cheeks, and the dirt that marked his ivory breeches, she decided he'd never looked more appealing. The lines of tension in his face that made him seem older had disappeared. She wondered how she could ever have thought him anything but handsome.

She stretched, replete, bruised in places she'd never felt before. How nice it had felt to awaken from the change, clean and warm, in her husband's bed. But she wondered how he'd known to find her at Bodhan's Pond. Intuition told her his knowledge of the grimalkin went far deeper than he'd admitted.

Even so, she rejoiced in his knowledge. No longer did she have to shoulder the secret of the grimalkin alone. Nicholas understood her and would keep her safe. Best of all, he'd admitted to caring for her. Perhaps one day he would return her love, and the grimalkin would be gone from their lives forever.

Mary gave them an odd look, raising an eyebrow as her gaze touched on the dirty washbasin and Catherine's bare shoulders. An unrepentant grin suddenly appeared on the girl's face, and her eyes gleamed above plump cheeks. Without waiting for Nicholas to invite her in, she bustled into the room and set the plate directly before Catherine.

Nicholas frowned, presumably at Mary's lack of decorum.

"I've brought ye a feast, for I ken ye've worked up a great hunger. Baps, mutton ham, kedgeree, eggs, more than enough for two." She poured Catherine a cup of chocolate.

"And I see you've worked up a great curiosity." Stomach rumbling, Catherine gave her a contented smile. "I shall need a dress from my rooms. The green velvet, I think."

"Right away, Cat." Mary slanted Nicholas an admiring glance before sauntering through the door.

Mentally vowing to find her cousin a husband at the first opportunity, Catherine lifted the lids off the breakfast plates. She didn't want to begin the discussion of the grimalkin until she'd eaten, or Nicholas might not hear her over her stomach's grumbling.

"Shall we eat?" She did not wait for his reply but sliced the mutton ham into large chunks and ate them, discarding ladylike delicacy in favor of hunger.

He drew a chair over to the bed and sat down, a plate balanced on his knees. "Slow down. You're going to choke."

"I apologize for the display," she informed him through a mouthful of baps, "but I cannot."

His eyebrows drew together for a moment before he nodded. "Ah, I begin to understand."

They ate in silence for the remainder of the meal. When Catherine had sufficiently filled her stomach, she set the tray aside and snuggled back against the pillows. She tightened the counterpane against her breasts, for she didn't want to distract him during this most serious discussion.

He, too, put his plate down and regarded her with an intent gaze. "It is time for you to tell me of the grimalkin. Leave nothing out."

Her mind spun with the magnitude of the task. "I don't know where to begin."

"Let me start, then." He rubbed his chin for a moment before looking up at her. "I've followed you several times in grimalkin form—"

"Pardon?" Catherine could hardly credit her ears. Questions about the grimalkin's habits sprang to mind, but most of all, she wondered how Nicholas had escaped harm. "And the beast didn't turn you into dinner?"

"Well, no. Actually, we've become good friends. I will tell you about it another time." His mouth quirked in a smile, as if he couldn't credit his ears, either. "But I have wondered if you retain any human intellect while assuming the grimalkin's shape."

"In a way." She paused, undecided on how much to tell him, how much he would comprehend without actually experiencing the change. "There is a dark place within me. I think of it as the grimalkin's lair when the beast lies dormant. When the change comes to me, the grimalkin surges upward from the dark place and takes over my body, forcing the human part of me into its lair."

She frowned, memories crowding in her head. "The first time I changed, I had just turned thirteen and thought I had gone mad. There is nothing quite so terrifying as the feeling that something is taking over your mind, stealing your body, and shoving you into a padded cell. A great deal of pain—agony, really—accompanies the change and my father hadn't prepared me for it, hoping to spare me worry. That first time, I almost welcomed the dark place when the grimalkin took over."

He tightened his lips at her explanation. "Does anyone other than your father know about the grimalkin?"

"All of the Scots in Kildonan know of the curse, but only my father knows I harbor the grimalkin deep within."

His mouth relaxed. "I admit I am relieved that no one else knows your secret."

"My father and I have worked very hard to keep that secret. You do not think me a witch, but I suspect many would disagree with you." She hesitated, realizing anew

Nicholas could reveal her secret and condemn her to death, or worse.

She hoped she hadn't made a mistake in trusting him. "Anyway, to answer your original question, I do not remember who I am while the grimalkin holds sway. I recall little other than sense impressions when I awaken from the change: the taste of blood in my mouth, the smell of my prey, the sounds of wild things in the brush."

Even though he looked grim, his eyes held a strange fascination. "These peculiarities of yours—your fear of the dark and of horses. They are related in some way to the grimalkin?"

She nodded. "The moon holds a particular allure for the grimalkin and without fail rouses it from the dark place. Horses seem to know I hold a beast—a predator, in fact—within my soul and react unpredictably in my presence. These are rules I have learned to accept."

"And yet, you used the grimalkin to your advantage when you saved that child in the village. How much control do you have over it?"

"Very little, I'm afraid. Once the change progresses beyond a certain point, I am lost."

Leaning forward, his hands on his knees, he switched to a new topic. "I have heard the grimalkin has existed for centuries. Are you the grimalkin in all these tales? Are you, in fact, hundreds of years old?"

A half-smile curved her lips. "No, I am only nine and twenty."

"Your mother . . . was she a grimalkin, too?"

"No. She gave birth to me, but I inherited the grimalkin's seed from my father. Likewise, my Aunt Morag inherited the grimalkin's seed from my grandfather. She died at the age of thirty-five, in a convent." She stopped, uncertain about how much family history to reveal to him.

"How did she die?"

"She died giving birth to a son. All women who carry the grimalkin and dare to become pregnant die in childbirth, as do their children."

He grew pale. "Do you mean—"

"Aye. If you place a babe in my belly, you sentence me to death."

"I'll be damned careful," he said, and silence grew between them as he digested that bit of information. After a moment he spoke again. "Are you the only grimalkin? Or are there more?"

"An interesting question. I find your perspective on the grimalkin quite refreshing."

"Do not patronize me, Catherine." He sounded annoyed with her.

"I'm not patronizing you." Nevertheless, she gave him a contrite smile. "I believe I am currently the only one. The grimalkin is a result of an ancient curse, placed by a Druidic witch, and is peculiar to my family."

"I assume if the grimalkin is a result of a curse, you do not willfully transform into the beast. Correct?"

"Quite so."

"I would like to hear more about this curse."

Dear Lord, she thought, *there is so much to tell!* She took a deep breath. "You have heard of the feud between the Clan MacClelland and Clan McQuade? Well, the curse is a result of that feud. In the fifteenth century, Niall MacClelland committed a terrible evil against Aonghas McQuade."

He nodded slowly, as if he'd expected this very explanation. Digging deep into her memory, she told him of the ambush at Bodhan's Pond, of Niall's brutal slaying of the McQuade chief and his subsequent blood-drinking. She discussed the Clan McQuade's long courtship with Druidic sorcery, and how their high priestess, Sileas, placed a curse on Niall MacClelland in retaliation. Nicholas remained quiet throughout the telling and seemed to stare right through her, as if transported back in time by her story.

"So you see," she concluded, "throughout the centuries MacClelland women have suffered the effects of the curse, passing from father to daughter the rituals and prohibitions that govern their lives. I, unfortunately, also bear the curse."

He rubbed his chin, his eyebrows drawn together. " 'Tis a fanciful tale, one I'd never believe if I hadn't seen the grimalkin myself," he admitted. "Putting disbelief aside, the story makes odd sense. You said you'd memorized the actual curse. Would you repeat it for me?"

"Of course. It is just as much a puzzle as it is a curse." Her voice low, she recited in English, the hairs on the back of her neck standing up at the power of the words:

"Killed my laird and killed my kin,
Only hatred beneath your skin,
Mixed and drank my family's blood,
Poured the remainder into mud,
A curse I place upon your daughters,
As the grimalkin they shall practice slaughter,
Until love grows between MacClelland and McQuade,
And the feud between us to rest is laid."

A thick silence permeated the room when she'd finished. At length, Nicholas softly repeated the last two lines:

"Until love grows between MacClelland and McQuade,
And the feud between us to rest is laid."

"What do you think it means?" He stared at the floor, evidently deep in thought. "I feel like I'm missing something. It's on the edge of my thoughts, but I can't quite isolate it."

Lower lip caught between her teeth, she hugged the counterpane to her breasts. Soon he would make the connection and realize Iain MacClelland hadn't forced him to marry her to save Rivendell from bankruptcy. Still, was the real reason they married—the hope that they'd fall in love and break the curse—any worse?

His fingers beat a light tattoo against the arm of his chair. "Until love grows between MacClelland and McQuade . . ."

She could stand the suspense no longer. "You, Nicholas, are a McQuade."

Eyes widening, he clutched the chair.

"I am a MacClelland," she ruthlessly continued.

A long moment passed.

"And you," he finished, his eyes abruptly narrowed, his

voice hard, "have used me more thoroughly than the most venal adventuress."

Hand held out, she implored him with her eyes. "Nicholas . . ."

He jumped up from the chair, shushing her with a chopping motion, and began to pace. "Yes, the MacClellands are in financial straits, but that is not the real reason your father insisted we marry."

"Aye—"

"You and your father plotted this scheme to make me fall in love with you, in hope of breaking the curse," he grated. "You forced me into a distasteful marriage to save your own damned skin."

"Nicholas, you must understand. My father waited until the day he died to tell me of his plan to blackmail you. I could not change his mind; I did not have the time. Regardless, I traveled to London at my first opportunity to release you from the blackmail. May I remind you that *you* dragged *me* to the altar."

He raised one accusing eyebrow. "I *dragged* you to the altar because I did not know your father was dead and could speak out against me no longer!"

"Fragprie swore he had told you Papa was dead—"

"So you claim. Still, I have only your word on this." A mirthless chuckle shook his chest. "By God, you and your family have roped me in quite neatly. All the lies, the deceit . . . they make my head spin. You never wanted money. You wanted my soul."

"Can you not at least attempt to understand my father's motive?" Catherine waved an arm, encompassing the whole room. "Surely there is no nobler purpose on earth than to right an ancient wrong through the power of love. Love cures all afflictions, heals all ills. He simply wanted to end the suffering between our clans and save his only child."

The counterpane slipped, revealing her breasts, and his gaze immediately dropped lower. A sneer curved his lips. "You seek to buy my love with your body? All of this sweetness, this innocence, has been a calculated attempt to make me fall in love with you, hasn't it? By God, you ought to try your hand at Drury Lane."

She glared at him. "Think about the curse, Nicholas. Love must grow between MacClelland and McQuade. It is not a one-way street. I must fall in love with you, too." Indeed, the words "I love you" hovered on her lips, but she bit them back, for she didn't think he'd believe her.

"You love no one but yourself," he informed her, eyes glittering.

"And you are a narrow-minded ass." How quickly their discussion had degenerated into the same old miserable name-calling, she thought. How could he ever fall in love with her now that he was pressured to do so?

"You've put far too much faith in love," he said. "What is love? How can you measure it? How can something as intangible as love end a centuries-old curse? You can't hold it in your hand. Indeed, what if you and I were to fall out of love? Would the grimalkin come back?" He stared at her, his mouth twisted into a frown. "I think, dear lady, that you have misread the witch's rhyme. The terms for release from this curse must be more tangible than love. In other words, you have gambled upon love and lost."

He clicked his heels together in a soldierly fashion and strode from the room, bumping into Mary on the way, who clutched a length of green velvet on her arm.

"I've brought ye the dress, Cat . . ." The maidservant trailed off when she caught sight of the thunderous look in Nicholas's eyes. She stared at his retreating back, and then clucked at Catherine, much like an old hen. "Can't ye two stop fighting? Good Lord, I've ne'er seen the like. First yer in his bed, then he's stomping oot o' the room."

Catherine punched the mattress. What a hellish coil. Well, she'd be damned if she'd let him walk out on her like that. Imperiously she gestured for the green gown. "Quickly, Mary, help me dress. The duke shall not get off so easily."

Nicholas stomped through the central hall and into the study he'd refurbished. Every time he blinked an eye, he found another facet to the MacClellands' perfidy. The family was beyond belief. Even worse, he'd discovered that he held the blood of a Druidic witch in his own veins. A chill gripped him, along with an odd pang of guilt. Tempered by some bizarre sense of ancestral responsibility, his fury with Catherine became diluted with confusion. He recalled the ring of sincerity in her voice as she'd told him she'd tried to prevent their marriage.

Had he been too harsh with her?

He settled himself into a velvet sofa drawn up to the fireplace and contemplated the shelves of books beside him. Each shelf stretched upward twelve feet, ending in an elaborately carved cornice that displayed local game birds. Busts of noteworthy Scotsmen—the same ones that had once graced his apartments—stood atop the shelves, their faces gray against the tapestries that now hid the stone wall. A patterned carpet spread across the floor, adding to the feeling of comfort.

He'd long been of the opinion that no room contributed more to a man's peace of mind than the study, and had consequently devoted a great deal of his own time supervising the reconstruction of this room. Now, as the quiet order and masculinity of the study soothed his frayed nerves, he guessed that as long as he and Catherine remained married, he'd be spending a great deal of time here.

He glanced out one of the arched windows, and in the distance he noticed a caravan of four post chaises. The armorial bearings on the carriages' panels, coupled with their drivers' blue and gold livery, revealed to him their owner's identity. The caravan wound through the village of Kildonan and toward Rivendell.

He sat forward, straining to see through the trees that lined the thoroughfare. "What the devil?"

The wealth of trunks strapped to the roof and back of the chaises indicated the traveler had come for an extended stay. Nicholas rubbed his forehead. It was bad enough having to watch one perfidious female, but two? "Damnation."

Sighing, he stood and made his way to the central hall. The carriages pulled into the circular drive and a bevy of sumptuously dressed servants jumped to the ground. The Scottish footmen squinted at the Londoners, their gazes traveling from their highly polished shoes to the tops of their powdered wigs. Nicholas heard the whispers of "popinjay" and "Sassunach."

Pasting a smile on his face, Nicholas placed his arms behind his back and braced himself, feeling much like a soldier preparing for an onslaught. The door to the first carriage opened, and an elderly lady dressed in a gray wool cloak glanced out.

Nicholas moved forward to greet her. "Mother. What a surprise." He took her hand and assisted her down. The coquelicot military feather poking from her bonnet swatted him in the eyes. It only increased his sense that Rivendell had just been invaded.

The Dowager Duchess of Efington laughed, her brown eyes alight with mischief. "La, Nicholas, have you not more enthusiasm than that?"

He placed a perfunctory kiss on her cheek. "I did not expect you. How long do you plan to stay?" Mentally he reviewed Rivendell's habitable rooms, deciding none would quite live up to the standards his mother had grown accustomed to. Her stay would be short, indeed.

"Until grouse hunting season concludes, perhaps longer." While adjusting her bonnet, she peeked up at him through her lashes. "I know I have placed myself beyond the pale by not informing you in advance of my visit. I hope you are not vexed with me."

He suppressed a sigh. "Of course not." Three months, he thought, of keeping both his mother and his wife in hand. He wasn't sure his heart could withstand the strain.

The door to the second carriage opened and a man wrapped in a burgundy greatcoat stepped down. He, in turn, assisted a small woman. They had their backs turned to him, but he knew they were quality by the cut of their clothes.

He nodded to the other travelers. "Friends of yours?"

Annabella lifted her eyebrows. "They're *your* friends, Nicholas."

At that moment, the couple turned around, and Nicholas found himself staring into the smiling countenances of Harry Rappaport and Clarissa Stonehaven. His jaw nearly dropped to the ground.

Harry rushed forward, not a blond hair on his head out of place. Likewise, his forest-green trousers and tan boots showed not the slightest wrinkle or mark. If it weren't for the bags beneath his blue eyes, Nicholas would have guessed the man had traveled the equivalent of a jaunt through the countryside.

"Nicholas, old friend. How good to see you. I hope you don't mind putting us up for a few weeks. You see, we're on our bridal tour."

Nicholas felt his gut clench in shock, not only at Harry's friendly attitude but at his announcement. The last time he'd seen Harry, in the study at Efington House, his cousin had nearly called him out. "Bridal tour?"

Harry put a possessive arm around Clarissa's shoulders. "We've been married for two months now. 'Twas our dream to spend our bridal tour on the continent, but as my coffers aren't quite as full as yours, we decided to share this precious time with you." His voice held a strange note of superiority, as if he'd bested Nicholas at a game and won the prize: Clarissa.

Eyes wide, Nicholas stared at Clarissa. She looked incredibly fragile, her face pale white, her neck as slender as a swan's, her brown ringlets peeping from beneath a straw bonnet. He realized that she no longer roused a protective instinct in him; indeed, he found her sweetness cloying.

Smartly dressed in a lilac sarcenet gown and matching wool pelisse, Clarissa gave him a cool smile. "Your Grace, we've missed you."

Nicholas sketched her a slight bow. "Congratulations to the both of you. 'Tis a fine match." The shock had begun to wear off, and in spite of Catherine's scheming, he silently thanked her for preventing his marriage to Clarissa.

The dowager duchess took Nicholas by the arm. "Where is the duchess?"

"She'll be down in a moment." Nicholas led his three guests into the central hall. "I'm certain you're all fatigued from the trip. I'll have rooms prepared immediately." He nodded to Fragprie, who had assessed the situation in an instant and had already directed a footman to remove the guests' trunks.

A flurry of servants came forward and removed the Londoners' outer garments. Harry looked around, his gaze touching on the worn plank flooring, the gray stone columns supporting the arched roof, the crossed claymores hanging above the front entrance.

Through Harry's eyes, Nicholas knew the hall looked rustic at best. The scattered Aubusson carpets and green velvet drapes Nicholas had purchased did little to detract from its barbarous splendor.

"Tell me, coz, how are you faring?" A touch of derision had entered Harry's voice. "Have you gotten used to these Highlanders yet?"

Nicholas raised an eyebrow. "I find I am like them in many ways." He felt more than saw his mother's intrigued stare.

"You have remained away from London far too long," Harry pronounced. Suddenly a teasing smile crossed his face. "Met any ghosts? Castles like this are reputedly full of them." Evidently hoping to twit Nicholas, Harry hugged Clarissa closer and dropped a kiss on her cheek. She pulled back from her husband ever so slightly.

"No ghosts. At least none that I cannot put to rest," Nicholas informed him. "But the castle is full of drafts, as you will learn."

"How about the grimalkin? Run into that legendary creature yet?"

Nicholas twitched. A slow, dull flush crept into face. "Grimalkin? Why, 'tis only a child's tale, meant to improve manners—"

A clatter interrupted him and he broke off. Catherine pelted down the large stone staircase at the end of the hall, two buttons of her dress open in the back, her bare feet flashing beneath the lace hem of her gown. "Nicholas, you won't dismiss me that easily. There is more you must hear."

All of the hall's occupants turned to watch her approach.

She skidded to a halt when she saw the assemblage, her honey-flame hair tumbling from her hastily arranged chignon. Her mouth fell open. "Who . . ." Evidently answering her own question, she trailed off and smoothed down the front of her skirt.

Nicholas strode forward and took her by the arm. "You remember my mother, of course."

Catherine closed her mouth and dropped into a curtsy. "Your Grace. How good to see you again."

"You may call me Annabella," the dowager said, patting Catherine's arm. "I apologize for this unannounced visit, but I often do things spontaneously, and I knew I would arrive at Rivendell before a letter would. I hope you are not too much put out with me."

Her eyes wide, Catherine murmured a suitable reply.

Nicholas knew all too well how she felt. He took pity on her and turned her toward Harry and Clarissa, sparing her from further conversation with his mother.

Harry pursed his lips and examined Catherine from head to toe. She stiffened beneath his perusal and buried her clenched fists in her skirt.

Nicholas gave her a supportive squeeze. "This is my cousin, the Honorable Harry Rappaport, and his new wife, Clarissa."

Mouth tightening, Catherine stared back at them with what could only be termed as belligerence. "I remember both of you well."

"How delightful." Harry gave her a brief nod.

Throughout it all, Clarissa had remained silent, her brown eyes considering.

Anticipating Catherine's imminent explosion, Nicholas cleared his throat. "Fragprie will show you to your rooms. We usually sup at five; I'll have a maidservant rouse you an hour before."

The three guests nodded their thanks and followed Fragprie up the stairs.

Her voice low, Catherine muttered, "What is going on here, Nicholas?"

"Come with me." He strode into the study and seated himself by the fire. Catherine followed him and perched on the edge of a chair.

She raised an eyebrow. "How long do they plan to stay?"

"I don't know." He rubbed his forehead. "Too long, no doubt."

"How will I entertain your relatives for weeks, perhaps even months? What am I supposed to do?" She stood up and began to pace. "My father never taught me these things, and I have no mother, and we didn't entertain. I don't even know the proper way to seat them at the table. Good Lord, what a nightmare."

"I'll help you."

She appeared to have not heard him. "My servants do not dress in uniform and will no doubt seem ill-mannered; Mrs. Finlay prepares only the simplest dishes; and I'm afraid moths have gotten into the table linen. Why did they come? Why?"

"I said I'll help you. We'll organize musical evenings, card games, a hunt, perhaps even an impromptu country dance."

"Why would you bother to help me? I thought you hated me." Her voice dropped to a whisper and she hesitated, her hands clasped together. "What if they discover my secret?"

Nicholas sensed she'd finally voiced the true source of her discomfort. He, too, found it a disturbing notion. "They will not. I'll keep you safe. Now please sit."

Frowning, she arranged herself on a chair.

Clouds had pushed across the horizon, darkening the study and throwing shadows across her face. Even so, the fire cast her with a burnished glow that reminded him of princesses and wood fairies. The red highlights that shot back from her forehead seemed alive in the dim light, quivering and sparkling as they melted into the molten honey of her hair. He looked into her emerald eyes and thought of humid jungles that only the most daring men explored.

With an effort, he forced his thoughts into more acceptable channels. "Earlier, you said there is more I must hear."

"Yes." Her shoulders slumped and she examined the carpet beneath her feet, her eyes heavy-lidded, her frown softer, tinged with sadness. She scuffed one of her feet on the carpet, hesitating, as though carefully choosing the words she wished to speak.

"I've wronged you," she finally said. "For different reasons, we've all wronged you. My father wanted to free his only child from a terrible curse, and I wanted a normal life. Fragprie wanted money. In our own ways, we've all proven terribly selfish."

Her gaze touched on him, then skittered away.

He cleared his throat. His own irritation lost its fiery edge.

"An apology would do little at this point." Pleating her skirt with her fingers, she took a deep breath. "But there is something I can do. Offer you your freedom. Again. I will sign any contract you wish, guaranteeing my silence on your parentage. Fragprie will prove more difficult, but if we think on it long enough, we might find a way to outmaneuver him."

"Fragprie will do as I say," he said, his tone harsh. He had recently confirmed some interesting gossip about the Scotsman. It seemed Fragprie had dallied with a McQuade clanswoman and gotten her with child. Since he'd revealed his knowledge to Fragprie, and wondered aloud how Robert McQuade would react to such news, the Scotsman had come to heel.

Justice had rarely tasted so sweet.

"Yes, you do seem to have gotten him under hand." She looked at the flames crackling in the fireplace. Moisture glinted in her eyes. When she spoke, her voice shook. "Do you have a solicitor you would prefer to engage?"

Moments passed, seconds in which he gazed at her and realized anew he wouldn't let her go. Not yet. There was so much about her that intrigued him, so much he admired despite her scheming, that he wondered if he would ever grow tired of their marriage.

He stood and walked behind her. His touch light, he brushed her cheek before placing his hands on her shoulders. Together, they stared into the fire.

"I do not wish to divorce you," he said.

"In that case, I shall use the MacClelland solicitor, a man named Donaldson—"

"I won't divorce you, Catherine."

She twisted around to view him with wide eyes. "You won't?"

He couldn't prevent a smile from twitching his lips. "No."

"But why?"

"Because I'm a fool," he said softly. "Because I won't leave you to face this curse alone." And in his heart, another truth echoed silently, one he refused to believe.

Catherine jumped up from her chair and faced him, the moisture in her eyes disappearing. "A fool? And what if I am the one who wishes a divorce?"

His smile became a grin. "I fear, lass, you are stuck with me."

Thirteen

Catherine gripped the leather-bound volume in her hand and tried to concentrate on the printed page. The tableaux on the far side of the drawing room had drawn her attention away from Milton's *Paradise Lost* most thoroughly. Nicholas, Harry, and Clarissa sat at a table covered in green baize. The men clutched a handful of cards, while Clarissa clutched Nicholas's thigh beneath the table. Surreptitiously Nicholas reached down, removed Clarissa's hand, and gave her a severe frown.

Clarissa smiled back at him, looking like an angel in her ivory muslin gown, and placed a few cards down on the table. Then she threw Catherine a sly glance from beneath her lashes.

With a start Catherine realized she'd gripped the book so hard her knuckles had turned white. She restrained the urge to yank the jade's brown ringlets, settling for a sip of Madeira instead. How would she ever win Nicholas's trust, his very heart, while Clarissa remained at Rivendell? The Englishwoman had an amazing repertoire of smiles and soulful looks, each of which she'd tried on Nicholas.

Harry, for his part, found another facet of the Scots to mock each night. If she heard his nasally voice imitating a brogue one more time, she might be inclined to strangle him. They both seemed to forget they were guests in *her* house, supping on *her* food, and sleeping in *her* beds.

She'd had no idea how difficult entertaining a houseful of guests could be. Nicholas had helped her at first, instructing her in the fine art of entertaining and preparing the Rivendell staff for the weeks ahead. She and Nicholas had discussed menus with Mrs. Finlay, ordered supplies and new table linen from Helmsdale, considered the seating arrangements, opened and aired the bedrooms, and planned an endless series of amusements.

But once he'd taught her the duties of a duchess, he'd left the task to her. She guessed he was trying not to undermine her authority at Rivendell, and while she appreciated the gesture, she'd had to work twice as hard this past month to keep the castle running smoothly.

A hearty laugh pulled her from her thoughts. Harry tipped a snifter of brandy to his lips, swallowed, and gave Nicholas a confidential wink.

"These Scots, Nicky, how do you stand them? The women run around barefoot and the men can hardly form a sentence. Why, the other night at the Temperance Inn, a man whose knuckles damned near dragged the floor cornered me and said"—Harry lapsed into an oafish brogue—" *'I would recommend to you, to keep at arm's length from me,'* simply because I expressed disapproval over the whisky served. 'Twas watered down, I'm quite sure."

Clarissa clucked in sympathy.

Nicholas, on the other hand, shook his head. "The Scots take great pride in their whisky. They even call it the *water of life.* You took a great risk complaining about the stock at the Temperance Inn."

A snort erupted from Harry. "Damned barbarians."

Catherine, who'd heard the entire exchange, imagined the feel of Harry's neck between her hands. Clarissa and Harry had proved themselves pests of the worst type. Indeed, the dowager duchess—who'd already retired for the night—was the only agreeable presence in the castle. She and the dowager had spent hours in the study examining tapestries and discussing the history behind them. They'd even taken a trip to the parapet to examine faded paintings of MacClelland ancestors.

But the dowager's questions about Robert McQuade had interested Catherine the most. It seemed Nicholas's mother sported an avid curiosity for her old lover. Catherine thought McQuade might return the dowager's sentiment, given their recent confrontation on the moors.

The flutter of cards being shuffled and dealt drew her attention back to the room. Would they never cease their interminable playing?

"Will you ride with us tomorrow, Clarissa?" Harry asked in a suave voice. "Nicholas and I are more than willing to delay our morning jaunt in favor of your presence."

Nicholas bestowed a smile on Clarissa, lighting his handsome face and making Catherine's heart ache with jealousy. If only he would look at her that way.

"You know I never arise before noon, but perhaps for you, dear, I shall make this one exception," Clarissa said, twirling one of the pink ribbons dangling from her sleeve. Although she spoke to Harry, her gaze remained on Nicholas.

"Tomorrow night we celebrate the festival of Samhain," Nicholas reminded her. "The hour could grow quite advanced before we return. Are you certain you wish to ride with us?"

Clarissa nodded, her curls bobbing. "I should love to."

"Jolly good," Harry said.

The three then picked up their hands of cards and began yet another round of loo. Again, Clarissa looked toward Catherine. This time the brunette permitted a tiny smile to curve her lips.

The words to Milton's *Paradise Lost* swam before Catherine's vision. She wished Clarissa would retire permanently. It was just like the hussy to rearrange her entire schedule to promote her flirtation with Nicholas.

She shifted on her chair, her thoughts turning to the daily pattern they'd all settled into. Nicholas and Harry usually arose at dawn to ride; the dowager and Clarissa emerged from their bedchambers long after noon. Catherine used her free time to pursue her duties, consulting with the staff and planning entertainments, as Nicholas had taught her to do. After luncheon, they often wandered the castle or gathered in the library to read or play games such as backgammon. Dinner was served at five o'clock and, with all its intricacies, usually lasted until eight or nine o'clock. They finished off the night in the drawing room, playing whist or cribbage and enjoying tea, coffee, and cakes.

Catherine found all of the activity exhausting. She longed for the days when she'd had Rivendell—and Nicholas—all to herself. Absently she reached for a dessert cake and took a bite. It was sweet and gooey, incredibly so, and she mused that if the dowager had tried one, her cork plumpers would have stuck to the insides of her cheeks permanently. Mrs. Finlay had attempted another French creation and, in Catherine's opinion, had failed miserably.

Of all the servants, the cook seemed most determined to put the dowager, Harry, and Clarissa at ease. Aware that no upper-class house in Edinburgh was without a French chef, she'd tried her hand at English and French cuisine. Privately grateful that the adventurous French cooking had remained confined to the circles surrounding the court at Holyrood, Catherine had choked down cows' palates, ox eyes, and coxcombs for one week before insisting on more staid Scottish dishes such as jugged hare and Partan Bree.

With a moue of distaste, she put the cake on a side table and took a healthy sip of Madeira.

Suddenly Clarissa folded her cards and swept the pile of ivory gambling chips aside. "Instead of wagering with these chips, I would like to stake words instead. The losers in a hand of loo must state something about their pasts that no one else knows. Agreed?"

Catherine swallowed her Madeira in one huge gulp and began to choke. Hastily she covered her mouth with a square of linen. Clarissa, both eyebrows raised, stared at her while she coughed, her expression of censure melting to a wide smile when both men nodded affirmatively.

Frowning, Nicholas dealt the cards out more slowly than he'd been wont to do. They played suits in quick succession, and in short order Nicholas won the round of loo.

Using the cards as an impromptu fan, Clarissa sighed.

"How ungentlemanly of you, Your Grace. Now I shall have to tell you some intimacy about my past."

Giving up the subterfuge of reading, Catherine fixed her attention wholly on the card players.

Nicholas shifted on his chair. "Clarissa, if you do not want to—"

"No, no, rules are rules." She gave the men a coquettish grin. "I shall tell you of my first kiss. A peer of the realm, who shall remain unnamed, drew me into the gardens at Lady Bessborough's fete two Seasons ago. He pulled the petals from a rose and let them drift across my bosom"—she slanted a look at Nicholas, who had grown decidedly red—"and then kissed me so long and hard I thought I'd surely faint."

Catherine closed her book with a loud snap. Envy coated the inside of her mouth like ashes. She stood and gave the three a cold stare.

"I believe I'll retire for the night. I suddenly find myself ill." Without waiting for their responses, she strode through the door a footman opened for her.

Back stiff, she marched up the stairs and gained the relative peace of her bedchamber. Mary sat in a chair by the fire, a pair of scissors in her hand. Adorned in a fine new uniform of wool plaid, she jumped up when Catherine entered.

Catherine raised one eyebrow in annoyance. Clarissa had already pushed her far beyond her limit. She hoped Mary wasn't about to hatch another scheme to improve her stylishness. "What are you planning to do this time, Mary? Cut the bodices of my gowns even lower? Perhaps you wish to have a go at my bonnets?"

"Oh, no, Cat, nothing so drastic as that." Mary began to fuss around Catherine, unhooking her velvet gown and untying her pantaloons and camisole.

The maidservant's hazel eyes held a zeal that made Catherine distinctly uneasy. "I've talked ye intae wearing kid slippers rather than those old brogues. Will ye not agree tae a haircut now? Short hair is all the style, and I'm wanting ye tae put that Sassunach wretch in the shade." She picked up the scissors and snapped them open and shut for emphasis.

Catherine stepped away from the pile of velvet and linen around her ankles and shrugged into the robe Mary held open for her. "Mary, I take pride in the way the staff has rallied on my behalf. You've all surpassed yourselves in your attempt to impress our London houseguests."

Indeed, their manners had become unobtrusive and their attention to detail impressive. Even though she missed the staff's easy familiarity, that sense of family that had so long been a part of her life, she thought the change a good one. Her servants had more pride in themselves and more confidence in carrying out their duties.

"But I remind you that not all attempts have been equally successful," Catherine continued. "Do you remember what happened when MacDuff tried to put that fancy saddle on Beelzebub? The stallion dealt MacDuff a kick that left him limping for days. Likewise, I shall kick you if you suggest one more time that I compete with Clarissa."

Mary cast her a knowing glance as she bent to retrieve the crumpled gown. "She's got yer dander up, poor lass. That Englishwoman is as cold as a kelpie, and about as black-hearted, too. She's havin' her revenge on ye, mark my words. Ye stole her man, and now she wants tae make ye pay."

"For once, you and I are in agreement. You may go, Mary."

Mary finished hanging the gown in the armoire, retrieved her scissors, and left the room on quiet feet.

After donning a wool nightgown, Catherine braided her hair and climbed into bed. Judging by Clarissa's sly looks and spiteful grins, revenge more than infatuation had inspired her flirtation with Nicholas. Still, Catherine could think of nothing but the smile Nicholas had given Clarissa earlier, one that had given him a boyish aspect he so rarely revealed. Her heart beating dully in her chest, she turned down the lamp and wished desperately for the oblivion that sleep brought.

Morning came swiftly. Catherine awoke in her lonely bed, an alien tension crackling through her veins. She realized with a sinking feeling that her day was about to become more complicated. The grimalkin was ready to emerge from its lair, and on the night of the Samhain *ceilidh,* of all nights.

She would have to find Nicholas this morning—alone—and warn him of the impending disaster. For once, the grimalkin had given her something positive: a reason to seek her husband out and rebuild the intimacy between them. In any other situation, she'd have preferred to have Nicholas by her side out of his own free will, not due to trickery or obligation. But the danger the grimalkin posed made those prideful sentiments unimportant.

Jumping out of bed, she rang for Mary and pulled on her camisole and pantaloons, thinking of the other Nicholas she'd glimpsed on those few occasions, the one who had teased her and kissed her and shown her a future most women only dream about. How she missed him.

She selected an emerald gown that would not only ward off autumn's chill but show her hair to advantage. Despite her earlier protests, she was more than a bit interested in competing with Clarissa. Minutes later, when Mary arrived with a tray of steaming chocolate, Catherine had clasped her crystal pendant around her neck. After Mary completed the final touches to her toilette, she hurried down the castle steps, hoping she'd find Nicholas alone in the dining room, enjoying a morning repast.

"Catherine, would you join me for a moment?"

She spun toward the voice, so surprised by his appearance that she wondered if she'd conjured him somehow.

He stood in the doorway to the laird's apartments, his tousled black head nearly touching the lintel, one large hand gripping the doorknob. White buckskin breeches and a blue hunting jacket clung to his body like a loving hand, and black boots encased his legs to the knee.

Gray eyes somber, lips turned to a frown, he looked most perturbed, and although his mien made her uneasy, she couldn't help thrilling to the private nature of his invitation. What better place to rekindle the warmth between them than his own bedroom?

"Of course. I, too, wanted to speak with you."

He didn't move completely out of her way, forcing her to

brush against him as she entered the laird's apartments. He felt hard, immovable, like a rough-hewn boulder. How she longed to melt that tough exterior and make him groan with passion.

The scent of Macedonian soap in her nose, she stopped by a damask chair. The furnishings in the sitting room made her feel distinctly small and feminine. Ponderous mahogany settees, chairs, and tables lay scattered about, looking so solid and timeworn that they'd overwhelm all but the largest men. Dark colors—burgundy drapes, a pine-green carpet, navy upholstery—implied only the most serious and stately matters were discussed within. Claymores hung on the stone walls, a decanter of brandy sat on the mantelshelf, and a length of MacClelland tartan covered a seaman's chest, all suggesting she'd entered a male stronghold.

At length she turned to face him. "What can I do for you?" Oh, she had a few answers of her own for that question.

He had positioned himself by the fireplace and leaned against the mantelshelf, one boot propped up against the hearth. Surrounded by medieval luxury, he reminded her of a primitive sovereign, his civilized veneer scarcely hiding the savage within.

"I am aware that several weeks have passed since the grimalkin has made an appearance," he said, pinning her with an intense stare. "I sense a restlessness in you, a strange anxiety that I've come to associate with the wildness. As you know, the Samhain festival will be held in the village square, beneath a full moon. I think it best you plead a headache tonight and remain behind."

An image of Nicholas and Clarissa dancing a Gaelic reel to wild Scots music suddenly formed in Catherine's mind. All her well-intentioned plans to stay in her room this evening crumbled. Yes, appearing at the festival might be dangerous. But leaving Nicholas in Clarissa's clutches was doubly so.

Her chin rose an inch. "My guests plan to attend the *ceilidh*. So shall I. Indeed, your mother has expressed a great deal of excitement over the event and has personally asked me to escort her. She would interpret my withdrawal as a snub."

He knocked his hand against his forehead. "Of course. My mother's amusement is worth any price, including the discovery of your secret. How silly of me."

"Have I not controlled the grimalkin so far? Harry's insistence that the drapes remain open at dinner and Clarissa's love of steak tartare do not make the task easy."

More than once Catherine had felt the grimalkin stir as she'd sat at the dinner table with her mouth full of bloody meat and moonlight shining upon her. Nevertheless, conscious of Nicholas's watchful gaze, she'd managed to subdue the beast and swallow with a brilliant smile.

"Indeed, I find your cousin and his wife most bothersome," she added, hoping to hear him echo her opinion.

Suddenly, like a hawk swooping down on a mouse, he grasped her shoulders. His lips hovered mere inches from hers. She throbbed where his fingertips touched her skin, reveled in the feel of his breath against her face. Almost without thought, she closed her eyes.

"How can I protect you if you willfully put yourself in danger?" Passion charged his voice. "Good Christ, Catherine, conditions are ripe for you to become the grimalkin. How could you even consider risking the festival?"

She moistened her lower lip with her tongue, unsure of how to seduce him but needing to become intimate with him again—in all ways.

"Look at me." Did his voice shake ever so slightly?

Lips parted, she opened her eyes and stared into an unexpectedly desperate gaze.

"You will remain behind tonight," he ordered.

"And leave you in Clarissa's tender hands? I think not."

"Clarissa means nothing to me." He squeezed her shoulders. "Your safety, however, means everything. Please, Catherine. Stay home."

"I suppose Sarah Spencer also meant nothing to you." The image of Clarissa's hand on Nicholas's thigh kept replaying in her head. She wasn't certain the grimalkin would appear, but she knew Clarissa would continue her seduction of Nicholas, if only to destroy their happiness, as Catherine had destroyed hers. "I have attended every year. I do not plan to stop now."

He gripped her harder, almost as if he wanted to shake her. "Madam, one day you will push me too far."

An eyebrow raised, she touched one of the lapels on his jacket. "Ah, and what would you do to me, Nicholas, if I pushed you too far? Give me a good, rousing tumble?" Heat flooded her insides at her own temerity, but she decided her lapse of propriety was worth the suddenly shocked, yet lustful look in his eyes.

"Good God." He spun away from her, muttering oaths. At the doorway, he stopped and fixed her with a gimlet stare. "You would try the patience of Job himself. Attend the *ceilidh* if you must, but know you risk far more than a rousing tumble."

Nicholas squeezed into the barouche, settling against the leather squabs next to his mother. Harry and Clarissa sat opposite, Harry smothering a yawn and Clarissa eyeing Nicholas with an intensity that had begun to annoy him. There wasn't a jot of passion in her eyes, just a wide-eyed stare chilling for its lack of emotion. Clarissa, he'd realized, saved all her seduction attempts for times when Catherine might see them.

If he hadn't known a lingering sense of guilt over raising Clarissa's expectations of marriage and then marrying Catherine, he would have demanded the brunette leave Rivendell. As it was, she'd arrived on Harry's arm, with his cousin's ring on her finger. He couldn't throw her out without alienating Harry. He hoped the words he'd exchanged with Clarissa late last night, bitter words that had ended in her tears, would suffice.

The barouche rolled down the drive and began the one-mile journey to Kildonan. Even from Rivendell he could see the bonfires in the village square, their yellow glow punching a hole through the darkness. A strange excitement snaked through him, as if the fires had stirred some ancient, tribal memory of war councils and witchcraft. He felt ready for anything, including the grimalkin, and would protect his wife's secret with whatever means necessary.

Dressed in plaid silk, the dowager duchess sat forward and peered out the carriage window. "I haven't attended a *ceilidh* since my last trip to Edinburgh, almost forty years ago. How exciting. Nicholas, are you sure the duchess will be waiting to greet us?"

"Quite certain. She has appointed herself your guide and will introduce you to all her clan." Exasperation crept into his voice as he remembered how obstinately Catherine had refused to stay home, how she'd teased him with talk of lovemaking. The wench knew all too well how to steal beneath his guard and prod him.

In fact, he'd wanted nothing more than to lift that emerald skirt and plunder the softness between her thighs, but pride had held him back. How could he make love to her, when the only reason she offered herself to him was to gain his love and break the curse? In the end, she'd break his heart.

"And will you serve as our guide, Nicholas?" Clarissa gave him a pretty smile, one that didn't quite reach her eyes. "You have become quite the Scotsman."

Her tone was all innocence, and yet Nicholas felt the jibe beneath the softness. She looked quite attractive, he admitted, her tiny form wrapped in an opaline silk gown trimmed with black ribbon and a matching spencer. Still, he'd begun to think those fine trimmings hid a core as spoiled as meat left too long in the sun.

"Harry knows nothing of the Scots," she continued. "I fear we shall feel quite lost amid all these Highlanders."

Harry smothered a yawn. His blond hair, perfectly coiffed as usual, glinted beneath the light of the oil lamp in the carriage. "I'm sure Nicky will escort us through these crowds of heathens. We shan't remain long, you know. I am not a scholar; I have no desire to study primitive cultures."

The dowager fixed him with a stern gaze. "If you find the Highlanders so abhorrent, why did you come to Scotland, on your bridal tour, of all things? You are being most rude, nephew."

"And you, dear Aunt Annabella, are the mother I never had." He grabbed her hand and planted a kiss on it. "When you scold me, you remind me of my childhood. I remember the generosity of spirit you showed me in those most difficult times."

Softening, the dowager cleared her throat. "Scamp."

Nicholas found himself wishing, not for the first time, that his three guests would end their visit and return to London.

After a few more endless minutes, their barouche pulled near the village square. Throngs of Highlanders—many wearing kilts and plaids, despite the fashion to the contrary—clustered around the square, preventing the vehicle from drawing close. Nicholas and his guests stepped down and paused on the outskirts of the crowd.

Sparks from the bonfires leaped toward the heavens and settled back to earth as dull embers. Torches crackled along the perimeter of the square, throwing light onto the excited faces of the dancers who spun past. Those who weren't dancing relaxed against improvised tables, benches, and stools. Men plied each other with rotund jugs of whisky and ale, apron-clad women tended the glistening haunch of venison that twirled over a fire, and cauldrons of apple butter spewed steaming, spicy clouds into the air.

Clarissa placed herself between the two men and grasped their arms. Casting an anxious gaze over the gathering, Nicholas allowed her arm to remain linked with his as he searched for Catherine. At length, he spotted her among the dancers in the center of the square, spinning and leaping to the ferocious pace of the Gaelic reel. She grinned up at her partner, a brawny youth who, based on his return smile, was enjoying himself far too much. They held on to each other tightly, as if their linked arms kept them from flying apart.

Nicholas felt a sour stirring in the pit of his stomach and quashed the desire to shake Clarissa off, grab his wife, and carry her home. He didn't want to thrust himself into the role of jealous husband again before all the villagers. He was an adult, damn it, not some hotheaded youth.

Rather, he scanned the heavens. The sun had already set, and although Rivendell basked in a waning gray light, the skies above the village were utterly dark. A large moon, painted a lurid orange, hung on the horizon. Even he found the sight mesmerizing, and he didn't see how Catherine could avoid the wildness this eve.

A footman trailed behind them, carrying a hamper of appetizers. Remembering his duties as host, Nicholas spoke to the footman, who then poured two glasses of ratafia and handed them to the dowager and Clarissa. He procured a jug of ale from a passing Highlander for himself and Harry.

Harry looked at him askance. "Do you really expect me to drink from a jug, Nicky? Good God, you have changed since you left London. I'm beginning to worry about you." He took the snifter of brandy that the footman proffered.

Enjoying the look of disgust on his cousin's face, Nicholas swilled ale from the jug. For one brief moment he wished he'd worn the ratty kilt and plaid MacDuff had given him. "And you, Harry, are far too stodgy. Shall we mingle?"

Harry pulled out a square of linen and held it to his nose. "If we must. Clarissa, darling, are you sure you don't want to return to Rivendell?"

Stepping gingerly on straw-covered mud, she glanced at Harry significantly. "I think the festival quaint. I should like to observe more. Perhaps we will even see the grimalkin."

Nicholas studied her briefly. What did the pair mean by these constant references to the grimalkin? Uneasiness coiled around his spine.

Could they have discovered Catherine's secret?

No. 'Twas coincidence, naught more.

"All right then," he said. "Follow me." Frowning, he led his mother and Clarissa into the crowd, nodding to those Highlanders he knew, occasionally using the few words of Gaelic he'd learned.

Clarissa tottered through the mud, her shoes leaving her feet with a sucking sound, her face bearing a pained smile. A pampered English rose among Scottish thorns, she garnered more than one lecherous grin from the kilted men.

Mincing across the village square, Harry held the scrap of linen to his nose as if he trod upon horse dung. "Do these people not know their station in life? How dare they raise their eyes to my wife."

"Scots are less formal than Englishmen. Indeed, many of these people are Catherine's distant relatives."

Harry stopped short. "Surely you jest."

A smile played about Nicholas's mouth. "Come along, Harry."

He steered his mother toward the half-cow turning slowly over open coals. He took quiet pride in the way she paid no attention to the muck and various odors. Walking by his side, she brushed shoulders with the meanest Highlanders and even stopped to pick up a child who had strayed from her mother. The hem of her gown splashed with mud, her gray curls turned golden by the firelight, she searched the crowd with a peculiar enthusiasm.

"Looking for someone in particular, Mother?"

"Yes," she answered, her tone distracted. "I'm looking for the duchess."

"Well, I believe she has found you." Indeed, Catherine had come up behind them silently, and now stepped forward to take his mother's arm.

"Good evening, Your Grace," Catherine said. A flush colored her cheeks and her eyes glimmered like a spray of stars on a dark night. An aura of magic hung about her, giving her the aspect of a sorceress mingling among mortals.

"You have a certain fey look tonight," he murmured, "as if you've dined with an elf."

Her eyes gained a look of reproach. "*Fey,* in the Scots tongue, means 'fated to die soon.' Surely you don't mean to suggest my death is imminent?"

Jolted by her comment, he quickly objected. "Not at all."

He allowed his gaze to rove over her form. Showing no concern about the importance of her position as duchess, she'd donned the same plaid skirt, peasant blouse, and arisard he'd seen her wear in the Temperance Inn. Her hair unfettered, her smile promising mischief, she looked so lovely he ached to hold her. He would never tire of her, not in a hundred years.

I've punished her enough, he thought. She knew how she'd displeased him by forcing him into marriage and understood how much he resented the situation. And although he'd become familiar with her traitorous side, these past few weeks he'd discovered another part of Catherine, a warm, gracious, confident side he admired very much. He had, indeed, married a duchess.

The time had come to let his anger go.

"Harry. Clarissa." Catherine gave them both a brief nod. "I'm so glad you could join us tonight."

The dowager linked arms with Catherine. "And I, my

dear, am thrilled beyond words that you've offered to escort me this evening. I'm hoping I might recognize a face or two from my earlier visit to Scotland. Surely a few of the nobility are here tonight."

Her eyebrows drawn together, Catherine peered at her mother-in-law. "Robert McQuade is the only Scottish peer living within a convenient distance. I did see him an hour ago, but as we aren't on speaking terms, I passed him by."

"Oh. I shall avoid him, too, then."

Nicholas noticed with something close to shock that a dull red blush had crept into his mother's cheeks. A suspicion began to form in his mind, one that left him dumbfounded. Nevertheless, he shook himself from the dark thoughts crowding in his head and grasped Catherine's arm when she began to draw his mother away. He had to try one last time to get his wife to safety.

"I should like you to leave with me. Now."

She lowered her eyes. "We have discussed this already. When I am ready to return to Rivendell, I will find you." Gently she pried his fingers from her arm and pulled the dowager into the crowd, leaving him with Harry and Clarissa.

Some of his excitement over the festival left with his wife. Sighing, he turned to his guests and did his best to entertain them, although, truth to tell, he found both Harry and Clarissa discouraging. They didn't want to dance, or drink, or talk to the villagers, or eat venison and half-cow cooked over the open flames. Harry insisted on his imprudent mockery of the Scots and Clarissa continued to wonder if she'd see the grimalkin.

After about an hour had passed, he decided they'd all had enough. Feigning weariness, he escorted Harry and Clarissa back to the waiting carriage and then went in search of his wife and mother. Another set of dances had started, the bagpipers and fiddlers coaxing lively music from their instruments. He waded through the dancers, their claps and laughter deafening in his ears, the smell of burnt wood and venison swirling around him. Someone pushed a pipe in his face, which he declined; another accidentally prodded him with a claymore—sheathed, thank God.

After searching the entire village square, he moved out past the tables and benches to the edges of the hills beyond. The subdued worry that had gnawed on him gave way to outright concern. Where the hell were they?

Angry voices drifted across the forested slopes. Immediately he strode toward the fracas, snatches of the argument reaching his ears:

"You could have asked for a divorce . . ." A man's voice, full of condemnation.

". . . would have killed you, you great Scottish clod." A woman this time, sounding suspiciously like his own mother.

"I see age has sharpened your tongue." The man again, his tone betraying unwilling admiration.

He bumped into his mother and Catherine moments later. Both appeared quite agitated, although Catherine looked furious and his mother heartsick.

"What has happened?" He scanned the group of fir trees behind them, looking for the man he'd heard.

The dowager brushed past him. "We're going home, Nicholas."

He looked to Catherine for enlightenment.

"Your mother had words with Robert McQuade," Catherine informed him in a hushed tone. "Never have I seen McQuade act that way before. Furious and desperate and possessive all at once. I couldn't decide if he was going to kiss her or turn his back on her."

Her words confirmed his earlier suspicion, and a feeling of betrayal washed through him, surprising him with its intensity. His mother still loved the Scottish earl. "McQuade is a blackguard."

"And a liar," Catherine added.

"I won't allow him to use her twice." Nicholas clenched his fists at the thought of what they'd all endured because of McQuade's selfishness.

The dowager marched back over to them and prodded Nicholas with a finger. "What are you two whispering about? I'm quite ready to leave."

Frowning, he started to talk, thought the better of it, and took Catherine's arm instead. The dowager didn't wait for them but started back toward the carriage. They followed in her wake, Nicholas reminded—as Harry had said earlier—of his days in a shortcoat.

Once they'd returned to Rivendell, Catherine and the dowager immediately sought their own rooms. Likewise, Nicholas extricated himself from Harry and Clarissa and stalked to his apartments. The worst of the trouble was over, he reflected. When—and if—Catherine changed to the grimalkin, she'd do so in the privacy of her own bedchamber. And he would be waiting for the grimalkin when she jumped from the window. The more he followed the wildcat, he reasoned, the more he'd understand the passions that ruled his wife.

Inside, Rupert helped him strip off his evening coat, waistcoat, stock, and boots.

"Lay out the kilt and plaid, Rupert, and then you may go."

The valet hesitated a few moments before answering, the closest he came to censure. "Of course, Your Grace." He indicated a decanter of brandy and a folded notecard. "Mr. Rappaport brought this up, Your Grace."

Nicholas glanced at the note, written in Harry's looping scrawl:

I hope this reminds you of your proper surroundings.
—Harry

He picked the decanter up, swirled its contents, lifted the stopper. A deep ruby red, the brandy had the texture and smell of a fine year indeed.

After the valet left, Nicholas collapsed on a settee and poured himself a brandy. Clad only in breeches and linen shirt, the brandy slipping down his throat with a refined ease, he'd hoped to get a few hours' sleep before his jaunt with the grimalkin. But thoughts of Catherine kept intruding, memories of her soft mouth opening beneath his, encouraging his exploration.

Women had no idea, he mused, what it was like to be male. The drive for coupling—particularly with a woman as beautiful and desirable as his own wife—could consume a man more thoroughly than even the most basic needs for survival. For some reason, Catherine seemed to exacerbate this drive more than any woman he'd ever known before, until he could think of nothing else.

At odds with his thoughts, a strange lassitude stole over him. The clock suddenly seemed to tick much too loudly, and the shadows created by the firelight leaped and danced on the walls like crazed gnomes. Deciding he'd had too much to drink, he put the snifter aside.

I'm tired, he thought. *Just a little nap, that's all I need.*

He stumbled over to the bed, the floor tilting and ceiling rotating with a speed that left him nauseous. Groaning, he flopped onto the mattress and stared at the pattern on the carpeting. When the woven circles began to writhe like snakes, he closed his eyes.

By God, that brandy was potent.

Suddenly he felt nimble fingers at his neck, undoing the studs on his shirt.

"Catherine," he mumbled. His alarm fled, replaced by the passion he'd tried so hard to deny.

A soft giggle floated through the air. Soon his shirt was gone and the cool night air caressed his skin. He felt soft pressure against the scar on his ribs, as if someone were kissing it.

"Ah, Cat, you've come to me." He reached down and tangled his fingers in silky hair. The room began to spin faster. He wondered if he was dreaming. "Lean closer, let me kiss you, smell you, touch you as I did on our first night." He hoped she could understand him, for the words sounded garbled to his ears.

A small female form pressed up against him. He felt slight breasts through gauze and imagined her long, honey-flame hair pooling about them. "God, how I've missed you. 'Tis a crime that we've only made love once, an error I plan to remedy. Now."

He reached out and grasped a mound of satiny female flesh. She was nearly naked, ready for him as never before, and the thought inflamed him further. "Drank too much," he muttered. "Can't get my breeches off. Will you help?"

"Of course, Your Grace," a breathy voice whispered. A

hand worked the buttons on his breeches, freeing his erection and then grasping him with delightful pressure.

A loud knock disturbed them. Without warning, the door opened and a female voice said, "You sent for me, Nicholas?"

Seconds later, a choked gasp filled the chamber. Nicholas opened one bleary eye, mentally preparing a harsh set-down for the maidservant that had dared disturb him, and found himself staring into his wife's horrified countenance. Fully dressed, she paused in the doorway, an oil lamp clutched in her hand.

If Catherine was fully dressed, then who . . .

He stared down at the hand that grasped him and slowly, disbelievingly, gazed at the face inches from his own.

Brown eyes sparkled with triumph.

The door to his apartments slammed hard enough to shake the frame.

"Damn you, Clarissa!" He was drunker than he'd ever been before, God help him, but still able to push her off. She landed on the carpet with a thud.

Too late, he thought, *too late.* Catherine hadn't seen his rebuff, she'd already left. Some sober corner of his mind noticed a fresh, penetrating odor in the room, as if lightning had discharged nearby.

Clarissa stood up and grabbed her robe. She shrugged. "How unfortunate that your wife interrupted us just as we were beginning to enjoy ourselves."

"Get out," he growled.

No sooner had she left than he began to retch, more from anguish than from brandy.

Fourteen

Sometime during the night, Nicholas awoke with a headache so severe he thought he'd cracked his skull. When he tried to sit up, his stomach churned as if he'd swallowed arsenic. He opened one eye and stared into the darkness, noting vague outlines of furniture and bed hangings. The smell of vomit lay heavily in the air. He couldn't remember what had happened, or even if he'd returned to Rivendell. A thick fog had settled into his brain, leaving him utterly disoriented.

He fumbled around until he found the edge of the bed, groaning as the foul concoction in his stomach slushed around. Unable to help himself, he began to retch over the side of the bed.

You're a swine, Efington, he told himself.

When he'd finished, he wiped his mouth against the corner of a sheet. He felt slightly improved, but wondered how he'd fallen into such a disreputable state. His head reeling, he swung his body off the bed and bumped into a stone wall. Velvet drapes brushed against his face. He grabbed them with shaking hands and pulled them open, flooding the room with moonlight.

Busts of dead Scotsmen stared down at him; claymores

mounted on the wall glittered with silver fire. Behind him, linen sheets and a burgundy counterpane lay in a tangle on his mahogany bed.

Apparently he had managed to return to the laird's apartments. He found an oil lamp and lit it, rang for Rupert, and then collapsed into a chair, trying to recall the night's events. By the time Rupert arrived, the pounding in his head had lessened to a dull ache and his memory had returned.

"Good evening, Your Grace." The valet frowned as he took in his master's condition, then knelt before the fireplace and began to coax flames from the half-charred logs.

Something akin to horror began to spread through Nicholas as Rupert prodded the embers. His inner eye had focused on the scene played out a few hours before. He remembered the hopeful sound in Catherine's voice when she'd first come into his apartments and asked for him. He tried to imagine what she'd seen: him, half-naked in bed with Clarissa, her hand around his shaft. His stomach churned even faster.

Good God, what a damnable situation.

He was beginning to think a demon hid behind Clarissa's sweet little face. He hadn't realized how far she'd go to wreck his marriage. He also couldn't believe he'd allowed it to happen. What was wrong with him? Was he some callow youth, to get so drunk he couldn't even tell whom he'd fondled? Harry would likely call him out if he learned of the matter, and he had every right to.

His thoughts darted to Catherine. Jaw clenched, he wondered why she hadn't run both him and Clarissa through with a claymore when she'd found them together. In her situation, he'd have been hard-pressed to display the same kind of control. She hated him now, of that he felt certain. He would have to work very hard to prove to her he'd left his wild youth behind and was ready to devote his heart to one woman.

He wanted her back in his arms.

The grimalkin mattered not.

Suddenly he realized the implications of what he'd been thinking. If he wasn't sitting in a chair, he thought he'd have collapsed.

" 'Tis almost two hours before dawn, Your Grace," Rupert announced, his gaze direct. "If I may be so bold, I suggest you need your sleep more than you need a morning ride with Mr. Rappaport."

Nicholas didn't answer. He stood, wavered for a moment, and then walked to the window, his thoughts on the woman he'd married.

Had he, despite his best intentions, fallen in love with the wench?

Surely love could explain his desire to prove himself to her, despite all of the difficulties between them. Marriage to Catherine was much like being whipped at the high cross every morning; only love could force a man to endure such a thing. But when had it happened? He recalled the night she'd danced for him at the Temperance Inn, their picnic on the moors, their marriage . . . their first dance at Lady Wisborough's ball.

He'd been snared, he realized, from the first day he'd met her.

He began to laugh.

"Your Grace?" The valet took a step forward, his hand held out. "Please allow me to escort you back to bed."

Nicholas shushed him with a hand gesture, his gaze on the frost-covered moors outside his window. Like the veriest idiot, he'd fallen in love with a woman who regularly transformed to a wildcat. Indeed, he remembered the fresh, penetrating odor that had permeated the room just as Catherine had fled, and he knew that the grimalkin had awakened. He turned from the window and gestured toward the pile of tartan draped across a rack.

"Get the kilt and plaid." He had little time left, none of which he planned to waste arguing with his valet. He loved her. He had to show her what she meant to him. But he had to find her first.

Rupert inclined his head. "Of course."

Every movement painful, Nicholas shrugged into the kilt and plaid Rupert held for him. Out of the corner of his eye, he noticed the decanter of brandy on the mantelshelf.

"Rupert . . ."

"Yes, Your Grace?"

"Are you certain this decanter of brandy came from Mr. Rappaport?"

"Yes. Mr. Rappaport delivered the decanter himself."

Nicholas picked the bottle up and swirled its contents. "The brandy had a most odd effect on me last night. Made me . . . downright ill."

Rupert paused, a length of tartan held in his hands. "When Mr. Rappaport delivered the brandy, he held a snifter in his free hand. It appeared to contain the same liquid as the one in the decanter. Shall I pour myself a glass and try some?"

"No, of course not." He replaced the decanter on the mantelshelf. Why would Harry have brought him poisoned brandy? To facilitate his wife's affair? The notion was ridiculous.

An eyebrow raised, Rupert finished arranging the plaid over Nicholas's shoulder and helped him draw leathern brogues onto his feet. After tucking a skean into his belt, Nicholas left the valet, crept through the castle, and out the servants' entrance. The moon had disappeared from the sky, and a rime of frost covered the earth, shrouding the moors in shadows and ice.

Cold predawn air froze the insides of his nose and forced the pain in his head to retreat even further. He walked the path toward the village, taking a shortcut he'd discovered to Bodhan's Pond. Two hours till dawn; hardly adequate to fetch Catherine, return her sleeping form to Rivendell, bathe her if necessary, and tuck her into her own bed.

And once she awoke, he'd face an entire new set of difficulties, the worst of which would be convincing her that Clarissa had taken advantage of him—a man who'd once kept two mistresses in the same house. Nevertheless, he would not rest until he'd repaired the damage Clarissa had wrought, now that he'd realized how deeply Catherine had engaged his feelings. And Clarissa, he vowed, would soon be on the road to London.

Wanting to pass through Kildonan unnoticed, he approached the village from the side and kept to the outskirts of the drovers' cottages. He'd nearly made it to the forest beyond when a gruff Scots voice stopped him.

"Halt. Identify yerself."

He spun around on one heel, his hand flying to the skean at his waist. None other than Robert McQuade stood about ten feet from him. He carried a torch in one hand, revealing boots smudged with dirt or ash. The sleeves of his red coat appeared dirty as well. With his free hand, he waved a piece of dark fabric at Nicholas with the same threatening manner one might brandish a pistol. The Scotsman's frowning countenance, coupled with that red coat, reminded Nicholas of a cardinal from the Spanish Inquisition.

"Don't try a knife on me, laddie." McQuade stuffed the fabric into his coat and drew a claymore from the sheath at his side. "Identify yerself." He prodded Nicholas's chest, the claymore's tip cutting through cotton.

Nicholas stiffened, his hand freezing above the skean. How ironic, he thought, that the man who'd brought him into this crazy world now wanted to usher him out. "Why are you skulking through Kildonan, interrogating passersby? Have you lost your mind, McQuade?"

His cultured English accent cut across the distance between them and, based on the way the torch suddenly wavered, surprised the hell out of McQuade. After thrusting the torch toward Nicholas, the Scotsman examined him, his gaze lingering on the kilt and brogues. He rubbed the few weeks' growth of a beard on his chin.

"Efington? Is that ye?"

"Yes, it is. Now, if you don't mind, I have some business to attend to."

"What are ye doing oot at this hour, dressed like that? Tell me the name o' yer tailor, so I can avoid him."

"Perhaps you would tell me why you're ready to pierce my heart with your claymore."

Eyebrows drawn together, the Scotsman sheathed his sword and took a step closer. "I'll have ye know, two o' my calves had their throats ripped oot this night. I found bluid everywhere—the straw, the sides o' the stall, the floor—and I found paw prints in the mess." His tone became confidential. "It had the look o' a wildcat's kill. But none o' the wildcats that roam these moors are big enough tae rip a calf's throat oot. I'm thinking tinkers have taken up residence in yonder moors."

The smell of whisky wafting from the laird made Nicholas's eyes water. Perhaps he'd inherited his recent proclivity for drunkenness from his father. "Tinkers?"

"Cattle thieves, laddie. Are ye daft?"

Nicholas glanced at the eastern horizon, resenting every second he had to spend with this mad Scotsman. "The last cattle thief hung long before Culloden, McQuade."

"Ah, but ye may be wrong." McQuade's eyes grew round. "Ye had tae see it. The calves' ruined throats, the bluid . . . only a tinker—or a wildcat—would take pleasure in killing cattle that way."

"You're the daft one . . ." Nicholas trailed off.

A shocking thought had suddenly occurred to him. Perhaps the grimalkin had killed the calves. Although the notion didn't make sense at a distance—in the past he had seen the grimalkin kill only small game—upon closer inspection, it made terrible sense. Catherine had observed him with Clarissa right before she'd changed. If her human fury had transferred to the grimalkin, the wildcat could have reacted with a savagery that explained the calves' torn throats.

Even so, part of him refused to believe Catherine capable of such an act, in either human or grimalkin form. But if the grimalkin hadn't killed the calves, who, or what, had?

His throat dry, Nicholas edged toward the forest. He had to find Catherine. "Inform me if you should learn of any new killings. Now, if you don't mind . . ."

"Watch yer back, laddie," the Scotsman said, dismissing him with a nod.

Nicholas forced himself to walk away, but as soon as he'd entered the forest, he began to run toward Bodhan's Pond, soaring over exposed roots and fallen tree trunks, tripping over a rock, and tumbling halfway down a knoll. The forest was much darker than the moors, and everywhere he saw razor-sharp claws, gleaming white fangs, the shadow of a wildcat coiled to strike. Brambles stuck to his kilt, as if trying to detain him, and suddenly found themselves torn up from the dirt. An image of ripped calves' throats and blood kept replaying in his mind, but he refused to acknowledge the worry that tightened around his chest like a vise.

After what felt like a lifetime, he reached the pond and peered into the grimalkin's cave. The stone chamber was even darker than the forest. After his eyes had adjusted to the gloom, he detected the faint outline of boulders, a dark patch of moss clinging to the wall. The leaves matting the floor rustled softly in a hidden breeze, and water trickled into a narrow channel running along the sides of the cave. Resigned to wait, he settled behind a gooseberry thicket and scanned the outlying woods.

At length, an acrid odor reached his nose, one that reminded him of moist, rusted iron. Tensing, he waited a suspense-filled minute before he saw the grimalkin padding toward the cave. As before, the cat disappeared into the opening and a blinding light erupted, draining him of energy. As soon as the light faded, he crept through the thicket and discerned the outline of a woman lying within the cave.

He bent his head, avoiding the low ceiling, and inched toward Catherine. The acrid smell gained strength with each step. Finally, he touched her. His hand came away slimy, as if he'd skimmed muck off the top of a peat bog. He tasted the liquid and almost retched for the second time that morning.

Blood! But whose?

Even as he stared at his hand, the cave lightened. The hour had grown dangerously close to daybreak. Aware he'd little time left, he found the brown sack and withdrew her cloak. He wrapped her within its velvet folds, lifted her, and carried her outside. A quick check of her shivering form told him she'd escaped wounding. Nevertheless, the amount of blood covering her body—her hands, feet, face, torso—chilled him to the marrow.

Although he'd like to believe Catherine innocent, he found it difficult to deny what his very eyes told him. He could not, he realized, declare his love to her until he'd solved this mystery and removed the specter of mayhem from their lives.

He rubbed the blood from her face with the edge of her cloak and returned her to Rivendell. Once he'd placed her upon her own bed, he rang for Mary and had the maidservant bring up a bucket of hot water. Then, his heart sinking, he opened the cloak and began to scrub the blood from her skin and beneath her nails.

When Catherine awoke, she found herself in her own bed, clean and dressed in a plaid nightgown. Pink light flooded the lace bedcurtains and settled across her face, but the world outside her bedchamber still slumbered. Everything remained quiet and peaceful.

Inexplicably, a knot of dread formed in her stomach. Some memory played hide-and-seek with her, one that was important and disastrous all at once. She closed her eyes and began to reconstruct her memory, until at length the knot in her stomach tightened and the most horrifying picture formed in her mind: Nicholas and Clarissa, in Nicholas's bed, Clarissa wearing a gauzy white gown and grasping his shaft the way Catherine had longed to do, Nicholas groaning . . .

The adulterous bastard. She was going to kill him.

She jumped out of bed, the stone beneath her feet frigid.

These past weeks, she'd damned near pined for him, swallowing her pride and attempting to earn his love. She'd played the role of duchess to the hilt, planning menus and entertaining his relatives, when she'd much rather have investigated new ways to improve her clan's welfare. She'd even turned the tasks she normally managed—such as the finances—over to him in an unspoken gesture of trust.

And for what? He'd bedded another woman at his first opportunity, making a fool of her and throwing her trust back in her face. Oh, how naive she'd been to think the Dark Duke had the capability to love. He would no sooner change his ways for her than he'd leap off a gibbet with a rope around his neck.

Their marriage was over.

Dressed only in her nightgown, she grabbed her dirk and made for the door. Betrayal ate at her insides like acid. How Clarissa must be gloating.

The Dark Duke had humiliated her for the last time.

Mary chose that moment to enter the bedchamber, a tray of hot chocolate in her hands.

Catherine almost gutted her.

The tray fell to the floor in a great clatter of silver.

Her eyes as round as crown pieces, Mary pressed herself against the wall. "Good Lord, Cat, what on earth are ye doing? Trying tae kill me?"

"Not you. The duke." Catherine attempted to brush past her, but the maidservant stubbornly positioned herself against the door.

"Ye canna kill him. I'll keep ye here till ye come tae yer senses." Breathing heavily, Mary crossed her arms over her chest.

"Out of my way."

"Nay."

Frustration welled up inside her. She knew that Mary's obstinacy could at times rival her own. "All right. We'll wait until you feel I've calmed down. Then I shall go and kill him." She jammed the tip of the dirk into a wooden bureau.

"I doan suppose ye'll tell me why ye're in such a foul mood, but I've seen plenty of mischief this morning, and I'll explain if ye have a mind."

Catherine, too, crossed her arms over her chest. "Of course, Mary. Gossip away."

The maidservant slumped but did not move from her position. "MacDuff stopped by the kitchen earlier for a bicker o' brose. He said there were killings on the moors last night. McQuade's calves, in fact."

"Killings?" Catherine froze. An unexpected memory of a terrible odor, one of death and hatred and corruption, flooded her mind, overshadowing her furious thoughts of Nicholas.

"Aye. O' the most vicious kind."

"How were the calves killed?" She swallowed, her pulse quickening as other sense impressions—the lowing of frightened cattle, a slick wetness beneath her feet—surfaced as well.

"McQuade thinks it the work o' a wildcat." Mary shivered and crossed herself. "There haven't been killings like these in almost one hundred years. Do ye remember the tales o' the grimalkin? Some o' the villagers say the grimalkin is back among us."

Catherine clasped her hands together to still their trembling. She couldn't possibly be responsible for the calves' deaths. The grimalkin had never before shown any malevolence. Why would it start now? "The grimalkin is just a tale. A story made up to scare children into good behavior. Surely you don't believe it."

"They found paw prints," the maidservant confided, her voice low. "Far bigger than that o' any normal wildcat. And Raonull swears he saw something skulking through his pastures about a month past." Her voice dropped to a whisper. "Something large wi' tawny fur and glittering green eyes."

"Oh, nonsense," Catherine exclaimed with far more force than necessary.

"Ye'd better be careful on yer morning walks," Mary warned her. "The wildcat isna the only beastie about. I hear McQuade almost gutted His Grace on the moors this morning."

"What?"

"His Grace went tae investigate the dead cattle and McQuade threatened him, thinking he'd caught a tinker. The man's daft."

Catherine steadied herself with a hand against the wall, her thoughts a muddle. No longer did she want to kill Nicholas. Indeed, upon hearing of McQuade's dead calves, her desire to shed her husband's blood frightened her. "Where is His Grace now?"

Eyes gleaming, Mary leaned closer. "In the study, with that English baggage. I heard them talking, low and furious. The duke, he told her tae leave—"

Before Mary knew what Catherine was about, she grabbed the maidservant's shoulders and shuffled her to the left.

"Cat, what are ye—"

"I must speak to His Grace." She nodded toward the dirk. "I'll leave that behind."

Paying little attention to Mary's wide-eyed stare, she slipped into the hallway, clad only in her nightgown. She couldn't afford the time to dress. She had to catch the pair together in the study.

Plaid flannel clinging to her legs, she hurried down the stairs and sidled up to the study door. Clattering echoed from the kitchen, but otherwise the castle seemed deserted. All the better, Catherine thought, her ear pressed against the door. She didn't want anyone observing her dressed in a nightgown, spying upon her own husband.

"You *will* leave Rivendell, Clarissa."

She discerned Nicholas's deep male voice easily, his tone full of command. Silently she cheered Clarissa's imminent departure, even if she didn't trust his motives. Was he trying to duck responsibility for his crime by removing the evidence?

"There was a time," a woman answered, "when you would have enjoyed my hand around you. Indeed, you begged me for it."

"That time has long since passed." He sounded even sterner. "Pack your bags and go."

"If not for your wife, we would have married. She has destroyed my happiness."

Catherine stiffened. The little jade!

"Thank God for my wife."

She heard an indrawn breath. Then a muffled slap. She pressed harder against the door. The wood was too thick; she couldn't hear. Lord, what was going on in there?

"Shall we be honest?" Nicholas again. Downright angry this time. "You don't want me. You simply want revenge against Catherine."

Catherine narrowed her eyes. He certainly sounded like the man wronged, and his attitude toward Clarissa doused some of the heat flicking through her veins. Even so, she couldn't help but wonder if he was the sort of man who thought he could dally with a woman, as long as he remained faithful to his wife in his heart, or at least in his mind.

"I do want you, Your Grace. I always will. But I admit Harry and I had another reason for coming here."

Catherine heard the throb of need in Clarissa's voice and clenched her jaw. She could imagine the brunette's brown eyes, as appealing as a puppy's, begging, beguiling, and utterly fake.

As silence grew behind the door, Catherine tensed. *Throw her out, Nicholas,* she silently pleaded. *Don't listen to her lies.*

"And what reason is that?"

Her shoulders slumped. Damn him.

Clarissa answered so softly Catherine couldn't hear her.

"Gambling debts? I see. I will confirm this story with my cousin, Clarissa, and if I find you've lied to me—"

Some more mumbling.

"No, I don't want you to end up in Newgate."

A gentle little sob. Catherine rolled her eyes heavenward.

"For Harry's sake," Nicholas said, his voice heavy, "you may remain at Rivendell until I've discussed the situation with him and found an acceptable solution. But I expect you to remain on your best behavior."

"Of course, Your Grace."

"Now, if you'll excuse me—"

Catherine scuttled backward and crouched behind a mahogany chest of drawers. Her cheeks burned with embarrassment. What would Nicholas think if he caught her eavesdropping on him? Surely such behavior was beneath a duchess, and more worthy of a chambermaid.

She held her breath as the study door opened and his tall form emerged. She willed him to walk toward the stairs, and not down the hall and past her hiding place. He paused for a moment, and then, as though obeying her silent command, he turned and made his way toward the foyer.

Her sigh was deep and heartfelt.

Skirts rustled near the study door.

"Ah, Lady Catherine. What an interesting position I find you in."

Frozen, Catherine stared at a clotted cream face and pink lips curved slightly upward. The brunette examined her from her bare feet to the top of her tangled curls, her brown eyes narrowed. "Do you often run about in plaid flannel, spying upon your husband and his guests?"

Her stomach churning, Catherine stood and smoothed her nightgown. "At least I do not climb into bed with them."

"According to Nicholas, you climb into bed with no one, not even he."

At Catherine's gasp, Clarissa laughed. "He will tire of you, and when he does, he will leave you in Scotland to find a woman more his class."

"And I suppose that woman is you?"

"No, Your Grace. I do not want him."

Catherine raised an eyebrow. " 'Tis just as well, for you will never have him."

"Ah, but I will have everything he owns."

"He won't divorce me to marry you, Clarissa."

"Who said anything about marriage?" With a little smile, Clarissa walked away.

Two weeks later, Catherine again found herself in the drawing room, subjected to a lengthy evening of card-playing and frivolous conversation. Clarissa, Nicholas, Harry, and the dowager sat at a table of commerce, while she concentrated on a book, *Dante's Inferno* this time.

"I hope, Harry," Nicholas said, his voice casual, "that this is the only gambling you engage in from now on, small games between family members who are not out to fleece you."

Harry examined Nicholas with a glint in his eye. "How fortunate I am to have your concern, coz."

Clarissa examined both men and then looked back to her cards, a sly smile twisting her lips.

Catherine had begun to think of Clarissa as a snake. The woman was crafty, playing upon Nicholas's concern for Harry to ensure her stay at Rivendell. She still wondered how Clarissa planned to own everything of Nicholas's without marrying him. Perhaps, a dark voice in her mind whispered, Nicholas had encouraged her in the bedchamber, and now that he'd tired of her, the snake planned to bribe him for her continued silence.

For her own part, Catherine refused to insist that Clarissa leave. Doing so would only reveal how much Nicholas's perfidy had hurt her. And she couldn't bear to give the Englishwoman any satisfaction. Instead, she remained silent and simmered like a pot of stew cooked too long with the lid on, ready to explode into an ugly mess.

Beyond the castle's walls, the wind swept along the moors, promising a frosty night. Tree limbs tapped against the windows and oil lamps flickered wildly in the draft that curled along the ceiling. Although decorated in warm tones of brown and tan and boasting an oversized hearth, the drawing room felt colder than a dovecote in a snowstorm. Grateful she'd worn her warmest gown—a robe of black velvet, trimmed with gold lace and tied together at the breasts—Catherine rearranged the dress over her gold-edged petticoat.

The card players had returned to circumspect wagering; a pile of ivory gaming chips lay next to each person. Clarissa threw some chips onto a central pile, her hands slim and white against the green baize. She'd ceased her overt flirtation with Nicholas and hung on her own husband instead. Harry, for his part, seemed quite pleased with himself, his quick smile and frequent toasts to Nicholas's health betraying an unusual animation.

Based on the easy camaraderie between Harry and Nicholas, Catherine reflected, Harry still didn't know about his wife's treachery. She wondered how Nicholas slept at night knowing he'd cuckolded his cousin. Indeed, the Londoners were a breed apart with their perfectly coiffed hair and well-fitting clothes, their obscure jokes and gossip and clipped accents.

"We must organize a hunt, Nicky," Harry said as he pushed a few more chips into the center of the table. "Fox-hunting season opens in two weeks. Perhaps we'll bring some civilization to the Highlands."

"Fox hunting is damned hard on the horses." Nicholas flexed his shoulders, as if cramped from the sitting position. Stretched beyond the limit, a seam along his coat of blue superfine split open.

She stared at the tiny rip, at the white linen beneath it, wishing she could run her hands along those broad shoulders and luxuriate in his virile strength. Instead, she bit her lip and focused on the pianoforte in the far corner of the room.

Her relationship with Nicholas had deteriorated to its lowest point yet. They'd had a terrible row the day after she'd discovered him with Clarissa. She'd accused him of dallying with the brunette, and he'd insisted on his innocence, and spoke of trust and honor, and they'd both said things better forgotten. Now they barely exchanged glances, let alone words, and although Catherine told herself she couldn't be happier, inside she wept. She still loved the bastard, and although her head told her to let him go, she found the task particularly difficult.

"You've ripped your coat, Nicholas," the dowager commented.

"Rupert will attend to it in the morning." Nicholas stretched his long legs out beneath the table and leaned toward Harry, making his cousin seem a dwarf in comparison. "If you are bored, Harry, perhaps you should return to London."

A chuckle rumbled from Harry's throat. "I simply like to hunt. The gratification that comes with bringing down either mighty buck or flying bird only increases with each shot."

Clarissa tittered. Gowned in a silver crepe frock over a powder blue sarcenet slip, sapphires dripping from her neck and ears, she appeared ephemeral, as if she might fly away on a fairy breeze. Catherine thought it more likely she'd cross the river Styx and descend to hell. If only the devil would take her now. "Poor, stupid animals." Clarissa toyed with one of her brown curls. "They have not a chance against you."

Catherine intercepted a covert glance between Harry and his wife. Uncomfortable, she shifted on her chair. What were the pair planning? "I would not suggest a hunt. My clansmen have set several traps. The participants could spring a trap and break a toe."

"Traps to catch the grimalkin?" Harry asked.

"No." Nicholas's voice brooked no argument. "To catch an ordinary wildcat. It seems we have a rogue animal wandering the moors."

Harry shrugged. "We will remove the traps before the hunt."

For once, Catherine applauded Harry's suggestion. She'd

worried night and day about those traps, hoping the grimalkin would be smart enough to avoid them.

"I, for one, believe the grimalkin has returned to Scotland." Clarissa shivered. "In fact, I believe I spied the beast a few nights back, its dark pelt glinting beneath the moonlight."

Nicholas shot a glance toward Catherine. She gave him a tiny shake of her head. Clarissa was spouting nonsense. The grimalkin hadn't appeared for quite a while.

She kept hoping, against her better judgment, that some large wildcat would prove the culprit in the killings before the next time the grimalkin appeared. But her sickening suspicions persisted. To date, her clansmen had yet to catch a wildcat. And no more killings had occurred.

"We are likely to have snow by All Saint's Day," she reminded them from her seat by the fire. "Surely such weather would confound your plans." As if to emphasize her point, a harsh blast of air rushed past the north window, rattling the glass in its frame.

"Not at all. Snow would only make a hunt more interesting." Harry glanced at her for a mere second before returning to his cards, clearly nonplussed by her effort to quash his hunt proposal.

The dowager tapped her cane against the floor. "I think it a fine idea," she offered, the cane at odds with her youthful gown of spangled India muslin. "We should invite all the locals within convenient distance. Catherine, I will assist you in this matter."

Catherine choked off an annoyed snort. Even Nicholas's mother, she mused, had become tiresome, meddling in Catherine's business and insisting on many trips into Kildonan. Catherine, who felt obliged to accompany her on her jaunts, suspected the dowager hoped for a glimpse of Robert McQuade. Yes, she often had to compress her duties as duchess into a single hour, sometimes less, just to promote the lovelorn aristocrat's *affaire de coeur*. No doubt the dowager saw a hunt as yet another opportunity to speak with McQuade.

"Very good," Harry pronounced. "A hunt we will have." A sly smile crossed his lips. "I will admit, however, to a certain feeling of ennui. I'm tired of cards. May I suggest another form of entertainment?"

Nicholas placed his cards on the table with a heartfelt sigh. "Of course."

"I would like to hear you play the pianoforte." Harry covered his mouth and coughed. The cough sounded more like a giggle.

The dowager froze. Nicholas made no response, but his gaze instantly darkened to a stormy gray.

Arrested by the silence that suddenly filled the room, Catherine closed her book. She wondered if she'd missed some terrible gaffe. Had Fragprie just pranced through the drawing room in only his underwear?

Clarissa's lips trembled as though she couldn't decide between a smile and a frown. Catherine noted a disquieting glint in the Englishwoman's eyes.

"I say, coz, will you not play for us? For your lovely wife?" Harry threw a hostile glance toward Catherine.

Lines of strain appeared around Nicholas's mouth. "I have not played for years. I could not do the instrument justice."

"Oh, now you are being modest." Harry tapped the dowager's hand. "He plays delightfully, does he not, Aunt Annabella?"

Her face white, the dowager gave her son such a somber look that Catherine jumped up from her chair and walked toward the group. She didn't know why the idea of playing the pianoforte affected Nicholas so, or why a gentleman of his status would bother to learn an instrument normally relegated to a lady's repertoire. But Harry's spite and Nicholas's obvious vulnerability roused remnants of loyalty in her heart. She would support him through Harry's attack, one so odd given Harry's previous good humor.

"I am in no mood for music," she announced when she reached the card players.

Clarissa gave her a moue of distaste. "You are never in the mood for anything."

"I agree with Catherine," the dowager said. "Let us retire for the night. I would much rather huddle beneath my counterpane than spend another minute in this infernal draft."

"Ah, but Clarissa would like to sing for us, wouldn't you,

sweet?" Like a vulture on offal, Harry refused to give up his idea.

Her gaze diverted to the floor, Clarissa hesitated for a moment before answering. "Yes, I should like to accompany a Haydn sonata. Do you know anything appropriate, Your Grace?"

Seconds passed, during which all gazes focused on Nicholas. He glared first at Harry, then at Clarissa. Lips tight, he finally stalked toward the pianoforte.

Disliking the pain she discerned in his eyes, Catherine placed herself in his path. "You don't have to play," she whispered.

"Oh, but I do." He stepped around her and settled himself on the bench, fingers poised above the keys.

Clarissa took up position next to Nicholas, while Harry lounged on a chair, his legs crossed. Catherine perched next to the dowager on a settee.

After staring at the keys for some time, Nicholas began to play. He hesitated at first, but then gained strength until the music poured from the instrument. A sad, haunting melody, it seemed to express an inner torment, some demon he had yet to purge himself of. Clarissa's singing, although adequate, only intruded on his playing, and Catherine wished she would close her mouth and sit.

Shoulders hunched, fingers long and sensitive, his song impassioned, he reminded her of the other Nicholas she had discovered these past months, the one she had fallen in love with. That Nicholas could feel. He had vulnerabilities, he hurt, he smiled and laughed like a boy. He would have been capable of loving her. How had she lost him?

"I hope I have relieved your boredom," Nicholas said, his gaze directed at Harry, his voice low.

Lost in memories, Catherine hadn't realized he'd finished the piece.

Harry nodded, his countenance solemn. "Oh, you most certainly have. Shall we ride at dawn?"

"I have other matters to attend to. Perhaps the following day." He stood, and after bowing toward his mother, Clarissa, and Catherine, he turned on his heel and left the drawing room.

Catherine stared at his retreating back. Questions tumbled through her head. Harry had obviously twitted Nicholas in some obscure way, but why? She wondered if Harry had discovered his wife's treachery and sought revenge on Nicholas in a devious manner, rather than confront him directly. After all, if Harry lost Nicholas's favor, he would find himself burdened by gambling debts and without a sou to pay them off.

Curiosity gnawed at her like a mouse at cheese. She decided to seek him out, if only to discover what lay behind the intrigue she'd witnessed in the drawing room. Doing so, she reasoned, would compromise neither her pride nor her self-respect.

Of course, a contrary part of her wanted to soothe his hurt. He was vulnerable and needed her. As a woman, she found that a very hard combination to resist, in spite of his dalliance with Clarissa. Nevertheless, resist him she would. She need only conjure an image of Clarissa snuggled in bed with him to strengthen her immunity, if need be.

Eyes narrowed, she examined Harry and Clarissa for several seconds before excusing herself and going in search of her husband. She found him the first place she looked: the laird's apartments. He bade her enter when she knocked, but didn't bother glancing at her as she walked into the room. Rather, he sat on a chair, his fingers creating a steeple, his gaze fixed on the crackling flames in the hearth. His jacket, waistcoat, and stock lay in a heap on the floor. Dressed only in breeches and a linen shirt damp with perspiration, he looked comfortable yet utterly cheerless.

"I did not know you played the pianoforte," she said, smoothing her petticoat, which peeked out from beneath the robe, with both hands. The movement pulled her bodice taut and forced her breasts to swell most alarmingly over the edge of her lace tucker. She wished he'd seen the display.

At length he looked at her. A small muscle ticked in his jaw. "Why are you here, Catherine? Do you seek to twist the knife further?" His voice, deep and husky, hinted at the vulnerability she'd sensed in him earlier.

She took a breath and, entirely for his benefit, smoothed her petticoat again. "Twist the knife? I don't understand what you're referring to. But I would like to." A single lock of black hair had fallen across his brow. How she longed to smooth his hair back and erase the lines of pain from his face!

You're slipping, she reminded herself. *Remain strong.*

"After all that has passed between us, I find your need to understand me rather odd. You do not trust me. You do not believe I have a jot of honor. Over these past few weeks, you have avoided me at every turn. Indeed, I thought you had intended to petition for a separation."

A bittersweet smile curved her lips. She didn't want to provoke another fight, not now. "You are a heartless rake. I am a lying Scottish tart. You bedded another, and I nearly gutted you with my dirk. I suppose my transgressions are nearly as wicked as your own."

He raised an eyebrow. "When did you 'nearly gut me' with your dirk?"

"The morning after I discovered you with . . . well, you know who I am referring to." She couldn't even spit out the Englishwoman's name.

"Ah, I see."

"Mary prevented me from following through."

"I will have to raise her wages."

Catherine walked over to the window, her back to him. As the trees outside bent with the force of the wind, his melancholy gaze bent her will to resist him. Shutting off such ill-advised thoughts, she shivered and pulled the drapes closed. "I do not want to talk about that Englishwoman, or about our disagreements. Rather, I'd like to know why playing the pianoforte was so difficult for you."

He discarded his thoughtful position and turned toward her, his gray eyes intent, his face a study of firelight and shadows. "I will tell you what you wish to know, but under one condition. First, we must discuss what you think you saw the night of the Samhain festival, in all its sordid detail. And you must promise to listen this time, rather than launch accusations at my head."

"You cannot talk your way out of trouble, Your Grace."

"I simply want a chance to explain what happened. First, what do you think you saw that night?"

She took a chair opposite him and picked up a snifter half-filled with brandy. She had a feeling she would need it. "I saw you, in your bed, half-dressed, your breeches open. The Englishwoman lay next to you, her hand around your—"

"That's enough," he interrupted. "You think you saw Clarissa and I enjoying an illicit tumble. In fact, you saw a very foxed man clutching a woman he thought was his wife."

"What kind of nonsense is this?"

"I was drunk, Catherine, terribly so. My vision was naught more than a blur. I said your name, several times. I thought you were in my bed, damn it. And dear Clarissa didn't correct my misconception."

How very much she wanted to believe him. "Prove it."

He rubbed his chin for a moment. "Why did you come to my apartments?"

"You sent a note, asking for me." Even as she said the words, she detected the flaw in her logic.

"Exactly." He jumped up with the same fervor as an eagle pouncing on a rabbit. "Why would I invite you to my apartments, knowing I had Clarissa in my bed? It defies common sense."

She nodded, hope flaring within her like a beacon on the darkest night. Her anger and humiliation had cut her adrift from all reason. "You have a valid point."

"Do you still have the note?" Hands clasped behind his back, he began to pace. "Perhaps if we examine it we can determine if the handwriting truly matches mine. Here, look at this."

He handed her a bill of lading he'd made some notes on. His handwriting was small, straight, almost illegible.

"The note disappeared," she said with growing conviction. "I thought I'd lost it." The Englishwoman, she thought, could teach Machiavelli some tricks. "But this writing looks nothing like the writing on the note. I remember thinking your handwriting looked like a child's—large, scrawling, with generous loops."

Nicholas ceased his pacing and clasped her hands in his own, warmer ones. She felt her heart beat faster at his proximity.

"Other than her ill-placed grip, nothing happened between Clarissa and I. Nothing. The entire incident was staged to cause trouble between us."

She believed him. Along with their careful review of the facts, the desperate honesty in his eyes, his dry, firm hand clasp convinced her. How she'd wronged him these past weeks. Amazed by the depth of treachery swirling around them, she shook her head.

"The following morning Clarissa and I exchanged words," Nicholas continued. "She revealed Harry's gambling debts and insisted if I threw them out, they'd end up in Newgate, unable to pay their duns. She promised to reform and begged for a chance to set things aright on her own. For Harry's sake I allowed her to remain at Rivendell and kept silent about her foray into my room."

Catherine felt heat flare in her cheeks. She knew most of this, but she dared not tell him why.

He pulled her closer. "Nevertheless, the twosome have overstayed their welcome. I'll arrange for an allowance for Harry and pack them off."

"Your mother grows tiresome as well," she admitted.

Nicholas nodded, a grin curving his lips. "Let us be rid of the three of them. We will organize a country dance the weekend after the hunt as a grand send-off. My mother, Harry, and Clarissa will return to London in time to celebrate the Yuletide, leaving us free to enjoy the holiday by ourselves."

He warmed her with the solemn promise in his gray gaze, the grin that had become teasing yet appreciative. The other Nicholas had returned to her.

Tears filled her eyes. "And a delightful holiday it shall be, Your Grace," she whispered a second before his lips descended to hers.

Fifteen

He held her for a long, long time. She leaned against his chest, breathing in sandalwood and leather and the unique male smell of him. Occasionally he tilted her chin up and kissed her with a soft pressure that left her weak, but he seemed unwilling to do anything more.

She didn't care. Never had she felt so treasured, so safe, so close to another human being. Yes, the grimalkin still remained between them, but right now even it didn't seem like an insurmountable obstacle. "I love you," she whispered.

He leaned his head down to hers. "What was that?"

"Nothing."

"As much as I enjoy holding you like this," he murmured, "I have yet to fulfill my half of the bargain. I'll ring for tea, and then I shall tell you about my childhood."

When he withdrew his arms, the warm cocoon around her crumbled. But she did want to hear about the pianoforte, so she nodded and sank into a chair. The anticipation of a lover's touch, she'd learned, could be just as sweet as the touch itself.

They talked of inconsequential matters until a footman

arrived, a tea tray heaped with Scottish scones in his hands. A large pot of honey stood next to the scones.

Catherine picked up a scone and began to spread honey over the pastry. "I have heard much about the Dark Duke," she admitted. "I look forward to learning about Nicholas, the boy."

A large dollop of honey fell directly into her cleavage. Warm and sticky against her skin, it dripped down, leaving a golden trail. She stared at the mess, amazed the honey had fallen in such an intimate location. An imp of the devil prodding her on, she yanked the tucker from her bodice, revealing over half of her breasts. "Lace is quite difficult to clean," she explained with a little smile.

Nicholas, who'd raised the teapot to pour, froze. He stared as well, his eyes gleaming. Just when she thought she'd begin to sizzle from the heat of his gaze, he poured them both a cup. "Have you ever tried a Dutch tart?"

Pressing her breasts together in an attempt to stop the flow of honey, she reached for a linen napkin. "I don't think so."

He drew the linen out of reach. "Shall I tell you how to make one?"

Heat flooded her breasts, turning them a soft pink. She'd seen that wicked sparkle in his eyes before and her insides tingled with impatience. Whatever a Dutch tart was, she felt certain she'd enjoy biting into one. "If you wish. Would you please hand me that square of linen?"

"In a moment," he said, a lazy smile spreading across his face. "To make a Dutch tart, you need honey, nutmeg, and cinnamon."

She wondered where a man of his stature had gained such culinary expertise. First the pianoforte, and now baking.

"First, you spread the honey, like this." He slipped his hand down into her cleavage, ignoring her surprised gasp, and began to spread the honey over her breasts.

She'd forgotten how gratifying it felt to have the man she loved stroke her. Eager for more, she untied the laces beneath her bosom, loosening the black robe, and pulled the ribbon from her chemise. His murmured endearment told her how much he appreciated the gesture, and immediately he stroked her breasts, his fingers warm and sticky. She leaned into his touch, her skin tingling, her eyes closed, head thrown back, a wanton ache curling between her thighs.

His voice grew deeper. "Then you sprinkle the honey with cinnamon and nutmeg. Dutch tarts are most delicious, I assure you. But I like them plain, too." He leaned down and began to lick at the honey between her breasts, pressing his face against their tender sides, his low groan of pleasure muffled.

He's done this many times, a voice whispered inside her head, and a spark of annoyance grew apace with the throbbing lethargy that stole through her limbs. She still hadn't fully relinquished her distrust of him, particularly when it concerned other women. "I suppose you've had more than your share of 'tarts.' "

"Ah, Catherine, do you think I lived as a monk before I met you?" He rubbed his chin against her sensitive flesh with dazzling expertise, provoking and torturing her, and she wouldn't ask him to stop, damn him, even if he'd loved a thousand other women. She grasped his hair in both hands and pulled, wanting him to know she objected but unwilling to end his blissful torment.

He pushed her back against the bed. "It matters naught, for now I kiss only you." Lips sweet with honey, he kissed her, moving his mouth slowly against hers, his shirt pressed against her breasts, her petticoat tangled between their thighs. She kicked at the muslin, wanting nothing to separate them, already anticipating the feel of his shaft deep inside her, probing, thrusting . . .

"But I'm afraid we shall have to wait," he announced, raising his head and giving her such a tantalizing grin she restrained the desire to slap him. "We must talk about a certain pianoforte."

"To hell with the pianoforte," she muttered.

He began to laugh and pulled her to him. "Once we get this behind us, I shall love you until you can no longer walk."

Grumbling, she snuggled into his side. "All right. If you must, tell me of the pianoforte."

He remained quiet for a moment, and Catherine had the

distinct impression he was reaching deep into his mind, retrieving memories that had long remained buried.

"Darkness dwells within every human being," he began. "In most people, these shadows are naught more than dreams and fantasies that vanish at dawn. But the man I'd thought of as my father, Ross Efington, was different than most. The darkness stained his soul like a great inkblot."

He played with the ivory ribbon on her chemise, his tone casual. Even so, she felt the tension that coursed through his body in the way he'd stiffened. "I have thought for many years about my father, wondered why he chose a path of evil. In the end, I believe he stagnated in a perpetual childhood. Lacking in discipline, he considered himself the center of all worlds and felt no one equaled him in either appearance, charm, or intelligence.

"He died when I'd reached the age of twenty."

"The thought that you haven't an ounce of his blood in your veins must comfort you," she offered.

"Ah, but I am the bastard son of a man you hate and a clan you have warred with for centuries. Is the McQuade blood an improvement?"

" 'Tis difficult for me to think of you as a McQuade."

A long silence fell between them. He kept his gaze fixed on the canopy above his bed and had ceased playing with her ribbon. Although he lay next to her, he was far, far away. When he spoke again, his voice sounded raw.

"Ross Efington fed on my fear, fed on the power he derived from his acts. He did not care that he'd harmed me. In fact, he regarded his floggings as great sport. When he died, Mother and I damned near danced on his grave."

She moistened her lower lip with her tongue, wishing she hadn't insisted on his confession. It was painful for her to hear; she couldn't imagine how difficult it was for him to tell of it. "Nicholas, if you can't tell me, I—"

"Specifically, with regard to the pianoforte," he forged on, ignoring her half-formed objection, "if I did not play Haydn to my father's liking, he would flog me with a riding crop, before all."

He turned to face her, his chin square and firm, his nose

straight and noble, his gaze distant. "Harry had attended many of these sessions."

The Englishwoman, Catherine recalled, had requested he play Haydn. "Oh, Nicholas." She couldn't think of anything else to say. Words weren't adequate.

"The tale is not over yet," he warned her. "My father always retained the hope that I would take an active role in the House of Lords. And so I set out to become a rakehell, my life filled with gambling and women—the antithesis of everything my father had wanted. I joined the Hell Fire Club, which was more an excuse for the bucks of London to indulge their deviant appetites than a coven, and I immersed myself in its rituals."

She'd heard of the Hell Fire Club and shuddered to think Nicholas had once belonged to it. Still, she now understood why he'd joined and felt heartsick at the appalling life he'd endured.

"One night a young girl—a paid prostitute—joined us in the labyrinth." He rubbed his knuckles against her cheek, his touch as light as an angel's wing. "I did not participate in the rape that followed, but I believe they killed her and disposed of the body. At that time I realized I had become so much like my father that I saw his face when I looked in the mirror."

His arm tightened around her. "From that point forward, I tried to turn my life around, tried to atone for the acts I'd committed. I renounced all things supernatural and became a man of science. Using Bacon, Voltaire, and Descartes as pattern cards, I began to think in terms of natural law and universal order."

She smoothed a lock of hair back from his brow. "You are the most logical man I know."

"You healed my heart. The grimalkin, however, turned my logic upside down."

Her pulse quickened at his subtle avowal of love. She lowered her eyes, suddenly feeling quite shy, and focused on the second half of his revelation. "Sometimes I wish I could see how I look when I change. I'll wager 'tis an amazing display. Terrible, too."

"I needed three months to come to terms with the sight,"

he admitted, "though even in that state you retain an exquisite grace. Now I find all aspects of the grimalkin fascinating."

Warming to their intimate discussion, she snuggled closer. Perhaps, she thought, he could help her understand the processes of the change better. "You say you are a scholar. How do you explain me?"

"I haven't explained you. Neither a priest nor the most learned men in society could explain you, either. That's what makes the problem so fascinating."

"But you have heard the tale of Niall MacClelland and Sileas McQuade's curse. Could it not be simple witchcraft?"

"I have not studied the grimalkin thoroughly enough to draw a firm conclusion." His eyes brightened, and although she preferred that to the bleak look they'd previously contained, she wasn't sure she liked the reason for his excitement.

Apparently caught up in the discussion, he stood and began to pace. Left alone in the massive bed, she abruptly felt like a rowboat adrift on the ocean.

"I want to understand the wildness, chart the process that makes you transform," he said. "In fact, I would give everything to experience the moors in the grimalkin's form, just once."

She pulled back from him, dismayed by his own transformation—from gentle lover to zealous scholar. " 'Tis obvious you haven't the slightest understanding of the grimalkin. If you did, you would not want to take the grimalkin's shape."

"That is why I have followed the grimalkin at night. I want to understand the beast better. The first night, there was a thunderstorm . . . oh, Cat, it was magical. You roared at the thunder, and I roared back. The feelings you roused in me breathed life back into my stained soul."

A strange jealousy surged through her, that he could have shared something so wondrous with the grimalkin. At the same time, his casual intermixing of the words *you* and *beast* offended her. Did he think her a beast? "You talk as if I were there. I wasn't. I do not remember what I experience in the grimalkin's form." She sounded as annoyed as she felt, and knew her reaction was completely illogical, but she offered no apologies.

He appeared to have not heard her. "The process of transformation does, to some extent, adhere to natural law. When you transform, you drain energy from the living beings around you. That energy then cloaks the grimalkin in a golden aura."

His objective tone made her feel like a freak. "Perhaps we should present ourselves at Astley's Royal Amphitheatre and perform tricks for money. You might serve as the grimalkin's trainer. Before long, you'll have the beast jumping through hoops."

He raised an eyebrow at her, inflaming her further.

" 'Tis a shame we can't have children," she declared. "You could train your entire family and thrill your audiences with your control over a pride of wildcats."

He fixed her with a candid gaze. "I don't yet understand why women who carry the grimalkin cannot bear a child, and I admit this is a problem for me, for I must have an heir. Still, there is much to learn, much to study."

Fists clenched, she glared at him. "I am not certain I enjoy being one of your experiments, Nicholas."

"You're not an experiment. You're a miracle."

"Why don't you just lock me up in a cage and ship me to Bedlam? There they could cut me open and compare me with the other animals they've studied." She felt her face heat up and knew it as a sign of an imminent explosion.

"Catherine—"

She'd had enough for one night. After those few moments of transcendental pleasure, their fall back to earth had shattered her into a hundred jagged pieces. "Please, Nicholas, don't. I shall not submit to any of your experiments, I do not want you following the grimalkin at night, and even if you asked me to, I would not attempt to bear your child. Good evening." She jumped up from her chair and made for the door.

"You're being far too sensitive." Nicholas arrived at the door before her and blocked her way. "Move into the laird's apartments with me. We'll discover the root of this problem."

"I have no desire to sleep in the same room with a . . . a fanatic who chases me about at night, taking notes on my behavior." With a neat twist she skirted around him, through the door, and up the staircase to her own room. Once inside, she closed the door and locked it.

Since she'd begun to change, she'd had two fears. She'd feared the thought of being accused as a witch the most, and had been quite relieved to learn her husband didn't succumb to superstition. But her other fear—that of being subjected to experimentation—had unfortunately come true. Even worse, the scholar was none other than the man she loved.

She threw herself on her bed, curled into a ball, and closed her eyes, feeling like a stoat caught in a trap. By loving Nicholas, she'd given him unequaled power to hurt her, and too often he'd used that power. Oh, if only she'd never met the man.

The day of the hunt dawned cold and clear. Exchanging smiles and mild conversation with his guests, Nicholas strolled through the crowd and paused to inspect the Scots delicacies arranged on tables. Occasionally he brushed shoulders with Catherine, who played hostess to the clan women.

His wife, he decided, outshone every other woman there, her dark blue pelisse of jaconet muslin and matching bonnet setting her hair afire. Since that night two weeks ago, when they'd discussed his scientific tendencies, she'd avoided him with more creativity than da Vinci himself might have shown.

He'd made many stupid blunders that night, kissing her breasts and then ranting about the grimalkin, and upon reflection had realized how callous he'd been. Apparently determined to nurse her injured pride, she'd refused to accept the apologies he'd offered on at least two occasions. He hoped time would heal her wounds, for they'd come too far to let mistakes keep them apart. He'd give her another week, then grovel if he had to.

Shouts echoed from the moors and forest, shaking Nicholas from his thoughts. In the distance, footmen thrashed through bushes and around trees, locating and blocking fox dens to prevent the foxes from finding cover. The huntsman, a Sutherland clansman from Kinbrace, tried to shush his pack of yapping hounds, without success. The cacophony of sound only added to the muted excitement filling the courtyard as men and women alike prepared for the hunt.

Nicholas and his guests had gathered outside the castle walls, the women in clusters before the open fires, the men huddled around jugs of mead, aquavit, and the inevitable whisky. Bows of MacClelland tartan decorated the lower branches of a giant hawthorn and flapped wildly in the November wind. They gave the courtyard a festive air.

Nicholas hadn't expected so many clans to respond to their impromptu invitation. Many had endured a two-day trip, arriving the night before and staying at Rivendell. Their dress surprised him, too. Although many of the tacksmen wore tartan finery, the chiefs paraded about in red hunting jackets, white breeches, and black riding boots. This fox hunt, he thought, appeared more English than a few he'd attended in Leicestershire.

He mingled among his guests, making a point to speak to the Countess of Sutherland, MacDonnell of Glengarry, and the Marquess of Stafford, undoubtedly the richest landowner in Britain. Once he'd pacified his most prominent guests, he moved on to the lesser-known, more boisterous chiefs.

Directly behind him, hearty male laughter blended with the snorts and whinnies of the hunters held in a makeshift stable. He felt a tap on his shoulder and turned, smiling, eager to join in the joke.

Instead, MacDuff stood behind him, gray brows drawn together, chin thrust forward. "There's a weasel in the stables, Yer Grace, a-stirring the horses and questioning the grooms."

"Does this weasel have a name?"

"Aye. McQuade." The head groom spit into the dirt beside them.

"Thank you." Trouble, Nicholas mused, seemed to follow his erstwhile father around.

When he reached the stable, he found McQuade, dressed in plaid and kilt, a dirk and sporran at his waist. The sight of his father dressed in traditional Scots attire pleased him. The man had many faults, Nicholas reflected, but at least he felt no shame regarding his origins. So many Highland chiefs had forsaken their heritage and had adopted English ways to the exclusion of all else.

His voice gruff, McQuade questioned a trembling groom and occasionally pointed at a saddle lying on the ground.

"Is there a problem?" Smoothly Nicholas inserted himself between McQuade and the hapless groom.

"Aye, there's a problem," McQuade said, a vein throbbing in his forehead. His eyes held no special significance, just anger and suspicion, and Nicholas had to assume his mother still hadn't told McQuade he'd sired a bastard.

"How do ye explain this?" McQuade waved what looked like a piece of cowhide, hair and all, beneath Nicholas's nose.

"Let me guess. You've taken up tanning."

The Scotsman narrowed his eyes. "Ye've got a smart mouth, laddie, and I have the inclination tae shut it for ye."

"Please, no fisticuffs," Nicholas said in his most neutral tone. McQuade seemed in danger of exploding in a whirlwind of fists, and the last thing he needed was a brawl. "If you would explain what this piece of cowhide means to you, and where you found it, I might be able to help."

"This cowhide is from one o' my dead calves," McQuade informed him, his voice rising, "and I found it stuck tae the stirrup o' one o' yer saddles."

Stiffening, Nicholas took the cowhide from McQuade and rubbed it between his fingers. "How do you know this belonged to one of your calves?"

"The color and the texture o' the hair. No one else in this valley raises roan shorthorns."

"That proves nothing." He handed the cowhide back to McQuade. "How do I know you're not lying in an attempt to implicate the MacClellands in the killings? I am aware of the ancient feud between the McQuades and the MacClellands, and from what I've heard, the two clans have gone to great lengths to cause trouble for each other."

McQuade reddened. "I doan like ye calling me a liar.

We'll see what the magistrate thinks about my theory." He turned and stomped out of the stables.

"McQuade," Nicholas called.

The old man turned around.

"I'll ask some questions, see what I can find out."

"See that ye do." With that, McQuade disappeared into the throngs of Scotsmen.

Nicholas focused on the groom. "Did you see His Lordship remove that piece of hide from one of our saddles?"

His Adam's apple bobbing in his skinny neck, the groom nodded. "Aye, Yer Grace. 'Twas caught in the stirrup, just like he said."

"Who generally uses that saddle?"

"Why, ye all do. I doan marry a saddle tae a man."

"Very well, then. Carry on." Nicholas left the stable and began to circulate among his guests once again. Although he'd learned nothing from the groom, his mood had improved. If McQuade had told the truth, he reasoned, the grimalkin couldn't have killed the calves, because the killer obviously rode a horse.

Catherine was innocent.

But then another thought occurred to him and he frowned. The killer had ridden one of *his* horses. That meant a vicious murderer of animals hid within Rivendell's walls, putting Catherine's and his mother's safety in jeopardy. Until he caught the culprit, he would have to insist Catherine and his mother cease their walks through the moors and into Kildonan. Indeed, he'd have to keep a very close watch on both of them, particularly his wife. She could not deny his company once she realized her safety was at risk.

Of course, if McQuade had lied about the cowhide, then Catherine could still be guilty of killing those calves, in grimalkin form. He pushed the thought from his mind, preferring to dwell on the alternative instead.

He rejoined the crowd and scanned the sea of leghorn bonnets, round hats, and Caledonian caps, looking for a certain honey-flame head. He found her by a table laden with grilled haddock, kippers, mutton ham, girdle scones, oatcakes—just about every kind of food one could imagine for a morning repast. Casually he selected a bannock smothered with heather honey.

She turned and gazed at him with eyes as green as clover. "Ah, Nicholas, are you enjoying your first formal gathering as laird of Rivendell?" Cold air had pinkened her nose and cheeks.

"How could I not enjoy such a well-organized feast? It seems the duchess has mastered the art of entertainment." He gave her his best smile. "You look quite fetching, by the way."

"You cannot disarm me with compliments. If you seek to pacify me, I suggest you try another method."

"I fear I am running out of ideas," he admitted. "Rather, there is a certain matter we must discuss. Robert McQuade found a piece of cowhide on a Rivendell saddle, and claims the hide belonged to one of his dead calves—"

"Surely you do not mean to suggest I killed McQuade's calves."

"Not at all. I merely wanted to explain the implications—"

"I already know the implications," she hissed, drawing him into a cove between two bushes. After making sure none of the guests had wandered within earshot, she continued, "You think the grimalkin killed McQuade's cattle. Well, not once has the grimalkin attacked anything larger than a rabbit. And never with that kind of viciousness. I really think—"

He swooped down and shut her jabbering mouth with one firm kiss. The faint taste of honey clung to her lips, which were tender and warm against his.

Stiff in his grasp, she fought him at first, pushing at his chest. "Let me go."

He moved more gently against her mouth, telling her he loved her with his kiss rather than words. Within moments she'd capitulated, opening her lips and melting into him, and he deepened the kiss, the possibility of their discovery only heightening his pleasure.

At length, he lifted his head and gazed at her. "I do not think the grimalkin responsible for McQuade's loss of cattle."

She put a hand to her forehead. "You've the touch of the devil. I forget everything when you kiss me like that." A shaky laugh suddenly emerged from her. "What did you say?"

He remained serious. "I do not believe the grimalkin killed McQuade's calves. I think, in fact, the perpetrator is human."

Quickly he outlined the meager facts he'd gathered regarding the killings, and proposed his theory that the killer had access to Rivendell horses and probably lived on Rivendell grounds.

"So you see," he said in conclusion, "you're going to have to forsake your walks through the moors and trips into Kildonan until we've found the offender."

Much to his relief, she nodded her acquiescence. "I quite agree. I shall pass the word to all of our servants."

Somewhere close by, a horn blew, its strident cry summoning all hunt participants.

He gave her a harassed glance. "I must go. We'll talk more of this later." After touching her lips with a finger as a gesture of parting, he went off to join the field.

Catherine watched as the cavalry of mounted aristocrats chased after the hounds to a suspected covert, their horses' hooves pounding like distant thunder. A bright splash of reds and whites against the winter-dull moors, the men wore an expression of savagery that seemed at odds with their tailored clothes. The women, for their part, blended in with the scenery, their riding habits of browns and greens quite drab compared to the men's brilliant plumage.

When the covert proved empty, the riders veered off deeper into the moors, following the huntsman's directions. She easily identified Nicholas, the tallest man in the pack astride a black hunter. He glanced at her as he rode away and a thrill shot through her at the promise in his gray eyes. Lips tightening, she espied Clarissa in her slate-gray riding habit close behind him. The hounds' baying faded as the riders disappeared over a knoll.

" 'Tis good to see you mingling with people of your own station, Duchess," a female voice said.

Catherine turned and met the cool blue gaze of Elizabeth Gordon, Countess of Sutherland. Her husband, the Marquess of Stafford, was perhaps the most notorious "improver" in the Highlands, driving the Sutherland clan off the land like dogs. Catherine had heard many tales about the Great Lady of Sutherland. Cozy within her English mansion, she'd mourned her clan's fate the same way marriageable women bemoaned the end of a Season.

"I'm quite pleased you found some time to visit us. Will you be staying the week?" Catherine glanced at the diamonds hanging around the woman's throat, at the rich braid trimming along her robe of *gros de Naples,* and decided the Countess of Sutherland was the most selfish woman she'd ever met.

The countess linked Catherine's arm in her own. "Of course we will stay. The country dance you've planned for Saturday sounds quite entertaining. Shall we walk?" She inclined her head toward a stone path around the castle, the ostrich plume atop her cork hat pointing at Catherine like an angry finger.

Catherine searched for a plausible excuse and found none. As detestable as she found the woman, she could not cut her directly; to do so would risk the anger of some of the most influential people in Scotland. "For a few minutes, perhaps. I have an errand—"

"Good." Lady Elizabeth pulled her down the path. "Much has happened at Holyrood since your last visit. Indeed, do you remember James Innes-Ker, fifth Duke of Roxburghe? He is in poor health, and many expect he will not see another year at Court. . . ."

Catherine allowed her thoughts to drift away as the woman prattled on. She touched her lips with one finger, remembering Nicholas's kiss. She had begun to realize that no matter how far she strayed from Nicholas, love would always bring her back to him. Nothing he said or did would change that fact.

Ultimately, these periods of hostility between them were not only tiresome but unproductive. She imagined some divine force had set two plates before her, one containing ambrosia and the other sheep dung. She had to eat one; and yet, she kept selecting the sheep dung. Did it not make far more sense to choose ambrosia and resolve this latest difficulty with Nicholas?

". . . and Fiona discovered her husband in that tart's bed. 'Twas quite a scandal, let me tell you." Lady Elizabeth wiggled her eyebrows almost comically, her sharp tone drawing Catherine back to the present.

"How shocking," she murmured. Tired of the woman's scandal mongering, she searched for an excuse to leave the countess's side. "I'm sorry, Lady Elizabeth, but I have an errand to run in the village that I can neglect no longer. A child has fallen ill, and I must bring medicines." She hoped the thought of mingling with commoners would deter Elizabeth from joining her on her "errand."

The countess shuddered. "Why, my dear, you cannot desert your guests. Have a servant run this errand for you."

Barely suppressing a smile at the success of her plan, Catherine spoke with feigned sadness. "I have taken a liking to this child and have personally attended her this past week. I will return within the hour, before anyone notices my absence."

"If you must." Nodding, Lady Elizabeth wandered away.

Rather than have the countess catch her in a lie, Catherine selected a basket of scones from a table, threw a linen cloth over the pastries, and started down toward Kildonan. The leaves in the distant forest had changed from oranges and yellows to a dull brown, and the sun had that peculiar glare it only displayed during winter months. Dead branches and dried stalks of wildflowers covered the moors, turning them a nondescript gray.

She'd just passed a peat bog coated with frozen muck when she heard a high-pitched laugh. Curious, she veered off the path and peered through a copse of denuded bushes.

A black hunter and a dainty gray mare stood tied to a sapling. Both horses sniffed the air and looked in her direction, and the hunter began to paw the ground. Nearby, a large man dressed in a red hunting jacket and white breeches examined the bare ankle of a woman, her slate-gray riding habit bunched around her calves.

Catherine drew in a deep, shocked breath.

Nicholas's head shot up, his gaze finding hers and holding it.

She began to step backward, away from the couple, air wheezing in her throat. The urge to confront them was almost as great as the urge to run. But as before, she refused to give Clarissa the satisfaction of knowing she'd made Catherine jealous. Her stomach clenching, she gave in to the urge to run, as fast as she could, down into the village.

Although stones and broken sticks littered the path, she made it onto the main thoroughfare without falling once. Rather than alert the entire neighborhood to her discomposure, she slowed and stalked toward the Temperance Inn, her head one large, throbbing ache. Sometime during her mad dash, she'd lost the basket of scones.

Not again, Nicholas, she thought. *Not again.* Sheep dung suddenly didn't seem so disagreeable at all.

Still, as her heart ceased to hammer in her breast and her lungs stopped burning, she began to think more clearly. She'd made many incorrect assumptions the last time she'd observed the Englishwoman and Nicholas in a compromising position. Clarissa herself had admitted she didn't want Nicholas, so perhaps the encounter was innocent, as Nicholas would no doubt explain.

As she passed the Temperance Inn, Catherine decided to give her husband a chance to defend himself. A mistake committed once, she reminded herself, is understandable. The same mistake committed twice, however, is stupidity. She would not let Clarissa fool her again.

Calm settled over her during the walk back to Rivendell. She stopped in the same spot she'd seen Nicholas and the Englishwoman, but they'd disappeared, along with her basket of scones. Her pace brisk, she left the copse behind and returned to the castle, where riders had already begun to return from the hunt. Harry rode at the head of the field, a brush, tail, and four pads affixed to his saddle.

A tentative smile curving her lips, she waved to the riders who dismounted near the stables. The other clan women surged forward to greet them, but fearing the horses' reaction to her presence, she remained in the courtyard. A few minutes later, Annabella rode in with McQuade, and as far as Catherine could tell, they seemed in harmony with each other. Mulling this development over, she almost missed Nicholas as he dismounted by MacDuff, his hair windblown and cheeks ruddy with vigor. His smile flashed at her across the crowd before several Scotsmen pulled him away.

Nicholas, she mused, would be less than pleased to learn how cozy his mother had become with Robert McQuade. But rather than waste her time worrying about something she couldn't change, she dismissed the pair from her mind and considered more pleasant thoughts.

She knew Nicholas would seek her out for another intimate discussion regarding Clarissa's latest stratagem. How ironic, she mused, that the Englishwoman, who'd sought to drive them apart, would instead bring them together. Justice had ultimately maintained an even and scrupulous balance.

Sixteen

Nicholas watched Catherine from across the dining room, trying to gauge her emotions. Clarissa, the sneaky chit, had again caused trouble for him. If she hadn't taken the jump so close behind him, he thought, her hunter wouldn't have hesitated and she wouldn't have lurched forward. Even so, he didn't quite believe the jump had twisted Clarissa's ankle, for her skin hadn't shown any signs of swelling, not even a red mark or scrape. As a gentleman, however, he'd have been lax in his duty if he hadn't stopped at her cry and offered assistance.

He could only hope Catherine would remember the Englishwoman's previous duplicity and withhold judgment until they'd spoken.

A warm draft blew through the room, fluttering the ends of the white linen tablecloth at his knees and even blowing out a candle. Footmen hustled forward to relight the errant wick, one of almost a hundred tapers set in sconces, chandeliers, and brass holders. The flames reflected off the diamonds and other gems dangling from the women's necks. Indeed, Nicholas thought this the most glittering, well-lit dinner he'd ever hosted. Unfortunately the decor outshone the conversation, for everyone seemed absorbed in maudlin

Jacobite fantasies. Even the mounted stags' heads on the wall drooped with boredom.

Accordingly he turned his thoughts to the scene with Clarissa earlier today. He remembered how the chit had sidled up to him, and afterward, how he'd realized he'd lost his skean. He'd worn the knife to display his approval of the Scots and their ways, but as knives went, it wasn't a prize. No jewels, no gold, just a sharpened piece of metal with an ivory handle.

Why would Clarissa have stolen it from him?

He shook his head. She couldn't have taken the skean. She had no reason to. He must have lost it during one of his jumps.

Catherine's laughter, rising above the conversation, caught his attention. Apparently MacDonnell of Glengarry, who sat next to her, had made quite a joke, for she'd convulsed with giggles. Nicholas felt like flinging a piece of beef at the redheaded laird. Although Glengarry appeared well over forty, he had a muscular physique and a certain twinkle in his eye that most women evidently couldn't resist.

Nicholas consoled himself with the knowledge that Glengarry had cleared his corner of the Highlands with almost as much fervor as the Marquess of Stafford. No blacker mark, in Catherine's view, could be placed against the man. She might be giggling now, but later, when they were alone, she would rail against the laird's selfishness.

He waved away a bowl of steaming parsley-potato soup, its aroma tempting him not. Instead, he kept his gaze focused on Catherine. Presiding at the foot of the table, she glowed with life, her honey-flame hair arranged in curls threaded with gold cord. Indeed, she looked like Venus herself, dressed in a flowing creation of gold tulle over white satin. Glengarry sent her an appreciative look from beneath his red brows, and Nicholas promptly decided the dinner had dragged on far too long.

His need to speak to Catherine about Clarissa's latest ploy had become a physical thing, gnawing at him the way a rat chewed into a sack of grain. He wanted to clear himself of wrongdoing in her view. As a fresh, penetrating odor swept through the room and Catherine stirred restlessly in her seat, he did a quick mental calculation and realized the grimalkin would soon awaken.

Prickling fear chased down his spine. Would someone find a dead calf on the moors tomorrow and undermine his belief in the grimalkin's innocence?

He gestured to the footman hovering by his side and spoke into his ear. "Have Mrs. Finlay send out the dessert course. Now. And tell her I want the desserts removed from the table no more than ten minutes later."

"Yes, Your Grace." The footman inclined his head and disappeared toward the kitchen.

In record time, a lavish spread of puddings, creams, and tarts graced the table. They disappeared back into the kitchen even more speedily. As a servant lifted the last dish off the linen tablecloth, Nicholas stood. "Ladies, I invite you to join my wife in the drawing room."

A few grizzly heads gave him an oblique glance of disapproval. Scotsmen, Nicholas had learned, enjoyed their dinner almost as much as he enjoyed tumbling his wife. Several obviously did not appreciate being forced to part with Mrs. Finlay's puddings. Remaining firm despite a chorus of grunts as the last tart left the room, he nodded to Catherine.

Following his lead, she led a troop of satin- and muslin-clad women away, leaving the men to more relaxed conversation and port or brandy. Nicholas, however, felt far from relaxed. His fingers tapping against the table, he waited a scandalously short amount of time before hustling his male guests into the drawing room with the women.

For once, the drawing room felt warm; the excess of bodies pressed together had heated it far more efficiently than the fireplace. Women clustered in twos and threes, some of them laughing, the more important personages holding court, and several old dames whispering. The card table that had so long been his companion was pushed up against the wall and now sported a series of tea, coffee, and fragrant cakes rather than ivory gaming chips.

He espied his mother by the card table and made directly for her side.

"Nicholas, boy, why have you joined us already?" the

dowager asked as he approached. "Can you not leave the ladies alone?"

"Not *ladies,* Mother, *lady*. Duchess, in fact. Where is she?"

"She complained of a headache and retired early." Annabella raised an eyebrow. "Have you two quarreled lately? I thought her more testy than a cat in a rainstorm."

Nicholas stiffened. His mother had not only struck far too close to the truth but had confirmed his fears as well. The grimalkin would indeed make an appearance tonight.

Ignoring the dowager's raised eyebrow, he turned to the assemblage. "I'm afraid I will have to retire for the night," he explained, forcing a note of fatigue into his voice. "I shall see you all on the morrow."

"Tell the truth, laddie," someone called out. "Ye're following yer pretty wife tae bed!"

Grateful that the lusty Scotsman had masked his own true motivation even further, he pasted a smile on his face and, amid laughter, left the drawing room. The servants had neglected to close one set of drapes in the central hall, revealing a bloated moon. Clenching his jaw, he raced up the staircase, strode down a drafty corridor, and stopped before Catherine's bedchamber.

He banged on the door. Made of oak and attached to the frame with iron hinges, the door looked strong enough to protect a maiden's chastity from the most energetic invader. "Catherine, open the door."

Nobody answered.

He turned the doorknob.

It didn't budge.

Footsteps echoed in the hall behind him. He swung around and startled a maidservant, who dropped the pile of bed linen she'd clutched in her hands.

"Have you seen the duchess?"

"Aye, Yer Grace. I heard her tell Mary not tae disturb her the rest o' the nicht."

He dismissed her with a nod and she scuttled away. Clinging to one last hope, he returned to his own apartments. Only a single oil lamp glowed from within the sitting room, leaving the furniture shrouded in darkness. A few embers glowed within the hearth, adding to the feeling of gloom. He imagined phantoms hid in the room's murkiest corners.

A loud snore caught his attention. Rupert lay on a settee, his mouth open, his chest rising and falling in the smooth rhythm of sleep.

"Wake up, man," Nicholas ordered, his exasperation with his servant tempered by the urgency of his own quest.

Rupert jumped to attention at the sound of Nicholas's voice.

"Your Grace. Forgive me. Another guest required my services and left me quite weary—"

"Find Fragprie and ask him for the key to my wife's chamber."

His face bland, the valet left the sitting room, only to return a short time later with Fragprie. The Scotsman's kilt rode askew on his hips and he searched the room with a wide-eyed stare. When he espied Nicholas standing in the shadows, he swallowed.

"The duchess possesses the only key to her bedchamber, Your Grace," Fragprie said, a tremor in his voice. "Is there a problem?"

Nicholas examined him with narrowed eyes. The man acted as if he'd committed a crime. "No, you may go," he said, resolving to watch Fragprie more closely.

Fragprie spun on his heel and left on quick feet. Rupert, however, hesitated.

"Both of you," Nicholas added. He heard the irritation in his voice and made an effort to calm himself.

Rupert bowed. "If I can be of further service—"

"Go!"

After the valet left, Nicholas strode to the window and searched the moors beyond. He'd lingered too long in the dining room with the men, he told himself. While he'd cast numerous glances at the clock, Catherine had returned to her bedchamber and the wildness had claimed her. Although the cold November air had edged the heather and thickets with frost, making outdoor excursions unlikely, he prayed that none of his guests had strayed into the courtyard and witnessed Catherine's transformation.

Almost shaking with urgency, he tore off his evening

clothes and shrugged into his tattered kilt and plaid. On the wall, a large, misformed shadow-man danced, copying his movements with mocking intent. As he pulled on his brogues, however, Nicholas noticed another shadow join his on the wall. An elongated, thin shadow, it stretched to the ceiling. He heard a soft footfall only a second before something very hard descended on the back of his neck.

Pain exploded in his head.

He clawed at the mantelshelf and fell to the floor, dragging the clock down with him. The clock smashed against the floor with a *pop,* sending springs and cogs in all directions. His limbs stunned, his gaze fixed on the large, clawed foot of a chair, he felt smashed, too. He couldn't move, couldn't even think—agony radiated along his spine, coming in waves, bringing tears to his eyes.

He moaned.

The clawed foot he stared at blurred and then doubled itself, spinning across his line of vision like a witch upon a frisky broom.

He closed his eyes.

How long he lay like that, he didn't know. Too benumbed to do anything more than groan, he heard several of his guests retire to their rooms for the night.

At length, the clawed foot ceased its spinning and his hands and feet began to tingle. Gingerly he drew himself onto one elbow and stared out the window. The eastern horizon remained a deep black, one that seemed to absorb light itself.

If he could get his arse moving, he told himself, he still might reach Catherine before dawn and bring her home. Someone very menacing roamed the castle and the moors around Rivendell. Although the blow to his neck had left him insensible for quite a while, Nicholas thought if it had been placed just a touch differently, it could have left him dead.

Questions and theories tumbled through his head. He speculated on who'd bludgeoned him, and why, and if it was linked to the calf killings.

Fragprie had acted damned strange tonight.

And Harry had shown his claws by taunting him about the pianoforte.

McQuade certainly had a reason to hate the MacClellands and anyone connected to the clan.

Indeed, the longer Nicholas speculated, the longer the list of suspects grew. All the while, some part him thought about Catherine, wondering if she was safe, or even now at the mercy of a vicious animal killer.

He groaned, his logic deserting him in the face of a lingering throb behind his temples. He had to find Catherine.

With that fundamental need urging him on, he hauled himself to his feet and waited several seconds for a bout of nausea to subside. When he felt capable of walking, he stumbled over to the seaman's chest. The blow to his neck had left him unable to turn his head, so he groped for the skean Rupert had procured for him, withdrew it from the chest, and tucked it into his belt. Then, with a dubious shuffle, he limped out of the castle and into the night.

His search for the grimalkin progressed slowly and painfully. He found not the slightest trace of the wildcat, even near Dun Strathnaver, the ancient broch that had once protected him from a thunderstorm. Cold air worked itself deep into his bones and he shivered, cursing the grimalkin even as he feared for Catherine. At length, he decided to wait for the wildcat by Bodhan's Pond, for he knew without doubt that she'd eventually return there. His gait awkward, he retraced his steps to Bodhan's Pond.

He craved a pint of Macallan whisky. He yearned for a crackling fire. As he settled behind the customary thicket near the grimalkin's cave, he longed for the grimalkin. But when his last desire was granted, he abruptly wished he were anywhere else. The same moist, rusted-iron smell he'd detected a month before wafted through the air like a noisome fog, heralding her appearance.

He grew stiff with suspense.

Thump crackle crackle . . .

Thump crackle crackle . . .

Glowing with an inner fire, the grimalkin hitched into the clearing, a large bag of some sort grasped between her jaws. Her tail low and ears back, she placed each paw carefully, making nary a mark on the dirt. Part of the bag dragged across the ground and left broken stems in its wake.

Thump crackle crackle . . .

She stopped and dropped the bag. It seemed to fall apart once it hit the ground. The smell of blood grew stronger.

Nicholas began to suspect that the bag wasn't a bag at all. Between the folds of brown fabric, he detected a glint of ivory, and a string—or a ribbon. Panic shot through him and he jumped up to get an unimpeded view of the bag. As he stared, his eyeballs grew hot in their sockets.

Good Christ, that's ugly.

The thought, unbidden, strayed into his head as he gaped at the mass of entrails that leaked from the woman's midsection. Bits of grass and dirt stuck to her glistening organs.

He'd never seen anything like this before. Ripped skin, loops of intestines . . . it looked so alien, so very wrong.

His gaze traveled higher. The woman's eyes were so wide he could see white all around, and her mouth had frozen in a rictus, as if she'd died in the middle of a scream. A cloak had twisted around her neck, hiding further damage. Although he didn't know her name, he recognized her face. She'd sat next to him at the Temperance Inn the night Catherine had danced for him.

He heard a wheezing sound and realized it was coming from him.

The grimalkin stared at him, her glittering eyes unfathomable. Abruptly she picked the body up by the tatters of clothing that covered it and began to drag it toward him like some grisly offering.

After a few seconds he became aware of a bitter smell, the relentless scholar in him identifying it as bile. He stood so close to the body—and the odor was so strong—that he could taste bile in his own mouth. He began to shake as if he were naught but a sapling caught in a gale-force breeze. Somewhere inside, he moaned.

She dropped the body at his feet, sniffed it once, and growled low in her throat.

What does she want me to do, he thought crazily, *call a surgeon?*

Evidently feeling she'd left the body in capable hands, the grimalkin turned and padded off into the forest.

Shock, horror, disgust—they stirred in his gut until he thought he would scream or go mad. Some heartsick part of him realized he'd found the calf killer. Just like last month, Catherine had discovered him in a compromising situation with Clarissa directly before she'd changed to the grimalkin. And as before, her human fury at Clarissa had transferred to the cat, this time encouraging it to brutalize this woman whose brown hair looked remarkably like Clarissa's.

He clenched his teeth. The grimalkin had become a killer of the worst kind, one with a taste for human flesh.

He could not hold back a groan. It forced its way through his teeth and echoed eerily through the clearing.

He would have to move the body. That much was obvious. He didn't want to attract any attention to this area, for fear of drawing villagers to the grimalkin's lair and accidentally revealing Catherine's secret. He'd also have to leave Rivendell at once. The stress of his appearance in Catherine's life had proved too much for her, turning her into a killer. Perhaps once he'd gone she would revert to rabbits.

A bray of wild laughter escaped him and startled a pheasant to flight.

Congealed blood stained his kilt and plaid as he picked the body up and began to pull it onto the moors. Pain lanced through his neck and upper shoulders, driving him to his knees several times. His gorge rose and he fought the urge to vomit as more of the woman's intestines flopped out of her midsection and dragged through the grass.

Then he did something he hadn't done since childhood. He prayed for strength to get through the night. But his pious words fell from wooden lips. Satan, he thought, would more likely answer his prayers, for his work this eve had more in common with hell than heaven.

After he'd put a suitable distance between himself and Bodhan's Pond, he found a niche between two boulders and dropped the body in, pity for the woman who'd died so horribly mixing with guilt over his own role in the affair.

Having disposed of the evidence, he stumbled back to Rivendell, and, ignoring the groom's audible gasp at his appearance—smeared from foot to chest with blood—he saddled Beelzebub and mounted. The horse, evidently distressed by the smell of blood, pawed and pranced and fought him every step of the way, but Nicholas barely noticed. Blessed numbness had stolen over him, one more emotional than physical, and many of the night's events had already begun to dissolve in a haze. *Have to leave,* he thought, the reasons behind his departure becoming more nebulous by the minute.

He kicked Beelzebub on the flanks. The great stallion took off like a stone released from a catapult. He guided the horse in the general direction of Kildonan, and in a few minutes he'd pounded down the main thoroughfare and come out the other side. Wind blew through his hair, taking some of the blood-smell with it, and he closed his eyes. Slumping in the saddle, he held on to Beelzebub's mane and let the horse take him where it would. He simply didn't have the strength to do anything else.

He did not become aware of his surroundings until Beelzebub stopped. Sides quivering, air blowing through his nostrils in puffs, the horse shook his head, the jingle of his bridle loud in the hushed night.

Nicholas lifted his head and stared at the ruins of Dun Strathnaver shimmering in the moonlight. He heard nothing but Beelzebub, saw nothing but stone, smelled only the fear and sweat on his own body. Preternatural stillness held the broch in its thrall, reminding Nicholas of a broken clock whose jammed gears strained to move forward.

"You great, stupid bastard," he muttered to Beelzebub, "you were supposed to bring me at least to the next village." Unnerved by the odd tension in the air, he pulled on the reins, swung the horse around, and urged him forward. Beelzebub stubbornly remained still. A few snorts blew from his nostrils.

The sense of expectancy in the broch heightened.

"Move, old boy."

The horse shifted on his hooves and began to backstep. Nicholas felt his saddle swell as Beelzebub took in a great breath of air.

"Good Christ, what's gotten into you?"

A large shadow that seemed to glow from within detached itself from the ruins of Dun Strathnaver and slunk toward them. Beelzebub began to stamp the ground, a low whinny issuing from his throat. Nicholas knew the horse was about to dump him, but as he didn't care to meet that shadow on his feet, he cleaved to Beelzebub's back.

The golden shadow crept forward and into a ray of moonlight. Nicholas felt his throat dry. Tawny fur, bright green eyes, four legs bunching with muscles . . .

"Move, damn it." Nicholas kicked the beast beneath him hard. He didn't want to end up the grimalkin's next victim. Indeed, he'd been the cause of the wildcat's ire, so it made sense the grimalkin would try to disembowel him next, as the ultimate resolution to her difficulties.

Beelzebub, however, had wholly fixed his attention on the grimalkin, and gave Nicholas no more attention than one might give an annoying fly. He hitched back and forth and then began to rear like a yearling with a weight on its back. On the third try the horse sent Nicholas flying through the air.

Barely missing a jutting boulder, he landed on his arse. The collision jarred his spine, sending a new shaft of pain through his body. If he made it through the night, he thought, it would be a bloody miracle.

The grimalkin sat back on her haunches and looked at him. Tail wrapped around her legs, a low hum emitting from her throat, she seemed completely at ease—and far from the ravening killer he'd imagined her to be.

Remaining perfectly still, he examined the clean lines of her, the well-formed muscles and sinews, the soft fur with a darker undercoat. Despite her aura, she appeared more gray than golden in the moonlight, and her ears now pointed upward, as if she remained respectfully at attention.

He glanced at her muzzle. Noted the clean fur, long whiskers . . .

Clean fur.

A mental image of the grimalkin carrying the body between her jaws formed in his mind. She'd grasped the body by its clothes, he recalled.

No blood.

There hadn't been a drop of blood on the grimalkin, anywhere.

He sat up, sending a fresh wave of agony through his body. His mind raced ahead of the pain.

Surely if the grimalkin had disemboweled that woman, he thought, blood would have smeared her from head to paw. Why, just by dragging the body across the moors, he'd damned near soaked his plaid and kilt with the foul stuff.

Had he made a terrible mistake?

He stared at her with wide eyes. "Why did you bring her to me?"

The grimalkin tilted her head, the hum from her throat growing louder.

"You didn't kill her, did you?" He hauled himself to his feet and took a step toward her, his eyes averted, palms up in a nonthreatening gesture.

Her legs folded and she lay down.

"You brought her to me to warn me," he guessed, making eye contact again. "Maybe you even thought I could help her."

She rolled onto her side, stretching nearly six feet across, her size intimidating him. Nevertheless, he continued to inch toward her until he stood close enough to stroke her. Trembling, he buried his hand in her fur, ready to jump away if she objected.

Playfully she swatted him with one large paw.

The wildcat's gesture had the same effect a benediction might have had on a congregation of sinners. Feeling like she'd forgiven him, accepted him, and decided to give him a second chance, he collapsed to the ground next to her and pressed his face against her tawny flank. His head and neck still ached, yes, but he felt the strength of ten men enter his bones. "You know who the killer is, don't you?"

She did not—could not—answer, but stretched beneath his caress. He inhaled the musky scent of her, his breath rustling her soft fur.

"Together we will find both this butcher and the answer to why he has killed a woman . . . and why he's taken to clubbing me."

An owl hooted somewhere nearby and wind whistled

across the heath as if mourning the loss of a loved one. A deer passed not too far in the distance, and both he and the grimalkin glanced its way.

The clock with jammed gears, Nicholas thought, had again begun to tick.

He relished the feel of her beneath his hands, the shape of her body as she sprawled in the heather. Never again would he doubt the grimalkin, for time and again she'd proved her goodness and loyalty. Catherine's heart beat strongly within the wildcat's body.

He cast a glance at the eastern horizon. The sky had changed from black to deep gray. Wishing he could extend these moments with the grimalkin a little longer, he rubbed her fur, noting how her golden aura cloaked his hand as well. He imagined they'd have many nights to learn about each other, he and his wildcat. He could not know this night would be their last.

Catherine awoke secure in her bedchamber, as usual. Beyond her windows, the sun had already begun its trek across the sky. She stretched, feeling an unusual contentment that only a night as the grimalkin could bring.

Good Lord.

She sat up abruptly, recalling bits and pieces of the night before. Her memory was hazy, but as she felt no lingering worry, she decided the change had occurred without incident. Nicholas must have carried her home from Bodhan's Pond. How pleasant it felt, after years of awakening cold and naked in a cave, to know Nicholas would care for her and protect her. He'd almost made the curse bearable.

Smiling, she snuggled beneath the counterpane. Over the last few weeks she'd noticed how his gaze followed her across the room, caught the wistful glint in his eyes when he thought she wasn't looking. He often cast a smile her way, one that revealed his affection for her without words. Indeed, he'd softened toward her considerably, and she couldn't help but hope that someday his affection would turn to love.

A loud knock interrupted her reverie.

"Come in, Mary," she called out, contentment bringing a smile to her lips.

The door swung open, revealing Nicholas rather than Mary. He strode into the room, the scent of soap trailing him. He looked out of place in her bedchamber, her delicate French chairs and bureaus making him seem absurdly large. The hair at the back of his neck curled, as if he'd recently washed.

"Nicholas. Thank you for bringing me home." She gave him an inviting smile and stretched again, pulling the bedcovers taut against her body. Yes, he'd said some foolish things to her lately, but *she'd* be the fool if she didn't learn to forgive him.

He removed his jacket and folded himself into a chair near her bedside. A lock of black hair fell across his brow, giving him a boyish aspect. The expression in his eyes, however, was far from lighthearted.

"We have much to discuss, Catherine. I fear your mood will not remain so positive once you've heard all I must say." He shifted his weight and stretched his long, buckskin-clad legs out before him.

The smile slipped from her face. She hugged the counterpane closer. "Has this something to do with the grimalkin?"

"I'm afraid so. As you must know, last night you transformed into the grimalkin. I followed you." He paused, evidently unsure how to continue.

"Please, Nicholas. What happened?"

"I found the remains of a woman on the moors."

She drew in a shocked breath.

" 'Twas the same woman—the brunette—who sat next to me in the Temperance Inn the night we celebrated the birth of MacDuff's grandson. Do you remember her?"

"Aye." Catherine more than remembered her. The woman's image had lodged itself permanently in her mind. Ample breasts, a triumphant smile . . . they still brought a sick feeling to her stomach.

But she'd never wished the woman dead.

Her heart beating wildly, she groped for courage. "How did she die?"

"Someone disemboweled her."

"Dear God! Do you think the grimalkin—"

"No." He clasped her hand and squeezed once, reassuring her. "The grimalkin found the body and dragged it to me. I smelled a bitter odor, evidence of ruptured organs that had not yet drained. The murder had obviously occurred just minutes before, and yet I detected not even a drop of blood on the grimalkin's fur. The cat simply wouldn't have had time to clean itself and then bring the body to me."

His clinical discussion of the woman stunned her almost as much as the revelation itself. And yet, she noted the stark frown on his face, the unusual paleness of his skin, and guessed he coped with what he'd seen by distancing himself from it.

She released the breath she didn't even know she'd been holding. "Thank God."

"There is something else," he continued. "The morning after McQuade's calves were killed, I found you in the grimalkin's lair, covered with blood."

"Oh, Nicholas, why didn't you tell me?"

"I thought to spare you worry. I had hoped the grimalkin, having assuaged its anger by killing those calves, would return to its normal patterns."

"The grimalkin, angry? Why?"

"McQuade's calves were killed the night you discovered Clarissa in my bedchamber. I had suspected your anger at Clarissa had transferred to the grimalkin."

Her throat constricted. "So you *do* believe the grimalkin guilty."

"No. Not anymore. The circumstances of the brunette's death fits those of the calves. The same person who murdered the calves killed the woman, and it is clear the grimalkin did *not* kill her."

"But that leaves us with one very big question. Who murdered her, and why?"

"Perhaps if we review all the facts," he offered, "we might reach a conclusion."

She nodded, encouraging him to continue.

Uncurling his large form, he stood and began to pace. Pink light flooded through the window and bathed him in a rosy glow. "First, we know that someone ripped the throats out of Robert McQuade's calves. Second, McQuade claims to have found a piece of his dead calf's hide on a MacClelland saddle. Third, someone clubbed me senseless yesterday after dinner."

She stiffened, her gaze flying to his. An ache settled around her heart at the thought of how close she'd come to losing him.

"And fourth, a woman was disemboweled on the moors last night."

He stopped by the window, shoulders slumped. "I do not see a pattern. Do you?"

Rather than answer, she climbed out of bed and joined him by the glass. Outside, an owl swooped into a dead patch of heather and clutched a mouse in its talons. Predator and prey then flew off toward the forest of Kildonan.

She touched the back of his head and felt a rather large lump. "Good Lord, Nicholas, you've a lump the size of a goose egg. Sit this instant."

"I'm fine, wife. Stop fretting."

"Nonsense." Prodding him on, she ushered him to a chair. He sat heavily and leaned his head against her bosom, his eyes closed. She ran her fingers through his hair as tenderly as she would for a child, carefully avoiding his lump. "I do not see a pattern, either," she admitted. "Let me ring for Mary. I will have her bring up some chamomile tea and a poultice to bring the swelling down."

At that moment, a knock sounded at the door and Fragprie entered without waiting for an invitation. Red blotches stained his face, as if he'd been crying. "Your Grace, Raonull discovered a woman on the moors this morning. 'Tis said she was under Robert McQuade's protection. The same wildcat who attacked McQuade's calves killed her."

Catherine drew in a breath, her shock only partly feigned. The notion of a madman wandering *her* moors both horrified and offended her. And the woman . . . to have suffered so.

Nicholas, however, remained stone-faced. "Why do you think a wildcat attacked her?"

"Raonull followed a trail of blood back to the place the woman had been killed. Paw prints—the same ones found around the dead calves—marked the forest loam all around." Fragprie wiped a hand across his forehead, blotting the sweat that had gathered there. "The MacClelland clansmen are becoming restless, Your Grace. They're talking about forming a posse to catch this wildcat and skin it alive. What should I do?"

"Make sure nobody does anything until our guests leave," Nicholas ordered. "My relatives and our Scottish friends will have left by next Monday, giving us the privacy to investigate the matter more thoroughly. In the meantime, warn all to remain within their houses from sunset to daybreak, and report anything that seems even the slightest bit odd."

Fragprie nodded and, shoulders slumped, left the room.

"Well, we have another piece to the puzzle," Catherine murmured, circling the chair to face him. "The woman was under McQuade's protection."

He nodded. "In fact, McQuade is linked in some way to every incident but one." A hint of tension had entered his voice. "His calves were killed, he found the cowhide on our saddle, and a woman under his protection was eviscerated. But I can't see any obvious connection between him and my bludgeoning."

He pulled her onto his lap. His mien, however, remained serious. "He could be trying to implicate the MacClellands in these crimes as a way of carrying on the feud between our clans."

She didn't answer right away. Rather, she luxuriated in the casual way he'd gathered her close. She'd seen that sort of intimate gesture between husbands and wives a hundred times over. He did not hold her with lust; no, he held her with a gentle ardor that told her how very much he needed her.

"Aye, McQuade's more than capable of organizing this kind of scheme, if not the murder itself," she eventually volunteered. "He's filed a claim in Helmsdale for Bodhan's Pond and the lands around it. Perhaps he seeks to discredit my family and sway the magistrate's decision in his favor."

Warming to their discussion, he rubbed his chin. "All right, we have one suspect. Who else?"

"Fragprie," she immediately answered. "He is a sneaky man with a long-standing hatred for Robert McQuade."

"Do you think him capable of murder?"

"Maybe. 'Tis hard to envision Fragprie ripping the innards from a woman's body."

They both fell silent. Catherine settled deeper into his lap and placed her ear over his heart.

Minutes passed, long minutes in which she traced his form with her eyes, trying to burn his image into her head forever.

"There is another possibility," he finally said. "Harry. He seems to take great pleasure in my discomfort lately. If I should die, Harry would inherit both my title and lands."

"But that does not give him a motive for killing those calves or the McQuade woman."

He nodded in agreement. "Harry worries more about the cut of his coat than the state of his bankbook. I find it difficult to believe he's been skulking through the moors, killing calves and women."

"What about Clarissa? She's made some rather odd statements lately."

"Such as?"

"Well, she insists she will own everything of yours."

He snorted. "She still thinks I will marry her."

"I don't think so. She said she doesn't want you."

"Good. My reprimands have finally had an impact on her." He leaned over and kissed her hair. "What you saw yesterday, during the hunt—"

"I know," she murmured, running a finger along his jawline. "She tried to drive another wedge between us."

"She took a jump too close behind me and claimed to have twisted her ankle in her stirrup. I had to respond to her cries of help or have her accuse me of the grossest negligence. I'm pleased you saw through her scheme."

"She is rather transparent. I admit I find it difficult to think of her as a murderess."

" 'Tis an impossible notion. She has neither the strength nor the cunning to kill those McQuade calves or the woman. I believe we can disregard her as a possibility." He began to play with the ribbons on her nightgown, drawing them taut but not quite pulling them free.

"You tease me unmercifully," she accused him.

He ignored her. "I can think of one more suspect."

"Who?"

"Myself."

"Nicholas, don't be foolish. I don't believe for a minute that you're responsible for any of this."

He remained perfectly still, his gray eyes harsh yet filled with longing. "Indeed, I am the bastard son of Robert McQuade. All of the incidents are affronts to McQuade. I would not blame you if you thought I invented the bludgeoning to turn suspicion away from my own guilty actions—those of revenge on a man who compromised my mother and sired a bastard upon her."

"Oh, posh!" She wagged a finger at him. "Don't try to scare me, husband. I know you far better than that. You are not capable of committing that kind of violence."

He grasped her head between his hands and kissed her hard. When he released her, she saw the gratitude in his eyes and wanted to cry. He needed her, despite all she was. And she'd given him something no one else could.

She was accepted.

She belonged.

"So, we have three suspects," she said, blinking the moisture in her eyes away. "McQuade, Fragprie, and Harry."

"Or the killer may be a rogue clansman, who kills for only one reason—pleasure."

She shivered. "What do you propose we do to flush out the culprit?"

"You will do nothing." Nicholas eyed her with a stern gaze. "I'll watch them. Wait for someone to make a mistake. And pray no one else is murdered before we discover the killer."

Seventeen

Catherine paused at the top of the staircase and watched the whirling dancers below her. Like a field of flowers caught in a breeze, the women swayed and turned to the music, their gowns of shell-pink, straw, malachite green, and crushed strawberry shimmering beneath tapers that lit the central hall. Their partners' uniforms of tartan kilt or blue superfine provided a neutral backdrop for their finery.

After smoothing her own skirt of coppery gold, Catherine descended the stone staircase. Jammed into buckram stays by the ever-diligent Mary, she felt as stiff and ceremonious as a warship setting sail. As fashion dictated, the stays shoved her bosom up to her chin, making a sort of fleshy shelf she thought nearly indecent.

Foot tapping to a blunt reel, she paused on the landing and nodded to the fiddlers and bagpipers who sawed and squeezed their instruments. She didn't dare dance for fear her bosom would escape from its silken cage. But Nicholas's admiring glances convinced her to endure the disappointment—at least until she met him alone in his apartments.

During the last week, she and Nicholas had danced a genteel mating dance, exchanging smoldering glances, soft touches, and thoughtful little gestures that kept them both breathing hard. Like a true gentleman, he'd refrained from further intimacy, instead courting her as she'd always longed to be courted, building a gentle bond between them, an understanding and respect more intoxicating than the most dedicated love play.

Eventually she'd realized that he waited for her to invite him into her bed. The notion that he would make love to her on her own terms both intrigued her and made her stomach roll. *Tonight I will have him,* she promised herself with newfound assurance in her own femininity.

Aware that Nicholas's hot gaze followed her progress across the room, she stopped to speak to MacDonnell of Glengarry and suffered the laird's intimate perusal. Noting Nicholas's frown, she smiled and moved on to less provocative guests, her heart singing over his jealousy.

Clarissa spun past on the arm of yet another swain, the hem of her lavender gown swishing against Catherine, her brown eyes alight with excitement. Occasionally the brunette's gaze locked with Harry's, some silent communication passing between them, and Catherine had to acknowledge the two seemed quite content with each other. She might even have felt happiness for them, if the killings on the moors hadn't left her so suspicious.

Instead, she observed Harry as he strolled into the drawing room. Could the fop be capable of murder, despite Nicholas's assurances? Curious, she followed him into the drawing room, which tonight served as an informal buffet and card-playing room, and checked to make sure each table remained stocked with Scottish delicacies.

Harry stood near the windows, talking to an old dame known for her deafness. The gray-haired dowager answered each of his sallies with, "Eh, my boy? What did you say?" Regardless, Harry remained at his irresistible best, lavishing the charm he'd inherited from his Italian forebears on her wrinkled face. Ever the dandy, his manners were so languid and clothes so extravagant a misinformed guest might mistake him for visiting royalty.

Suddenly she heard a most distinct noise and shot a glance in Harry's direction. He, too, looked at her, and a light flush crept over his cheeks.

Harry had just broken wind.

Pretending she hadn't heard the noise, Catherine busily adjusted the blond lace edging her sleeves. But they both knew she'd caught him.

Grasping the old dame's arm, Harry drew her out of the drawing room, sending Catherine a look of undiluted malice as he passed. Catherine had a feeling that she could have done no worse to Harry than to witness him in such an ill-bred slip. She smiled to herself and bit her tongue.

Nicholas, she thought, was right. He couldn't have murdered those calves and that woman. He wouldn't have risked dirtying his jacket.

Outside in the central hall, gongs sounded from the tall-case clock, signaling the hour had reached eleven. The fiddlers and bagpipers abruptly ceased playing and muted conversation filled the air.

The Countess of Sutherland poked her head into the drawing room and beckoned to Catherine. "The duke plans to make an announcement. He is asking for you."

An eyebrow raised, Catherine threaded her way into the central hall, Lady Elizabeth trailing in her wake. Nicholas stood three steps up on the staircase deep in conversation with a footman. He noticed her approach and smiled. Mischief glinted in his gray eyes. "I have a surprise for you," he said sotto voce.

"You look far too pleased with yourself. Should I feel nervous?" When he laughed, she added, "Why don't you give me my surprise in the laird's apartments? Indeed, I have a surprise for you, too."

Without answering he turned toward the assemblage. Although soft chatter filled the hall, all gazes had turned toward him. "I'd like to thank you all for joining us in this Yuletide season. In celebration of this glorious holiday, I would like to present my wife with a gift."

She felt her cheeks grow warm as the last talk died away. "Oh, Nicholas, really."

"Fragprie, bring it in," he ordered.

The servant nodded and walked to the doors leading outside. With a flourish, he opened them, revealing two clansmen and a large cart. A blanket covered the top of the cart, concealing its contents.

A hushed expectation filled the central hall as the two footmen wheeled the cart in, its wheels creaking and groaning under the weight of her gift. Muscles straining, they pulled the cart next to her, and with a wide grin, Nicholas yanked the blanket away.

Everyone strained forward to see what the cart contained, including Catherine.

Loud laughter broke out through the room.

"What kind o' present is that?"

"Are ye planning tae make her harvest the fields?"

"Eh, laddie, ye got a good sense o' humor," a male voice said, his observation echoed by a series of similar remarks. Her face contorted with mirth, the Countess of Sutherland covered her mouth.

Catherine felt her eyes fill with moisture. "Oh, Nicholas."

The cart contained a windmill-like apparatus attached to a wooden box. Metal glinted from within the box. She touched it with a shaking hand.

"Oh, Nicholas," she repeated. "A threshing machine."

"Twenty-five threshing machines, to be exact," he said, his grin melting into a tender smile. "One for each clan family and a few to spare."

The moisture in her eyes became tears that ran down her cheeks. She knew what his gift meant. No longer would she have to worry about her clan's welfare. Just as he protected her, he would protect all who depended on her.

How she loved him.

She climbed the steps, threw her arms around his neck, and kissed him thoroughly. Amid a few surprised grunts and general applause from the assemblage, he kissed her back. When she finally let him go, he withdrew another package from beneath his coat. Wrapped in gauze and silken ribbons, it rattled as he handed it to her.

"This, too, is for you," he said.

"You will undo me before all our guests." Sniffling, she pulled the ribbons. The silk fell apart, revealing a malachite box, which she opened.

"I will undo you alone, tonight," he whispered.

Inside the box, a handful of emeralds and diamonds, connected by a fine gold chain, sparkled against black velvet. She touched the necklace with one reverent finger. " 'Tis beautiful." The urge to cry returned with even more force.

"No more so than you," he told her. His hands sure, he unclasped her crystal pendant—the same one that contained his wedding ring, twisted in a figure eight.

Gooseflesh erupted across her skin.

Like a bank of storm clouds that had blotted out the sun, the pendant seemed to take all the heat away from her body. She stared up at the beloved planes of Nicholas's face, at the crystal pendant he held in his hand.

I will lose him to darkness.

The mad notion popped into her mind and she quashed the desire to snatch the crystal teardrop from his grasp and settle it back around her neck. The pendant, she told herself, was nothing more than glass and metal.

Stop acting the part of a superstitious fool.

Surprised at her own whimsical fancies, she bent her head forward. He picked up the diamond and emerald necklace and fastened it around her neck. His breath blew against her nape, and suddenly she felt a kiss pressed against the spot where her hair met skin. Smiling, she leaned into him.

"That's more like it, Your Grace," that same male voice said. "Ye can't bed her if ye doan bribe her."

Laughter once again filled the central hall. The men surged forward to thump Nicholas on the back, and the women clustered around Catherine to examine her necklace. Catherine felt the gaze of a certain Englishwoman burn into her, but she ignored the enmity in that gaze and smiled.

No one, not even Clarissa, would spoil this night, she promised herself.

Catherine's response to his gifts couldn't have pleased Nicholas more. He'd tried through deeds to tell her how much he loved her, and tonight, after the last guest had either left or retired to his rooms, he would tell her through words.

Leaning against one wall, Harry by his side, he watched

a footman approach her with a piece of folded paper on a salver.

"You're quite the charmer tonight," he said to Harry, his gaze focused on Catherine. "Several ladies have asked me for an introduction."

Catherine retrieved the paper, opened it, and read it. Her brows gathered together and a frown curved her lips.

Harry straightened the lapels of his pea-green coat. " 'Tis the Yuletide season, coz. Brings out the best in me."

With one quick look around the central hall, Catherine hurried after the footman toward the servants' quarters.

Harry continued talking, but Nicholas dismissed him from thought. A small knot had formed in his stomach. Catherine looked far too worried to suit him.

"I say, Nicky, what's wrong?" Harry leaned closer. "You haven't heard a word I've said."

Nicholas cast a distracted glance in Harry's direction. "My wife left the room with undue haste."

The dandy laughed low in his throat. "I never thought I'd see the day. His Grace, the Duke of Efington, in service to a skirt."

"She's my wife."

"For God's sake, relax." Harry shook his head, the movement stiff due to the height of his necktie. "Your Mrs. Finlay probably ran into some difficulty that only the mistress of the house could resolve. Cooks are flighty. They need constant reminders of their own worth."

Nicholas hesitated. He did not want to hover around Catherine like an overzealous nanny and didn't think she'd appreciate such attention, either.

He felt a tap on his shoulder and turned around. Rupert stood behind him, his face uncharacteristically red.

"You have a visitor in your apartments, Your Grace," the valet said.

"And this visitor's name?" Reluctantly he turned his thoughts from Catherine.

"His Lordship, the Earl of Bucharrie." Rupert curled his lips into a frown of distaste. "Shall I have him forcibly removed?"

Nicholas stiffened. He wondered if he was about to unmask the murderer. "No. Thank you, Rupert. I'll attend to it myself, right away."

He excused himself to Harry, and after stopping in the study to retrieve the pistols that had just arrived from London, he entered his apartments and found the laird pawing through the wooden wardrobe in his sitting room. Several jackets of blue superfine lay scattered across chairs and settees.

"Hold, McQuade," Nicholas warned, the pistol aimed at the Scotsman's back, "before I have you arrested for thievery." He assessed the jumble McQuade had made of his clothes. "Had I known you'd grown so fond of English attire, I would have sent you to my tailor."

McQuade turned around slowly, his face suffused with red. He had one hand shoved deep into a pocket of his own jacket. Behind him, several empty hangers hung on a wooden rack. "Are ye a ghost, tae sneak up on me sae quietly?"

Both eyebrows raised, Nicholas lowered the gun and crossed his arms over his chest. "You have the blush of a guilty man, McQuade. Why are you looking through my clothes, and what do you have in your pocket?"

"This." The Scotsman withdrew a swatch of dark fabric and extended it toward Nicholas. "I thought I might find a match for it in yer closet. But unless ye keep another set o' coats somewhere, I can see I was wrong."

Examining the fabric by the light of an oil lamp, Nicholas noted its fine texture and questionable color.

Puce superfine.

Fabric used in a man's evening coat.

"I don't understand," Nicholas finally said, thinking his father had again strayed into the realms of daft reasoning.

"O' course ye don't, laddie. Ye wouldn't unless you'd killed my calves. I found this piece o' wool near the place my calves were butchered. At first I thought the killings the work o' a wildcat, but no wildcat wears a gentleman's evening coat."

Vaguely Nicholas recalled the laird brandishing a piece of dark fabric at him in Kildonan the morning he'd gone to fetch Catherine from Bodhan's Pond. The same morning, in fact, that McQuade had discovered the calves. And McQuade's voice held the intensity of truth.

Still, the Scotsman seemed the most likely suspect for the killings. Nicholas decided to prod him, hard, in the hope he'd reveal something incriminating.

"How do I know you're not hiding compromising evidence in my wardrobe in an attempt to implicate me in the murders? Will the magistrate be stopping by tomorrow? Good God, man, you're transparent."

As if someone had lit a fire beneath his feet, McQuade became bright red. His limbs shook and his gaze nailed Nicholas to the floor. "This is the second time ye've suggested such a thing. Do ye think I'd kill a woman simply tae implicate ye? For what purpose?"

"There's a certain border dispute between the MacClellands and McQuades regarding Bodhan's Pond. Surely the magistrate would decide in an innocent man's favor before a murderer's?"

"Aaarrrggghh!" McQuade swung out, his hamlike fist connecting squarely with Nicholas's jaw.

Nicholas staggered back a few steps before catching himself on a settee. He rubbed his jaw. "Quite a punch you have there, McQuade."

In the shadows beyond the doorway, he noticed Harry, standing with his fists clenched, ready to charge the laird. He gave his cousin a negative shake of the head.

McQuade advanced on him, shoulders hunched, eyes narrowed. "Do ye know who that woman was? My sister's daughter. I wouldna murder my own niece for a bloody pond." Spittle flew from his mouth.

"I'll have ye know, Efington, yer factor was shagging her every night. Got her wi' child, he did. 'Twas on her way home from a tryst wi' Fragprie that the killer murdered her." McQuade stopped, his face mere inches from Nicholas's. "He was going tae marry her. But I forbade the marriage. A McQuade would never stoop tae marry a MacClelland, nor anyone in service to the MacClellands."

Nicholas felt his eyes widen at these new revelations. The dead woman, also Fragprie's lover? He remembered Fragprie's odd behavior the night before, the way the Scotsman's kilt had ridden askew on his hips. When he'd asked for a key to Catherine's bedchamber, Nicholas thought, he must have interrupted Fragprie in the middle of a tumble.

Would Fragprie have murdered the woman he wished to marry, and who carried his child?

Not likely.

Would McQuade have killed his own niece in an effort to discredit the MacClellands?

Not likely.

A chill came over him. That left two possibilities: a rogue clansman, or Harry.

McQuade poked Nicholas in the chest. "What have ye tae say, Efington?"

Nicholas had to admire the old bastard. He had the ballocks of a longhorn—tough as shoe leather and twice as hard. "I had not known the victim's identity. I apologize for suggesting you had some hand in the deed." He made a placating gesture. "Tomorrow, my guests from London are leaving. Shall we work together to banish this killer from the moors?"

Some of the fire left McQuade's gaze. He took a step backward. "I have not told anyone about this piece o' fabric, for I doan want tae give the murderer a reason tae fly. I ask ye tae keep it a secret, too."

"Of course." Nicholas nodded. If McQuade hadn't compromised Annabella all those years ago, he mused, he might even like the old duffer. He had fire in him, a welcome change from the apathy of the London peerage. "Would you like to meet here, or at Kinclaven?"

"Kinclaven. Noon." Back stiff, McQuade turned on his heel and marched away, sparing a disgusted sneer for Harry.

Harry sauntered into the room, shaking his head. "Quite a scene, coz. McQuade's daft, is he not?"

"Perhaps." Aware of a queer protectiveness for McQuade, Nicholas said no more. Rather, he studied Harry through narrowed eyes. The dandy looked so harmless, with his graceful airs and charm and lazy smile. They went back years, he and his cousin. Harry had always been a diffident child. Could he have turned into a monster when Nicholas wasn't looking?

No. He simply couldn't believe Harry guilty.

Together they turned and walked back into the central hall. Nicholas's mottled chin—evidence of fisticuffs—drew several stares, but propriety dictated he remain with his guests. Propriety also dictated, he thought, that his wife remain with their guests. Where was she?

Nodding to acquaintances, Nicholas procured a glass of wine from a passing footman. "Do you see Catherine anywhere?"

Harry took up post nearby. "Can't say that I do. Shall we look for her?"

"Well . . . yes." Nicholas ran a hand through his hair.

The two men split up and began to work their way through the crowd of dancers. Nicholas paused to question those who stood on the outskirts of the dance floor, but no one seemed to know where his wife had disappeared to. When his mother danced by on the arm of an elderly Scottish statesman, he tapped the Scotsman on his shoulder and took his place.

"You've been in a scrape, I see," Annabella said, her gaze fixed on the entryway rather than his chin. Indeed, she watched the entrance more than her footsteps. After stamping on Nicholas's boot, she tripped over the extended leg of some English dandy.

Nicholas caught her just in time. He had an idea who his mother was hoping to see, and the thought irritated him. "Well, Mother, you seem to have no more grace than a herd of elephants tonight."

The dowager's cheeks flushed pink. " 'Tis a terribly rude thing to say to your mother. At any rate, I can't imagine what's come over me."

"Don't be coy. We both know McQuade's come over you. I found him up in my apartments, pawing through my wardrobe, not even half an hour ago. By now he has long departed for Kinclaven. You may stop watching the door."

"He was going through your clothes? Whatever has gotten into the man?"

" 'Tis a long story," Nicholas admitted, "one I will tell you later. Have you seen Catherine recently?"

"You've lost your wife again? For shame. Can you not keep your household in order?"

Gritting his teeth, he forced a pleasant smile to his lips. "If you should see Catherine, please let her know I would like to speak to her."

"Of course." Nodding graciously, she moved off, her back ramrod straight.

Nicholas searched the central hall, looking for a pea-green coat. He espied Harry near the staircase, his head inclined toward a serving maid. The dandy nodded once and strode across the ballroom toward Nicholas.

"That little wench over there insists Her Grace left to meet her cousin in Dun Strathnaver. Now where the hell is Dun Strathnaver?"

" 'Tis a broch near the border of McQuade's land," Nicholas said, his mind racing. A terrible feeling came over him. While he and Harry had tussled with McQuade, the murderer had gotten to Catherine. As he'd suspected, Harry was innocent, and the culprit was a rogue clansman, one who killed for pleasure. He started toward the entryway. "I'll return shortly."

Frowning, Harry fell into step beside him. "Is your wife in trouble? I'll come with you." He put his hand to his waist, as if checking for a pistol.

"No. You'll slow me. Gather Fragprie and MacDuff and follow me, instead. Both Scotsmen know where Dun Strathnaver is."

Without waiting for Harry's reply, Nicholas strode away. His pistol stuck in his waistband, he raced outside and ordered a groom to saddle Beelzebub. When the groom didn't move fast enough, he pushed the man away and saddled the horse himself. After jumping aboard the stallion's back, he turned in the direction of Dun Strathnaver and dug his heels into the horse's flanks.

He wondered if he was overreacting, but quickly decided it was better to overreact than to lose Catherine. Good Christ, if he lost her, his own life would be over. It would be a blow he'd never recover from.

The land passed quickly beneath the horse's great stride as they charged through the moors. Ponderous clouds sped by overhead, challenging man and beast to a race. Beelzebub jumped a boulder and landed neatly on the other side, not missing a step; nevertheless, Nicholas's heart tripped in his chest at their breakneck pace. It would take only a single foxhole to break the horse's leg and send Nicholas flying. Still, a heightened feeling of alarm forced him to kick Beelzebub's flanks and urge him to even greater speeds.

Over the pounding of the hooves he heard another horse, following fast and hard. Harry hadn't wasted a moment of time, Nicholas reflected, feeling his own burden ease at his cousin's presence.

He gripped the bridle in his hand and fixed Catherine's image in his mind.

I'm coming.

After a jolting trip through Kildonan's forest of oaks, horse and rider pounded past Bodhan's Pond, throwing up dirt and sand in their wake. Nicholas stood in the stirrups, never touching the saddle, wanting to interfere with the horse's gait as little as possible.

Finally he detected the faint shadow of Dun Strathnaver in the distance. Breathing hard, he steered Beelzebub directly to the heart of the broch, not allowing the pace to slacken until the last minute, when he pulled sharply on the reins. Brought to such a sudden stop, Beelzebub reared and neighed shrilly.

Nicholas jumped down, his boots landing in muck that splashed across his legs. A sour stench rose from the muck, which had split apart like a sack of rotten grain.

Fear sharpening his senses, he strode into the broch. Despite the skittish moon that hid behind the clouds, he could see the contours of every stone, hear each twig break beneath his boots, feel each tuft of grass scratch against his breeches.

"Catherine!"

Silently he cursed the butcher that had made his home unsafe and began to search the ruins, checking each corner, yelling Catherine's name. She did not answer.

She wasn't here.

His pulse began to slow, and he began to feel like the

biggest fool ever. He'd jumped to conclusions. Catherine wasn't in danger—

A low groan floated on the air.

He froze.

"Catherine?"

He ran toward the groan, the air around him heavy, full of ominous portent.

Pounding hooves in the distance. Getting closer.

Harry would be with him soon.

He glanced behind him, scanned the rocks, his jaw clenched so hard his teeth ached. Somewhere close by, the murderer hid. Danger was all around him. In the shadows. Beneath the scummy surface of the peat muck. Behind the stone walls. Hiding beneath the moss that clung to the broken walls. He felt it but could not see it.

"Catherine!"

The groan again, low, tortured.

He pulled out his pistol, cocked it.

As if guided by a divine hand, the clouds parted and a ray of moonlight fell directly on the far corner of the broch. It lighted on the figure of a woman. She sat hunched in a strange position, her head focused toward the ground.

He'd found her.

He sprang from the tumbled stone he'd perched on, scraping his fingers on granite, running toward her, hoping he wasn't too late, praying the killer hadn't hurt her—God, he was supposed to protect her from this, and he'd failed.

A memory of savage innocence returned to him and he roared, filling the broch with the sound of his fury and desolation.

She looked up at the sound, her eyes dark pools.

Behind him, the pounding hooves grew louder.

She began to shake her head back and forth, telling him no, insisting he go away.

She had obviously mistaken him for her abductor.

"I'm coming," he shouted.

Her eyes became wide and another low moan drifted from beneath the gag stuffed into her mouth, raising in pitch until it became more of a scream than a moan.

At the last second he realized she wasn't afraid *of* him, she was afraid *for* him.

Danger became death.

And death had found him.

Crack!

The pistol shot rang out through the moors a second before something hard and hot scorched his forehead. He yelled with the pain of it and launched himself from the ground as his legs gave way, even in his extremity trying to reach Catherine.

He hit the dirt with a bone-crushing blow, still several feet from Catherine. Choking, unable to breathe, he stared at the horse and rider that pounded by. The rider wore a black cloak and Wellington hat, his features dark and impenetrable.

He felt for the pistol at his waist.

His hand closed on air.

"Bloody hell," he wheezed.

He looked toward Catherine. Her eyes had filled with tears that ran down her cheeks. Hands tied behind her back, ankles bound by rope, she looked sorely used. He struggled to pull himself closer to her, searching her soiled copper gown for signs of blood. Finding none, he assumed she hadn't been cut or maimed. But had she been raped?

His body grew cold with a savage need to bury his hands in her abductor's flesh and tear it asunder.

Blood dripped into his eyes and down past his lips. Gagging on the salty taste of his own imminent demise, he put one hand to his forehead to stanch the flow and tried to haul himself to his feet.

Catherine moaned.

A shadow loomed next to him and, with a low, mocking laugh, kicked his knees out from under him. He fell back to the moss-covered ground, his wound a spear of agony that hurt so badly he thought he'd pass out.

"Ah, Nicky, begging will get you nowhere. 'Tis the time of reckoning."

Harry's smooth drawl floated across the air. His blue eyes appeared unnaturally light in their dark sockets, the effect as strange as the grimalkin's eyes but immeasurably evil.

Hand wrapped around a flintlock pistol, the dandy assumed an indolent posture that was all the more frightening for its ordinariness.

Nicholas sagged against the ground as he stared up at the man he'd regarded as a lifelong friend. His head ached, his body trembled like a plow horse's at the end of harvest day, and his spirit felt as if it had tumbled into a dark well. Regardless, he swore to finish Harry before Harry finished them.

A little frown curved Harry's lips as he brushed a few invisible horse hairs from his dark breeches. "How I hate these types of scenes. So very messy." The pistol dangled and Harry stared off into space, evidently caught in some demented reverie.

Now, Nicholas thought.

He struggled to draw air into lungs that suddenly felt flat.

Knock him off his feet.

But before he could tighten his muscles to jump, Harry shrugged and life returned to his gaze. "Can't be helped, I suppose." He walked a large circle around Nicholas, occasionally prodding him with the toe of his boot, the pistol trained on Nicholas's heart.

"The Dark Duke, vanquished at last. How long I have waited for this moment." Then he doffed his top hat and bowed to Catherine. "Thank you for drawing him here. Did you like my friends? I brought them up from London and paid them a quid to abduct you. One English pound for one Scottish whore. Seems a fair trade, does it not?"

She glared at him, her eyes full of hate.

Nicholas sought to turn Harry's heavy-lidded stare away from Catherine. "Let me guess. You are angry that Clarissa has found you lacking and prefers me." Unwilling to reveal how much fear and the loss of blood had weakened him, he, too, kept his voice bantering.

"She does not want you, coz, she wants your money. She wants to become a duchess. When you and Catherine are found dead, I will have your title, your lands, everything. And Clarissa will have her dreams fulfilled. We have long plotted for this night."

Harry shook out his lacy shirt cuffs and, without warning,

leaned close to Nicholas's ear. "Everyone thinks the grimalkin has committed the murders. These fool Scots and their superstitions." He giggled, the sound edged with lunacy, rising and falling through the broch like the cry of a starved wolf. "Rather ingenious of me to take advantage of their naïveté, no?"

Swallowing against the pain in his head, Nicholas grinned. "You always did know how to make the most of a situation."

Harry bowed like a virtuoso receiving his due. "The grimalkin's legend intrigued me when I first heard it. A few more months and I had the entire scheme worked out. What better way to set the stage for your murder than to commit several crimes in the grimalkin's name? When your eviscerated body is found next to your wife's, no one will question the killer's identity. The local clansmen are quite eager to believe such nonsense."

"You surprise me, Harry. I didn't think you'd have the stomach for murder. Nor did I think you'd risk ruining your jacket."

"The woman died quickly, with little mess. The calves, however, were far more foul. But why worry? When your fortune is mine, I will order a hundred coats to replace the two I've lost."

Blood began to leak out from beneath Nicholas's hand and a red haze washed over his eyes. Palm slick, he applied even more pressure to the wound. He wasn't certain if blood had obscured his vision or unconsciousness drew near.

"By the way, I killed the woman with your knife, the one Clarissa extracted from you on the day of the hunt," Harry confided. "If anyone should have enough sense to question the existence of the grimalkin, he will find a trail of evidence that leads to you."

Nicholas drew a quick breath. Harry had been diabolically thorough. "So you clubbed me over the head a week ago?"

"Yes. And I delivered laudanum-laced brandy to your room the night the grimalkin killed the calves." Harry positioned himself with his back toward Catherine, his shadow blotting her out as the moon eclipses the sun.

"Both nights you stated a desire to retire early. As I am

a very flexible man, I chose those very nights to set the stage for your eventual murder. I knew that once you'd gone to your apartments, you wouldn't emerge, nor would anyone disturb you. To make sure you didn't change your mind, I . . . shall we say, *ensured* your fatigue. Once I'd finished with you, you had little chance of discovering my plans or interrupting me at an inconvenient moment."

Nicholas groaned at the irony of it. The only reason he'd retired early those nights was to follow the grimalkin. Unwittingly he'd encouraged Harry to murder the very same nights Catherine had transformed into the grimalkin. "You are very calm. If you hate me so much, why aren't you angrier?"

"Oh, Nicky, I don't hate you. You are simply in my way."

The clouds spread apart for a moment, permitting even more moonlight into the broch. Nicholas saw his own pistol laying on the moss not five feet away.

Harry tilted his head to better view Nicholas. His eyes held not the slightest bit of remorse, just a childlike interest. "Clarissa knew I planned to send you drugged brandy the night I murdered McQuade's calves. I permitted her to climb into your bed, for I understand her need for revenge against your Scottish whore. She never wanted you, Nicky. She wanted to destroy Catherine."

"You and she are well-suited," Nicholas gritted, his ears ringing with the sound of his own labored breathing.

"Would you like to meet the grimalkin?" Lips pulled back from his teeth, Harry inclined his head. "Please. Allow me to introduce you."

Nicholas glanced at the pistol, a litany repeating itself in his mind.

Grab it.

Aim at his heart.

Shoot him.

Survive.

With a flourish Harry picked up a sack, opened it, and withdrew a cane. The cane sported a silver animal's paw as a handle. "Wildcat prints," he said, and pressed the silver end of the cane into the ground.

"Jesus, you're well-prepared," Nicholas muttered, his

heart creeping up into his throat, each beat strangling him. Perspiration wet his shirt and dripped into his wound, stinging like vinegar. The pistol was too goddamn far away.

Harry preened. "And this . . . this I consider a flash of pure genius." He pulled what looked like a furry black pelt out of the sack and slung it over his shoulders.

Then, his face cracked in a wide smile, he began to hop and jump in a circle, his eyes bright, gibbering, "I'm the grimalkin, I'm the grimalkin, I'm the grimalkin . . ." Like some demented fiend, he chanted in a singsong voice, his pistol raised to the heavens.

A shaft of fear arrowed through Nicholas, leaving his gut ice-cold. Harry had left the realms of sanity quite some time ago. That made him more dangerous than a bull with an arrow lodged in its neck.

Kill him now.

Save Catherine.

Survive.

Nicholas heeded the voice that spoke inside his head. With a grunt of defiance he sat up and reached for the pistol, his gaze straying toward Catherine. She strained against the ropes that held her, her eyes glowing with anger as well as alarm. An unusually warm draft of air blew through the broch, rustling through his hair like a familiar caress.

She caught his stare for a moment and then closed her eyes.

Without even thinking about it he knew what she planned to do.

Perhaps realizing his audience had deserted him, Harry ceased his gibbering and took off the pelt. "So, coz, any more questions before I dispatch you to hell?"

"Not for the moment," Nicholas said as a fresh, penetrating odor invaded the ruins. He temporarily halted his advance toward the pistol, realizing Catherine's plan had more merit. Once she'd distracted Harry, he'd grab the pistol and blow a hole through his old friend. "But I do feel I ought to point something out to you. You've made a terrible mistake."

"Mistake? Whatever are you talking about?"

Nicholas smiled. "The pelt you wore was black. The grimalkin is golden."

Frowning, Harry put his hands on his hips. "How do you know this?"

"Look behind you." A glow enveloped Catherine, falling on the boulders and lighting the moss with sparkling gold.

His mouth dry, fascinated despite the circumstances, Nicholas watched as the ropes around her ankles and hands and the gag around her mouth twisted into a series of distinct fibers before breaking and falling away. He prayed Harry wouldn't kill her out of fear. But this was their best chance, and they were about to die anyway.

"Do you think me so stupid as to fall for that old ruse?" Wagging his finger at Nicholas, Harry shook his head. "I can see that wound in your head has far from incapacitated you, and I imagine you are still capable of causing me a bit of trouble. 'Twas one of the things I admired most about you, you know. Your brutish strength." Harry fell silent, examining Nicholas with the same expression one might regard a poisonous snake.

Nicholas bided his time. Behind Harry, Catherine curled in quiet agony, her mouth open, her spine curving, bands of tawny fur erupting across her torso.

"There's a light behind you, Harry. Don't you see it?"

Harry kept his gaze focused on Nicholas with singular intensity.

Clicks and pops filled the air, along with a wet scrunching noise.

"Do you hear it, Harry? 'Tis the sound of the grimalkin coming for you."

The glow surrounding Catherine flashed brighter.

Suddenly Harry spun around just as the glow became the brilliant white of ten thousand candles.

Nicholas threw his arm over his eyes to protect them.

Harry screamed and clutched his head.

Even as the transformation completed, the grimalkin sprang, her jaws open wide, claws unsheathed, her body a smooth killing machine. She hit Harry square in the chest and bowled him over.

"Catherine, no!"

The momentum carried Harry back and he fell, striking his head against tumbled stones that had once formed a wall. The grimalkin drew one unsheathed paw across his chest, shredding his jacket, waistcoat, and shirt down to the skin.

Nicholas scrambled for the pistol and pointed it at Harry's chest. "Catherine," he begged, "do not kill him." She could not live in human form, he knew, with a man's death on her conscience, no matter how evil that man had been.

The grimalkin paused, teeth bared, within inches of striking.

"No," he said.

She growled low in her throat.

"No."

The growl trailed off and she looked at him.

"I love you," he whispered.

She turned and padded off into the moors. The pistol dropped from his numbed hand. Arms aching to touch her, to hold her, he watched her go.

Eighteen

Harry lay crumpled on the ground, his face as white as bleached bones, an oily pool of blood gathered beneath his head. His eyes stared sightlessly at the heavens.

Nicholas shivered miserably in a cold, wet wind. Although he knew the notion irrational, he half-expected Harry to rise from the dead and wrap still-warm hands around his neck.

Dried twigs snapped and leaves rustled behind him.

Footsteps.

He struggled to his feet and swayed like a newborn foal.

A dark shape lumbered into the broch.

"Efington? Is that ye?" The old laird's face, round and pale in the darkness, came into view.

Nicholas pressed a hand against his forehead. "McQuade," he whispered a second before he pitched forward.

McQuade caught him and helped him over to a standing stone.

"I heard a pistol shot on my way home tae Kinclaven," the Scotsman said, his breath smelling of whisky. He examined Nicholas with dark eyes and began to fashion a bandage from a piece of tartan. "What have ye been up tae, laddie?"

"The grimalkin," Nicholas croaked, and glanced at Harry's form. "I've got to find her."

McQuade followed Nicholas's gaze and stiffened. "Here. Press this tae yer wound." He stuffed the bandage in Nicholas's hand and knelt by Harry, his fingers tracing the grimalkin's marks on Harry's chest. "Ye say the grimalkin did this?"

"No," Nicholas mumbled, realizing too late that in his confusion he'd implicated Catherine. The wind that had sprung up turned the blood that oozed from his wound to ice. Strength leaking from his limbs like water from a sieve, he collapsed to his knees.

"Well, he's dead. We canna do anything for him now." McQuade pulled Nicholas to his feet. "I'll take ye tae Kinclaven, laddie. 'Tis a short walk only."

Nicholas slung his arm around McQuade's shoulder. Slowly, leaning most of his weight on his father, he hobbled toward Kinclaven. At some point during the trip he must have passed out, for he awoke in a small room.

Shelves of leather-bound books stretched from floor to ceiling and a sepia-tone globe sat upon a desk in the corner. Quills, pens, stacks of paper, and plans for what looked like a steam locomotive littered a nearby table. A worn tapestry hung above the mantelshelf, lending a medieval air to an otherwise modern room.

McQuade had placed him on a velvet settee near a fireplace. The flames that had already thawed his body began to thaw his mind.

Catherine!

A figure stirred in a nearby chair. "Sae, ye've returned tae the living."

"How close is it to dawn?"

McQuade stood and poked the logs in the fireplace. "Ye need not worry about the time, laddie. Ye've got tae recover."

"Harry . . ."

Shaking his head, McQuade prodded a log with vicious force. "I've dispatched a footman tae return the body tae Rivendell. I take it he shot ye by mistake, while trying tae defend ye from the wildcat." He turned to Nicholas, his face calm, his gaze deadly. "We'll kill the beast, have no doubt o' it."

"Kill the beast? What do you mean?"

"My clansmen and yours have banded together in unholy unity. Even now they are searching the moors around Rivendell, looking for the wildcat. As soon as yer mother arrives tae take care o' ye, I plan tae join them."

Nicholas stared at McQuade, blood surging wildly through his veins. "I don't want you to harm the grimalkin."

"I ken ye think ye saw the grimalkin, but that beastie's just a legend. 'Tis a rogue wildcat that has committed these murders."

A feminine swish of skirts sounded in the hall. Seconds later, Annabella burst through the doorway, her eyes wide and staring, her muslin gown spotted with mud. When she saw Nicholas, she looked to McQuade for reassurance. "Dear God, is he all right?"

McQuade placed an arm around Annabella's shoulders and drew her to Nicholas's side. Nicholas noted the gesture and frowned.

"Aye, he'll live," the Scotsman said. "He may be the spawn o' the devil himself, but he's a strong one."

Nicholas silently agreed that he was, indeed, the spawn of a very large, very disagreeable Scottish devil.

Her hand trembling, she touched the wound on Nicholas's forehead. "How bad is it?"

"Not terribly," McQuade informed her. "I'd say a pistol shot grazed him. A few days' rest and the wound will mend nicely. Now, if ye'll excuse me, I have a wildcat tae catch." The Scotsman squeezed her shoulder and strode toward the door.

Not if I catch her first, Nicholas thought. He swung his feet over the couch and prepared to stand.

Annabella quickly leaned over, grasped his legs, and forced him back onto the settee. "A few days' rest, my boy. You heard what the earl said." She turned to McQuade. "Thank you, Robert."

McQuade walked a few steps back and touched her on the cheek. "Ye ken I'd do anything for ye, lass." They stared at each other for a moment before the Scotsman left the study.

Annabella pulled a chair next to Nicholas. "You'll stay here until I can arrange for a surgeon to see you."

"I cannot."

"Yes, you can."

"I have to go." He swung his legs over the couch and stood, holding the mantelshelf for support.

At first the whole world spun around him with dizzying speed and his stomach churned in protest. But the longer he stood, the slower it spun, until finally it settled down altogether. Unfortunately, his stomach continued to twist like an overwound spring.

"Nicholas, do I need to call for assistance?"

"Give me a moment. I'll be fine."

His mother eyed him with a skeptical stare and fussed around him, urging him toward the settee.

Resolutely ignoring her, he waited for the bout of nausea to subside. His gaze strayed to the tapestry hung above the fireplace. The woven colors remained remarkably vibrant despite the tapestry's antique texture. Nutmeg, copper brown, gray, and clover green combined to portray a castle.

Annabella, too, glanced up at the tapestry. " 'Tis quite beautiful, but now is not the time to admire it. Lie down."

He shushed her with an impatient gesture. The longer he stared at the tapestry, the harder the images pulled at him. His roiling stomach forgotten, he took a step away from the fireplace to better view the pattern ingrained in wool.

The castle dominated the cloth. A line of demarcation dissected the castle in half; on the left, pouring rain and lightning pounded the castle, and on the right, the sun shone benevolently on its turrets. As he traced the ramparts and notched battlements of the castle, he realized the tapestry depicted Rivendell. Indeed, a small woven hawthorn grew in the courtyard, the sapling just a shadow of the giant tree it had become.

"Nicholas, I am going to call a footman," his mother warned. "You're as pale as milk."

He swallowed, sensing he was on the edge of a momentous revelation. "Hush!"

Annabella fell silent, staring at Nicholas with the same intensity he stared at the tapestry.

An open door stood in the middle of the castle. Within the door, two figures—lovers—entwined. The man wore somber clothes of black that matched his black hair, whereas the woman wore gold. Her hair twisted around her head like fire. He could even detect the tiny outline of a teardrop-shaped pendant around her neck.

Tension surged through his veins. He clutched the back of a chair for support.

His gaze darted to the rain-shrouded side of the castle. Within the bushes and flowers he discerned a golden catlike form. A woman whose hair writhed like snakes stood above the cat, her face twisted with grief. She clutched two pieces of tartan in her tiny hands, one the McQuade tartan, the other MacClelland.

Good Christ, he thought, the rhyme! What was the witch's rhyme?

Killed my laird and killed my kin,
Only hatred beneath your skin . . .

Could the woman whose hair writhed like snakes be the witch Sileas McQuade, the same one who'd placed the curse of the grimalkin on the MacClellands?

Excitement bubbled up in him like the froth on a tankard of ale.

He stared at the sun-drenched half of the castle, a field of ivy and flowers twined around it. A small boy with honey-flame hair, hidden in the ivy, took shape beneath his gaze. Like the witch, the child also held a piece of tartan in his hands, but his fabric was a strange combination of both MacClelland and McQuade tartan.

A mixture of MacClelland and McQuade . . .

His mouth fell open.

I know how to free her.

Wave after wave of astonishment rippling through him, he recalled the tale of Niall MacClelland's heinous deed, committed all those years ago. Just as Niall mixed the blood of the McQuades to celebrate their deaths, he reasoned, so must the blood of a McQuade be mixed with that of a MacClelland to celebrate their love.

He and Catherine must conceive a child.

A chuckle built deep in his chest and he began to laugh, with joy, with relief, with hope.

"I fear that bump on your head has done more damage than anyone suspected," Annabella said. "If you do not lay down this instant, I shall force you to the settee myself." She hunched her shoulders and prepared to do battle.

His laughter died away. "You remind me of my wife," he said, and stepped around his mother before she knew what he was about. The movement renewed his dizziness for but a second before it melted away. "I am returning to Rivendell, with Catherine. You will find me there."

"Nicholas, please—"

"Hush," he said again, a finger on her lips. "Everything will be all right." Indeed, everything would be perfect—if he could find the grimalkin before the clansmen.

"Take this," Annabella insisted, a cloak held in her hands. It was a woman's cloak, but he didn't have the luxury to spout missish complaints right now. He took the cloak and slung it over his shoulders, its full cut providing him with more coverage than he'd expected.

A collection of claymores and dirks decorated one wall of the study. He selected a wicked-looking dirk, tucked it into his waistband, grabbed a thick wool blanket from the settee, and left the study.

After a few wrong turns, he found the front door and stepped onto frozen ground. Clouds, lit with the gray of predawn, had gathered thicker than before, promising to coat the ground with snow. Wind blew at his cheeks and nipped his earlobes, the cold invigorating him. He began to walk in the general direction of Bodhan's Pond, certain he could find the grimalkin before the villagers. After all, he'd followed the wildcat many a night and knew her patterns.

As he walked through the stand of trees surrounding Kinclaven Castle, branches plucked at the blanket he held in his hands. He twisted between gnarled trunks and made his way onto the moors, the ruins of Dun Strathnaver gray and dead far in the distance. Several torches, bobbing their way to the broch from an opposite angle, cut through the darkness like miniature beacons.

Shouts and commands twisted toward him on the night air:

"Follow the tracks, laddies."

"I see something moving. Just ahead."

And a higher-pitched voice, tinged with awe and fear, "It *is* a wildcat, by God."

He picked up his pace, striding with something close to panic in his gut. Soon he'd accelerated to a dead run. His wound throbbed in his forehead. Dizziness assailed him. He fought it off, his mouth dry with fear for Catherine. Just as the grimalkin had nosed around the earlier killings, she'd returned to Dun Strathnaver to investigate the site of Harry's death. The smell of blood had drawn her as a flame attracts a moth.

More shouts pierced the shadows.

"Corner it. Quickly."

A pistol report rolled over the hills like thunder.

"Ye got it!"

For a second or two, all remained silent. Then the grimalkin's throaty roar split the night in two. Nicholas imagined the sound full of pain, of dying. His knees nearly collapsed beneath him. He barreled into the broch at full speed, toward the Highlanders clustered in a half-circle. Their faces appeared demonic in the flickering torchlight.

"Stand aside," he growled, and forced his way to the front of the circle.

They had hemmed the grimalkin in between themselves and a crumbling wall behind her. The men closest to her held dirks and makeshift clubs. One fool brandished a pistol. She crouched low to the ground, her tail up and curved like a scorpion's. Ready to attack.

His stomach a cold, tight stone of dismay, he examined her fur, her limbs, her torso for signs of damage. Although blood splattered her paws, she seemed untouched. A bullet hole marked the stone behind her.

Frowning, he tore the pistol from the Highlander's grasp. He knew the man as Gearald, the innkeeper whose daughter Catherine had saved.

The grimalkin tensed.

Eyes wide, Gearald stared at him. "What are ye doing? Do ye want tae die?"

"Be quiet," Nicholas muttered, "and don't move."

His every step placed carefully, he moved around the remaining Highlanders until he stood in front of the half-circle. The wildcat's gaze burned into him. He looked over his shoulder at the astonished men. "I won't have it hurt."

"Help me grab him," a grizzled old man whispered, his attention lingering on Nicholas's feminine cloak. "He's lost his senses."

Two Highlanders edged toward him, their eyes wide and panicked, reminding Nicholas of spooked horses. Muscles quivering, the grimalkin transferred her attention to them.

"Move again and it will kill us all," Nicholas hissed.

The two stopped in their tracks.

He regarded the men with narrowed eyes. "The first man who injures the wildcat will be driven from Kildonan."

Whispers threaded through the broch: "He's daft."

Nicholas took a step toward the grimalkin. The grimalkin swiveled to watch him, her green gaze locking with his. Slowly, every step placed with the utmost care, he edged toward her, his hand out, palm upward. *Catherine,* he thought. *See me. Know me. Remember.*

Behind him, utter silence reigned.

Closer and closer he came to the grimalkin. Always he watched her eyes, looking for a change in them, a sign she would attack. His limbs felt stiff, from fear as much as bruising, for he knew if she jumped for him the Highlanders would kill her. Then he would never know the happiness he sensed could be theirs if he protected her this one last time.

His breath hitched in his chest. When he stood near enough to touch her, her whiskers started to twitch and she nosed forward, catching his scent, skimming his hand with her fur. He remained still, letting her investigate him, and in her impossible green eyes, something flickered.

Her muscles relaxed.

Trembling, he caressed her head, slipping his hand around behind her ears.

A slow rumble began in her chest.

Excited murmurings chased through the Highlanders.

"Back away," he ordered them, still caressing the wildcat.

The grizzled old man nodded, and slowly the men edged backward.

Nicholas waited until the torchlight had dimmed, leaving them in shadows. Then he turned to the grimalkin.

"Come with me."

Aware that the villagers continued to watch, he walked along the wall until it crumbled to nothing, and rounded the corner to the far side of the broch.

The grimalkin followed, her tread soft, making nary a sound.

His limbs grew weak with relief. He stumbled against a rotting timber and caught himself. The wildcat paused, her eyes wide, but when Nicholas moved on, she kept pace with him, always a foot or two behind. As the minutes passed, the glow from the villagers' torches faded in the distance.

Bodhan's Pond, he thought. *I've got to bring her to Bodhan's Pond.*

Somehow, he stumbled his way across the moors, the grimalkin his silent companion. The village of Kildonan, separated from the moors by a stand of trees, twinkled in the mist. Soon the first waves of Bodhan's Pond came into view, and scanning the hills and valleys for Highlanders, he crashed through the thickets surrounding the pond.

Thorns poked beneath his cloak and attached to his crumpled evening coat, trying to slow him down even more. His footsteps muffled by sand, he limped toward the grimalkin's lair, pushed the bushes aside, and collapsed onto a mat of dried leaves.

The stone ceiling above him swayed and danced.

Something large and very warm curled up next to him.

Darkness descended.

When he awoke, heat surrounded him. Soft female curves pressed against his back and legs. Eyes burning, he rolled over and gathered his wife into his arms. She still smelled musky, the wildcat's scent clinging to her skin. Christ, she felt so good. Hands shaking, he separated from her for a moment and pulled off his cloak, evening coat, waistcoat, breeches . . . everything, until he was as nude as she.

She made a little sound, almost like a sigh.

He lay back down, pulled her to him, and covered them both with the wool blanket. Leaves scratched against his bare arse and worked their way around him, surrounding him in a pillow of warmth. Luxuriating in the feel of her silken form cuddled into his, he listened to the wind blow outside the cave, breathed deep of forest loam and rotting leaves, stared at the dull expanse of stone above him, and knew he'd never made love in a more provocative place than this.

So primal. So fitting.

"Wake up, love," he whispered.

Dark, thick lashes fluttered against porcelain skin.

He buried his nose in her honey-flame hair, touched the spot where her hair met her skin.

She was his. All his. Forever.

"I'm in love with you, Catherine," he said.

She stirred against him and yawned, her backside rubbing against him with tantalizing softness. Heat began to build between them, trapped by leaves and the wool blanket. Playfully he turned her on her side and cupped her breasts from behind. They fit in his hands perfectly, their fullness pressing against his palms. He stroked her and nuzzled her neck until she moaned.

"Wake up," he murmured. Surely, he mused, she had the most exquisite body in all of creation. A long, smooth back, tiny waist flaring to generous hips, a gorgeous rounded bottom, and long legs that would put a thoroughbred to shame. His gaze returned to her bottom, to the small cleft of honey-flame curls snuggled between her thighs, and he groaned.

She stretched in his grasp and turned over. Her eyes opened halfway. "Nicholas. How nice of you to invade my dreams."

" 'Tis no dream, love." He showered her with kisses, his own need building to a fever pitch within him.

Her eyes opened wider and her gaze settled on the bandage on his forehead. She grasped his head between her hands, holding him still, and touched the bandage with one shaking finger. "What happened? Where are we?" She glanced at the stone walls surrounding them.

"We're in the grimalkin's lair, love. I thought I'd warm you before I brought you home. And that," he said, pointing to his head, "is the result of a foolish miscalculation. 'Tis nothing." He began to kiss lower, running his tongue along the sweet curve of her breast, hoping her customary memory loss would prevent her from recalling Harry's perfidy, at least for a while. The afterglow of their lovemaking, he thought, would cushion the shocks.

"Oh." Her arms snaked around his neck and she pressed against him, her body soft and yielding. "We have waited far too long, husband, to try this again."

"My thought exactly." He captured her face in his hands and kissed the pink tip of her nose. "I love you, wife." Desire, he saw, had turned her eyes a brilliant green. "You have, I fear, found yourself a husband whom you'll never be rid of."

She stilled against him, her fingers buried in the hair on his lower stomach. Even her chest had ceased to rise and fall. "Please, say that again. I'm not quite certain I heard you correctly."

"I love you." He released her and smiled, certain he'd found the most beautiful, most noble, most *perfect* woman in the world.

But rather than melt at his words, as he'd expected, she narrowed her eyes and pulled back from him. "You love me because you want to free me," she said, referring to the witch's curse.

He chuckled deep in his throat. His wife—forever the wildcat. "I love you, you silly wench, because I cannot do otherwise."

Pressing her cheek against his chest, she hugged him close. He felt a peculiar wetness where she'd nuzzled him, and his own throat constricted with unspoken avowals.

"You wish to talk of love?" Her husky voice enfolded him like an enchantment, bringing a strange tingle to his limbs.

She leaned back to look at him, her lashes spiked with tears. "Well, I loved you from that first day I saw you. How I cursed you, even as I longed for you to kiss my bitterness away. But I did not think any man would love me, knowing I had a beast within." She closed her eyes halfway, her voice melting to a whisper. "Indeed, I still cannot believe it."

He pressed his lips to her forehead, wanting to erase every last doubt from her mind. "Shall I shout of my love from the highest hills? Announce it at the Temperance Inn? What will convince you?"

"Perhaps a kiss," she offered, and grinned impishly.

"Of course. Anything to please a duchess." He kissed her, tenderly at first but then more furiously, her breast silky and warm against his palm. She squirmed as if trying to slip beneath his skin, pressing closer and exploring him with as little shame as if his body were an extension of her own. He encouraged her with soft words of love, his limbs nearly quivering with intense desire.

"You drive me mad," he said. He had to take her soon. She was too damned beautiful, too damned provocative. No man could withstand such a combination for long. He slid his hand down her stomach and explored the moistness at her thighs. She opened herself to him, encouraging further intimacy.

She was ready for him.

Dizzy with sensations he hadn't known possible, he spread her thighs and thrust deeply, her small moans inflaming him further. His gut tight, he brought them both to the peak of pleasure, Catherine crying out with a wild abandon that knew no restraint. As he felt himself begin to explode, he threw his head back and plunged into her as far as he dared. She clung to him, breasts heaving with the heat of their passion, her body trembling with her own fulfillment.

Afterward gentleness replaced the frenzied desire that had consumed him. He pulled her pliant form against him and kissed her tenderly, wondering if even now a child had begun to form in her womb. The tapestry had depicted a small boy with the honey-flame hair. Was he destined to have a son first? Whatever the case, he planned to fill Rivendell with the sound of their children's laughter.

"Catherine, I've discovered how to break the curse," he said, his voice hoarse.

"Curse? What curse?" Mumbling, she did not even look

at him, but ran a hand through the hair on his chest, her fingernails softly scratching.

He felt a glimmer of masculine satisfaction that he could have brought her to such a state with his passion. "You don't care that the grimalkin is gone from our lives forever?"

"What?" Abruptly she sat up, clutching the wool blanket to her breasts. "You've discovered the terms of release? Tell me!"

"A child, born of MacClelland and McQuade, will break the curse." Amid her surprised gasps and knowing nods, he told her of the tapestry and his interpretation of it.

When he'd finished, she shook her head. "What you've said makes sense, but I can still feel the grimalkin's presence, hovering deep within the dark place. You may have planted a seed in me, but I fear you misread the tapestry."

She caught her lower lip between her teeth for a second. "Oh, Nicholas, what if a child forms within me even now? Then the baby and I shall die when I give birth, as do all women who carry a grimalkin."

He put an arm around her, her desolate tone raising protective instincts in him he hadn't known he possessed. "I'm sure I had the meaning right." He went over the tapestry in his head. A castle, two lovers entwined in the doorway, the crystal pendant . . .

The crystal pendant.

"Wait. There is something I forgot."

His evening coat lay in a crumpled heap near the mouth of the cave. He checked the pocket, found the teardrop-shaped pendant snuggled safely inside, and withdrew it. "You must wear the crystal pendant."

She eyed it uncomfortably. "What will happen when I put it on?"

"I do not know."

"Let me dress, then," she said, and pulled a drab wool gown from a sack. "I'll feel better prepared to meet whatever surprises the pendant has in store for me if I am clothed properly." Each movement one of extraordinary grace, she pulled the gown on and waited patiently as he buttoned it.

As he reclaimed his own clothes and dressed, he almost

smiled at their systematic approach to the situation. In fact, he felt more like a cook than a man steeped in magic. "According to legend, Aonghas met his death near the edge of the pond," he said, a smile finally breaking out. "I suggest we stand in approximately the same location."

"Do you find this amusing?" Eyebrow raised, she scowled at him.

"In a way, yes. We're being so damned logical. I feel as if I'm making a rather complicated confection. Two cups of sugar, butter, a crystal pendant, a pregnant lass, mixed together and cooked by the icy waters of Bodhan's Pond . . ."

She punched him on the arm. "You have a most disconcerting sense of humor. Have some respect. Besides, I thought the logical approach appealed to you."

She grasped his hand and led him to the edge of the pond. Dark water swirled beneath a crust of ice and broke free just as it reached the shoreline.

He pulled the crystal pendant from his pocket. "Are you ready?"

"Aye." Her knees wobbled but her eyes glittered with excitement.

His entire body tense, he settled the pendant around her neck. As soon as it touched her skin, a brilliant yellow light exploded from her and she cried out.

Fat, lazy snowflakes began to swirl down from the sky.

"Oh, Nicholas, it tingles. . . ."

Suddenly afraid for her, he reached for the pendant, ready to rip it from her neck.

She stopped with an upraised hand. "Nay. Stand back."

Eyes closed, she began to tremble and raised her arms to the sky. A warm wind, at odds with the falling snow, stirred her skirts and unbound hair. Arms lifted like a supplicant's, her bosom heaving, the elements swirling around her, she looked like she held the power of life and death in her hands.

Awestruck, Nicholas felt his mouth hanging open. He didn't bother to shut it. She was an angel fallen to earth, begging to return to divine realms.

Don't leave me, he thought.

Coalescing in thin air, balls of silver stardust joined the

snowflakes and hit the ground, exploding in a shower of sparks. Each impact sounded like a hammer striking metal.

The very stars were crying.

Don't leave me.

The wind became a whirling dervish that lifted her up and spun her around, her body contorting to the grimalkin's and changing back to human, bands of hair erupting across her torso and then disappearing. Each change occurred more quickly until her features became indistinct and fire began to lick at her feet.

His wife, he thought, was going to burn alive before him. and he could do nothing.

Tendrils of flame slowly wound around her torso, surrounding her in a red-hot glow. Golden vines twisted up past her face and through her hair, lifting each honey-flame strand away from her scalp until she seemed more fire than human, burning, consuming, sizzling.

The sight terrified him and he fell to his knees.

"Catherine," he breathed, looking at her face, which was a face no more but a brilliant conflagration of flesh and magic.

Each snowflake that struck her instantly became steam, and as the fire devoured her, clouds of mist began to swirl about her, amorphous shapes that clung to her like bees to honey. The wind began to blow harder, blurring the fire, scuttling across the ground with a sucking sound, as if trying to draw her up to the heavens.

He detected an odd smell, that of burning hair. It took him several seconds to realize that his eyebrows and the stubble on his chin had caught fire. He rubbed his face against his coat and pushed himself backward, crablike, from the unquenchable blaze that had been his wife.

She could not possibly survive this.

Tears squeezed out from his eyes.

She had feared death by immolation most.

The first pink rays of dawn broke over the horizon and lit upon her form. In the very center of the fire a white teardrop formed and began to pulse a brilliant rainbow of colors, each one more dazzling than the last.

He stared at the colors with childlike wonder, his heart throbbing dully in his chest. The sight of Catherine's transformation was becoming too much for him. Just as he felt certain he'd go mad, a sudden, tremendous gust of air rushed past the pond, bending saplings and uprooting thickets. It blew the fire away, revealing the woman beneath, suspended in midair. It flapped against her tattered gown and lifted her hair off her neck one last time before she dropped to the ground, her eyes sealed tight.

Her hair looked even more lustrous than it had before, and her skin remained milk-pale. Indeed, he had thought it impossible for her beauty to grow, but grow it had. Her face and limbs had gained a certain refinement that bordered on perfection.

She had entered the forge as iron and emerged as finely tempered steel.

"Catherine?"

Her chest, he saw, did not rise and fall.

He grew light-headed with fear.

The snow began to fall harder, covering her with a mantle of white.

"Oh, Cat." He crouched beside her and touched her hair, his teeth clenched to keep the sobs inside.

Without warning, her eyes flew open, their green irises now ringed with gold. She convulsed and drew in a great breath of air.

He let out a whoop of joy and gathered her to his body, sheltering her, protecting her, swearing nothing and no one would ever threaten her again. Rocking back and forth, he stroked her arms, her neck, rained kisses down on her soft hair.

After many minutes had passed, she touched his face. "My God, I'm free." With trembling fingers she stroked the pendant that still hung around her neck.

He gazed at the teardrop, his chest tight. The crystal no longer contained a gold ring twisted in a figure eight. Instead, a golden grimalkin lay within, forever trapped, its green eyes staring out at the world beyond.

"It's over," he whispered, and rose to bring her home from the grimalkin's lair for the last time.

Catherine paused at the entrance to Lady Wisborough's Egyptian-inspired ballroom, her hand resting on a marble column. Before her, society's glittering finest danced a stately cotillion, the satins and figured silks and wools of their attire creating a patchwork of gentility. She searched the gathering for a certain large frame, discovering him near the card-playing room, in easy conversation with a few of his cronies.

Inside her, the baby kicked. Surprised at their son's strength, she touched her middle and smiled.

Her gaze met his across the room.

A long moment passed.

Finally he broke the spell and strode toward her, his black hair gleaming blue like a crow's wing beneath the gaslights. He'd exchanged his traditional evening garb of blue superfine for black wool breeches and a coat, its lapels lined with black velvet. Embroidered vines twined on his white waistcoat and a snowy cravat encircled his neck, the simplicity of his attire emphasizing the broad, clean lines of his powerful form.

A head taller than most of the men present, he cut a dashing figure and received adoring looks from several of the ladies, Clarissa not among them. The lethal Mrs. Rappaport would remain at her dead husband's estate in Surrey—for the rest of her life—or risk exposure as an accomplice to murder.

Nicholas reached her side, eyebrows drawn together, a little frown curving his lips. "Are you feeling well, love?"

The baby turned a somersault within his warm prison, his gymnastics startling a squeak out of her. Eyes wide, she touched her stomach again.

"You're going back to Efington House," he said, his eyes dark. "I should not have allowed you to attend this ball. Good God, you're naught but three months away from your time! You should be home, in bed."

His concern, his unreasoning fear for her health, made her chuckle. Men simply didn't understand the nature of childbearing. "Pshaw, Nicholas. You worry too much. Have women not made babies for hundreds of years, in conditions less propitious than mine?"

"Wicked wench," he muttered, "I'll see you home in

bed." He leaned closer and whispered, "And I'll turn your laughter into something infinitely more pleasing."

She shook her head, her amusement growing. He did not want her to dance on her feet, but he had no compulsion against dancing with her in bed. Nicholas, she decided, was the randiest man in England. Or Scotland, for that matter.

And she loved him all the more for it.

"Invitation accepted," she said, her hand curled around his forearm. "But first, let us dance one country dance. 'Twas here we met, 'twas here we fell in love. Shall we not complete the circle and dance here as husband and wife?"

"An excellent suggestion." An arm placed protectively around her waist, he led her onto the marble dance floor, several gray heads bending together in urgent gossip as they passed.

". . . his mother, remarried to a Scotsman! Ross Efington is rolling in his grave, mark my words."

Catherine felt a smile curve her lips at the way love had blossomed around her. Annabella and McQuade had married within weeks of the country dance at Rivendell, and although she'd had to prod Nicholas most dreadfully, in the end he'd attended the ceremony. Shortly afterward, Annabella had told her new husband he'd sired a son: Nicholas.

McQuade had been shocked at first, then overjoyed, and hadn't left Nicholas alone until Catherine and Nicholas had left Kildonan for London. Nicholas had mixed feelings about the Scotsman, and she understood his dilemma all too well, for she had yet to resolve her own feelings of dislike for McQuade, built on hundreds of years of feuding.

But the love Robert and Annabella displayed for each other, and their happiness over their coming grandchild, made them difficult to resist. With time, she knew they'd banish the ghosts that haunted them from the distant past.

She and Nicholas joined three couples who'd formed a line. An orchestra, hidden in an alcove, struck up a Gaelic reel, and the lead couple began their figures. Behind them, the tongues wagged.

". . . Angel of Mercy has reformed the Dark Duke . . . look at them, so besotted, so in love . . . it's positively vulgar."

She leaned into him, her extended belly keeping them

farther apart than she'd have liked. Even though she was bulky with child, he managed to make her feel small and feminine. His broad shoulders and arms encircling her like a warm cloak on a cold night, he hugged her, filling her with both contentment and wild anticipation. She cast a glance at the tallcase clock in the corner and noted they would soon be able to leave without causing a scandal. After all, they'd arrived at least ten minutes before.

She chuckled. "Did you hear that? The Angel of Mercy has reformed the Dark Duke. 'Tis rich to think of it. Indeed, the Dark Duke has liberated the Angel of Mercy."

He pressed a kiss against her hair, his warm breath tickling her ear. "I think, perhaps, 'twas a little of both."

Turn the page for a preview of
Heart of the Dove . . .

Bedfordshire, England, 1856

Richard Clairmont sat straight up in bed. Light-headed, he took deep breaths of air. For a long moment he stared into the darkness, focusing on the moon, which had almost passed beyond his window. The nightmare had smothered him as surely as if a pillow had been pressed to his face.

That one had been worse than most.

He marveled at the twist his subconscious had put on his dream tonight. Miss Drakewyck, the charlatan who had plagued his thoughts during the day, had begun to plague his nights, too.

Breathing somewhat easier, he disentangled himself from the linen sheets that twisted around his waist. Dreams didn't predict the future. Miss Drakewyck wasn't in danger, nor was she worthy of his concern. She probably snuggled in her virginal bed, thinking of bats and toads and whatever else concerned aspiring witches.

Still, he knew sleep would elude him. He hauled himself to his feet, drew a glove onto his damaged hand, and walked to the window. Moonlight glittered upon well-tended gardens and turned the fountain into a pool of silver. Crickets chirped and bats wheeled through the sky—ordinary occurrences on a midsummer's eve.

He glanced at the clock on the side table. Two in the morning. He remained by the window, preferring the moonlit grounds of Castle Close to the lonely sheets on his bed. The air smelled moist and rich with earth, the same way it had in the glen where he'd met Lucinda Drakewyck. What an odd sight she'd been in the woodlands that day, spinning and curtsying to a tree. His lips twitched and he almost smiled.

But then her mother's face—Vivien Drakewyck's—rose to the surface of his thoughts and his amusement fled.

Lucinda Drakewyck was the very image of her mother, and judging by her antics in the glen, she planned to become a so-called clairvoyant just like Vivien. The elder Drakewyck had bilked both rich and poor alike with her predictions, and although a few prophecies had come to pass, Richard ascribed her success to coincidence rather than clairvoyance. People couldn't see into the future. Magic didn't exist.

But greed did exist, and greed was a quality the Drakewycks possessed more than their share of. Eventually Lucinda Drakewyck would open her spell-casting parlor for business, and when she did, he would be her first customer, ready to reveal her for the charlatan she truly was. The memory of his own mother—trapped by Vivien Drakewyck's predictions and soaked in brandy—demanded no less.

After one full minute he changed his position, glanced down at the fountain, and noticed a darkness against gray stone, a moving shadow that blotted out the dewy-sparkle of the grass. He leaned forward just in time to see the shadow slip into the room below him.

Good Christ, a thief! And on his first night in Castle Close, no less.

Energy flooded his limbs. He thrived on this kind of situation. In fact, he'd almost expected it, given that nightmare he'd had. Each movement smooth and purposeful, he yanked on his shirt and boots, grabbed a silver candlestick and flint, and crept out of his bedchamber. Body pressed against the wall, he stalked down the corridor toward the stairs, ready to subdue the criminal with his fists if need be.

As he reached the balcony, he realized the shadow was moving up the stairs toward him. He ducked into a musty bedchamber and, with the door ajar, waited for the shadow to pass by.

A whisper of fabric brushed the carpet directly outside. His body tingling with the need to fight, he gripped a fleshy part of the shadow and yanked it into the bedchamber. It felt soft, like velvet.

A little squeak emerged from the depths of the velvet.

"Do not move," he said, his voice cold.

"Squire Piggott?" a small, feminine voice asked.

He withdrew the flint from his pocket and lit the candle. Light flared in a dim halo, revealing a face darkened by the folds of a hood. He couldn't identify her. Even so, the black velvet, coupled with that ladylike voice, sent his thoughts in other directions. Perhaps he'd prevented a rendezvous between Squire Piggott and an old mistress rather than thwarting a burglary. This woman obviously hadn't heard he'd bought Castle Close from the squire.

"Explain yourself, madam," he ordered, at the same time yanking the hood from her head.

Large brown eyes, shot with gold, stared into his.

"Miss Drakewyck!" He waved the candlestick in her direction. He'd dreamed about her, and now here she stood. He wondered if he'd fallen back asleep without realizing it.

The tips of scissors, pointed his way, glinted within the folds of her cloak. "Captain Clairmont!"

They both took two steps away from each other.

She nodded toward the candlestick, her bosom heaving. "Do you plan to bludgeon me?"

"Of course not." He lowered his weapon, his gaze falling on the scissors. "Do you plan to skewer me?"

She shoved the scissors into a pocket. "No." Her full lips curved in a forced smile. "Once again you have caught me in a most compromising position. I can't decide whether to faint or flee."

"Neither will work, I assure you." Evidence, he thought, would suggest Miss Drakewyck and Squire Piggott had formed an intimate liaison. The knowledge didn't surprise him. Hadn't Vivien Drakewyck sampled half the men in Bedfordshire?

"I daresay I would rather have encountered Squire Piggott than you," she said, her voice trembling. "I don't suppose you'll let me go."

"I'm afraid not." He thrust the candlestick onto the shelf and lit an oil lamp. A nimbus of light sprung outward, illuminating her face.

She was as striking as he'd remembered. Candlelight sparked molten highlights in her cinnamon brown hair, and the black silk edging her cloak accentuated the smoothness of her complexion. Her soft, full lips pouted at him, as if begging for a kiss. And those eyes held a golden promise of passion amidst their innocence—a combination irresistible to any man.

Even so, her cheekbones were more pronounced than he recalled, and the shadows under her eyes spoke of many nights without sleep. "Why are you traipsing about your neighbor's house at two o'clock in the morning? Have you given up witchcraft in favor of thievery?"

Her hand fluttered to her throat. "I am guilty of many things, Captain Clairmont. Thievery is not one of them."

"Then why are you here?"

She swallowed and touched a lumpy object she'd concealed in her cloak pocket. Crystal glittered within folds of velvet, and he realized she'd brought her magic dove with her.

The muscles along his neck tensed. Despite his warnings, Miss Drakewyck seemed hellbent on taking up the family trade. He tightened his lips at the thought of the townfolk she'd cozen, the self-serving predictions she'd make. He still remembered Vivien Drakewyck's visits to his own home, Clairmont House; the way Vivien had looked at his father, her gaze full of hot secrets. They'd had an affair; he realized that now.

"Miss Drakewyck, I demand an answer!"

"My uncle owes Squire Piggott five thousand pounds," she blurted, then clapped a hand over her mouth. Her gaze flew to his face.

He stared at her, surprised at the confidence given so freely to a hostile stranger.

"If we cannot repay him, we will lose Drakewyck Manor," she added, her voice weak.

He suddenly realized that a shared secret—such as the one she'd revealed—often created an intimacy between a man and a woman. Did she seek to gain his silence with secrets and familiarity? This little fraud knew how to gain an advantage. "So you steal from Squire Piggott in order to repay his loan. Outrageous, Miss Drakewyck. Did your uncle teach you nothing of ethics?"

"Do not bring Uncle George into this. Anyway, I am not here to steal." Her chin raised up a notch. "I shall resolve the debt with the Squire in another way."

In another way? What did a debt-ridden woman have to give but herself? Blood rushed through his veins, hot from both anger and desire. How eagerly she assumed her mother's role in all ways! "The Squire is a willing participant, I assume?"

"Well, not quite," she admitted.

So, she had to convince the Squire to take her, like any streetcorner harlot. He found himself growing angrier by the second. She looked so young, so . . . fragile. Did she really understand what she was proposing?

"Five thousand pounds. A hefty sum. Do you suppose you are worth it?"

Her eyebrows drew together. "I . . . don't understand."

He allowed his gaze to rest on the soft folds of velvet which draped across her breasts, noting the flush that came to her cheeks. She was so very beautiful, with her white skin and pert nose and soft brown hair which swept across her shoulders in a chocolate wave. Dainty, her limbs small and soft, she would fit him perfectly.

"Perhaps you *are* worth it. I will pay your debt to the squire, and then you will pay your debt to me." His voice—low, scornful—nevertheless had a throb to it, one he despised. She'd made him weak, this witch.

"As much as I appreciate your offer, Captain, I must refuse it." She shrugged, her gaze forthright. "As I said, I have already hit upon an acceptable solution involving Squire Piggott and no other."

He tightened his jaw. "And what is this solution? Please, tell me if you dare."

Heat flooding her cheeks, Lucinda dropped her gaze to the carpet. What could she possibly explain? That she'd come to snip Squire Piggott's cloak for a magic spell? He'd have her arrested, if not thrown in Bedlam! And his questions . . . they hinted at something she neither understood nor appreciated.

Oh, why had she confided in him? He wasn't a knight in armor come to rescue her, no matter how much he looked the part. That glint of compassion she thought she'd seen in his gaze had been a trick of the candlelight. Captain Clairmont didn't help "frauds" like her—he prosecuted them.

"I had anticipated encountering Squire Piggott, but not you," she said, her voice steady, at odds with the trembling in her limbs. "Do you often stay with the squire?"

Arms crossed against his chest, he regarded her

closely. "Do not suppose you can divert me. I want an explanation."

"If I confess, will you let me go?"

He lifted her chin with one gloved finger, forcing her to meet his gaze. "Not likely. I wish to know how you plan to satisfy this debt, and why you prefer Squire Piggott to me. Are you in love with him?"

She drew in a quick breath. A bolder man she'd never met, or a more presumptuous one. Growing resentment stilled the trembling in her limbs. She slapped his finger away. "Preposterous! I have no feelings for the good squire, nor will I entertain such familiar inquiries! Now, I believe 'tis your turn to answer *my* question. Why are you here, at Castle Close?"

He slowly rubbed his full lower lip with the ball of his thumb, his gaze assessing her from the hem of her cloak to the curls that sat atop her head. His ocean blue eyes blazed with male appreciation before he dropped his lids halfway. He wasn't so very handsome, she observed; his cheeks were too angular, his nose strong, and his chin far too square. But somehow, on him, they weren't faults at all. They combined to give him a very masculine appeal, one that could change from gentle to harsh, given his mood. Right now he appeared quite inflexible.

"Squire Piggott and I have just finished negotiating a real estate contract." He took a step closer. "Now, how do you plan to resolve your debt with the squire?" The glint in his eyes warned her not to toy with him further.

"By retrieving something of the squire's," she hedged, and slipped behind a chair to keep him at bay. "Something insignificant, which he will likely never miss."

His brow furrowed as if he'd expected a different answer. "A nonsensical excuse, Miss Drakewyck. You will have to do better."

"I can tell you nothing more. Please try to understand."

"Understand what? You haven't explained anything."

Nostrils flaring, he circled around the chair toward her. "Let us examine the evidence more closely. You have crept into Castle Close in the dead of night, dressed in a concealing cloak, with all the stealth of a thief. You profess a desire to *retrieve* something. I have heard of criminals hanging for less at Tyburn."

"It sounds damning, I know." He had her trapped. Right now he thought her a thief. If she explained her true purpose, he'd think her mad. She couldn't decide which was worse. A sudden wave of disgust washed over her. As usual, she'd bungled the situation. "Oh, why did I have the misfortune of encountering you, of all men!"

His eyes widened as if she'd slapped him. "On the contrary, you are quite lucky I discovered you. Do you have any idea of the repercussions you will face by toying with the squire in this manner?"

"I know the evidence is difficult to explain, but you must trust me—I meant no harm. Please let me go."

"You are a fraud, Miss Drakewyck. Do you really expect me to trust you?"

"If you reveal my presence here, you will ruin my reputation. I will have no choice but to marry the squire. Let me go. Please."

"Do you not think marriage a more noble path than the one you've chosen? By God, the squire should marry you."

"I am not a sack of goods to be bartered in payment of a debt!"

He gripped the chair next to them with one large hand, his fingers curled into the damask upholstery. "You are bartering *yourself,* Miss Drakewyck. I cannot believe you would turn down an honest alternative in favor of intrigue."

"I will marry no man unless I love him." She, too, gripped the chair.

"Then you're a fool."

She threw up her hands and glared at him, heat inflaming her cheeks. "I thought long and hard before deciding to come here tonight. Despite the circumstances, my purpose is not criminal. Had you slept at Clairmont House, where you belong, this would not have happened. If you want, turn me over to Squire Piggott. Or let me go. But please, stop badgering me!"

He closed his eyes in the manner of a man at the end of his patience. "You belong at Drakewyck Manor, Miss Drakewyck, in your own bed."

She didn't like the inflection he placed on the words "own bed." In fact, she found his entire demeanor vexing. "And you, like most men of your ilk, take great delight in telling me what to do. I am not interested in your advice, *Captain.* Nor will I inform you why I am here."

" 'Tis not necessary. I have already guessed. Love and lust can make a king forget his country." His tone became low, suggestive. "Surely they will make the Squire forget about your debt."

Shocked at how quickly he'd discovered her plan to cast a love spell, she gasped. Her arms fell to her sides. "Please, tell no one—"

"This is not a lark, Miss Drakewyck." He caught her arm and held it tightly. "The dangers are very real. What you propose to sell, many would take for free. Allow me to demonstrate."

In one brisk move he grabbed her shoulders and yanked her against his body. He slipped his hands beneath her cloak and eased it downward, the tie at her throat loosening in response to his gentle pressure. Soon it had pooled in layers of black velvet at her waist, exposing her arms and breasts—clad in a thin muslin dress—to the musty night air.

His palms were hot against her as he ran his hands down her back, beneath the folds of the cloak, to her bottom, kneading her flesh all the while, his thumbs rubbing hard enough to remind her she was utterly helpless, that he could do as he wished with the smallest effort. She froze at the intimacy, unprepared for the sweet tremors that chased through her limbs, for the delicious vulnerability he roused in her.

"Have you any idea what you do to a man with that defiant mouth?"

She twisted against him, to no avail. "Release me this instant."

"Surely you would not begrudge me what you offer Squire Piggott so casually." His lips thinned to a hard line. He tightened the embrace to one of bruising force, trapping her with arms so strong they could crush her in an instant. He traced her spine, touched the nape of her neck, fondled the sides of her breasts, each intimate caress drawing the bowstring of sensation within her tighter.

"I offer the squire nothing, and you even less," she said, striving for a imperious tone but failing miserably. She could see nothing but his face, harsh yet unreadable; could smell nothing but the clean male scent of him, soap and bay rhum and freshly washed linen. Drowning, she levered her foot back, ready to kick anything solid, desperately trying to ignore the feel of his heart beating against hers, the practiced vitality of his touch.

He sensed her intention and trapped her with one rock-hard thigh. "A token resistance only sweetens the kiss." His voice was a throaty purr, deep, musical, almost as mesmerizing as the dark glow of desire that had replaced the harshness in his eyes. "But you understand this already, no?"

"I have no desire to kiss you," she hissed, knowing she'd lied as another pleasurable jolt weakened her. He moistened his lips with his tongue, his gaze never leaving hers. Slowly, still stroking her bottom, he lowered his head and covered her mouth with his own, his kiss gentle at first, drawing her will from her body.

She tried to hold back. Effortlessly he shattered her resolve, his tongue and mouth tormenting her so thoroughly that her legs buckled. He pulled her even closer, so close she nearly straddled him, her breasts crushed against his chest.

Abruptly he broke the contact between them, lifting his head to stare at her with eyes both harsh and full of longing, anger and desire at war. "Is this what you seek from Squire Piggott?"

"You have misjudged me," she said, her voice wavering. She knew her defense was halfhearted at best. Heaven help her, she didn't want to end the intimacy, the excitement, the rapture he promised her with one burning gaze. She clung to him, dizzy with unfamiliar need, begging him with her eyes to kiss her again, to bring his plunder to its conclusion. He'd brought a part of her to life that she hadn't known existed, and she gasped at the potency of her own desire.

With a ragged sigh he bent his mouth to hers and claimed her again, thrusting his tongue forward, filling her mouth, robbing the breath from her lungs.

"So sweet," he murmured, and reluctantly she surrendered to that strong male form, that even stronger will, to the pure magic his lips wrought inside her. He deepened the kiss but she didn't stop him, didn't protest; he assaulted her every sense until she could think of nothing but him.

Without warning, he ripped his mouth from hers and released her. She swayed backward and seized the chair for support.

"I won't allow the past to repeat itself," he muttered, his eyes dark, chest heaving, a lock of black hair falling across his brow. "I'm bringing you back to Drakewyck Manor."

She stared at him, shocked to the core, not by his words but at her complete loss of control. Her heart was pounding so hard she thought it might jump into her throat. Slowly, the jolts of pleasure in her limbs subsided, leaving an icy chill in their wake. When she felt her legs would hold her, she released her grip from the chair.

She hadn't believed anyone, or anything, could subvert her own will so thoroughly. Richard Clairmont had taught her a valuable lesson today. Never again would she lose her head to any man, particularly one as disagreeable as he.

She mentally shook herself. "What do you mean, history repeating itself? I met you only a month ago."

"Pull your cloak back on," he said, an unspoken accusation in his eyes. "I'm taking you home."

"But—"

"Your cloak, Miss Drakewyck." He pointed to the garment, which hung in sloppy folds around her waist, the glint in his eyes suggesting she'd made an awful display of herself.

"And who pulled my cloak off? You've taken liberties no gentleman would dare!" She fought to keep her voice lowered, but outrage was getting the better of her. How dare he act the righteous prig after kissing her into oblivion? And, more to the point . . . damn the man for conquering her so easily!

She thrust her chin forward and glared at him.

Never again.

As if he wished certain words to remain unsaid, he tightened his lips and yanked her cloak up around her shoulders. She began to tie the strings at her throat, but he pushed her hands away and tied them himself, quickly, knotting them.

Before he'd released the strings she spun away from him. He moved even more quickly and took her arm. His touch none too gentle, he hustled her toward the door.